QUEEN OF EMPIRE

By HR Moore

Titles by HR Moore:

The Relic Trilogy:

Queen of Empire

Temple of Sand

Court of Crystal

In the Gleaming Light

http://www.hrmoore.com

For Chris and for Alice.

FAMILY TREES

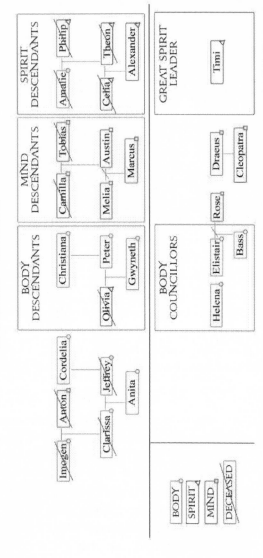

BODY DESCENDANTS

Imogen — Anton — Cordelia

Clarissa — Jeffrey

Anita

Christiana

Olivia — Peter

Gwyneth

MIND DESCENDANTS

Camilla — Tobias

Melia — Austin

Marcus

SPIRIT DESCENDANTS

Apollie — Philip

Cetia — Theon

Alexander

BODY COUNCILLORS

Helena — Elistair — Rose

Bass

Draeus

Cleopatra

GREAT SPIRIT LEADER

Timi

BODY
SPIRIT
MIND
DECEASED

THIS FAMILY TREE CAN ALSO BE FOUND AT WWW.HRMOORE.COM/QUEENTREE

CHAPTER 1

The river's crystal cold water kissed Anita's toes as she dangled them over the bank's edge. She tapped lightly at the surface, the sound blending with the trickling of water falling over rock. She lay back on the grass, looking up through the trees at the clear blue sky above, hot rays of sunlight beating down on her skin. Anita closed her eyes, imagining that she was just a normal girl, enjoying a moment of peace by the water.

The crunch of footfall shattered the silence. 'You won again?' said Cleo's familiar, excited voice. Cleo dropped down next to Anita, prodding her in the side until she sat up.

Anita fixed Cleo with impatient grey eyes. She inhaled, lines appearing on her forehead as she raised a questioning eyebrow. Anita had entered and won every challenge in Empire since she was twelve years old. She'd been so far ahead of those her age, that when she'd turned thirteen, they'd made her compete with the adults. By the time she was fifteen, none of the adults could keep up with her, and now people cared more about who came second, as that's where the real competition was.

'So nonchalant,' Cleo teased.

'It's hard to get excited about winning when you know you're going to win.'

'I don't know... Bass has got pretty close to you a couple of times,' said Cleo, mischievously. Her eyes glinted as she threw her long, silky, black hair over her shoulder.

Cleo onto her favorite topic of conversation so soon... that must be a record. 'Bass, beat me?'

Cleo barked a laugh, clapping her hands in delight.

Anita rolled her eyes. 'Come on. We'll be late if we don't get a move on, and it's Mind class first.'

Cleo was a Mind, but Anita was definitely a Body. She could take anyone on when competing in Body disciplines, and she had a fair amount of Sprit in her blood too, but Mind had always been a challenge.

She didn't understand why everyone had to continue with these ridiculous classes for years after school. She was twenty-five, but formal weekend education had to continue until thirty, the age when one's 'Centre comes together', whatever the bloody hell that meant. Allegedly, at the mystical age of thirty, one's Mind, Body and Spirit would blend into one. From that point, developing any one skill would become more of a challenge.

Well, Anita found Mind enough of a challenge anyway, and seeing as nobody she knew had morphed into some new magical being at thirty, she suspected it was all just propaganda. The Descendants and their council had a passion for the theatrical. However, today was not the day to challenge the Descendants' vision. She didn't want to have to play chess for hours on end with a councilor, the punishment for being late, so it was best to be on time.

* * * * *

'Oh, look who's here,' said Cleo, playfully. She shot a sly sideways glance in Anita's direction as they approached the temples.

Anita looked around and saw the cause of Cleo's sudden excitement. She'd clocked Bass, with his tall, muscular frame, angular features, and short, sandy colored hair. Bass exuded his normal relaxed demeanor, leaning back against the base of a large oak tree, soaking up the sun's hot rays. His legs were bent, arms resting on his knees.

'He's looking for someone... I wonder who that could be...' Cleo was in her element, mincing her sparrow-like legs gleefully as they approached.

Anita gave Cleo a rough shove, putting an end to the strutting, but knowing all it would really do was encourage her.

'I see him every day at the observatory,' said Anita. 'He's probably looking for that girl we saw him with.'

But Anita knew Cleo was right: Bass was waiting for her. She could feel his energy perk up every time he saw her. It was a sharp intensification that directly corresponded with the wide, endearing smile that would spread across his face. Thank the Gods not everyone could feel energy, the fundamental life force that drove everything in their world, and nobody knew she could. It was a skill reserved for the Spirits, but she had always been able to, ever since she could remember.

* * * * *

They rotated through their classes. Mind was first, where today the aim was to move an object using only the energy of one's mind. Everyone thought this was ridiculous; no one could do it, not even the councilor leading the lesson. A girl at the back had a hysterical moment, swearing she'd moved the flower she'd chosen, but she couldn't repeat the feat.

Anita wasn't a fan of the Mind Temple. Its gothic features made it oppressive, like the walls contained secrets and the doors might suddenly slam shut, locking you in, never to let you go.

They escaped the gloomy space and moved onto their next class: Spirit. Anita had always loved the Spirit Temple. It was so lofty and light, sunlight streaming in through enormous slit windows that extended up the clean lines to a spired point miles above. The flowers everywhere were free and wild, flitting spontaneously in the light breeze that played across the open expanse of the temple's floor.

The Mind Temple had closed off, secluded areas, full of dark corners where it was easy to hide, conspire and observe. In contrast, the Spirit Temple was one enormous open space. Soaring columns that seemed too few and too high to hold the walls in place loosely sectioned the temple. Obviously, Anita was most loyal to the Temple of the Body, but she had always felt an inexplicable pull towards the Spirit Temple.

The lesson focused on joint meditation, where two people sat opposite one another to meditate to a shared mental space in one or the other's mind. Here, they would have a shared experience invisible to the outside world.

This again had seemed ridiculous, until several months ago, when Anita and Cleo had paired. They had each meditated to a boat on the sea. They hadn't seen one another there, but through much in depth comparison, they'd found that the details of the boat, the weather, the sea, had all been identical. Now they always tried to pair with each other to see if they could repeat the feat, or even get a step further.

Today, however, Bass jumped in before Cleo and Anita could pair up. As a result, Anita spent a couple of very uncomfortable hours trying to ignore Bass' soaring energy and closing herself off to anywhere his mind wanted to go.

It wasn't that there was anything wrong with Bass. He was gorgeous, with a tall, athletic frame, olive skin, and classic good looks. He was a kind, loyal friend, Anita's only real friend apart from Cleo. He usually came second to Anita in Body challenges, not to mention that he was intelligent, in an academic sort of way, ran the energy observatory, and came from a well-connected council family.

It was just that Anita had never seen Bass as anything other than a friend. She saw the girls swoon when he walked by. Most of them would have, just because of his family connections, social climbing rife amongst Empire's well to do. Mothers with nothing better to do spent their days plotting how to marry their daughters off in advantageous ways. In addition, Bass was handsome, clever, and didn't have a big head about his background, making him Empire's most eligible bachelor.

But Bass' energy never shifted with other girls like it did with Anita. She'd tried to make it obvious she didn't see him that way; for her, there was no chemistry, but he'd never quite taken the hint.

Next up was Body class, where they learned how to use their energy to influence the actions of their bodies. The lesson was on knife throwing, but seeing as Anita was a better shot than any of the councilors, she skipped it. In fact, she hardly ever went to Body lessons. She'd only show up if something like yoga was being practised, and only because there was a crossover with the Spirit disciplines.

Anita usually went for a run or a ride during this time, meeting up with Cleo and Bass afterwards to walk home. Today she stayed in the Spirit Temple; she could do with some actual meditation after her session with Bass…

* * * * *

Two long hours of not being able to concentrate later, her mind not in the mood to relax, Anita wished she'd gone for a run after all. She was getting ready to leave, when a sudden surge of energy filled the temple. Her head snapped up, a shot of adrenaline coursing through her as she searched for the source.

Her eyes snagged on a movement in the center of the temple, a man emerging from a newly formed circular hole in the floor. His mind was elsewhere, face angled towards the floor, the stone slab sliding closed unnoticed behind him. He started walking towards where Anita sat, transfixed, at the back of the temple.

He seemed weightless, moving apparently without effort, yet purposefully, with the grace of a highly trained dancer. He was tall with broad shoulders, and an athletic, lean frame. She assumed he was a councilor.

He looked up, towards the entrance, and Anita's breath caught involuntarily in her throat. He was ruggedly handsome, eyes a bright, piercing blue. They had both a depth that could have been a century old, and a life that hinted at a rebellious intelligence. Tousled blond hair framed his face, neat enough not to be outlandish, but messy enough not to be conformist. His jaw was locked, lips pursed and twitching, brow furrowed, deep in complex thought.

Tanned, muscular forearms protruded from a loose, white shirt with casually rolled-up sleeves. A heavy, red, floor-length cloak flowed around him.

Anita's blood stood still in her veins. Her energy bubbled uncontrollably inside her. It rose rapidly, as though riding on the back of a bird, frantically flapping its wings. It catapulted upwards from her stomach to her chest. Here, she could contain it no longer. It burst free with a force so strong that Anita feared there might be an actual hole, not that she could muster the will to tear her eyes away and look.

The man snapped out of his thoughts, immediately alert. His radiant energy diminished as he tracked her. His eyes found her without difficulty, scrutinizing every contour of her body, assessing the threat before his shocking blue eyes locked with hers.

Anita couldn't begin to read what she saw there. Confusion? Aggression? Wariness? Intrigue? It was all she could do to hold his gaze with her own inquisitive eyes, her energy shamelessly betraying her interest as he considered her from afar.

He stood stock still, she sat spellbound, considering her next move, when a crisp, impatient voice rudely shattered the silence. 'Alexander,' it said, as a second man strode confidently into the temple.

Alexander? It couldn't be... Anita's energy shifted, defensive and panicked. Alexander smiled, intrigued by her reaction.

'I'm coming, Marcus,' he responded, not taking his eyes off Anita for a second, 'is Gwyn ready?'

Shit. She struggled to regain some composure. Why were they here? Anita gathered the tremendous strength required to tear her eyes from Alexander, moving her gaze to Marcus. She was completely unprepared for what she found. Holy Gods; he too was perfect. He was as tall as Alexander, but his thinner form made him seem somehow more refined.

Whereas Alexander was wearing a loose shirt, slacks, and beaten up soft leather mules, Marcus was impeccably dressed in expensive, well-cut attire. Everything seemed flawlessly in place, from his shiny leather brogues, to his pressed white shirt and expensive gold knot cufflinks, to his perfectly quaffed, short, dark hair and chiseled cheekbones.

His eyes were dark and opulent and contrasted with Alexander's for reasons more integral than just color. Marcus had none of Alexander's grounding. His eyes flitted playfully, looking for something, anything of interest. They were impulsive, giving the impression that life bored him. Like their sole occupation was to find something entertaining, to supply at least a small diversion before returning to the usual dull monotony.

Marcus too sported a floor-length red cloak, but he wore it with a different kind of authority, an audacious authority. Whereas Alexander seemed to flow when he walked, Marcus was more overtly commanding, arrogant, with clipped, impatient strides. His energy was the most potent she had ever felt, and as it flowed over her, it had a drug-like effect. Once again, the pressure in her chest built, nothing she could do to stop her energy from erupting.

Alexander turned casually back to look in her direction, the side of his mouth twitching almost unnoticeably. He raised one, infuriating, mocking eyebrow, flicking his eyes over her once more. This was mortifying.

'Come on. We haven't got all day,' came a curt, officious, female voice from the entrance. Anita couldn't see the woman, so focused instead on the vain struggle to get her energy under control.

Marcus spun briskly, striding past Anita to join the woman outside, without sending as much as a glance in Anita's direction. Alexander followed him, but stopped as he came close to where she sat.

'You should learn to control your energy,' he said, in a voice low but commanding. 'With energy that strong, you're a very desirable asset.'

With that, he flowed out of the temple, leaving Anita dumbfounded, head spinning, drained and empty, wondering what in the world had just taken place. That he could read her energy was horribly embarrassing, but why had her energy reacted like that towards both Alexander and Marcus? That had never happened to her before. Her energy was usually so static, unless of course she found a new challenge... was this a challenge? How? What did Alexander mean about her energy being so strong? And what did he mean about her being an asset? Most of all though, why were the Descendants in Empire? They usually lived in Kingdom, close to the Grand Temples... they rarely came out here...

Anita spilled out of the temple and almost ran headlong into Bass and Cleo, who had just finished their Body lesson. 'Oh my Gods, did you see her?' Cleo practically sang. She was bristling with delight, wildly swishing the ends of her thin cotton scarf; Cleo's equivalent of rubbing her hands together with glee.

'I saw them in the Spirit Temple. Alexander appeared out of the center, and then Marcus came in, and then a woman, I think Gwyn, called them from outside. Gods... what are they doing here?' said Anita, the words a jumbled rush.

'Three of them?' said Cleo, jealousy all over her tone. 'We only saw Gwyn. She appeared from the center of the Body Temple, all flowing golden locks and cloak. What are Alexander and Marcus like? I bet they're gorgeous, just like everyone says.'

Anita felt a pulse of aggression in Bass' energy. Given she wasn't sure she could find the words to adequately describe them, even if she tried, she changed tack. 'More importantly, why are they here?'

'Don't know,' said Bass. 'Nobody in our class knew either. I mean, the councilor probably did, but he wasn't letting anything slip.'

'It'll give me something to find out at work then,' said Cleo. 'I'll see you there later?'

Cleo worked at The Island, a bar on an island, in the middle of the river, on the outskirts of town. It was pretty much the only place to socialize in Empire, so that's where everyone went.

Cleo used her place of work to keep abreast of anything and everything going on. She wasn't above slipping a few free drinks across the bar to help people on their way, not to mention that her skills of persuasion were the stuff of legend. So, she was right of course, the quickest way to find out why the Descendants were in town, was through Cleo, at The Island.

'Have fun,' said Anita, shooting Cleo a knowing smile. Cleo was about to be in her element; fun was an understatement.

CHAPTER 2

Bass went back to the observatory and tried to persuade Anita to go too. He'd been paying close attention to the energy since the recent death of Philip, the reigning Spirit Descendent. He wanted to see if there had been any movement in the last few hours.

Interested as Anita was to see the effect this was having on the energy, she wanted to mull over what had happened at the temple. She opted for a run by the river instead. She would stop by the observatory and pick up Bass later, so they could head to The Island together.

After her brief encounter with the Descendants, Anita was like a coiled spring. She was angry at herself for her uncontrollable and embarrassing energy, and Alexander's cryptic comment about her being an asset had left her feeling vulnerable. She didn't understand why they were here, but the whole thing was deeply unsettling; she didn't like it one bit.

She ran for miles along the river, her long, muscular legs eating up the ground. The shallow, meandering water usually took her mind off any preoccupation, but today it was no help. She ran faster and faster, but it just made it worse. She was more frustrated by the end than she had been at the beginning, and by the time she got to the observatory, she was in a foul mood.

* * * * *

'So, are you going to ask her?' asked Patrick, Bass' lab assistant. He had floppy brown hair, blotchy, almost translucent skin, and exceptionally bad fashion sense, although he thought he was the height of cool. He had been probing about this for weeks.

'Maybe,' Bass replied, feigning exasperation, but he was fooling no-one, least of all Patrick. Patrick, like everyone else, saw the way Bass looked at Anita, and knew there was nothing Bass wanted more than for her to want him too. Patrick, frankly, had always thought Bass was crazy. He could have his pick of any other girl in Empire, and it wasn't like they didn't throw themselves at him. But Bass only had eyes for Anita.

He just didn't get it. Anita was alright, he supposed; she was quite good looking, had a cracking body, if you liked the toned, athletic, boarder-line menacing look. But she was unpredictable and stubborn, she did not suffer fools, and was used to winning everything. Patrick found Anita intimidating and unfathomable. Maybe that's what the attraction was… that she was mysterious.

A light started flashing on the dashboard in front of Bass, showing a spike in the energy in the immediate vicinity. They usually used the sensor to alert them to an approaching Descendant. Strangely, Anita had the same effect, her energy so strong that it set off the alarm.

'Well, now's your chance to *maybe* ask her,' said Patrick. 'I'll make myself scarce. See you at The Island later.'

* * * * *

'Hi, Patrick,' said Anita, as she clunked up the spiral metal staircase into the room. Anita had no idea why Patrick always seemed to be leaving as she arrived. How was his timing so impeccable?

'Hi, Anita,' he replied. 'I'm off to The Island. See you there later?'

'Yep, sure,' she said, her tone terse. The last thing Anita wanted was to be left alone with Bass. Patrick turned and grabbed hold of the express exit, a pole through the floor, winking annoyingly at Bass as he slid out of view.

The observatory was an incredible building. The Descendants had commissioned it four generations back, so they could keep tabs on the energy. Bass' family were known for their study of energy and had helped design the building. They'd been in charge of research from the start, earning Bass' ancestor a council position. Bass' father now held that position, and it would be Bass' in time. His family had been instrumental in understanding both energy volatility, and how everything in their world linked together.

The observatory was over three levels. Downstairs was a large, perfectly round, midnight blue pool of water that was always eerily still. It helped to absorb any background energy 'noise'. The middle floor contained dashboards that provided readings of energy levels in various locations around the world. A gentle humming filled the air as the energy flows were processed. Dials whished backwards and forwards and lights flashed in a way meaningless to the uninitiated.

The top floor contained the instruments that actually recorded the energy waves, and it was Anita's favorite. Numerous instruments adorned the roof, each trained in a different direction, and all with golden

17

receiver dishes that were shaped like the energy waves themselves. The receivers were of various sizes so they could pick up different frequencies of energy from different distances, with the biggest so large it had to rest on the floor of the roof. Anita loved to lie on that one and stare up at the stars, the large, lolloping energy waves reverberating through her, off to be recorded downstairs. Of course, this affected the readings, so Bass wouldn't let her do that at a time like this, when a ruling Descendant had just died, but she climbed to the roof anyway to look out over Empire.

Empire had a regal look about it, sort of understated yet effortlessly elegant. It was balanced, embraced, and contained by the river. Beautiful, arched, red brick bridges stretched across the meandering waters, connecting the wealthy center to the other side. The bulk of the town hid the less desirable areas from view.

The center of Empire spanned an area about the size of a square mile, built in an era before anyone saw a need to put up walls. The imposing spires of the temples dominated the skyline, seeming to watch over and protect the buildings around them.

Surrounding the temples were several well-to-do areas, with fully stocked food markets, jewelry shops, clothes shops, perfumers, stationers, and restaurants serving an array of new and fantastical concoctions.

Then, of course, there were the lovely, large, red brick houses with eccentric gardens. The fashion was for ostentatious, perpetually blooming, sweet-smelling, climbing flowers. The plants were perfectly at one with their owners.

The most desirable houses, lived in by councilors, along with properties owned by the Descendants themselves, were on the outskirts of town, or in the surrounding countryside. They usually sat atop imposing hills or nestled against ancient woodland, all gloriously picturesque, secluded, and with spectacular views.

Empire had once been the world's premier city, where trade was done and Gods were worshipped. Kingdom, a much more impressive metropolis, had long since claimed that title. Empire was now in retirement, basking in previous honors and glories, living out a dignified and well thought of old age.

'I'll never tire of that view,' said Bass, coming through the window onto the roof behind Anita, nodding towards the town. 'It's beautiful at night.'

Anita moved further onto the roof, so Bass wasn't standing so close. She sat on a pipe connecting to the instruments downstairs.

Bass leaned against a receiver, Anita appraising him as he struggled with some internal debate. The muscles around his mouth clenched uncharacteristically, tension filling his torso and powerful arms, energy spiking with... something. Anita held her breath, dread filling her.

'So, are you going to the ball?' he blurted, trying to make throwing caution to the wind sound casual.

Anita turned away to hide the look on her face, her body rigid, hands clasping the pipe for support. 'No, I don't think so,' she said. 'The ball isn't really my thing. Sucking up to councilors, watching everyone make idiots of themselves in front of the Descendants, pretending to fawn over every word they say.'

'Oh,' said Bass, energy tumbling.

Anita felt bad; maybe she'd gone too far. Bass was, after all, going to be a councilor one day, but there was nothing she wanted less than to go to the ball with him. Or, at least, not in the way he wanted... argh. She was useless at this. And aside from the obvious, that it would give him the wrong impression, she didn't want

19

every girl in town to hate her. People already thought she was weird for winning all the challenges; she didn't need the scheming mothers on her back too.

'Found anything new with the energy?' she asked, hoping the change of subject would lift his mood.

'No, nothing yet. There was a small downshift when they announced Philip's death, but it seems to have come back up again. I'm expecting Alexander's Crowning to lift the energy further; it's exciting to have a new ruling Descendant.'

The death of Philip, Alexander's grandfather, was cause for concern around the energy. Everything was connected, and a fall in the energy meant there was less to go around. If it fell enough, it could impact crop yields, the weather, and many other things besides. 'It's Christiana's death I'm really worried about… the Body bloodline…'

'Hopefully we won't have to worry about that for a while,' said Anita, getting to her feet. 'We Body types are stronger than we look.'

Anita shot Bass a smile that was supposed to say both, 'sorry' and, 'chin up'. Bass smiled optimistically, his energy giving a little jolt: message not received, again.

* * * * *

The Island was nothing more than a shack, really. Strips of wood thrown precariously together decades before to form a building initially intended as a warehouse for traded goods. Since then it had been embellished inside, laid out over two levels.

A short, stubby bar adorned the wall on the lower level to the right. Bottles of all kinds of mysterious looking liquids balanced perilously on the uneven shelves behind. This level also had a private room

20

behind the bar, ample space for standing, a couple of tall tables, and ledges here and there to place drinks on. One of these ledges partially obstructed a shady-looking passage to the back door. Despite appearances, it led to a pretty wooden deck with benches overlooking the river.

To the left of the door was a set of three squeaky wooden steps that groaned agedly every time a pair of feet touched them. They led to a raised seating area with a series of booths and rough wooden tables, affording varying degrees of privacy. Weird and wonderful trinkets adorned the walls; trophies from successful trading expeditions to the Wild Lands.

The place was packed. Clearly news that Descendants were in town had spread like wildfire, and everyone wanted to know why. Luckily, Cleo had grabbed a booth at the end of her shift, and Bass and Anita pushed their way through the crowd to join her.

'Before we get into the gossip, let me get you a drink,' said an overzealous Cleo, by way of a greeting. She flagged down a bartender and ordered a bottle of Ginger Champagne.

'What are we celebrating?' asked Bass, surprised. Ginger Champagne was rare and usually only saved for special occasions. Luckily, being friends with the owner's favorite bartender and only daughter meant they never had to pay for such luxuries, even so, this was an extravagant move.

'We're celebrating my brilliance at extracting the gossip I am about to tell you from a councilor,' Cleo replied, carefully annunciating each word to make sure they could all hear and therefore marvel at her achievement. The bartender placed three glasses on the table and filled them with champagne.

'The gossip mill comes up trumps again,' said Anita, wishing that Cleo would just get on with it, but knowing there wasn't a speck of hope on that front. At least the promise of gossip had lifted her mood.

'Indeed, it does,' said Cleo, taking a moment to build suspense, savoring the attention before beginning her story. 'So, we know so far that the ruling Spirit Descendant, Philip, passed away a couple of weeks ago, meaning that Alexander, Philip's grandson, will succeed to the throne soon. We also know that Christiana, the ruling Body Descendant, is getting on a bit.'

Cleo paused, the silence pregnant.

'What we didn't know, until tonight, is that Christiana is more than getting on a bit.' Cleo looked between them, her voice hushed. 'She's dying.'

'What?' Bass and Anita said together, their voices low.

'That's going to have a significant effect on the energy,' said Bass, livid. 'The bloodline…they have got to prepare people for news like this.'

'But why would Gwyn, Marcus, and Alexander come here if Christiana is dying?' asked Anita.

Cleo looked smug. 'Why indeed?'

'Cleopatra, we know you're brilliant, and for that we're eternally grateful, but we're dying over here. The suspense is literally killing us,' said Anita, barely covering her frustration.

'Alright, alright. They're *all* here, not just the young ones, and they've brought Christiana here to die. There's something here she wants to make peace with before she goes, but nobody knows what it is. All I know is that she's currently on her death bed below the Temple of the Body, and that Austin is fuming about the whole thing.'

Austin, Marcus' father, the ruling Mind Descendant, had a reputation for being venomous. He, as with most Minds, thought himself superior to everyone, including the other Descendants, so it wasn't surprising that he was cross at having to be in Empire at the whim of another.

'They're going to hold the Chase, the Crowning, and the ball here, instead of in Kingdom. They're going to hold off for a couple of weeks, as the likelihood is it'll be a double Crowning, with Peter succeeding Christiana.'

'They're going to let him rule?' asked Bass. 'Surely it would make more sense to pass straight to Gwyn? It's supposed to be a female line…'

'Nobody knows if either of them is eligible to rule, given that Christiana has no direct female heir. The bloodline could be broken anyway, and the prophecy could already be dead,' said Anita, trying to take in the magnitude of what she'd just heard.

'Gwyn certainly doesn't think it's dead, given the way she was strutting across the temple earlier,' said Cleo.

'So, they're having the Crowning here, but where will it take place if not by the Relic?' asked Bass.

They'd built the three temples as triangles, with three tips, one from each temple, meeting at a point in the middle. In Kingdom, the main areas of the Grand Temples were open to everyone, with a central section that only the Descendants could use, and the joined tips, which housed the Relic, were also open for everyone to visit.

Crownings usually took place by the Relic, so that everyone could see them, but in Empire, the layout was slightly different. The temples were open to everyone, but underneath each temple were chambers that only the Descendants could use. Underneath the joined tips was a sacred area, but nobody, apart from the Descendants, and a few select councilors, knew what was there. On the main level, the area of the joined tips was closed off to everyone but the councilors, who used the hexagonal chamber inside to host council meetings when in Empire.

'The rumor is that most of each Crowning will take place in the public center of the relevant temple,' said Cleo. 'The Descendants will then go to the sacred center underneath the tips to perform part of the ritual, and then will come back up to complete the ceremony.'

Cleo really had excelled herself this time.

'And the Chase? Where and when will that take place?' asked Anita, as offhandedly as she could.

Cleo and Bass smiled. 'Bet you can't wait to get your teeth stuck into that one,' said Bass. 'See if you can't beat the Descendants...'

Luckily, at that moment, there was a ruckus across the bar, and Anita took the distraction as an opportunity to evade a ribbing and head to the restroom. But what Cleo had failed to mention was that the young Descendants were in the back room. The commotion was the result of them leaving, and Anita found herself trapped directly in their path.

A mass of bodies closed ranks behind her to gawk at the Descendants as they passed, and she couldn't go forward without attracting their attention. There was nothing she could do but duck her head and try to keep her energy under control.

Gwyneth came first. Cleo was right, she did have flowing golden locks, her long blond hair glimmering in the light. She was tall and thin; unpleasantly thin. Her floor length silk dress and red cloak made her look the part, but she had the air of someone trying just a little too hard. She wasn't unattractive, but nor was she a great beauty, her nose too long, eyes set a little too close together.

Gwyn walked past Anita without so much as a glance in her direction. Unfortunately, the same luck was not to be had with the next Descendant, Alexander.

As soon as she saw him, her energy lifted. She did everything she could to suppress it, but Alexander's head turned slowly, carefully, searching for the source. Here we go again, thought Anita, desperately trying to push back through the crowd.

He found her, of course, piercing blue eyes looking down into hers, this time only a meter away. Neither said a thing as they held each other's gaze. She searched for any hint of what he was thinking, but his expression gave her nothing to work with. The crowd watched with growing interest, but Anita was determined not to break first. He might affect her, but she wasn't going to let every victory be his.

Marcus, who had been talking to a couple of councilors at the bar, sauntered over to see the cause of the crowd's interest. Alexander moved on, following Gwyn outside.

'Well, that was interesting,' Marcus drawled, standing close and looking down with flirty eyes. He smelt of vanilla, and as it wafted over her, she inhaled greedily, momentarily disorientated as her pulse reacted, racing, energy singing, color rising to her cheeks. She told herself to snap out of it, exhaling sharply, trying to get a handle on her out-of-control emotions.

'Alexander rarely deigns to interact with anybody... even if he didn't talk to you, I would call that an interaction, wouldn't you?'

'I'm not sure what I would call it, other than weird,' Anita shot back, a little too sharply.

Marcus smiled. 'We're heading to my family's residence just outside of town. Why don't you join us?'

She couldn't take on the Descendants all at once, and certainly not on their territory. If Anita had had a social climbing mother, what she was about to do would be cause for disinheritance. Seeing as she didn't, and that, to Anita, winning was more important, she had no choice but to refuse.

'I'm terribly sorry, but I have a prior engagement,' she said. 'Please excuse me.' And with that, she forced her way through the shocked crowd, heading for the back exit, out onto the deck.

'Holy Mother of the Gods,' Cleo exclaimed, bounding after Anita. 'What were you thinking?'

'I couldn't go with them,' said Anita.

'You have just committed social *suicide*.'

'*Social suicide*? How?' Anita spat. 'Where exactly was I in the *social standings* anyway? They're just people, Cleo. People like you and me. They just happened to be born into a different bloodline.'

'They're powerful. You need to be careful.'

Alexander's earlier words came back to her, *you are a very desirable asset*, and it halted her tirade. She knew Cleo was right; her abilities often made her reckless, but staying off the Descendants' radar was the smart thing to do.

'Look, I know I shouldn't have done it like that, but I couldn't go to Marcus' residence and be their plaything for the evening.'

Cleo nodded. 'At least you didn't make a complete swooning idiot out of yourself like half the other girls in there would have.'

'Look, Cleo, I think I'm going to head home. Thanks for the champagne and say bye to Bass for me?'

'Sure, no worries,' said Cleo, shaking her head as Anita turned and walked back inside.

CHAPTER 3

Alexander got up and made his excuses. There was only so much of Gwyn and Marcus proclaiming they were masters of the universe that he could take. He had never enjoyed spending time with them, but since Philip's death, he found them tedious.

He would go back to the temples and see how Christiana was doing; she was always a sound source of advice. Maybe she could help him understand why the Body girl was having such an effect on him.

He, unlike the girl, could control his energy, so no-one would know, but he couldn't stop thinking about her. Maybe it's her energy, he thought, as he descended through the center of the Temple of the Spirit into the lower chambers; raw and unrefined. She has no idea how powerful she could be.

But he knew that wasn't all it was. His brain flashed endless images of her pale lips, smoky eyes, slender hands, creamy skin, dark hair, the dip between her neck and collarbone, the curve of her toned arms...she invaded his every thought. For some inexplicable reason, his mind kept drawing him back to her.

Alexander entered the plush private chamber that now belonged to him underneath the Spirit Temple. His spacious accommodation consisted of a study, a bedroom, a bathroom, a sitting room, and a small kitchenette. His grandfather, Philip, had had the whole place overhauled when he had ascended to rule. Alexander hadn't even thought about changing it; he didn't see the need.

He pushed a small square at the side of the worn wooden paneling covering the wall at the back of his study. It was the only wall not covered in bookcases laden with Philip's dusty old manuscripts. A secret door sprang open. He ducked through into the gloomy corridor beyond, lit only by the occasional lantern, and followed it towards the chambers underneath the Temple of the Body.

Alexander's mind wandered as he walked... wandered to her. He barely noticed the twists and turns, feet seeming to follow their own path. But as he approached Christiana's chambers, the sound of muffled voices jarred him back to life.

The only people allowed down here were the Descendants, a handful of trusted and very well-paid servants, and occasionally a councilor, accompanied by a Descendant. Alexander listened, picking out the harsh tones of Austin, the Mind Descendent, and Christiana's weak replies.

Unsettled energy radiated from them both, and Alexander knew something was wrong. He snuck forward as far as he dared and hid behind an ornate grey pillar. He positioned himself so he could see what was going on, and strained to hear their every word.

'I've got to find her; I have to tell her. She's here. What we did...' said Christiana.

'You're going to tell her?' said Austin. 'I thought you just wanted to find her and see her. What good can telling her do now?'

'The energy. Once I'm gone, who knows what will happen. Only the Gods should have the power we took. It's my greatest regret.'

Alexander felt Austin's intentions. Waves of malicious, negative energy rolled off him, rising to unprecedented levels. Christiana would know; she had surprising Spirit skills for a Body.

'Austin, she will find out. The prophecy will be fulfilled and the true bloodline will be restored,' said Christiana, her voice strained.

'No, she won't,' Austin sneered, brushing Christiana's words aside. 'We're the only two who know the truth now Philip's gone. And soon it will just be me.' His voice was a terrifying mix of wistful longing and startling cruelty. Austin reached down and put his hand on the pillow next to Christiana's head, his brutal intention plain. Christiana didn't fight. She had accepted what was to come, her face relaxed, energy calm, unconcerned with the imminent danger.

'The true bloodline will be found, Austin,' Christiana repeated, her voice soft but insistent, like this was so obvious an observation that anyone would be a fool not to see it. 'This is bigger than you; it's in the hands of the Gods,' she said, pausing and looking openly up at Austin, her eyes still sparkling, full of life, a smile playing around her old, thin lips. 'The Gods who you are about to help me join.'

Austin's eyes flew open. He grabbed the pillow and furiously covered Christiana's face, using all his weight to hold it resolutely in place. Christiana didn't struggle. She lay totally still until Alexander could feel her energy no longer. He could have intervened. Should he have? But Christiana could read energy; she would have known he was there, and she hadn't appealed to him. He had a better chance of fulfilling her last wishes if he wasn't at war with Austin, but now he knew exactly what Austin was capable of, and it made him sick.

Alexander turned and left, navigating quickly back through the black corridors. He rushed into his chamber, swinging the panel swiftly and firmly closed before retreating up into the temple and out into the night.

He vomited violently as he reached the cool night air, still not quite able to believe the act he had just witnessed. He left the temples and somehow stumbled to the river before letting his legs give way, sinking gracelessly to the hard ground of the riverbank. He sat all night, not feeling the cold or the damp that penetrated his clothes, numb, barely even hearing the river swirling by.

Eventually, as the sun rose, a greyish light illuminating the water, tears trickled down his cheeks. He held his head in his hands, staring into nothing, a deep sense of loss growing inside.

Hours later, when the sun was fully in the sky, but blocked out by determined black clouds, he returned to his chamber, full of questions. What had Christiana meant about taking the power of the Gods into their own hands? And about the bloodline, and the prophecy? Did Christiana have a female heir? Was that who Christiana had wanted to find? What had they done and why? His grandfather, Philip, had known something and never told him? Had Philip been involved in whatever this was?

There were too many questions to answer all at once, but Alexander knew the place to start his search was in the archives. Maybe an examination of the birth and death records would cast some light.

* * * * *

Ever since the encounter at The Island a few days before, Anita had been restless. People were gossiping, trying to determine why she had attracted the Descendants' attention. Anita wanted nothing more than to fade into the background. She had gone to the observatory every day and had been sullen and moody with Bass and Patrick. For that, she felt bad, which made her even more frustrated.

She had turned to Body pursuits, but no amount of riding, sailing, climbing, or swimming could seem to lift her mood. To add insult to injury, the Descendants had gone quiet since that night at The Island. Nobody had seen them or heard from them, and even Cleo had nothing to share. They could be anywhere. They could have left Empire. Nobody knew.

Anita desperately wanted to understand why her energy had reacted to Marcus and Alexander. She didn't know how to *control her energy*, as Alexander suggested she should.

Today's attempt at distraction was a run by the river, with her grandmother's springer spaniel, Thorn. Surely the combination of exercise and playing with Thorn would pick up her spirits...

Anita was preoccupied with thoughts of embarrassing displays in bars when she felt powerful energy approaching from behind. She was instantly wary, her automatic reaction to most people since Alexander's words in the temple, as she spun to see who was there.

Her energy leapt when she saw Marcus' blissful form coming towards her. For Gods' sake, get a grip, she said silently to herself. Unfortunately, this seemed to spur on her energy's disobedience, Anita feeling once again like she might explode. At least Marcus didn't seem to have Alexander's reader skills; that should save her one embarrassment, at least.

'Well, hello,' drawled Marcus as he approached. 'Fancy seeing you here.'

'Hmm,' Anita replied, feigning disinterest and calling to Thorn.

'Mind if I join you?'

'Umm…'

Anita was trying to think of a suitably offhand reply, when Marcus said, 'Great!' His smile that of a naughty five-year-old.

'Right,' she said, setting off across the field, not pulling any punches. Marcus kept pace with her, but he wasn't in any state to make casual conversation. Anita smirked and increased the pace.

They reached the fence and Anita jumped straight up, making to climb over into the next field. Marcus reached out a surprisingly strong hand, grabbed the back of her top, and pulled her roughly back down.

'I think that's enough of that,' he gasped, trying to catch his breath. 'You've made your point.'

'I'm sure I don't know what you mean,' said Anita. The run had improved her spirits no end, and now she was in a mischievous mood. She liked the way this encounter was going.

'I think you've got a fair idea,' Marcus fired back, having recovered enough to assume his usual superior stance. 'How did you get so fast?'

Anita shrugged. 'I don't know,' she said, softening a bit. 'I've always been fast and strong and able to beat anyone I've competed against. At first people thought I cheated, but now they just think I'm weird.'

'Well, I know what that's like.'

'What you know is adoration and envy and jealousy. Nobody thinks you're weird.'

'What's so different about how people treat me? They stare at me, they talk and point, they whisper and snicker…'

'… ahh, the poor little Descendant…'

Marcus exploded forward, his face inches from Anita's, the smell of vanilla washing over her. Her stomach dropped, her heart rate rocketed. The informality of the run had made her bold; had she pushed him too far?

'You think it's funny? You haven't got a clue.'

His energy was… all over the place; he was an intriguing animal. 'Then enlighten me,' she said, her voice soft.

The side of Marcus' mouth curled into a smile. He inched forward, crowding her, Anita instinctively stepping back, but a tree blocked her escape, her back now flat against its bark. There was nowhere for her to go.

Marcus placed his arms on either side of her, pinning her in place. Her pulse quickened. He leaned his head down, looking straight into her eyes, amusement dancing across his features. To her surprise, Anita liked it, despite his misguided assumption that he was in control.

His features smoothed, and the mood between them shifted. There was a tension in the air as they waited for what seemed like forever to see what would happen next. Faces inches apart, eyes boring into each other, breath mingling, Anita's pulse beat loudly in her ears. The intoxicating smell of him invaded her lungs, clouding her mind. She tilted her head up slowly, holding his gaze, challenging him to make the next move.

His eyes flicked to her lips, a shot of triumph punching through her. He bowed his head warily, watching her cautiously, as though she were a wild, unpredictable animal. He brushed his lips against hers, a shocking jolt of electric energy running between them, her head twitching in surprise. She fought the urge to pull away as Marcus pressed his lips more purposefully to hers, the feel of it so intense. He was surprisingly gentle, moving his hands to her face, kissing her more deeply.

She relaxed into the kiss, mind racing, not sure if she were really in a dream, her lips responding willingly, seemingly without instruction. He finally pulled back, slowly running his thumb across her now sensitive lips, before replacing his hands on the tree. He leaned back in towards her, flirting, making her think he was heading for her lips once more. He changed course at the last moment, moving his mouth to her ear, where he softly commanded, 'Come to the ball with me.'

Anita froze: she had not expected that. A flurry of thoughts poured into her mind, adrenaline-fueled panic filling her body. Given what had just happened, she was struggling to think at all, let alone clearly. She had to buy herself some time…

Anita looked down at the ground, searching for inspiration, before taking a deep breath and returning his gaze once more. She paused, savoring his confusion, impatient intrigue in his eyes. 'Maybe,' she said, huskily, then quickly, before he had time to process her response, ducked under his arm and out into the open field.

'Maybe?' Marcus called after her.

She put her fingers to her lips, still tingling from his touch, gazing back at him. 'Maybe,' she confirmed, sporting a triumphant look as she turned, called to Thorn, and ran back the way they had come.

Marcus sank to the ground, leaning back against the tree trunk. He took a deep breath and ran his fingers through his perfectly quaffed hair. Why the Gods did he like her?

Anita's mind exploded as she ran. What should she do? She didn't want to hurt Bass, who she had already turned down. She didn't want the other girls to hate her, or to have the attention that going to the ball with Marcus would bring. But Anita had kissed plenty of guys, and she had never felt an energy jolt like that before. In fact, she had never felt an energy jolt at all. Had Marcus felt it too?

She sprinted home. She would avoid Marcus; give herself time to think about her answer... and why did the memory of Alexander striding across the Spirit Temple keep invading her mind?

* * * * *

Alexander had spent the last two days buried in the archives. He'd waded through the birth and death records for the ten generations of Descendants before Christiana, but couldn't find anything suspicious. It looked like she was authentic, so he turned his attention to Christiana's heirs. The problem was, although everyone else had to register babies with the relevant council, Mind with Mind, Body with Body, Spirit with Spirit, the Descendants could enter their births into the records themselves. There were two entries in Christiana's line. First, Peter, on 21st May 1310, and then Gwyneth, on 20th March 1337. Again, it looked fine.

The only thing he could find was that they had waited for three days after Gwyn's birth to enter her into the records. Other than that, there was nothing. No other children of Christiana, and no sign of record tampering. It was a dead end.

Alexander had also looked through the newspaper archive, hoping for a clue in some seemingly innocuous article. He'd found a story about a woman dying from childbirth a few days after Gwyneth was born; not a regular occurrence, but not unheard of. There was an article about a strange shipment of chocolate from the Wild Lands that had had to be burnt; again, not regular, but no obvious connection. And the multitude of articles about the bloodline and whether it was still

35

intact was to be expected, given that the birth of Gwyn's father, Peter, had meant the end of the all female line.

Alexander wasn't surprised not to find anything, given the control the Descendants had over the newspapers, but a small part of him had hoped.

He put back the book that held newspaper articles from March 1337, then moved further down the row of records. He stopped by the book for March 1340, the month his father, Theon, had died in a fire in Empire's Body Temple.

Nobody knew why Theon had been there late into the night. Everyone assumed he'd been in his chamber beneath the temple, coming out to help when he realized a fire raged above. The whole thing was deeply suspicious.

Alexander's mother, Celia, had died shortly afterwards, which everyone had attributed to a broken heart. Alexander's grandparents, Philip and Lyla, had brought him up, but every time Alexander had tried to bring up the subject of his parents' death, Philip had looked pained and swiftly changed the subject.

Alexander had tried, of course, to find answers, but other than the archives and family libraries, there was nowhere to look for clues. The ruling Descendants tightly controlled information. He had tried to identify people to ask, who would have been around at the time, or who might put him onto a new lead, but there was no one obvious. That, and Alexander didn't want to risk getting some poor, unsuspecting person into trouble by probing where he shouldn't.

Now it seemed there was something more that Philip had been hiding, and Alexander desperately wanted to know what it was.

CHAPTER 4

Anita entered the observatory, still reeling from her latest encounter with Marcus, and still with absolutely no idea what to do. On the upside, her mood had improved considerably. She managed a beaming smile at Bass and Patrick as she reached the top of the stairs.

'Morning,' she said, happily.

'Morning,' Patrick and Bass responded in downbeat tones.

'What's up?' asked Anita. It was unlike these two to be so down in the dumps.

'They're about to make an announcement, totally out of the blue and with no preparation,' said Bass, bitterly.

'No...' stammered Anita, 'she hasn't... surely not so soon?'

'Yep, dead,' said Patrick, darkly, but with the edge of something else in his voice... excitement, maybe. 'Found in her chamber a couple of days ago. Apparently passed away in her sleep.'

Anita knew why Patrick wasn't entirely unhappy; this would be the most significant energy event the world had ever seen, and the three of them had front row seats. Despite this, Anita couldn't help but be annoyed at Patrick; he was so insensitive.

'That explains why the Descendants disappeared over the last couple of days,' said Anita, keeping to herself that she had seen Marcus, who had displayed no obvious signs of mourning.

'They're going to stand on the steps of the Body Temple and make an announcement,' said Patrick. 'Broadcast it over the airwaves, so everyone knows. Just like that.'

Anita turned her back on Patrick, shocked to find that Bass had gone pale. 'Bass? Are you alright?' she asked. He was usually so strong in a crisis.

'Aside from the fact that we're about to see an unprecedented fall in energy, that will probably destabilize our entire world, I'm peachy, thanks.'

'Right, I see. Fair point.' Anita shot a questioning look to Patrick, who shrugged in a way that said Bass had been like this all morning.

'They're about to start,' said Patrick, looking at his watch and walking over to the radio receiver to make sure it was correctly tuned. 'Here we go,' he said, almost as though he were announcing the start of a fairground ride.

A brusque yet buttery male voice cut across the room. 'Citizens of the world, we have come here today, to the Temple of the Body, to announce a terrible tragedy.' The voice paused, the trepidation of the crowd palpable. Whoever it was speaking, Anita didn't like him.

'It is with deep regret that I have to inform you that Christiana, ruler on earth for Tatiana, Goddess of the Body, has moved on from this world.' The crowd gasped. 'She passed peacefully in her sleep several nights ago.

'We, the Descendants, have been making preparations for her funeral, which will take place here in Empire, in the Temple of the Body. Her funeral will

38

take place one week from today.' Another pause, the crowd silent.

'Peter, Descendant of Christiana, will succeed to the throne to rule on earth for Tatiana, Goddess of the Body. There will be a joint Chase, Crowning, and ball for the succession of Alexander, Descendant of Theon, and Peter, Descendant of Christiana.

'Christiana was a vibrant, skillful leader of the Temple of the Body. In her honor, we expect a competitive Chase and a lively ball. I, Austin, ruling Descendant of the Temple of the Mind, understand that this will be a difficult time. We must, however, not only mourn the loss of one great leader, but celebrate the rise of two new ones. I would urge everyone, regardless of your temple allegiance, to embrace the ethos that Christiana would have wanted and celebrate our new beginning. Christiana has left us to join the Gods, and may the Gods look down favorably upon us all.'

That was it. To the point, perfunctory, nothing superfluous to the very base of what was required. Nothing that might help reassure the people that there was still hope in the world. No mention of the prophecy, or the broken female line. No declaration that, of course, the Descendants were still battling on behalf of the people, to free them from the energy instability of the Gods. Nothing.

In perfect unison with the close of Austin's speech, every light on every dashboard flashed an angry red. Bass yanked off his headset, slammed it onto his chair, then stormed out towards the roof.

'Well, I think this is an, *I told you so* moment, don't you?' said Patrick.

It amazed Anita how Patrick could be crass, even in the most dire of circumstances. Anita rolled her eyes and followed Bass up to the roof. He was sitting on a pipe, staring out over Empire. She walked slowly towards him, pausing for a moment, inches away, looking down into his cloudy eyes.

She stepped into his space and wrapped her arms around him, his head against her torso as she held him tight. He relaxed into her and she stroked his hair, a hand running down his back, trying to sooth the ridges she found there. The tension was ebbing from Bass' energy when he suddenly stood, his hands on her hips. Upright, his hard, strong body inches from hers, he pulled her towards him, hands moving to envelop her shoulders, drawing her into him.

Anita responded without thinking, wrapping her long, lithe arms around his muscular form, lowering her head into the crook of his neck. She wanted to take away his pain. They stood there for minutes, Bass caressing her back, Anita not sure how this had happened, but his energy wasn't soaring in the way it might have.

They pulled apart, Bass avoiding her eyes, wordlessly moving to the edge of the roof and sitting, legs dangling over the side, staring out towards the temples.

'At least the view's still good,' said Anita, immediately wishing she hadn't; she really needed to stop spending time with Patrick.

Bass didn't say a word, and Anita dropped down beside him. They sat in silence for an age before he finally broke it.

'My family has run this observatory for five generations,' he started, quietly, guardedly. 'You would think they might have learned to listen to us by now.'

Anita sought words to respond, but found she didn't have any, so she let the silence stretch, waiting for Bass to continue.

'My father told them what would happen if they came out with it like that, but Austin wouldn't listen, and he's the only Descendant with any legitimate power right now.'

Bass paused again, struggling. Anita felt useless, desperately wanting to help, but with no idea how.

'We told him we would see this. A sudden, dangerous drop, and then, who knows what? But it's unlikely to bounce back like it did with Philip. People think it's over. They think we'll never be free from the Gods, that the energy will be unstable forever. We've never seen anything like this, and we still don't really understand how energy works; anything could happen.' He hesitated, Anita sensing that they were about to get to the heart of Bass' rambling. 'Tens of thousands could die, and we failed to stop it.'

The words hit Anita like a train, and her reaction was immediate. 'What?' she said, with such force it surprised even her.

Bass exhaled sharply and looked away.

Anita shuffled around so she could see more of his face, placing a hand on his arm. 'You can't be serious?' she said, gently. 'You did everything you could. You stood up to Austin, who doesn't sound like a bundle of joy, and we can still find a way to bring the energy back up.'

'How are we going to do that?' said Bass. 'All gather round and politely ask the Gods if they would mind very much leaving us alone, so we can live happily ever after?'

Anita was more than a little shocked. She had never seen Bass like this, and he had certainly never spoken to her like that. She dropped her hand and turned back to face Empire, until finally, a logical argument popped into her head. 'The energy… it didn't fall until the announcement?'

'It exactly coincided with the speech. You saw the dashboards,' he said, pithily, taking a deep, loud breath that said he was humoring her, but she had better get to the point soon.

'But Christiana died several days ago,' she said. 'Austin said so himself. In which case, it wasn't Christiana's actual death that sent the energy plummeting, but peoples' reaction to the news.' She grabbed his arm in excitement. 'Which means there's at least a chance we can bring the energy levels back up. If we could make people believe we can still get rid of the Gods, then we might head off disaster.'

Bass wasn't biting. 'Come on Bass, you know I'm right. As you've suspected for some time, it's not the actual events that cause energy fluctuations, but peoples' emotional responses. It's people that control the energy, so there's still a chance we can turn this around.'

'Even if you're right, you think Austin's going to let us interfere? He's dead against any kind of intervention. He thinks we just need to accept the inevitable and get on with our lives.'

'I didn't say it would be easy,' Anita replied, her tone reflecting her irritation at Bass' uncharacteristic negativity, 'but I'm yet to find a challenge that I want to turn down, and I'm afraid this one will not be the first. So, you can either help me, which would make my life a lot easier, seeing as you're the energy expert, or you can wallow in your depression and help to pull the energy down further.'

Bass inhaled again, this time resigned; he knew she was right. 'Alright. Count me in,' he said, rolling his eyes.

Anita threw him a victor's smile.

'You can be really annoying sometimes, you know,' he said, fighting the upward turn of his lips.

'Thanks. I'll take that as a compliment,' she grinned.

* * * * *

Bass sat outside the chamber in the center of the temples. He was staring into the mid-distance, thinking about what he was going to say to the Grand Council. His father came out and put a heavy hand on his shoulder.

'We're ready for you,' said Elistair, Bass' mid-height, grey-haired father, who looked almost lanky next to Bass, even though his shoulders were broad. 'Are you ready?' His kind, perceptive eyes searched Bass'.

'As I'll ever be,' Bass replied, giving his father a knowing look.

Bass and Elistair walked into the chamber, and every pair of eyes turned to look at them. Bass ignored every single one. The hexagonal room had always fascinated him, so he let that occupy his mind instead.

The councilors from the three temples sat along three of the walls, with the Descendant for each temple sitting in the middle of their wall of councilors. On the floor, in the middle of the room, was a circle that had to remain uncovered. No one was even allowed to walk over it, the area directly above whatever sacred thing lay below the temples' points.

Opposite the middle wall of councilors was a lectern, to which they summoned guests like him, to give presentations and updates to the Grand Council.

Bass made his way purposefully to the lectern. He wouldn't let them intimidate him, so he didn't rush. He moved across the room as though he were born to be here, which, as with most of the others, was in fact the case. Regardless, he was glad to reach the safety of the lectern, where he could bring up the illustrations of his results and encourage everyone to focus on those, instead of him.

'Good morning, Descendants, councilors. It is a great honor to be here today,' said Bass, noticing that the chairs for both the Body Descendant and the Spirit Descendant were empty. Alexander and Peter were each sitting to the side of the chair that in a few days would be theirs. Presumably, Bass thought, because Austin had insisted on it. It was a petty power play that seemed redundant; like anyone would ever question who held the power here…

'As you can see,' Bass continued, using an energy wave to bring up a projection of a graph in mid-air, 'the world experienced a significant and instantaneous negative response to the news of Christiana's death. The moment Austin's speech concluded, the energy plummeted to unprecedented levels, and it continued to drop for three consecutive days. It finally slowed and levelled out last night to where it is currently, here,' he said, letting everyone take in the dramatic drop, pointing to a place on the graph that matched his words.

'To put it bluntly, we do not know the effect this drop in energy will have on our world. However, it is likely to have a profound impact on our agriculture, fish stocks, weather, and on the psyche of our people. This last point is the most important, as this is something over which we can exercise at least a modicum of control.

'Three days ago, when Austin gave his speech on the steps of the Temple of the Body, Christiana had been dead for several days already. There was no impact at all on the energy as a direct result of her death. It was only when Austin told the world that Christiana was no longer with us, that there was an instant and dramatic decline.

'Clearly, this shows that it is our perception of events and the state of the world, and not actual events and the real state of the world that have the most profound effect, indeed, any effect, on the energy. This means that if we can find a way to influence the general populous, if we could give them hope that there may yet be a way to free the world from the Gods, then we stand a chance of bringing the energy back up, of saving our world from destruction.'

Bass paused, surveying the room. 'If we don't do this, the decline in energy is likely to have increasingly negative effects. People will see the energy level as proof that their worst fears are being realized, which will, in turn, drag the energy down further, in a vicious and destructive spiral.'

Austin, who looked like Bass had just casually sauntered over to his chair, slapped him in the face, taken a bow, and then strutted back to the lectern, took to the floor. He looked down at Marcus, sitting to his right, before theatrically addressing the Grand Council. 'Councilors,' he said, in the same buttery tone he had used for the radio broadcast, 'let me start by expressing my gratitude to Bass for coming and speaking to us today.'

Austin had declined to address the other Descendants directly, self-righteous idiot.

'I'm sure it is a daunting task for one so... young,' he drawled, the condescension such that Bass had to fight quite hard the urge to punch him. Instead, he looked over to his father, who gave him a *we knew this would happen* kind of look, before turning his head back towards Austin.

'Now, it would be easy for us to jump to conclusions at this troublesome time, when we are all still grieving the loss of Christiana. However, we simply cannot try to keep alive the hope of freeing the world from the Gods. Not when that hope is gone.'

Cold silence rippled across the chamber. It was one thing to think thoughts like that, but quite another to come out and say them. The words were shocking... and dangerous.

'We have seen energy dips before,' he continued, seemingly oblivious to the effect of his words, 'and it always bounces back when people come to terms with the events that caused it. In a few days we have the Chase. This is a high-spirited event known to boost the energy, and after that, we have a double Crowning and ball. These, I am sure, will lift the energy, and I am confident there will be no...,' Austin looked pointedly at Bass, '... *destruction* for us to worry about.'

The way Austin lingered over the word destruction made it a challenge; *prove me wrong if you dare.*

Nobody in the room had the power to challenge Austin. Even if Peter and Alexander had been crowned already, it would be a bold move to take on Austin this publicly, especially so early in their Descendancies. So the room remained silent, stunned at what they had heard.

Austin's look told Bass his time was at an end, so he retreated towards the door. An aide opened it for him, and he walked out into the sunshine, weather that did not reflect his mood.

Just as expected, Bass thought, as he waited for his father. The energy update had been the last topic of the day, so they would walk home together.

Elistair exited the chamber with a collection of councilors, saying his goodbyes as they reached where Bass stood. They walked a short distance in silence before Bass could contain his emotions no longer. 'That was a complete waste of time, and to top it all off, Austin made me look like a childish idiot.'

'You know as well as I do that most people in that room knew you were talking sense.' Elistair's soft yet authoritative voice had its usual calming effect. 'Austin knew you were talking sense too. The question is, why is he so set against doing anything?'

They walked in silence as they considered the question. 'Regardless,' said Elistair, 'we will continue to monitor the energy and provide reports to the Grand Council. With so much energy wiped out, crops will fail. Austin will have no choice but to act eventually, unless he wants an uprising.'

'That would be a sight I wouldn't mind seeing,' said Bass. 'It would remove the smug smile from Austin's face. Although, I'm not sure food shortages would suit me…'

'Who knows, maybe the new Descendants will see sense,' said Elistair, although his tone didn't project confidence. 'But before anything else, the councilors need to organize a Chase,' said Elistair, chuckling. 'It was news to everyone in that room that the Chase will take place before the funeral. You should have seen James' face! I don't think he'll be getting much sleep over the next few days.'

Bass laughed wholeheartedly, glad for a diversion.

'They'll start with an announcement early tomorrow, I should think, so make sure you're watching the energy,' said Elistair. 'Anyway, enough of all that. Shall we pop in on Anita and Cordelia on the way past?'

Bass could feel his father's intent gaze at the mention of Anita's name. 'Yep, sure, why not,' said Bass, his smile faltering.

'Do you think the Chase and ball will cause an energy uptick?' Elistair asked, as though it were an unconnected, casual comment.

'You think I can't see right through you?' said Bass. 'You're so obvious it's painful. No, I'm not going to the ball with Anita. She isn't going to the ball; says it's not her thing. And no, I do not want to go with some desperate, vacuous councilor's daughter, thank you very much.'

'You've got to take somebody, and Missy is very nice; not vacuous at all.'

'Firstly, what kind of name is Missy? Secondly, that you focused on the fact that she *isn't* vacuous means that she *is* desperate, which means she probably looks like the back end of a bus.'

'Very well. Have it your way,' said Elistair, failing to hide his exasperation, 'but you've got to take somebody.'

'Oh, sod off would you,' said Bass, although there was no real fire behind his words.

* * * * *

Cordelia's house was, in fact, a small and ramshackle cottage covered in white climbing roses. It was a perfect, with a beautifully maintained garden, four pretty little windows, and a sweet, flower-lined path to the rustic front door.

As usual, Bass and Elistair veered off the path and made their way round the side of the cottage to the back door, which was wide open. They could hear voices inside, so knocked and walked straight in, calling an upbeat, 'Hello?'

'Hey,' came Anita's cheerful response as she recognized the voices. She greeted them both with a hug. Anita knew Elistair well; he was a longstanding friend of Cordelia's, which is why she and Bass had become friends. Elistair had given Anita her job at the observatory, and because of that, she saw him a lot. He would often pop in to see how research was going and to offer his opinion on any fluctuations.

'Tea?' Cordelia shouted, from the front of the house

As the others walked into the sitting room, Cordelia placed the kettle on top of the wood-burning stove, an orange glow visible through the glass. It was becoming Autumn, still warm outside, yet Cordelia always liked to have the fire burning. She said it made her feel safe, although it wasn't clear from what, and it gave the house a cozy quality.

Elistair plonked himself down into a well-worn armchair, and Bass dropped onto a sofa that had seen better days. They happily accepted steaming cups of tea and a piece of homemade chocolate and beetroot cake from Cordelia.

Anita looked around as she sat down next to Bass, curling her feet up under her, thinking how different Cordelia's house was to Elistair's. Cordelia's was small, dark, cozy, well-worn, and a total jumbled mess, whereas Elistair's was light and airy like the observatory. Elistair had filled his house with antique energy meters and devices, everything with its place, and his furniture was old and comfortable, yet smart. It was a remarkable mix of antique and modern, and Anita, normally poised and in control, always worried she was on the edge of breaking something priceless when she was there. It was curious how at home they always seemed here, she thought, helping herself and Bass to their second pieces of cake, given how they lived in different orbits…

In fact, it was strange that Elistair and Cordelia had become such good friends. Cordelia must be twenty years older than Elistair, and there was no obvious reason for their friendship. Anita couldn't think why she hadn't asked them about it before.

'How did you two meet?' she asked, cutting across the conversation.

Cordelia and Elistair turned and looked at her in surprise, Cordelia giving her a sad look. Neither immediately responded.

'Oh, I don't know,' Cordelia eventually ventured, her voice delicate yet decisive. Her tone, as usual, contained a sharp undercurrent that made people think twice before disagreeing with her. 'It was so long ago, I can't think exactly how we met.'

And with that, Elistair changed the conversation to focus on how Anita and Bass had hated each other at first, when Anita had come to live with Cordelia at the age of three. He started recounting embarrassing stories of how, through Bass' unwavering determination, they had finally become friends.

At last the torture was over and Elistair and Bass headed for home, but the look her grandmother had given her bounced around Anita's mind. She would do some digging on Cordelia and Elistair's friendship; they were hiding something.

Cordelia came back from showing Elistair and Bass out, an intriguing smile spreading across her face as she sat. 'So,' she started, meaningfully, 'I hear rumors that *somebody* wants to take you to the ball.'

What? A look of panic shot across Anita's face, a rush of adrenaline coursing through her veins. How could she possibly know? How did anyone know? She looked questioningly at the dog before inwardly chastising herself. 'I don't know what you're talking about,' she said too quickly, trying to brush the comment aside.

'Well, the whole of Empire seems to be talking about it.'

'Talking about what?' Anita asked, confused. Had Marcus told everyone?

'Whether you'll say yes, obviously.' Cordelia laughed, shaking her head in bewilderment.

'I haven't decided yet,' said Anita, only just able to form a response.

'Well, that's a turn up for the books; Bass must be thrilled!'

'Huh? What do you mean?'

'That you didn't say no outright,' said Cordelia, looking at Anita as though she might have hit her head.

'Oh...' and it all made sense. 'Bass and I are just friends, and will only ever be friends. I don't want to give him the wrong impression.'

'I see,' Cordelia replied, frowning. 'In which case, who were you talking about?'

Cordelia leaned forward in her seat, really interested now. Anita was furious at herself and got up to leave. 'I'm going for a swim, see you later,' she said, throwing the words back over her shoulder as she hurried away. Cordelia stared after her, intrigue plastered across her face.

CHAPTER 5

Two days later, Anita made her way to the riverbank opposite The Island, to where the Chase contestants had gathered. She spotted Bass and moved towards him, hoping he'd shaken off his grim mood. They had announced the Chase yesterday, the day after Bass had presented to the Grand Council. However, this had caused practically no shift in the energy, and he had been in a foul mood ever since.

'Hey,' said Anita, her tone light.

'Hi,' Bass responded, visibly perking up at the sight of her. 'Ready?'

'I was born ready,' she said, cockily. In reality, she was nervous, not that she would ever admit that to anyone. Anita had never competed against the Descendants. She'd never even seen them compete, so she had no idea what she was up against. The thought that they might beat her was unsettling.

A councilor appeared and ushered the contestants away from the rapidly growing crowd towards the top of the nearest hill. When they reached the summit, they found the Descendants already there, cloaks on, looking regal, standing in a line behind three boxes, Austin in the middle. Austin beckoned to James, the organizer, who brought him an energy speaker, so his voice would carry to the crowd below.

Austin strongly reminded Anita of Marcus, but with a few notable differences. He was older, grey hairs rippling through his dark locks, face more tanned, with lines both from age and too much time spent out in the sun. He was a little broader, a lot fuller, and had not a hint of Marcus' fun-loving disposition. Instead, he radiated a menacing authority, enhanced by cold eyes that confirmed Anita's suspicions; he was just plain mean.

'Descendants, councilors, contestants, children of the Temples of the Mind, Body and Spirit,' said Austin. 'We are here today to celebrate the beginning of a historic and momentous occasion: the Crowning of Alexander, son of Theon, and Peter, son of Christiana. As is customary, according to our traditions, those Descendants not currently in power will compete with any and all challengers to become Chase Champion.

'The Chase Champion will open the dancing as guest of honor at the ball. I am thrilled to see such a turnout to compete here today,' he said, pausing as he surveyed the contestants, 'and I do hope we have a competitive and fair Chase.'

Austin eyed Bass suspiciously, obviously sizing up Marcus' competition. It's not him you need to worry about, thought Anita, smiling to herself.

'Contestants, please take your positions.'

With those words, Alexander, Marcus, Gwyneth, and Peter took off their cloaks with a theatrical flourish, handing them to a waiting councilor. Marcus is attractive, Anita thought, watching him hand over his cloak… Gods, she needed to focus.

She forced herself to look away; she had to keep her eyes on the prize. Anita would need her wits about her today, as she suspected the 'fair' part of Austin's speech would be ignored.

The contestants lined up behind the Descendants, who were now in front of the boxes, facing down the hill towards the crowd below. The boxes contained homing pigeons, each with its home in a different location. Austin would pick one box at random, so that, in theory, nobody would know which way the pigeon would fly. He would then release it and the contestants would chase it to its home. Here, the winner would claim their prize, normally just the glory of winning, but today with the added honor of a prominent role at the ball.

They used homing pigeons, as it was easy to track their energy, and each contestant would use an energy meter to lock onto and follow the pigeon. Often contestants struggled with this part, having to either drop out right at the start if they couldn't lock on quickly enough, or follow the other contestants. Anita found locking on easy, probably because she was a reader. I must watch Alexander, she thought; he'll be off to a flying start too.

The other problem contestants often ran into was blindly following their energy reader, instead of also thinking about the best route to take. Contestants might end up at the top of a vertical incline with no easy way down, or swimming across a river without realizing there was a bridge fifty meters downstream. At least she was on home turf; that should be an advantage.

James was moving around, handing out energy meters, and Anita took the small golden box handed to her. Here we go, she thought, as the meter sprang to life in her hand. She took her place behind the Descendants at the brow of the hill.

'In the interests of fairness, I shall choose a contestant to pick the pigeon you will chase,' said Austin, motioning to a girl standing beside Bass to step forward. 'Which box shall it be?' he asked.

The girl, looking a little dazed at the responsibility, pointed at the left-hand box. 'That one,' she said, in a small voice, before stepping back into line.

'Splendid,' proclaimed Austin. 'Contestants, please ready yourselves,' he ordered, reaching forward and unhooking the latch on the left-hand box. 'I declare this Chase... open,' he roared, flinging the lid open, a pigeon launching itself into the sky.

Anita watched the pigeon in what seemed like slow motion as it paused for a split second in mid-air. She used the opportunity to point her energy meter at the bird and lock onto its energy, then hurtled down the hill with the rest of the contestants. About halfway down, someone shoved her, sending her sideways. She stumbled and almost fell as Gwyn whipped past. Bitch, thought Anita; two can play at that game.

Anita launched herself off a ledge at the bottom of the hill. It was like she was flying. Not missing a beat, she landed, completed a forward roll, and picked up her pace again. The stunt gave her a bit of a lead, as most other contestants, including Gwyn, she noticed smugly, were taking the path all the way to the bottom, now stuck in single file where the path narrowed. But Anita knew Bass would take the route she had, and the other Descendants were right behind her, so she picked up her pace.

Anita pelted at full speed across a rickety bridge, over the river into dense woodland the far side. Anita sensed someone coming up behind her, and with energy that strong, it had to be a Descendant. She didn't know which, and wouldn't waste the time and energy required to look.

She soon found out. As she came out of the woods, vaulting the fence into an open field, Alexander landed to her right, recovered from his own leap, and raced away. Anita picked up her pace to match

Alexander's, not quite believing how fast he was for a Spirit. They flew across the grass, easily jumping the stream that ran through its middle, and leapt at the steep incline to the far side. It was exhilarating. This was the first time she'd ever truly been challenged, and that spurred her to new depths of determination.

They reached the hill's summit and picked their way down the other side, back to the river. 'You could at least pretend to use your energy meter,' Alexander jibed. 'I've already warned you once.'

'You seem to have a callous disregard for your own safety, whilst being particularly concerned with mine,' she shot back. 'Any specific reason for that?'

'I'm the Spirit Descendant; people would mock me if I couldn't read energy. You, on the other hand, are a Body, with what seem to be exceptional skills. You are not what you might call normal, and this is a dangerous climate in which to stick out.'

'You seem to have remarkable Body skills for a Spirit. You seem to be fine, so I'll take my chances,' said Anita, as they reached the river, jumping from rock to rock to cross it.

The next group of challengers, including Gwyn, Bass, and Marcus, had reached the summit behind them. Anita made a show of holding up her energy meter and pointing in the direction the pigeon had flown. 'Happy now?' Anita called over her shoulder as she launched into a sprint along the riverbank. Alexander pelted after her.

They carried on at full speed for an hour, going up and down hills, across the river, over fields, through woods, until, at the summit of a small hill, Anita's energy meter started playing up. It indicated that she should head east, when she could feel the pigeon's energy heading north.

'That's weird,' said Anita, as they ran down the slope, 'my energy meter's telling me to go east. What does yours say?'

'It says to head north,' said Alexander, showing Anita his meter, 'and I can feel its energy heading that direction.'

'I can too,' she said, Alexander's face hardening.

'Austin…' said Alexander.

'Um, why?' Anita asked, as they reached the flat and headed north.

'He must have tampered with the meters because he wants a Descendant to win. Energy meters don't just stop working. They lock onto one source of energy and don't change until they're given a new target. Are you sure you didn't accidentally set it to a new target?'

'No, of course not. I'm not stupid,' she said, indignantly. 'I work at the observatory for Gods' sake; I know how to use an energy meter.'

'You work at the observatory?' he said, clearly surprised. 'You're an energy expert too?'

'I wouldn't go as far as expert,' she said, upping the pace a little, 'but I work with Bass and help him monitor the energy.'

'Brilliant,' he said, sarcastically. 'You're an energy reading Body who also knows all about the… issues we face. It doesn't get much worse than that. You've got to lose the Chase.'

Anita laughed. 'You're off your rocker if you think I'm going to do that.'

'You've got to. Austin will know you're a reader if you win.'

'How? I'll say I saw the pigeon heading north and that your meter was pointing north, so I headed north. It's not entirely untrue.'

'And what about when we get to the end? How are you going to explain how you actually find the pigeon?'

'I'll get lucky.'

'You'll get lucky? Yeah, sure, no one will suspect a thing.'

Anita had had enough. 'You stay here and keep spouting doom and gloom if you want to, but I'm going to get a move on.'

Alexander couldn't do much but pick up his pace; he would have to make sure he got to the pigeon first.

Two hours later, both Anita and Alexander knew they were nearly there. The pigeon had stopped, and its energy was getting closer. They leapt over a gate from one field to another and a beautiful farmhouse, several rickety old barns, and a massive crowd came into view.

They raced across the field and a cheer went up from the crowd. All eyes turned towards them as they competed to take the lead. As they reached the courtyard, Alexander was slightly in front. They sensed the pigeon's energy behind them at the same time, both immediately whipping around, turning in perfect unison, like dancers performing a routine. They headed for a barn, Anita now slightly ahead, having benefitted from the sudden change in direction.

As she entered the barn, she saw the pigeon sitting on a low stack of rectangular hay bales. Alexander's energy was immediately behind her, so strong that it felt like it might envelop her, but she reached out and snatched the scroll at the pigeon's feet just ahead of his large, muscular hand. She somehow leapt on top of the bales to avoid directly colliding with them and tried to slow herself down. Alexander had no option but to do the same, bowling into Anita with such momentum that he pushed her off the other side. He landed on top of her, leaving them in an awkward heap on the floor, luckily not totally in view of the growing crowd.

'Happy?' Alexander hissed.

'I will be when you get off me,' she retorted. 'You know there's nothing worse than a sore loser.'

Alexander looked spectacular, in a terrifying sort of way, his face inches from hers. She cocked an eyebrow. He stood and stalked out of the barn, visibly trying to regain his composure.

Anita got up as gracefully as she could and found herself face to face with Austin.

'Well, that was interesting,' he said, in a sing-song voice, pinning her with cold and dangerous eyes. 'Congratulations… um…'

'Anita,' Elistair said, coming to the rescue, 'congratulations. A startling performance, as ever. Austin, this girl has won every contest she has ever entered, and she hasn't disappointed again here today. Well done, Anita.'

Thank the Gods for Elistair.

'The presentation, Austin?' prompted Elistair.

'Yes, of course, follow me.'

Anita followed Austin out of the barn, Elistair stuck firmly to her side. As they emerged into the courtyard, Anita saw a few other contestants finishing, with groups of stragglers still following behind. Anita caught Bass' eye. He sported both a huge grin and an enormous graze down one of his legs. She gave him a questioning look. He inclined his head in the general direction of Gwyn and Marcus, and Anita was glad she hadn't had to deal with the two of them. Poor Bass.

Elistair ushered Anita after Austin, who was giving off extremely strong negative energy. Maybe Alexander was right; maybe she should have kept a low profile. Well, too late for that now, she thought, as she stepped up in front of the crowd.

'Descendants, councilors, contestants, children of the Temples of the Mind, Body and Spirit,' said Austin, back in his element. 'Today we have witnessed a spectacular, competitive Chase, with our worthy contestants having battled for three long hours, over difficult and varied terrain. But, as is always the case, there can only be one victor, and today, by an excruciating margin–better luck next time, Alexander– the victor is Anita, of the Temple of the Body.'

A roar went up from the crowd, much to Anita's surprise. Normally everyone was indifferent when she won; they must be happy that someone other than a Descendant had finished first.

'As is customary for a Chase of this importance, we have a spectacular prize for our winner. Along with being guest of honor at the Crowning Ball, and leading the ball's first dance, I present to you, Anita, a vintage energy meter from my own private collection.'

The crowd gave another roar as Austin took the energy meter from James, who had been nervously hovering with it at the side of the stage, and handed it to Anita. Austin looked pained.

'That concludes today's festivities,' said Austin. 'I trust that you all had an enjoyable day and I thank the contestants for playing their part. Please make your way to the energy trains, which will return you to Empire.'

The crowd dispersed and Anita made her way towards Bass and Elistair, but before she could reach them, a hand closed around her arm. The hand belonged to Austin, who looked like a small boy about to pull the wings off a fly.

'Our champion can't travel back with the crowds. You *must* travel with us,' he said, in his horrible, over-the-top voice. He pulled Anita towards a floating golden carriage with plush, overstuffed red velvet seats. It probably cost more than Cordelia's cottage.

The carriage already contained Marcus and a driver, and her energy leapt as they neared. Great; this won't be awkward at all. She took a deep breath and gave herself a talking to; she could handle one brief carriage ride. How bad could it really be? But as she reached the steps, an unwelcome hand blocked her path.

'Allow me to help you,' said Alexander, in his charming, chocolate voice. He took Anita's hand, then moved aside to help her climb the steps. 'Austin, I thought I would ride back with you. I trust that will be okay,' he said, climbing in behind Anita without waiting for a response.

'Of course,' Austin snarled, as he too climbed aboard. 'Let's get a move on then,' he barked, once he'd sat down next to Marcus. Alexander took the seat next to Anita.

They travelled in awkward silence for several minutes, Anita looking out over the countryside, avoiding her travelling companions. She hoped this would be enough to discourage conversation, but knew it was unlikely to be that easy.

'That was quite a show, Anita,' said Austin, dangerously.

Anita had no choice but to look at him now, his hard, brown eyes glinting as he stared menacingly at her.

'Very impressive,' said Marcus.

'Thanks,' she said, in the sweetest, most innocent tone she could conjure. 'I've always had a knack for Body contests.'

'I see,' said Austin.

'Yes, congratulations,' said Alexander. 'It was close at the end there, but the best contestant won.' The sliver of air between them hummed with tension, so she looked away, eyes snagging on Marcus, who seemed to be sizing up Alexander. It looked as though he might be about to launch an attack across the carriage. Anita couldn't understand why...

'It was especially impressive how you turned so quickly at the end, when you both realized you were heading in the wrong direction,' said Austin, resuming his campaign.

Anita looked him straight in the eye, trying to project an air of non-threatening, naïve confidence. 'Well, as you know, we Body types are prone to lightening reactions. When I saw Alexander turn, I did the same. When I turned around, I saw the open entrance to the barn, took a punt, and got lucky.

'The strangest thing happened in the middle of the Chase... my energy meter broke. Luckily, I saw the pigeon heading north, and, of course, could see Alexander was still heading north, so I continued that way, but it's such a strange occurrence for an energy meter to go wrong like that. Have you ever heard of that happening before?'

Austin's gaze turned murderous. His energy went from playful boy to hostile animal. Alexander stiffened beside her, his energy defensive. Anita's energy intensified, not focused on Austin, as it should have been, but distracted by Alexander. Alexander's energy softened, almost imperceptibly, and then turned hard as steel.

Bloody hell, thought Anita, wondering what might happen next, when to everyone's surprise, Marcus threw her a bone. 'Most likely you reset the meter to track something else by accident. It happens.'

Marcus, the diplomat. This was surprising, although Anita didn't miss the plea in his eyes. 'Yes, probably,' said Anita, pulling herself together with a slight shake of her head. 'Luckily, I was with Alexander, and I could follow him, otherwise I would have been out of the race. Given how competitive I am, that would not have been an attractive sight.' She laughed, hoping self-depreciation would move them to safer territory.

'Well, luckily you did have Alexander to follow, so we have the good fortune of your company on our journey home,' said Marcus, again taking everyone by surprise.

Anita went bright red, thinking instantly of the kiss in the field, and Marcus' invitation to the ball. Shit, she thought, please don't bring that up now. This time, it was her who sent Marcus a pleading look. Alexander came to the rescue, obviously feeling her energy shift. He asked Austin about the history of the energy meter Anita had won. Alexander would now suspect something was up with her and Marcus, but she would take that over Marcus discussing the ball in front of Austin any day.

Austin, glad the attention was once again back on him, launched into a story about how the meter had belonged to his father, Tobias. The story lasted all the way back to the city.

Anita zoned Austin out, watching the countryside whip past. She took deep breaths, desperately trying to subdue her out-of-control energy, but with Marcus and Alexander so close, there was nothing she could do. Alexander shifted in his seat and his hand brushed against hers. It sent a shiver of energy up her arm, into her brain, the feeling so intoxicating, it almost made her gasp.

She was horribly confused and couldn't have been happier when the carriage pulled up outside Cordelia's cottage. She could say goodbye and retreat to a place where there were no readers to scrutinize her energy, nor spectacular specimens to cause it to spike.

* * * * *

Anita headed to The Island later that night to see Cleo; it had been ages since they'd hung out. She walked into the bar, hearing Cleo before she saw her.

'I knew she would win. I told you. She's never been beaten, and she wouldn't let a few Descendants stop her.'

'Hey Cleo,' Anita called across the room, waving at her best friend. Anita made gestures which hopefully meant *I'm going to get a drink, I'll come over in a minute*, and headed to the haphazard little bar to place her order.

The Island was packed full of people who'd been at the Chase, both those who'd been in the crowd and contestants, but thankfully the Descendants didn't appear to be around. At least that gives me more time until I have to give Marcus an answer, thought Anita, suddenly unbalanced as an overexcited Cleo yanked her sideways.

'YOU DID IT!' Cleo squealed, wrapping Anita in a frenzied embrace. 'WELL DONE!'

'Thanks. It was a bit close for comfort this time; I made it by a whisker.'

'I knew you would do it. Now, let me buy you a celebratory drink.'

Anita put her hand up to protest, but Cleo shot her a warning look so ferocious that she immediately backed down.

'Thanks. I'll have an Empire then, please,' a cocktail made of a curious mix of spirits that Anita had never quite managed to determine.

This, Cleo seemed pleased with, presumably because the drink was both extremely potent and suitably extravagant. Cleo called the order to the bartender, who said he would bring the drinks over, then dragged Anita to her table. Cleo shooed away the guys she'd been talking to then leant in conspiratorially; there was clearly something Cleo wanted to discuss.

'So,' Cleo started, still totally over the top, 'I've heard a rumor.'

'Oh, a new and different pastime for you. I'm thrilled you're branching out...'

'Sarcasm is the lowest form of wit.'

'No, really?'

Cleo gave her a chastising look, but couldn't contain herself any longer, so pressed on. 'I've heard that Marcus is inviting someone outside his usual circle to the ball.'

'Really?' asked Anita, with a slight flutter of panic. 'How do you know that?'

'Well, you know James, the Mind councilor who organized the Chase?'

'Yes.'

'His son Henry has invited me to the ball!'

'Oh my Gods! No way!' said Anita, with genuine excitement.

'Thanks,' said Cleo, looking smug. 'We can discuss how I pulled that off in a minute, but anyway, he came in to see me last night for a drink, and we drank a little too much Island Punch. He started saying that Marcus' friends have all been teasing him about not having a date for the ball. Pretty much everyone else in their circle has one, most of them with each other, obviously, apart from Marcus, Henry, and one other notable exception,' said Cleo, eyeing Anita deviously. 'Some girl called Missy, who will attend the ball with Bass.'

'What kind of name is Missy?' laughed Anita. 'And who is she?' she asked, both relieved and a tiny bit jealous, if she was being totally honest. She didn't want to date Bass, but something about their long friendship made her irrationally possessive of him.

'She's the daughter of some senior councilor. Their parents probably orchestrated it... but anyway, Henry said they were all been teasing Marcus about it

65

yesterday, and he said he had options outside the normal crowd. Apparently, he said he's not telling anyone who he's taking, because he wants it to be a surprise on the night.'

Anita sat very still, not saying a word. Should she tell Cleo? It would be good to talk to someone about it. But before she got a chance, Cleo was already speculating about who it could be.

'I think it's that girl in our Mind class; the useless one who thinks she's a gift from the Gods. Or maybe the girl that Austin let pick the pigeon this morning; maybe he's in on it too. I can't imagine Austin would like it if Marcus turned up at the ball with someone outside their circle, unless he knew about it first.'

'Cleo,' Anita said quietly.

'Uh huh,' Cleo replied, at the same time as thanking the waiter for their drinks.

'There's something I need to talk to you about,' she said, 'um… outside.'

Cleo looked worried. 'Is everything alright?'

'Yep, but it's crowded in here.'

'Okay,' said Cleo, picking up their drinks and heading to the back door.

They sat on a bench overlooking the river, and Anita took a long sip of her toxic cocktail. 'Delicious, as always,' she said, racking her brain for the right words.

'You didn't bring me out here to talk about cocktails,' replied Cleo, energy full of anxious excitement, presumably because she'd caught a tantalizing whiff of gossip.

'No,' said Anita, still wondering how to approach this. 'You know the other week when I turned down Marcus' offer to go back to his place with the others?'

'No,' gasped Cleo, 'you went?'

Anita smirked and shook her head. 'No.'

'Oh. Sorry, carry on.'

'A few days later, I was running by the river, when Marcus ran up behind me. He asked if he could join me for a run, so obviously I put him through his paces.'

Cleo smirked.

'We got a fair distance before he wanted to stop for a break, and we chatted for a bit.' Cleo's face froze in a look of open-mouthed disbelief, and Anita had to stifle a laugh as she continued. 'He asked me to go to the ball with him. Well, it was more of a command than a question really…'

'… you're the one he's taking to the ball?'

'I'm not sure.'

'You're not sure? What do you mean, *you're not sure*? You said yes?'

'Um.'

'Um?'

'Well, I told him, *maybe*.'

'You told him *maybe*?' Cleo repeated in a disgusted tone.

'Yes.'

'Right.'

They sat there in dumbfounded silence for a minute before Cleo piped up again. 'As you know, this doesn't normally happen to me, but I'm basically speechless. You've got to go to the ball with him.'

'Why?'

'Why? Because he's a Descendant, and can you imagine the look on bitch-face Gwyneth's face if you do? I saw her shove you at the start of the Chase.'

'That's probably the best reason I've thought of so far,' laughed Anita. 'But other than that, I just don't know if it's a good idea.'

'Why not?'

'I don't want to draw attention to myself.'

'You didn't stop to consider that when you won the Chase this morning.'

'I know.'

'Even so, why not? A bit of attention might be fun.'

'Hmmm.'

'You have to lead the first dance anyway, so it may as well be with someone who'll look good, and by the Relic, does he look good.'

'That makes it even worse; leading the first dance will be like asking everyone to speculate about what's going on between us. It's more of a punishment than a prize, if you ask me.'

'Let them speculate and enjoy the attention; that's what I'd do.'

'Yes, well, you've always been better at that than me.'

'You should go with him. Enjoy it. Put two fingers up to Gwyn; you know you want to.'

'I'm still thinking about it. Don't worry, you'll be the first to know what I decide. But in the meantime, don't you dare tell anyone.'

Cleo looked hurt. 'Me? Gossip? *Never.*'

'Come on, let's go inside. I think I need another drink.'

CHAPTER 6

The following day was Christiana's funeral and Anita walked to the Temple of the Body with Cordelia, Alastair and Bass. Cordelia and Anita found seats in the open section at the back, whereas Alastair and Bass walked the seemingly endless distance to the front, where seats were for councilors. As was customary, those belonging to the Temple of the Body had priority over the newly laid out seats. Those belonging to the other temples took any seats left over, or stood.

The Body Temple didn't have the same colossal, open expanse as the Spirit Temple. As opposed to sky-high pillars holding up the roof, the Body Temple had a series of high arches splitting the space into distinctly separate, but relatively open sections. Every temple had a clear run from at least one entrance to its altar. In the Spirit Temple, every entrance had this, but in the Body Temple, many had to sit in side chambers with views obstructed by intricate stonework. The Mind Temple was a total nightmare for large public events, the spaces so closed off that only a very fortunate few ever got to see anything. That's how the Mind Descendants liked things; small and elitist.

Twenty minutes later, the seats were full. A massive crowd stretched out behind the temple, penned by ropes designed to keep a clear path for the coffin.

Christiana had been extremely popular, mostly for her fairness and generosity, and many people had travelled from Kingdom to attend.

Music wafted back through the temple from a harp at the front, bouncing around the arches and up to the spire above. It was vibrant yet haunting, the hair on the back of Anita's neck rising as the procession of the coffin and Descendants began.

Everyone turned in their seats to watch as the coffin, carried by six Body councilors, entered the temple, Peter and Gwyn following immediately behind. They were both wearing black cloaks and Gwyn had a black birdcage veil across her face, with small white flowers in her hair. Theatrical, thought Anita.

Behind them was Alexander, also with a floor-length black cloak, his disheveled hair a little more tame than usual. He sported his customary regal-yet-rugged look, like some ancient knight about to wield a sword in pursuit of the righteous. His energy was less prominent than normal, Anita wondering how he masked it. Finally, Austin and Marcus entered the temple, also in black cloaks, but theirs with a red trim running around the edge.

Austin walked in front of Marcus, looking every inch the evil dictator as he sauntered in. Marcus, however, looked regal, chiseled features as glorious as ever as he strode confidently after his father. He spotted Anita, looking directly at her, locking his eyes with hers as he ascended the steps. Anita held his gaze, hoping nobody noticed; she couldn't make herself look away.

Marcus neared where she sat, breaking eye contact to keep from having to turn his head, continuing up the aisle to join the other Descendants. Cordelia looked sideways at Anita, but said nothing. She knew Austin and Marcus had given Anita a lift home after the Chase, had probed for every detail; she would be insufferable now.

The funeral was short and emotional. Austin gave the opening speech, which caused a ruffle in the crowd. He explained it away in his normal, cloying tone. 'As the only current reigning Descendant...' Anita rolled her eyes.

There were several moving tributes to Christiana and the spectacular Body feats she had achieved during her life, along with accounts of her generosity to those of all temples. Peter gave a gripping insight into life as the child of someone so exceptional, however, the most moving account was the last, from Alexander.

'... and at five, when I had recently lost both my father, in a tragic fire in this very temple, and my mother, of a broken heart, just a few months later, it was Christiana who guided me. Over the years, she was a source of unparalleled council.

'She was a leader but not a dictator, she was competitive, proud, stubborn, but above all compassionate. She observed the world around her, striving not to control, but to understand. She was a source of hope, believing in honesty and doing what was right, even when this path was the most difficult and dangerous of all.

'But Christiana's mortality was part of what made her great, and her time had come, as it will for us all. Our deep and painful loss is truly the Goddess Tatiana's gain.'

At the end of the funeral, the Descendants and councilors processed out with the coffin. Christiana's body would be transported back to Kingdom, where she would be buried alongside her ancestors. The crowd dispersed as soon as the procession left the temple.

Cordelia turned to Anita and fixed her with a curious look. 'I didn't realize you and Marcus were such good friends,' she said, in a low voice that only Anita could hear.

'We're not. Why would you say that?' she asked, getting up to file out of the temple with everyone else.

'You know just fine why I say that... we can talk about it later.'

Cordelia had spotted Elistair and Bass and made a beeline for them. Anita was following in her wake, totally preoccupied by thoughts of Marcus' alluring gaze, when a presence blocked her path. She looked up, shocked to find Marcus inches in front of her, her energy immediately responding.

Get. A. Grip. Anita. She silently yelled.

'Hi,' he said.

'Hi,' she replied, eyeing him with a *can I help you* kind of look, conscious of all the watching eyes around them.

'I was wondering if you'd given any more thought to my invitation?' he said, in a low voice.

'Oh, was that what it was?' she asked, feigning surprise, her voice not much more than a whisper. 'You see, I was under the impression that it was more of a command than an invitation.'

Marcus assessed her for a beat, a disorientated look morphing into a playful one. 'I see. Well, for that I must apologise, Anita. I should attempt to clarify.' He cleared his throat in an elaborate manor before murmuring, 'Anita, Champion of the Chase, would you do me the exceptional honor of attending the ball with me?'

'I'm not sure that invitation possessed the level of gravity required for something so important. How am I to know your request is earnest?'

'Your concern is the sincerity of my proposal?' said Marcus.

Was that a real question…? 'There was a certain frivolity to it,' she replied, not meaning to take the flirting to quite this level in such a public place, even if their tones were hushed, 'but I suspect your invitation is sincere.'

'In which case…' he said, looking expectantly at her.

Anita paused, considering how to respond. Should she say yes? Cleo would certainly be happy… She tilted her head up, searching his eyes, reminded of their encounter by the river. Judging by the catch in his breath, he was there too, his eyes flicking to her lips.

Luckily, at that moment, Austin's voice boomed, shattering the moment.

'Marcus, there you are,' he said, seeing Anita as he reached where they stood. 'Ah, the champion. How are you, Anita?'

'Very well thank you, and you?' she said, surprised he'd asked.

'Yes, yes, very well,' he said, casting her aside. 'Come on Marcus, we have lunch to get to.'

And without another word, Austin dragged Marcus away, Marcus briefly looking back at Anita, who flashed him a smile as she mouthed the word, 'Maybe'.

Anita spotted Elistair, Bass and Cordelia, and made her way over to them, elated. She'd put off giving Marcus an answer and had the last word.

'Where have you been?' asked a suspicious Cordelia.

'I spotted a friend and said hello,' she said, which wasn't entirely untrue.

'We're heading up to Elistair's for lunch,' said Cordelia, 'I take it you don't have any other plans?'

Bass looked at Anita, clearly hoping she would join them. 'I'm free as a bird,' she sighed. 'Lead the way.'

* * * * *

After lunch, Anita took her wine out onto the balcony. She adored the view from here, at the top of the hill, looking out over the wild countryside and river below. She would love to live up here, in this dramatic setting, just outside of Empire. The house was prominent and modern yet not overpowering, with clean, angular lines. If only she were in love with Bass; life would be divine.

Bass slid the door closed behind him as he joined her on the balcony, standing close as he leaned on the wooden railing, their arms touching.

'You're one lucky guy,' she said.

'How so?' he laughed.

'You can wake up and look at this wild, beautiful view every morning, then go to the observatory and stare out over Empire to your heart's content.'

He laughed again, eyes twinkling. 'Yep, I'm exceptionally lucky when it comes to magnificent views; can't argue with you there.'

They stared out in silence, taking in the scenery for a few moments, before Bass said, 'The ball…'

Anita looked at Bass, anxiety screwing up inside her. Don't do it, Bass, she silently pleaded. 'Yep,' she replied, as calmly as she could.

'I know you said you weren't going before, because it wasn't your thing, but now that you have to go… well, I've asked this girl, Missy, but only because her father is a friend of Dad's, and I said I'd do it as a favor…' He paused, taking what looked like a difficult breath, '… but if you would want to go with me, I'll tell her there was a misunderstanding or something,' he said, rushing the words out. 'I'd hate for you to have to do the first dance on your own…' He nudged her arm playfully.

Anita took a long inward breath. 'Bass.' She turned to look at him, barely bringing herself to hold his gaze when she saw the hopeful look in his eyes. 'Any girl in this town would jump at the chance to go to the ball with you; you know that. I'm sure Missy is really looking forward to it…'

'… yes, but…' Anita put a hand on his arm to silence him. She had to put an end to this. Maybe the wine was making her bold, or maybe it had something to do with the arrival of Marcus and Alexander in Empire, but it wasn't fair to let Bass think there was hope.

'I love you, Bass, but I love you like a brother. I wish I felt differently; it would make everything so simple… but, I'm sorry, I just don't see you that way.' She paused, racked with guilt at his crestfallen expression. 'You should go to the ball with Missy; I'm sure she's great.'

Bass turned away, gazing at the river. 'Maybe if we went on a date, maybe if…'

'… it wouldn't make any difference.'

He turned back to face her. 'But, what if… I mean, we could still go to the ball together.'

'No. That wouldn't be fair on Missy, and it wouldn't be fair on you either.'

He sighed and ran a hand through his hair, the cogs of his mind visibly turning. His eyes met hers, flicking from one to the other, searching her soul. Eventually, he nodded, turning back to rest on the railing, his energy betraying deep hurt, but also resignation. 'Who are you going with then?'

'That's not yet confirmed,' she said.

Silence settled over them as they leaned on the railing. They stood there for a minute, marinating in their changed dynamic, letting a new equilibrium settle.

Anita eventually squeezed his arm before turning back towards the house, moving towards the door.

Bass let her go, the flame of hope that had kindled for so long in his core, finally fluttering out.

* * * * *

The following day, Anita felt lighter. She would never want to hurt Bass, but was glad he finally knew her feelings. She had even survived her grandmother's questioning about Marcus on the way home, telling her instead about the conversation with Bass. Cordelia had been indignant. She thought Anita and Bass were perfect for each other and couldn't imagine why Anita didn't recognize that she was onto a good thing.

Given her good spirits, Anita felt like a ride, so headed to a small stable yard on the outskirts of Empire. She'd helped there since she was twelve, in exchange for free riding, and now had her pick of the horses.

She galloped across an open field, heading for the woods, flying across the ditch in the middle, hurtling towards the trees at breakneck speed. But as she approached the woods, she felt extraordinary energy coming towards her. She slowed to a canter just as a colossal black stallion sailed over one of the enormous jumps out of the woods. The rider circled wide into the field, heading over the next jump back into the woods.

Given the power of the rider's energy, along with their disheveled hair, Anita knew it was Alexander. This was confirmed moments later when a bay stallion, also bearing a rider with powerful energy, soared over the fence into view and completed the same wide circle before hurrying back into the woods. Without thinking, Anita spurred her grey mare back to a gallop, heading for the corner of the woods. She hoped she could catch them and join in with what was obviously a race.

Anita easily cleared the fence into the woods. As she landed, she heard hooves thundering just in front of her and to her right. She maneuvered her mare, Iona, through the trees, and came out just behind Alexander's black stallion, preparing to launch them over the next jump.

Anita hurriedly collected her mount and followed Alexander over, urging Iona up beside him when they landed. Alexander's head swiveled as she came level.

'What are you doing here?' he shouted.

'I was out for a ride and saw the fun, so thought I'd join in,' she replied impishly, flashing him a disarming smile before ducking to avoid a branch.

'Has spectating ever occurred to you?'

'Ha!' she laughed. 'Don't be ridiculous.'

Alexander pulled in front to clear the next jump, this one taking them back into the field. The other side he hurtled towards the hedge between this field and the next, Anita once again following him without hesitation.

Marcus emerged from the woods and was gaining ground, his stallion fast across the flat open field. He urged his horse faster still, catching Anita, who had dropped behind.

'Fancy seeing you here,' Marcus shouted.

'Is that the only line you know?'

'If you ever agree to spend some time with me, maybe you'll find out,' he replied, as Alexander cleared another fence back into the woods. Anita followed, landing safely, but Marcus clipped the fence as he jumped. His stallion lurched forward as they landed, Marcus thrown clear into the undergrowth, his horse bolting.

Alexander and Anita, hearing Marcus' expletives as he thudded to the ground, reigned in their mounts.

They turned back to see if he was alright, Marcus' horse thundering past.

Anita leapt off Iona and ran to where Marcus had landed. He was trying to sit up as she got there and smiled when he saw it was her.

'We meet again,' he said.

Not too badly injured then. However, before she could come up with something good in reply, another voice chimed in.

'How careless of you to lose your steed, Marcus,' said Alexander, as he walked his horse back towards them. 'I do believe you owe me your next shipment of chocolate.'

Anita felt Marcus' energy turn, red hot anger raging through him. Alexander's energy brightened as he sensed Marcus' rage. He was enjoying himself, but Anita couldn't see why. Marcus had lost, Alexander hadn't won.

'And to lose in front of your girlfriend… in fact, to withdraw… how embarrassing for you.'

Anita had never known energy as hostile as Marcus' was now.

'She's not my girlfriend,' he said, through gritted teeth.

'I see,' said Alexander, lifting an eyebrow, 'you can't even get someone like *her* to go out with you. Interesting.'

Anita scowled. It was one thing to goad Marcus for loosing, even if he was taking it too far, but it was quite another to bring her into it. Anita's energy ignited with such ferocity that it forced Alexander to sit up straight.

'I may not be his girlfriend,' she said, 'but we are going to the ball together.' Anita almost laughed when she saw the look on Marcus' face.

Alexander gave a small smile, then turned and galloped away. He forced his energy to remain light until he was out of Anita's range, then released the damper on his feelings. Anita's venom had taken him by surprise, but even more surprising was that it hurt.

His plan had worked; he had wanted Anita to be under Marcus' protection. It was unlikely that Austin would harm Anita while Marcus had feelings for her, but Alexander hadn't planned for it to happen like this. He hadn't wanted to make her hate him; he wanted to help her. Alexander cleared the fence out of the woods and galloped towards home.

Marcus sat, gob smacked, staring up at Anita. 'You're coming to the ball with me?'

'It would appear so,' she said, as surprised as Marcus and needing to escape, to consider what she had just done. 'Have a pleasant walk home,' she said, mounting her horse.

'What? You're just going to leave me here?' Marcus' indignant, disbelieving tone was comical. 'You tell me you'll go to the ball with me and then you just leave?'

'It would seem so.'

'But I'll see you before the ball?'

'I'll probably be at the Crownings, so you might see me there.'

'But where should I pick you up?'

Anita thought briefly about this. 'At my grandmother's. Where you dropped me off the other day.'

'Right, well, I'll let you know what time?'

'Great. I'll look forward to it,' she replied, her manner sterile.

'Me too,' said Marcus, at a loss for words as Anita turned and cantered away.

* * * * *

Anita and Cleo sat by the river. Anita had been to work at the observatory, but Bass had been so down in the dumps that she'd left early. She wasn't sure if it was because of what she'd said to him, the energy, or both, but she couldn't bear to be around him when he was so depressed.

'I told Bass it's not going to happen,' said Anita, absentmindedly looking down at the river.

'You did?' Cleo turned to look at her, amazed. 'I didn't think you'd ever get round to putting the poor guy out of his misery. At least that explains why he's been in such a foul mood.'

'I hope that's not the only reason.'

'Why else?'

'The energy.'

Neither Anita nor Cleo knew in any exact way what that meant, but they knew whatever effects the downturn would have, they would not be good.

'Also, I'm going to need your help,' said Anita.

Cleo practically fell into the river. 'Who are you and what have you done with Anita?'

'I'm going to need your help getting ready for the ball.'

Cleo's reaction was immediate, and as expected, totally disproportionate. 'Oh my Gods! No! Really? With Marcus?'

Anita nodded, throwing Cleo an indulgent look. Cleo grabbed her and hugged her excitedly.

'This is too exciting,' she squealed. 'So, we need to get you a dress, and work out what to do with your hair, and your make-up… have you thought about make-up? And jewelry, and what about shoes? How high can you go? Marcus is tall, right?'

'Um, well, he's taller than me,' she said, reliving the encounter by the river. She'd had to look up at him to meet his eyes. 'I'm, what, five foot ten? He's definitely over six feet.'

'Yep, that sounds about right,' said Cleo. 'All the Descendants are tall, apart from bitch-face, obviously; the good genes skipped her generation. Ridiculous heels it is then, and I'm taking you shopping. You need something spectacular to wear, and I'll get my hairdresser to do your hair. We need all the help we can get in that department,' said Cleo, eyeing Anita's almost shoulder length dark hair suspiciously. It would definitely pose more of a challenge than Cleo's long, silky, black tresses, but some kind of up-do would work. 'Hair up, subtle makeup, floor-length dress…'

'… everyone will be in floor-length dresses,' Anita laughed.

'Just clarifying, in case you get some crazy idea in your head and go shopping without me.'

'I see,' said Anita. 'Well, I'll leave it to you, my style guru. Just don't tell anyone who I'm going with, okay?'

'Okay. We can go shopping tomorrow. This is too exciting for words!' she said, giving Anita another quick squeeze.

* * * * *

'Is Marcus any good at dancing?' Cleo asked, as she helped herself to a piece of Cordelia's pumpkin and walnut cake. They'd just got back from Temple Mews, where they'd bought Anita's dress and shoes for the ball.

'How should I know?' said Anita. 'But I would imagine so, given that the Descendants seem to be trained for every eventuality.'

'You know Cordelia is a genius,' Cleo garbled through a mouthful of cake. 'She really is.'

'Thank you, Cleopatra,' came a voice from the corner.

Anita whipped round to see Cordelia looking smug. How had she come in without them hearing? Great, now Cordelia knew; she would never live this down.

'You're going to the ball with Marcus?' Cordelia asked, clearly amused.

Anita glared at Cleo, who shrugged apologetically. 'She was going to find out, eventually.'

'Yes,' sighed Anita, 'I'm going to the ball with Marcus.'

'I knew you were up to something,' said Cordelia, settling into an armchair. 'Come on, tell me everything.'

Anita recounted the story about the run by the river (leaving out the kiss), the encounter after Christiana's funeral, and the ride in the woods, Cordelia listening intently, fascinated.

'We need to get you a dress,' said Cordelia, when Anita had finished. 'Something show-stopping, and shoes, and what are you going to do with your hair?'

Cleo jumped in before Anita could utter a word; there was no choice but to go with it. Anita showed Cordelia her dress and shoes and listened to how she would have her hair and makeup. She observed Cordelia and Cleo's childish excitement as they speculated about the first dance. After what seemed like an eternity, Cleo got up to leave.

'See you tomorrow at the Crowning,' she said, making her way to the door. 'Don't forget to get your beauty sleep; tomorrow is a big day.'

'Yes ma'am,' said Anita, half saluting, half waving as Cleo left the room. Cordelia turned to face Anita square on. 'I know, I'm sorry...' Anita started.

'... sorry for what?' Cordelia said, cutting her short. 'I'm thrilled for you and you two are going to look fabulous leading the first dance; you're such a wonderful dancer. Wait here, I've got something for you.'

Cordelia disappeared out of the room and came back a minute later carrying a large wooden box. She opened the lid and fumbled around inside before lifting out a beautiful gold and diamond tiara. It had a swirling pattern with a string of upward points designed to sit low on the wearer's head. Anita sat and stared, totally speechless.

'It was your mother's,' said Cordelia. 'She would have wanted you to have it and it will go perfectly with that dress.'

Cordelia rarely mentioned Anita's mother, Clarissa. Anita assumed it was because Cordelia didn't know that much about her. Cordelia was Anita's paternal grandmother, not that she ever really spoke about her son, Jeffrey, either.

'It's beautiful,' said Anita.

'It will look beautiful on you,' said Cordelia, closing the wooden box.

Anita had tried to probe about her parents on countless occasions, but Cordelia simply would not open up; it seemed too painful. Anita had rummaged around the cottage enough to know that Cordelia kept nothing that gave any clues. She had even been to the archives, but they had been useless. She only hoped that one day Cordelia would decide to fill in the blanks.

CHAPTER 7

The following day, Anita woke early, as always, and headed to the garden for a yoga session. Surrounded by the smell of her grandmother's flowers and the sound of the gurgling stream at the bottom of the garden, it was easy to forget the world.

She lay on the ground afterwards, arms outstretched, and couldn't stop her mind from speculating about the day and night ahead. Leading the first dance didn't worry her; that would be a walk in the park. What did worry her was how everyone would react to her turning up with Marcus. And then there was Alexander. One minute he wanted to 'help' her, and who knew what that meant... the next he was insulting her.

She lay there, eyes open, watching the puffy white clouds as they slid seamlessly across the powder blue sky. She was contemplating going back inside when a wave of powerful energy hit her senses, approaching from the road. She held her breath, adrenaline spiking through her veins, poised to take defensive action.

'Fancy seeing you here,' drawled a voice from near the house, and Anita relaxed.

'Still a master of originality I see,' she said, smiling, not moving from her position on the ground.

Marcus walked towards her, Anita feeling his energy intensify as he came closer, hers responding in the same way. Thank the Gods he wasn't a reader, she thought again.

'Did you come for any particular reason, or just to watch me doing yoga?' she flirted, turning her head to watch as he approached.

Marcus said nothing, but kept coming steadily towards her until he was standing right over her. He crouched, and she pushed herself up on her elbows. He took hold of her hand, seductively kissing the back.

'Are you always so feisty?'

'As a general rule.'

'I came by to say I'll pick you up at seven o'clock, if that's to your satisfaction?'

'Seven o'clock it is,' she said, flashing him her sweetest *see, I'm not feisty when I don't want to be* smile.

'In which case, I will look forward to seeing you then,' he said, with a matching *now that wasn't so hard was it* nod of his head. He stood, gently released her hand, and disappeared back the way he'd come.

Anita slumped heavily back to the ground and took a long, deep lung full of air, relishing the bunch of anticipation in her stomach. Butterflies fluttered, their wings brushing her nerves, sending tingles to her brain. Eventually she got up and headed back inside; she would be late for the Crownings if she didn't get a move on.

As she approached the back door, an enormous bouquet of dusky pink peonies stopped her in her tracks. She opened the attached card, reading the words, 'Until later...' scrawled, in perfect, old-fashioned script. She rolled her eyes; trust him to have perfect handwriting.

Anita showered and got dressed, paying quite a bit more attention to her appearance than she normally would. She told Cordelia it was because she wanted to look her best in case she had to deal with any unwanted attention. Cordelia gave her a look that said she knew it was a lie.

Anita walked with Cordelia to the temples. She didn't hear a word Cordelia said, a faint smile playing across her lips all the way.

As it was a double Crowning, they would use both the Temple of the Body and the Temple of the Spirit. Most of the ceremony would take place in the Temple of the Body, but Alexander's actual Crowning would take place in the Temple of the Spirit. This would happen after the Descendants had gone to some secret location beneath the temples, to do whatever thing it was they had to do.

Anita and Cordelia once again sat at the back of the Temple of the Body. Luckily, this time, Marcus was already at the front. No opportunity for embarrassing looks as he walked past, Anita was relieved to discover.

Once again, music flooded the temple. At Christiana's funeral it had been haunting, but today, the hidden organ boomed out a theatrical, moody, full-bodied piece as the procession began.

First came the Spirit and Body councilors, clad in full length cloaks, hoods up, so no-one could see their faces. Nobody was sure why they did this. It invoked powerful visions of cult members preparing to sacrifice to the Gods; utterly terrifying.

After the councilors came Peter. Someone had done a good job of dolling him up. But despite his swept back hair, smart suit and cloak, he didn't have the air of a Descendant. He was tall and reasonably good looking, but had a sort of scrawny, wispy look about him, his wavy dark hair tinged with grey. He looked tired, with none of the gravitas of the others.

Next was Alexander, cloak billowing around him as he strode, God-like, towards the alter, his hair cut shorter for the occasion. Anita's energy rose the second she clapped eyes on him, as he ascended the steps into the temple. If Alexander felt it, there was no outward sign, but then again, every female pair of eyes had locked onto him, transfixed. Her energy was probably lost in the mix.

Last and most melodramatic of all was Austin. He had his floor length red cloak on, but also had a hood over his head, so nobody could see his face. He moved theatrically down the aisle, relishing his moment to shine. Anita wondered what the new dynamic would be like. She got the impression that Peter would go along with whatever Austin wanted, but wasn't sure Alexander would be so easy to control...

By the time Austin had reached the front, the councilors had taken their seats. Peter and Alexander sat on the elaborate gold thrones in front of the altar. Austin stopped just in front of them, turning to face the congregation before dramatically lowering his hood.

He paused, surveying the scene, a taut silence settling over the crowd. 'Descendants, councilors, children of the Temples of the Mind, Body and Spirit. We are here today to observe a momentous occasion in our history; the Crowning of two Descendants, Alexander, son of Theon, and Peter, son of Christiana.

'As ever, a Crowning evokes mixed emotions; a sense of loss for those who have moved on from this world, and joy for the instatement of two new Descendants, beginning their reign. As the ceremony is being held here in Empire, rather than in Kingdom by the Relic, some of the ceremony will take place privately, below the temples. However, this will form only a small part of today's proceedings.

'Peter's Crowning will take place here in the Temple of the Body, and Alexander's in the Temple of the Spirit, with the main part of the ceremony taking place here.

'I would like to take this opportunity to say how proud I am of both Peter and Alexander for the way they have handled this difficult time, and I look forward to having them join me as reigning Descendants.'

Patronizing bastard. How *proud* he is of them? Please.

As Austin moved to his front-row seat, a Body councilor got gracefully to her feet, moving slowly and purposefully to the center of the altar behind Alexander and Peter. She still had her hood up, cloak falling elegantly from her shoulders, but Anita knew this woman, Helena, well.

She was the cousin of Alexander's mother, Celia, and she lived here in Empire. At thirteen, given Anita's considerable Body abilities, Helena had helped her to harness and use her skills. She'd been a source of counsel, guidance, and competition. Even now, at fifty-five, Helena could push Anita like most others could not.

Helena had been there when Anita was teased about being different, when children were scared to play with her, when people whispered the Gods had sent her.

Despite her involvement, Helena had always kept Anita a safe distance away, and had never been a motherly figure. She was not warm and cuddly, far from it, she was the most formidable person Anita knew; she made even Austin look like a pussycat. But she had always been there when Anita needed her. There was a curious connection between them that Anita found both strange and oddly comforting.

Anita had hardly seen Helena for the last few years. She was now the most senior Body councilor, hence why she was performing today's ceremony. She spent a great deal of time with the academics, studying and teaching Body skills to those, like Anita, who displayed potential.

Helena had invited Anita to join the academics a couple of years back, but she'd turned her down. Cordelia hadn't been keen on it; she'd never really liked Helena, and anyway, Anita had been more interested in continuing to study the energy. Luckily, Elistair had offered her a job at the observatory a few weeks later, so it had been the right decision, but Helena and Anita had barely been in touch since.

Helena bowed her head, facing the audience, but not looking at them directly. She paused for several moments before lifting her head to reveal her deep green eyes. She raised her arms out and upwards, cloak fanning out with her arms. The congregation held their breath, anticipation almost palpable.

In a low, controlled, powerful voice that instantly commanded the attention of everyone who heard it, she began.

'In the beginning, there were three Gods; Theseus of the Mind, Tatiana of the Body, and Jeremiah of the Spirit. The three Gods created three worlds, each with a mix of the three Gods' skills.

'In each world they created people who lived to serve the Gods, and in return, the Gods kept the energy stable, so resources would be plentiful. The people built temples to thank the Gods for their generosity, and worshipped the God to whom they belonged.

'For hundreds of years, the people of our world lived like this, in harmony. We served the Gods, and the Gods provided prosperity for all. But then, in the year 769, the Gods made a change.

'In that year, they sent three people to the world to rule for them; Janus for Theseus, God of the Mind, Georgiana for Tatiana, Goddess of the Body, and Julius for Jeremiah, God of the Spirit. Each was known as a Descendant, and each would pass their Descendancy down to their children, Janus and Julius through their male heirs, and Georgiana through her female ones.

'The Descendants would rule the world for the Gods, responsible for energy harmony. Although the Gods never explained why they had been sent, the people showed great respect for their new leaders; there was accord for over two hundred years. Then, at the turn of the century, the Gods made another change; they revealed the Relic.

'With the Relic came a prophecy, that one day the Descendants would return the Relic, an act that would free the world from the Gods. When that happens, the energy will be forever stable, and the people will be free to rule as they please, to choose their own leaders.

'The Relic brought great hope, yet great disruption. The world's energy has been volatile since that day, and we live in hope with each generation of Descendants that they will be the ones to free us from the Gods.'

Another councilor joined Helena at the altar, one from the Temple of the Spirit that Anita didn't recognize. He was a short man who looked as though he'd enjoyed one too many long lunches and a great deal too many cigars. He too faced the congregation, standing directly behind Alexander, Helena moving to stand behind Peter.

'Children of the temples,' the Spirit councilor said, in a voice that conveyed more authority than his stature suggested, 'we have heard the history and the prophecy, and it is now time for our Descendants to begin their journey to rule.' He paused and raised his arms as Helena had done earlier. 'Alexander, son of Theon, of the Temple of the Spirit, do you promise to uphold the quest for energy balance, to seek, before anything else, to fulfil the prophecy, and to rule according to the wishes of Jeremiah, God of the Spirit?'

'I do.' Alexander's unwavering reply floated through the temple.

Anita's energy rose at the sound of his voice, but she didn't even notice, too busy gazing at Alexander's ethereal form. He was every inch the confident ruler, a tad disheveled perhaps, but only in a way that seemed to enhance his right to reign. By the time Anita snapped out of it, Helena was talking.

'Peter, son of Christiana, of the Temple of the Body, do you promise to uphold the quest for energy balance, to seek, before anything else, to fulfil the prophecy, and to rule according to the wishes of Tatiana, Goddess of the Body?'

'I do,' answered Peter, in a confident, clear voice, but that still somehow hinted at nerves. Alexander conveyed a sense that he was meant to be here, but with Peter, it was as though he wasn't sure. Then again, as the first man to lead the Body line, he was probably worried about being mobbed on his way out... what if the prophecy truly was broken?

'The Descendants will now withdraw to the sacred place below the temples for the next part of the ceremony,' said the Spirit councilor.

Alexander, Peter, Gwyn, Marcus and Austin got up and approached the circle in the floor in the center of the temple. Anita didn't know where to look; both Marcus and Alexander were walking directly towards her, both looking directly at her. Her energy rocketed, so she concentrated on trying to get that under control, trying desperately to tear her eyes away. She failed on both counts.

As they descended the steps, through what was now a hole in the floor, both Alexander and Marcus smiled. Marcus, presumably, because he thought he alone was the one making her look awkward. Anita made a mental note to put him firmly back in his place later. More embarrassing was Alexander's smirk, doubtless because he could feel her ridiculous energy.

Both reactions made Anita cross, which meant Cordelia had a rough fifteen minutes trying to make conversation while they waited for the Descendants to return. Cordelia gave up after a few attempts and resigned herself to listening to the music that was once again filling the temple.

Almost exactly fifteen minutes later, the party of Descendants returned. Austin looked a bit put out, but the rest of them seemed to be in high spirits as they made their way back to the altar. This time, instead of sitting in front of the altar, Alexander sat in the front row with the other Descendants. His throne had been moved out of the way so Peter's actual Crowning could take place, and Helena was once again directing proceedings. Peter sat alone, all eyes on him.

'Peter, son of Christiana, I summon you to the altar of your Goddess to make public your allegiance to your ruler,' said Helena.

Peter stood a little too quickly and made his way to the altar where he knelt, arms open, looking up towards the ceiling. 'I, Peter, son of Christiana, of the Temple of the Body, declare myself at the disposal of my ruler, the Goddess Tatiana.'

Helena, who had conjured a crown from nowhere, stepped in front of Peter and held the simple gold band above his head.

'I, Helena, councilor of the Temple of the Body, and servant of the Goddess Tatiana, crown you, Peter, son of Christiana, of the Temple of the Body. May the Gods always guide you as you seek to free the world.'

Helena slowly lowered the crown onto Peter's head. Remarkably, it fit, which seemed strange given that it was a crown made for a female head. Had they resized it?

Helena removed her hands and took a couple of steps back as a fanfare flooded the temple. Peter stood, looked at Helena, who gave him an uncharacteristically reassuring nod, and stiffly turned around to face the crowd. As he did so, the congregation begrudgingly bowed. Peter paused, seemingly unsure what to do next, when Austin rose and made towards the aisle.

This seemed to galvanized Peter, who hastily led the procession back out of the temple and into the sunlight beyond. Anita avoided looking at either Alexander or Marcus, and felt smug because of it.

The procession immediately turned to head towards the Spirit Temple, where the same ceremony would take place for Alexander. Unfortunately, the Spirit Temple was full of Spirits, which meant that Anita and Cordelia had to stand outside at the back. Anita scaled a pillar, which gave her a pretty good vantage point from which to view Alexander's majestic performance at the altar.

When Alexander turned to make his way back down the aisle, there was no hesitation; he confidently strode out of the temple and through the cheering crowd. He shot Anita a quick glance as he approached her perch. This time, it was Anita's turn to feel Alexander's energy rise at seeing her, which improved her mood significantly. She was almost jovial by the time she dropped back down to where Cordelia waited below.

* * * * *

By the time Anita and Cordelia got home, Cleo had set up shop in the sitting room. She had brought with her a chest full of ancient torture devices and immediately set about using them on Anita. It was four o'clock by the time they gave Anita a break, and only because Cordelia appeared with some sandwiches and a carrot and ginger cake.

At four thirty, the hairdresser and make-up artist arrived and got to work on Cleo. Harry was picking her up at six thirty as everyone had to be in place and ready by seven for the Descendants' procession at seven thirty. Cleo didn't want to be late.

When they finished with Cleo, she looked extraordinary. Her hair was in a loose up do; several delicate plaits woven in her silky locks, accentuating her spectacular cheekbones, her eyelids a shimmering palette of bronze and gold.

'Wow, Cleo, you look amazing,' said Anita. 'I mean, you always look great, but you've somehow reached a whole new level.'

'Thanks,' Cleo laughed, 'just wait until you see the dress!' She practically skipped upstairs to get changed.

While Cleo dressed herself, the hairdresser and makeup artist began on Anita, building her updo around her mother's gold and diamond tiara. The results, even Anita had to admit, were good. They'd somehow made her look imperial, yet soft and approachable, her makeup understated, yet striking.

Anita was admiring their handy work in the mirror when Cleo re-entered the room. 'Bloody hell,' said Anita. Cleo was a vision in a floor-length, golden, shimmering, figure highlighting, sleeveless dress, with a low v at the front. It fitted her magnificently and suited her, even if it pushed the boundaries of acceptability.

She had simple, sky-high gold sandals on her feet, which, of course, she moved in effortlessly.

'Stop staring and put on your dress,' chastised Cleo, grinning at Anita's reaction.

Anita went up the narrow stairway to her cramped bedroom, where she slipped on her flowing red dress. It was a rich, blood-red silk, cut straight across the front with a deep, seductive v that showed off her perfectly toned back. It had a band around the front that fitted Anita's athletic waist as though made especially for her, and dropped straight to the floor, kicking out at the bottom so it swished beautifully as she walked.

She grinned as she zipped herself up and did a quick twirl so the fabric poured around her legs; maybe this wouldn't be so bad after all.

She stepped into the ridiculous black stiletto sandals with silk satin tie straps that Cleo had also convinced her to buy in Temple Mews. Thank the Gods her mother had left her some money when she'd died; shopping in Temple Mews would have been out of reach on her observatory salary alone. She winced at the thought of the damage to her bank vault.

She returned downstairs, to a gaggle of approving comments and her face cracked into a broad smile.

'They'll call you *Queen of Empire* in that tiara,' said Cleo, 'and your dress will match lover boy's cloak like a charm.'

Anita rolled her eyes and gave Cleo a playful shove.

'Can you believe I'm actually looking forward to this?' Anita said once the hairdresser and makeup artist had departed.

'By the Gods, if we can get you to look forward to a ball, then there's nothing we can't do,' giggled Cleo.

Cordelia, who had just got back from walking her dog, Thorn, entered the room.

'Ha! Did she just say she was looking forward to tonight? It's amazing what a bit of makeup and a pretty dress can do! You both look beautiful,' said Cordelia, 'effortlessly elegant.'

'Thanks,' they said together, giving independent twirls, then laughing like kids playing dress-up. A rap sounded on the front door.

'That will be for me,' Cleo squealed, giving Anita an excited half hug, then rushing to the door, pausing for a moment to regain her composure before swinging it open. 'See you later!' she called over her shoulder, gliding through and saying, 'Hello Henry,' in her most sassy tone.

Anita and Cordelia could just about make out Henry's stuttering, 'Hello,' as Cleo closed the door behind her.

'Poor thing doesn't know what he's got himself into,' Anita joked.

Cordelia laughed. 'She always was a determined one.'

'That's an understatement,' said Anita, 'but if he can't even say hello, I'm not convinced he'll last the night!'

Five minutes later, Cordelia tactfully removed herself. 'I'm off to sit by the stream for a while. You look lovely, Anita, and I hope you have a wonderful time.' Cordelia gave Anita a brief hug before heading for the back door, Anita suddenly emotional. She took a deep breath and shook it off.

She checked the clock. Six forty. Plenty of time to contemplate both how to handle Marcus and what to do about the Alexander problem. She perched on the arm of a sofa, thinking the situation through, surprised when she heard the gate squeak.

She jumped up and looked through the window to see a parked town car and Marcus striding up the path towards the front door. Anita retreated from the window and took a couple of deep breaths. 'Well, guess I'll just have to wing it,' she muttered, taking a deep breath as Marcus rapped forcefully on the wood.

Anita waited a few moments before making her way slowly to the door. He deserved to sweat; he had, after all, turned up twenty minutes early, a most ungentlemanly thing to do. In fact, maybe that should be her opening line…

She swung the door open, revealing each to the other, and they stood in silence as they took in the sight, Anita's chastisement forgotten. Marcus' energy made a sharp, upward turn, and she heard his breath catch in his throat. Her own energy soared as she surveyed the impeccably dressed, dazzlingly handsome man in front of her.

Anita smiled, relishing the flutter in her stomach. Marcus took glorious control. He stepped towards her and kissed her slowly, seductively, on each cheek, Anita's energy tingling delightfully as he did so.

'Good evening, Anita,' he said in her ear.

'Good evening, Marcus,' she replied, as he took a step back. 'I think you'll find you're early.'

'I couldn't wait a moment longer,' he said, at least a hint of sincerity in his tone, 'and there's somewhere I want to take you before we surround ourselves with people.'

Anita stepped forward, raising an eyebrow, Marcus closing the door behind her. He turned and offered her his arm. 'You are exceptionally beautiful,' he said softly, leaning in.

Anita tilted her head and smiled, letting him guide her down the path and through the gate.

By the time they reached the car, Marcus' chauffeur was holding open the door to the very spacious back seat. Marcus helped Anita inside. He waited until she'd settled herself before climbing in.

'What is it you want to show me?' asked Anita, intrigued, after a couple of minutes of driving. The ball was at Austin's estate just outside of Empire, which was where they seemed to be heading, and Anita was keen to know what lay in store.

'It's a surprise,' he shrugged, boyishly, as though it were something he couldn't tell her even if he wanted to.

She shot him a simmering look before smiling in submission.

They travelled in silence, Anita watching the scenery, Marcus watching Anita, both pacified by the rhythm of the car and mellow music playing from the front. They were up in the woods above the river now and still climbing. Anita assumed that Austin's estate would be at the top of the hill, with a spectacular view; that would be where she would choose to live if she were in his position.

They passed a pair of imposing gates, enormous, protective lions on pillars either side, and Anita threw Marcus a curious look.

'We're going in a different entrance,' he said, confirming Anita's suspicions that this was it. About a mile further through the woods, the chauffeur turned the car through a pair of much smaller, far less intimidating gates. The car popped out of the tree line into open parkland soon after. This ran to the edge of a cliff, affording spectacular views of the surrounding landscape, including both Empire and the observatory.

The chauffeur pulled up near the cliff's edge, got out, and came round to open the door. Marcus stepped out and helped Anita do the same. She walked to the edge and studied the vertical drop to the river, a long way below. It was incredible.

She turned to look back at Marcus, but as she did so, caught sight of something behind him that was altogether more impressive; an enormous, imposing castle, complete with fairytale battlements and turrets. Bloody hell.

The chauffeur unloaded a picnic basket and blanket before nodding to Marcus and striding off into the woods.

'Where's he going?' asked Anita. 'You're making him hang out in the woods?'

Marcus laughed. 'No, even the evil Descendants aren't that mean. There's a summer house. He's gone to make himself a cup of tea and put his feet up until I call him back. Come on, we don't have long until we have to put on a show,' he said, taking her hand and leading her to the blanket.

They sat, Anita as elegantly as she could, given the restrictive dress. She sent a silent thanks to the Gods that she wasn't wearing the figure-hugging number Cleo had on.

Marcus opened the wicker basket and produced two beakers and a bottle of Ginger Champagne. 'Sorry,' he said, expertly popping the cork and pouring generous quantities into each beaker, 'I couldn't find any champagne flutes that Dad wouldn't have killed me for bringing out here, and the caterers for the ball were watching theirs like hawks.'

'How unjust,' she teased, as he handed her a beaker. Hearing Marcus call Austin 'Dad' made Austin seem almost human. Anita had visions of Marcus as a small boy being chastised by an exasperated father and found it quite endearing.

'It's quite some view you've got here,' she said, turning to look at the landscape, taking a sip of the delicious wine, bubbles fizzing gently on her tongue.

'I thought you'd like it,' he said. 'I come out here a lot. My mother often comes with me.'

The mention of Marcus' mother shocked Anita. She'd assumed she was dead... had she been at any of the events over the last couple of weeks?

'I look forward to being introduced to your mother,' said Anita, hoping he would offer more information.

'You might have to wait awhile for that,' said Marcus, heavily. He saw Anita's inquisitive expression, so tentatively continued. 'My father and mother don't see eye to eye anymore, on anything, so they lead separate lives. My mother comes out here when Dad's in Kingdom, and she goes back to Kingdom when he comes out here. I go between the two, although I spend more time with Dad now, obviously.'

'That must be hard,' said Anita.

'Not especially,' he shrugged. 'You're used to what you're used to, I suppose. Like I imagine you're used to living with your grandmother and not seeing your parents.'

'My parents are dead,' she said, watching for his reaction.

Marcus' eyes flew open. 'Anita, I'm so sorry. I had no idea.'

She smiled. 'Why would you? It's fine. I don't even remember them. As you say, you're used to what you're used to. Living with my grandmother seems normal to me, anything else would be strange.'

Marcus topped up her beaker, a comfortable silence setting over them as their eyes wandered across the horizon, the seriousness of their revelations ebbing away.

Marcus turned to look at her, a mischievous smile playing on his lips. 'Ready for the first dance?' he asked, the air charged with flirtation.

'It's not the first dance I'm worried about,' she said. 'I'm more concerned about how everyone will react to me turning up with you. I can almost hear the ripple of whispers as we walk in already.'

'Ah yes, the gossip mill. It's surprising your friend Cleo kept our secret; even Dad hasn't found out about you, which is I think a first for him.'

Anita's guts tightened at this news. It was one thing to deal with the gossip mill, it was quite another to have to deal with a blindsided Austin.

Marcus got up and walked over to the car. 'Anyway, I wasn't talking about the first dance in there,' he nodded towards the castle. 'I meant the first dance we are about to have out here.' He turned on the car radio, a vibrant, sassy melody rippling out of the speakers. He sauntered back to Anita and held out his hand.

She looked at it for a beat, making him wait before she took it. 'I do hope you know how to lead,' she said.

'I'm more concerned that you might not know how to follow.'

Anita smiled. 'Touché,' she said, raising an eyebrow. 'I suppose we're about to find out.'

Marcus used her hand to pull her to him, placing his free hand on her waist, drawing her close, bodies pressed together. He took control, and Anita let him. They danced for what seemed like forever, flirting, testing, teasing.

Marcus spun Anita out before guiding her back into his hold. Not bad, she thought, enjoying herself. Not quite as good as Bass, but the first dance would be a long way from an embarrassment.

As the song ended, Marcus bent Anita gently backwards, holding her there as the last remnants of the song floated away into the twilight. Stillness filled the air and Marcus gently pulled her back to him, their faces inches apart. They stilled, pulses racing, before Marcus leant in, his intention plain. Anita pulled away.

'You'll smudge my lipstick,' she breathed, her eyes throwing him a challenge.

Marcus grabbed her hand as she moved away and pressed it lightly to his lips, meeting both her eyes and her challenge.

'As you wish…,' he purred.

* * * * *

'Anything new?' Austin snapped at the man in front of him, dressed head to toe in black; a guard from his security team sent to give him an update. Austin didn't know who he was, nor did he care. He was annoyed that Amber hadn't deigned to come herself, and this man seemed as good a person as any to take that out on.

'We know who Marcus has asked to accompany him to the ball this evening,' the man said. He spoke with care, taking time over every word in a way that Austin found intensely irritating.

'Oh?' replied Austin, his interest piqued, though he didn't show it, making a mental note to get Amber, the Head of his Security and Research Team, to sack this dithering imbecile.

'Anita. The girl who won the Chase. By all accounts she's an excellent dancer, so the first dance should be quite a spectacle,' he prattled, when he really should have stopped the moment he'd uttered Anita's name. Austin's face was dark as night.

'You mean to tell me that *my* son is bringing to a Crowning Ball some girl he has met only twice? Some low life, unorthodox girl that everyone thinks is peculiar?' His voice was chilling, but the imbecile continued confidently, seemingly oblivious to Austin's reaction to his words.

'She seems exceptionally skilled, Sir,' he said, in an enthusiastic tone.

'I know that, you simpleton, that's why I have a security detail on her. Why else do you think you currently find yourself in my employment?' Austin's voice was louder now.

The man tried to stutter a reply, but a cool, enticing female voice put him out of his misery, before he could dig himself into any further danger. 'Thank you, Thompson, you can go.'

The woman was on the tall side of average, lithe, with heavy auburn hair that she wore cut short in a bob. Her skin was porcelain white and flawless, her eyes cat-like and treacherous. Thompson didn't need to be told twice and made his way swiftly past the stiff, heavy, leather drawing room furniture, past where Amber was standing seductively by the crackling fire, towards the ancient oak door. She waited for him to leave before meandering her way towards Austin, his face still alive with fury. She pouted provocatively as she approached him.

'Austin,' she said sulkily, putting one hand on each lapel of his dinner jacket and kissing him lightly on the lips, 'aren't you going to tell me how enchanting I look?' She spoke slowly, lingering over the word enchanting, stepping back to complete a slow turn as she said the words.

'Amber, you look captivating, as always, but your feminine charms won't get you out of this one,' he growled, perhaps not quite as aggressively as he could have done. 'Why didn't you know Marcus was bringing our number one suspect to the ball?'

'I had my suspicions,' she said, stepping forward and playing with his bow tie, 'but I didn't want to tell you until I was sure. And now I'm sure, so here we are.

'They may have met more than twice, as we previously thought, but they have only ever met briefly. It makes perfect sense. She's powerful, and Marcus has always been attracted to powerful people. You can hardly blame the boy; I can only imagine how dull it is to have to spend time with all the airheads he normally hangs around with. At least Anita has a bit of fight in her. I would quite like her,' she looked up through her lashes, 'if she wasn't number one on my hit list.'

They had been on a constant lookout for powerful girls of about Anita's age, especially powerful people from the Body Temple, ever since Christiana had told Austin they were coming to Empire to look for the girl.

'Speaking of your hit list, have you made any progress?' asked Austin, his thunderous mood abating as he absently caressed her lower back; he loved to discuss the hit list. Amber arched into him.

'We have one or two more to add to the list, both members of the Institution, but Anita still outstrips them all,' she said. 'In fact, Marcus might be doing us a favor; we have the perfect opportunity to study her more closely.'

'Which is great, until he falls in love with her, and she turns out to be the one.'

She smiled a slow, ruthless smile. 'Marcus is far too much like you to do something as stupid as falling in love. It's lust and infatuation, nothing more,' she said, pulling back from him.

Austin smirked, using the hand at the base of her spine to pull her roughly back against him, noses almost touching. 'Is that what it is?' he said.

Her eyes flashed. 'I would say so,' she said, then bit his lip to the point of pain.

Austin pushed her away in retaliation. 'My adoring public awaits,' he said, heading for the door.

Amber had placated him... for now.

* * * * *

Austin came out of the drawing room just as Marcus and Anita were climbing the steps through the front door into the imposing entrance hall. They were a breath-taking couple, even Austin had to admit it. They looked positively regal as they ascended the stairs, Anita's arm laced through Marcus'.

Marcus, oblivious to Austin's presence, turned his head to look down at Anita in a way that was half predator, half puppy dog. Anita looked up at Marcus and smiled. Austin's mood blackened; that had better be what lust looked like.

Anita detected a sudden shift in energy ahead and looked up to see who it belonged to. Spotting Austin, she tried to pull away from Marcus, but Marcus, who had also spotted Austin, held her resolutely in place.

'You're late,' snapped Austin.

'Father, you remember Anita?' Marcus said brightly, ignoring Austin's formidable tone. 'Our guest of honor this evening?'

'Anita,' Austin nodded, before whirling around and striding towards the great hall, cloak billowing out behind him.

Marcus turned to Anita and gave her an apologetic look.

'That went well,' said Anita, as they followed in Austin's wake.

'Ignore him. He was obviously in a foul mood already,' Marcus whispered.

They approached the huge, studded oak doors that led into the great hall and joined Peter, Gwyn, Alexander and Austin, who were already there.

Alexander turned as they approached, and Anita didn't miss the spike in his energy, or the darkening of his eyes. His eyes lingered on her for a beat too long before Marcus stepped in between them, snapping the moment.

Anita shot Marcus a hostile look, motioning to indicate the lack of dates for the other Descendants.

'We don't normally allow non-Descendants in the procession,' he murmured in her ear, 'but seeing as you are the guest of honor, we'll go last.'

Great. One more thing to make her stand out, as if there wasn't enough already. At least Marcus and Alexander looking as dashing as ever would draw some of the female attention away from her.

Gwyn sported an impressive emerald and diamond necklace that Anita's eyes kept darting back to. But Gwyn's dress seemed to wear her, rather than the other way around. It was black, low cut, and velvet, complete with a very high slit up the side. It was beautiful, but she couldn't pull it off. Maybe that would attract the attention of the bitchy girls; Anita might get off lightly.

The hum of chatter that had been audible through the doors faded abruptly into silence, hauling Anita back from her thoughts. The Descendants lined up, ready to process. First Gwyn, then Peter, then Alexander, then Austin and then Marcus and Anita. Marcus offered Anita his arm, and she begrudgingly took it; it would, she reasoned, look odd if she didn't.

They could hear the muffled sound of a councilor instructing the room to stand for the procession and the scrape of chairs as everyone obliged. The councilor then announced their arrival, the thick doors swinging easily open when he finished. Gwyn immediately and confidently led the way through.

Silence reigned for a few moments as all eyes tracked the procession, and then, just as Anita and Marcus reached the entrance, the band started to play. Anita could not have been more appreciative and from the moment it began, the experience was abstract, almost dream-like. She floated through the hall in her own little bubble of a world. It was surprisingly easy to block out the indelicate eyes that followed her.

The hall contained three enormous banqueting tables, one down each side and a third across the top to form a horseshoe. They were heading for the top table, where the dates of the other Descendants, along with some of the most senior councilors, were waiting. They processed past the other two, packed tables, set with an impressive array of silver and glassware, all eyes fixed intently on them.

They passed underneath many spectacular crystal chandeliers, mesmerizing works of art hanging on the walls. They were modern pieces, depicting energy waves in abstract ways, yet were somehow perfect for the grand old environment. It made the place almost contemporary, devoid of stuffiness.

As they neared the top table, Anita noticed Cleo, already looking bored, next to Henry, who was positively beaming. That's going as expected then, thought Anita, spotting Bass sitting next to a girl she could only assume was Missy. Missy looked nice, although very plain, and she needed someone like Cleo to take her shopping, her dress extremely conservative.

Anita felt Bass' energy pick up as she went past, and she shot him a warm smile. Elistair was sitting on the other side of Missy, but looked preoccupied with something. He barely noticed the procession. Anita wondered what it could be, realizing just in time that they had reached the top table, where they had to split from the others to get to the far side. Anita, Marcus and Alexander went to the right and Austin, Peter and Gwyn to the left.

Austin sat in the middle of the top table, which Anita thought reasonable, it being his castle after all. Anita sat to his left, as the guest of honor, and Gwyn to his right. Marcus sat on Anita's other side, and he had some councilor's daughter, then Alexander, and then Helena to his left.

Other than Gwyn and Peter, Anita didn't recognize anyone at the other end of the table. Peter's wife and Gwyn's mother, Olivia, had died during childbirth and Peter had never had another public relationship. Anita hadn't yet spoken to Peter. He seemed to keep himself to himself, and she imagined him to be shy.

Everyone sat except Austin, who remained standing to make the opening speech, his voice creamy as ever. 'Descendants, councilors, Children of the Temples of the Mind, Body and Spirit. I welcome you to my home for the celebration of a truly significant moment in our history; the Crowning of not one, but two Descendants.

'Tonight, we bring to a close the Crowning traditions, having had a fantastic Chase and a poignant Crowning ceremony, both with record turnouts. We shall, of course, look forward to our Chase Champion and tonight's guest of honor, Anita, leading this evening's dancing. But first, let us toast our new Descendants, Peter, son of Christiana, and Alexander, son of Theon.' Austin picked up his Ginger Champagne, saying, 'To Peter and Alexander,' as he lifted his glass in the air.

The rest of the hall mirrored his actions, standing and lifting their champagne, echoing, 'To Peter and Alexander.'

Austin finished his uncharacteristically brief speech with, 'Bon appétit.' Austin sat and the gossip erupted, accompanied by many obvious glances, and even some pointing.

'Just as I thought,' said Anita, leaning into Marcus, as a mountain of food landed in front of them.

He squeezed her hand under the table and whispered, 'They're saying how beautiful you are.' Her energy spiked and she forced herself to look away, not wanting to give the crowd any more fodder.

Anita made it through dinner without enraging Austin. He asked her a series of probing question, such as how Alexander had run so fast at the Chase. Apparently he had never previously displayed Body skills quite like it. Anita replied that she'd had to slow down to Alexander's speed, because of her broken energy meter, although this was definitely a lie.

Austin asked about Anita's family life and her parents in a way that suggested he already knew the answers. He asked why Marcus had kept it a secret that he was bringing her to the ball, to which she replied, truthfully, that she didn't know. But most surprisingly, he was interested in her relationship with Helena, and why, given her considerable Body skills, Anita had chosen not to become an academic. Anita told him the truth; that she had wanted to study the energy. He did not seem satisfied with her answer.

Luckily, at that point, Gwyn interrupted with some inane comment, shooting Anita a death glare, drawing Austin into conversation with her. Anita couldn't have been more pleased and turned towards Marcus, ensuring that by the time Austin turned back, she would be engaged in another conversation.

As she turned, she spotted Cleo speaking animatedly with the man to her right and Henry trying desperately to get involved. She also glanced in Bass' direction. He was, ever the gentleman, doing his best to chat to Missy, although this appeared to be a struggle. Elistair, she noticed, still didn't seem to be in the mood for a party.

Marcus was discussing the Chase with the girl to his left. On the other side of her, Alexander was talking in low tones with Helena. Anita sat for a moment, looking down at her food, following the ebb and flow of Alexander's energy as he conversed with Helena. She found it comforting.

Alexander's energy picked up and Anita felt a warm pressure at the edge of her energy field. She'd never experienced anything like it and looked up cautiously to see what was happening, but Alexander wasn't looking at her, he was still deep in conversation with Helena…

After three enormous courses and a significant quantity of various types of wine, Anita decided it was time to open the dancing. In line with tradition, there would be no announcement. Anita and Marcus would take to the floor at a time of their choosing, throwing a signal to the band and surprising the audience by launching into their dance.

Marcus reached over and took Anita's hand. She inclined her head toward the open space between the banquet tables, and he smiled in agreement. He led Anita around the top table, waving to the band as they passed. The band changed pace, beginning a jaunty number, and the room quietened in expectant anticipation.

Anita could hardly contain her excitement. She loved to dance, and, leaving Marcus by the edge of the tables, she spun her way to the middle of the floor. Marcus ran after her and caught her just as she stopped spinning. He leant her backwards, then restored her to an upright position in a slow, fluid, silky movement. They smiled at each other as they came face to face, each reminded of their dance on the cliff. Then Marcus, almost violently, spun Anita out and back in again.

They tangoed around the floor, paying no attention to the audience, who watched open-mouthed at the display. A polite waltz was the customary dance to kick off proceedings. No one had expected this.

After a couple of minutes of the borderline inappropriate spectacle, complete with too much body contact, several improper looks, and the suggestive backing track, the others eligible to join the first dance got up and made their way to the floor. All except Austin, whose face was like thunder as he watched the exhibition.

Marcus and Anita finished their opener with a flourish, Marcus spinning Anita around so they were back to back before lifting her high on his shoulders, her arms outstretched. He spun several times before letting her slide back to the floor, having masterfully positioned them to join the formal dancing. He kissed her hand racily, throwing her one last risqué look as they took their places.

This part was a group dance, where two couples danced a set routine together before moving round to dance with another pair. The band changed the tone significantly, launching into what was almost a jig. Marcus and Anita started with Alexander and his date.

First Anita and Marcus, and Alexander and his date danced a few steps with each other, then they all danced a few steps together, before they swapped partners for a couple of twirls. Anita took Alexander's proffered hand, and a tingle of energy ran through her. If he felt it too, he didn't let on, looking at her indifferently the whole time they danced together, Anita frustrated she had no clue what he was thinking.

The music went on and Anita and Marcus cycled through many more couples. They danced with Gwyn and her date, Cleo and Henry, where Cleo threw Anita so many meaningful looks that Anita almost burst out laughing, and Bass and Missy. Missy was an uninspiring dancer, moving in a stiff, uncomfortable way. Bass, on the other hand, danced easily and gracefully, and lifted and twirled Anita when they came to dance together, embellishing the set routine and looking dashing while he did it. Anita beamed at him as they moved on.

The dance came to a close when Anita and Marcus met up with Alexander and his date again. The band finished their jig with a flourish, and the couples bowed and curtsied. Alexander led his date away and Marcus took hold of Anita's elbow, steering her as far away from Austin as he could. He'd noticed Austin's expression too then.

Marcus led Anita out through the doors of the great hall, across the lobby, and into another large room. The room had a bar that, during the day, had views over where Anita and Marcus had danced by the cliff edge. Marcus grabbed two glasses of Ginger Champagne, handed one to Anita, and headed for the open door out onto the balcony.

'You do like to ruffle feathers, don't you,' said Marcus, with mock disapproval, his eyes glinting.

'Me?' said Anita. 'I think you'll find you were leading.'

'Well, we'll just have to agree to blame the band then, who, for some reason, selected a raunchy number for the first dance.' He over-emphasized the shrug of his shoulders and perplexed look.

Anita's eyes flew open. 'That was you?' she said, punching his arm not quite hard enough to cause any harm.

'I don't know what you're talking about,' he said, raising his arms in protest. Luckily for Marcus, before Anita could launch a proper attack, a squeal invaded the air. Cleo bounded over to Anita and wrapped her in a hug.

'You. Looked. A-MAZING,' she sang. 'You should have seen everyone watching you. I cannot believe you just did that. But the way your dress kicked out... a superb choice, and he isn't a terrible dancer,' she gushed, nodding her head in Marcus' direction, squeezing his arm.

'Thanks,' replied Marcus, rolling his eyes. 'I'll get more drinks.'

* * * * *

Alexander had finally ditched his date. She'd proven a great deal more clingy than he'd expected, so it had taken a bit of work. Luckily, Cleo seemed to have done the same thing to Henry, so Alexander had left her with him.

He made his way into the library, where, thankfully, no one else had ventured, and helped himself to a shimmering crystal glass full of Austin's brandy. He sat down heavily in a chair by the open doors onto the balcony and contemplated the night's events so far.

Firstly, there was the conversation he'd overheard two of Austin's security guards having just before the procession. They'd been talking about Austin's hit list, and it was clear from what he'd overheard that Anita was at the top. Austin was always scouring for powerful people, to either recruit or get rid of, but this search was more frenzied than usual. It must have something to do with the bloodline; was Anita the girl Christiana had wanted to find?

Alexander needed to find a way to tap Austin for information. His trip to the archives had left him with nothing to work with, and there was no one else to ask.

Then there was his conversation at dinner with Helena. She'd all but tried to recruit him into the Institution, an underground movement that wanted to set aside the return of the Relic, in favor of some other method of stabilizing the energy. Trying to recruit him would have been a bold move under any circumstances, but was downright dangerous under Austin's roof, and right under his nose.

Austin hated the Institution and would no doubt hate them even more right now, with all the controversy around the prophecy. And Anita... her energy was extraordinary, like nothing he had ever known; such a potent mix of Body and Spirit. The tingle when they'd touched... so rare that no one knew what caused them.

Anita fascinated him, and although he was trying to keep it firmly hidden, he was drawn to her. She was reckless. The way she'd won the Chase, exposing her reader abilities to everyone... the way she'd danced around the floor... she was incredible, but it would only enrage Austin, and she was already in danger. Alexander was relying on Marcus to keep her out of harm's way, but with stunts like this evening, that would be difficult. Austin hadn't even tried to hide his fury.

Voices on the balcony interrupted Alexander's thoughts. 'I'm looking for Alexander, have you seen him?' said a whiny female voice Alexander recognized as his date's. In one swift movement, Alexander rose from the worn leather chair and made his way to the library's side door. He ducked through just as the voices reached the window, heading for the stairs.

Only Descendants and a handful of the senior councilors would dare to go upstairs in Austin's castle without permission; he would be safe up there. Alexander took the steps two at a time and turned left when he reached the top. He headed out onto a large internal balcony that wrapped its way around the four sides of a courtyard below.

This was his favorite part of Austin's castle, the courtyard exposed to the night sky, but the balcony covered, with pillars all the way around to hold up the roof. Climbing plants crawled all over the pillars, wispy braches covered in flowers falling down over the stone benches below.

The courtyard was the creation of Marcus' mother, Melia, and was a perfect demonstration of why Austin and Melia now lived separate lives. Austin was transactional and controlling, but Melia was hard yet fair, with far-reaching openness, just like her plants.

Alexander walked to the far side of the balcony and lay down on one of the stone benches. He placed the brandy glass, which he had fortunately had the foresight to pick up during his escape, on the floor.

He found it wearing being around other people for too long, all their energy waves bouncing around. It was a relief to be on his own, where he could think without interruption.

He'd been lying there for only a few minutes, listening to the muffled sounds of the party, when he heard the courtyard door creak open below. Two sets of cautious footsteps make their way through, Alexander easily picking up their energy, one anxious and the other angry.

'What is it?' questioned a fierce voice that Alexander recognized as Elistair's. 'We agreed we'd never talk about this again.'

The anxious person didn't immediately reply, pacing around the courtyard. 'That was before Austin went on this vendetta.'

Peter's thin voice was a surprise, and Alexander's interest piqued. What could Peter possibly be wrapped up in?

'What is that supposed to mean?' asked Elistair.

'It means that Austin's put together a hit list of powerful girls. Anyone between twenty-three and twenty-seven years of age. He's trying to track her down to finish off the prophecy for good.'

Alexander couldn't believe his ears. Peter knew what Austin was looking for? Had Christiana told him? So their being here did have something to do with the prophecy and the bloodline…

'But how does he know?' Elistair spat.

'He knew there was a chance she'd got away, but assumed even if she had, she would never resurface. When Christiana told him why she wanted to come to Empire, Austin went crazy. He ordered Amber to double her *researchers* and told her we're not leaving Empire until she's tracked the missing girl down.'

'Does he know?' The concern in his voice was palpable.

'No. Not for sure, but she's at the top of his hit list. Just her winning the Chase would have been enough to keep her there, but her reader stunt has wound him into a frenzy. He wasn't hiding his feelings about the display earlier either. She's signing her own death warrant; you've got to do something.'

Alexander's mind raced. How did Elistair and Peter know anything about this? And why was it Elistair's responsibility to do something?

'What exactly do you suggest I do?'

'Take her into the Wild Lands and keep her there.'

Elistair laughed. 'Aside from the obvious difficulty of kidnapping someone as adept as Anita, how do you suggest I keep here there? Lock her up? Stay there and supervise her myself?'

'Persuade her to go with you. Say you're going on a trip to record the energy or something.'

'That would never fool her, or my son. And even if it did work, Marcus is besotted with her. You think he would just let her go? He's Austin's son, regardless of how much of Melia he has in him. He'll turn out to be just as ruthless and just as possessive; you can see it in the way he looks at her.'

'Well, you've got to do something, otherwise she's going to wind up dead.'

Elistair became angry. 'I should never have got involved. Anything we do now to try to save her will be the final nail in her coffin, and will expose us too. Listen to me very carefully, Peter. Do nothing. Absolutely nothing, you hear me? Do not so much as mention her name to anyone. Do not contact anyone who knows. And never, I repeat, *never* talk to me about this again.'

A silent chill filled the courtyard as the enormity of Elistair's words sunk in. Elistair turned sharply and left, furious. Peter, now beside himself with worry, hung around for a few minutes more. He paced up and down, getting his emotions under control before following Elistair out.

Alexander lay there in shock; he couldn't believe what he'd heard. The prophecy wasn't dead? There was a female heir to the Body bloodline? That's why Christiana had insisted they come to Empire... to find her... and... Anita was that girl. Anita was a Descendant. That was the only thing they could have meant. Unless there was some other way to fulfil the prophecy... but everyone knew there was only one way; the Descendants had to send back the Relic. Either way, Anita was in serious trouble.

* * * * *

117

Marcus endured a few more minutes of Cleo's overexcited squealing before cutting past her, placing his hand firmly on Anita's waist, and drawing her away. 'If you will excuse us, Cleo, there's something I promised to show Anita.'

Cleo raised an eyebrow, Anita's face flushing a soft shade of red. Marcus placed his hand on Anita's back, guiding her inside, into the hall, and up the stairs.

'You promised to show me something?' said Anita. 'That the best you could come up with?'

'Does that girl ever tire of talking?' he said, ignoring Anita's jibe.

'Not that I've witnessed'.

'And anyway, there is something I want to show you.'

'Oh?' Anita looked at him warily.

'This way,' he said, when they reached the top of the imposing staircase, his hand refusing to leave Anita's back as he ushered her through a vast door.

They were in a large sitting room, with floor to ceiling windows and light curtains that wafted softly in the breeze. Anita looked at Marcus, her eyebrows raised. 'This is my suite,' he said. 'I wanted you to have a good view.'

'Of what?' she asked.

He led her out onto the balcony, this one directly above the one they'd been standing on minutes before, just as the night sky lit up with an explosion of twinkling lights. 'Of that,' he smiled.

Anita walked, open-mouthed, to the stone railing. She leant against it as the next release of energy hit the sky. It was beautiful, and she'd never seen anything like it. Not only could she see the smoky, shimmering lights, but she could feel them too. It was extraordinary, a series of small bursts like popping candy on her skin.

Marcus couldn't take his eyes off her; a light seeming to radiate from her as she watched the display. He walked up behind her, placing his hands on her waist. 'I thought you'd like it,' he murmured, as he bent his lips to the base of her neck, gently brushing them against her delicate skin.

The movement sent delicious shivers down Anita's spine, all the way to her toes, then back up to rest where Marcus' fingers caressed her through her clothes. Could he feel that too?

Marcus slipped his hands around Anita's waist and pulled her back towards him, enfolding her in his embrace. She didn't fight him, leaning her head back against his shoulder, resting her hands on his arms. They watched the rest of the display in silence, Anita's skin greedily drinking in the sensory assault.

It ended, and Marcus drew her back inside, her skin still tingling, both from phantom energy bursts, and the continued contact between Marcus' skin and hers. 'We had better go back downstairs,' he said softly, 'unless we want to give the gossip mill something else to talk about.'

Anita smiled in agreement, hiding her disappointment. 'I suppose you have a point. Can I use your bathroom, and I'll join you down there? I'm assuming you have a bathroom up here?'

'Through the bedroom,' he said, pointing to the right. 'You might want to wait awhile before coming to find me; I'm going to apologize to Dad. It's better to do it when the castle is full of people. Hopefully, he'll be full of Ginger Champagne or something stronger by now.'

Anita laughed. 'Good luck,' she said, heading for the bedroom.

To her surprise, Marcus' bedroom had windows on both sides. One side looked out onto the balcony where they'd just been standing. The other… who knew?

The bedroom was exactly what Anita had expected. There was an enormous four-poster bed, covered with the most comfortable looking duvet and pillows Anita had ever seen. Someone had tuned down the bed, a sprig of lavender on the pillow. Of course, they have people to turn down their beds.

The rest of the room was sparse. A large wooden chest at the end of the bed, a mahogany dressing table in front of the balcony window, and a round table with a chessboard inlaid. The chess pieces were beautiful, made without embellishment in silver and gold. The pieces were mid-game, and Anita wondered who Marcus let in here to play.

Once she'd freshened up in the bathroom, which came complete with a spectacular roll top bath, Anita headed back into the bedroom. She couldn't resist seeing what was on the other side of the mystery windows, so walked over to have a look.

As she approached what she could now see were, in fact, doors, she sensed powerful energy on the other side. Peeking through the curtains, Anita found Alexander's familiar, delectable form lying on a stone bench. Without hesitation or thought, she opened the door and stepped through. Alexander sat up as she appeared.

'Anita,' Alexander blurted, both his tone and his body language communicating his surprise.

'Hi,' she said hesitantly, for once keeping her energy under control; probably something to do with all the alcohol she'd consumed. 'What are you doing here?'

'Getting away from everyone downstairs,' he said. 'Sometimes all the energy waves get to be too much.'

'I know that feeling... where's your date?' she asked, relishing the opportunity to fish for more information about this mysterious man. 'What was she called again?'

'Patricia.' Alexander's face cracked into a clandestine smile. 'She's probably got a search party out looking for me by now. Excruciatingly boring and wildly stuck up,' he said. 'I only agreed to come with her as a favor to her father.'

'I see,' she said, raising her eyebrows, surprised by this sudden rush of information.

'Anyway, what are you doing up here? I'm surprised Marcus let you out of his sight after your show earlier.'

Alexander's tone was brisk, but she could sense his interest in her too, although his upfront appraisal took her by surprise. It was one thing to think things like that, but quite another to come out with them. She paused, moving to sit down next to him, just far enough away to mean their skin didn't touch, but close enough for agonizing awareness of his proximity.

'He's gone to find Austin to apologize for our dance,' she said. 'Judging by the way Austin was glaring at us, I can't image it's going to go well.'

'No, I wouldn't have thought so,' Alexander said slowly, studying her. 'Austin is a dangerous man to cross, and you've done it more than once.'

Anita waved her hand dismissively. 'Why does it matter? You'll all go back to Kingdom in a couple of days and Austin will forget he ever knew I existed,' as will the rest of you, she didn't add.

'Is that really how you think this will play out?'

'Yes,' she said firmly.

Alexander propelled himself to his feet, then turned to face her. 'Anita, Austin doesn't just forget about people like you. You're powerful. Very powerful.

121

As I've told you before, you'd be a valuable asset for someone like him. And Austin isn't the only one who's interested in you, especially after your display at the Chase, and after tonight's performance, you'll take some forgetting.

'Austin will view what you did tonight as a public humiliation. Not only did you have the audacity to turn up with his son, but you made a spectacle of the first dance. People will talk about that for years. Austin will never forget.'

The mood between them had shifted from open and light-hearted to fierce.

'So what?' He was lecturing her, and she didn't like it. 'Even if he doesn't forget me, what's he going to do? And what do you mean I could be a valuable asset? And who else is interested in me? You talk in riddles,' she said crossly, mainly at herself, because she hated when she couldn't keep up.

Alexander took a frustrated step away, running his hands through his disheveled hair. 'Did you see the woman downstairs with ginger hair?' he said, turning round with a sharp purpose that Anita found distracting. 'The one that's always hanging around, not too far from Austin?'

Anita nodded dumbly. Now she thought about it, there did always seem to be a woman fitting that description hanging around.

'That's Amber, and she's head of Austin's private security and research team.'

'His what? What does Austin research?' Anita smirked, even more confused.

Alexander threw Anita a menacing look, wiping the smile from her lips. 'He researches people like you. Powerful people who he wants to either use or get rid of.'

The words landed and Anita went pale. 'What do you mean *get rid of*?' she asked quietly, the wind snatched from her sails.

'I mean kill, Anita.' He rounded on her to bang the point home, looking like he might shake her.

Anita looked up at him, confused. '*Kill*?' The word hung in the air like a threat. 'And Marcus? Does he want to use me or kill me too?'

'No,' he said quickly, reassuringly, a shadow flashing behind his eyes that Anita had neither the ability nor the inclination to process. 'Marcus doesn't know the full extent of Austin's activities. Either that or he ignores them. Your best bet is to stay as close to Marcus as you can. Austin won't risk losing Marcus.'

'Won't risk losing him?' she said, not understanding.

Alexander's exasperation was palpable. 'If Marcus falls in love with you, which he seems well on his way towards, and he finds out that Austin is a threat to you, there's a risk that Marcus will choose you over Austin. That would drive a split through the Mind line, and Austin can't afford for that to happen in the current climate.

'Austin needs all the support he can get, and he'd rapidly lose supporters if there were another rift in his family. He suffered too many defections when he and Melia separated. Austin won't risk losing Marcus too.' He rushed the words, as though this were obvious, something that merely required a quick recap.

'What do you mean, defectors?' she demanded. He was making her feel obtuse, and she was nothing of the sort.

'You really know nothing, do you?'

'It would appear not,' said Anita, standing up too, turning her back on Alexander and walking over to lean against the railing.

She felt Alexander's energy soften, heard him take a deep breath.

'The Descendants rule by right; that much is true,' he said. 'But that doesn't mean we don't have politics. We're not the only influential players. The academics and the councilors are both formidable groups in their own right. They have powerful individuals, those with significant energy, and they know secrets about various Descendants; secrets we wouldn't want to get out.

'Melia was a senior Mind academic when she and Austin married, which brought Austin supporters. Those supporters abandoned him when they split. Another rift may cause Austin to lose more support, something he would like to avoid.'

'But what if Austin lost all his supporters? What difference would it make?'

'Worst case scenario? It could lead to a total loss of confidence in the current system, especially if it coincided with a large drop in the energy... ring any bells? Ultimately, it could lead to an uprising and the Descendants being overthrown.'

Anita gave him an amazed look; was he mad? 'But that would never happen. It would mean we'd never be free of the Gods.'

'The prophecy may already be broken. Some think it's better to take an eternity with the Gods than a lifetime with the Descendants. The balance is fragile, far more fragile than most people realize. Austin is only too aware of its fragility, so the safest place for you is next to Marcus.'

'And if I don't want to be next to Marcus?' she said, spinning round to look at him.

'You do,' he replied simply. 'I can read your energy, remember?'

'Don't worry, I remember,' she said, searching his eyes, looking for... something. 'How do you hide your energy?'

'What do you mean?'

'Do I have to spell it out for you?' she said, trying to recover some balance.

Alexander said nothing, holding her gaze until she continued.

'You have extremely powerful energy, but I've only had glimpses of your true power. Most of the time you hide it, or suppress it, or something. You've told me I need to get my energy under control, I'm asking how?'

'It's not as simple as that,' he replied. 'It takes practise. I'd have to show you; it's not something I can easily explain.'

'Then show me,' she said.

'Now is not the time, and I doubt Marcus would be pleased.'

'Why do you say that?'

'He's like a child with a toy; he doesn't like to share. Now, if you will excuse me, I should probably find my date and offer to take her home.'

Alexander headed back inside, but turned just before he reached the door. 'Do not tell anyone about this conversation, especially not Marcus. Do not let on you have any idea about any kind of politics. Do not try to find out more. Stay as close to Marcus as you can; make him fall in love with you, and avoid Amber and her henchmen at all costs.'

With that, he disappeared through the door, leaving Anita infuriated, confused, deflated, excited, full of questions, and above all, intrigued. She had to get him to show her how to hide her energy...

Anita was still preoccupied when she reached the top of the stairs, almost bumping into Marcus, who had

125

just ascended them. He reached out and grabbed her arms to stop them from colliding.

'I was going to send out a search party,' he teased, leaning his head down towards her, the heady smell of cigars on his breath.

'Sorry,' she breathed, trying to pull herself together. 'I was just admiring your suite and enjoying the time away from prying eyes. How did it go with Austin?'

'It could have been worse,' he shrugged, quickly changing the subject. 'I think we should get you a drink,' he said, leading her back downstairs and into the bar.

Marcus handed Anita a glass of Ginger Champagne before they joined Bass, Cleo, Missy, Henry, and, to Anita's surprise, Gwyn, on a group of sofas around a low table in front of the fire. Cleo was leaning against Henry; obviously they'd reconciled. Bass, Missy and Gwyn were sitting awkwardly on the opposite sofa, Bass not sure what to do with his arms, wedged between the two women.

Marcus and Anita sat on a third sofa, their legs touching. Marcus stretched out an arm along the sofa's back and Anita leaned in, getting comfortable, ignoring Bass' regular glances. They sat chatting and laughing for hours. Henry made pompous comments, Bass tutted about the energy wasted on the light show, and Missy barely said a word. Gwyn was paying Bass more attention than was strictly necessary, and Cleo shoehorned as many provocative comments in as she could.

Marcus and Anita laughed easily along with the rest of them, but Anita couldn't shake the feeling they were being observed. Amber was nowhere to be seen, but Alexander's warning had made her uneasy.

Eventually, Bass got up, saying it was time to leave. He was taking Missy, Cleo, and Henry back to Empire and offered to take Anita too. Anita nodded. 'That would be great, thanks.'

Marcus looked crestfallen as he walked them to the front door, where Bass' car was waiting. The others climbed in, but Marcus pulled Anita back towards him. A look of panic swept across her face, concerned that Marcus would try to kiss her here, in front of everyone, including Amber, who had just appeared at the door. Instead, he leaned in and whispered, 'This is not finished.'

A thrill of excitement shot down her spine. 'Goodnight, Marcus,' she said, holding his gaze before climbing into the car with the others, to be whisked down the magnificent drive and back to Empire.

* * * * *

Anita was the first to be dropped off, and they let her out at the end of Cordelia's road so they wouldn't have to make the tight turn outside the cottage. Anita climbed out of the car and called her goodbyes to its drunken occupants, picking her way along the uneven ground.

She had given up on her shoes and was carrying them in one hand, holding up her dress, now too long, with the other. Wisps of hair had escaped their pins, falling around her face, and her mind was foggy from the wine. She couldn't wait to fall into bed.

It was misty and the only light came from the moon, Anita glad she knew the road so intimately. She approached the cottage, surprised by the powerful energy she could feel up ahead, and immediately tensed, on guard. She kept moving cautiously towards the house, trying to make as little noise as possible. Her heart raced as she considered whether she should stay and fight, or turn and run. But out of the mist emerged

127

a familiar, lean figure leaning against the garden wall, still clad in his dinner jacket, bow tie and top button undone. Anita stopped dead when she saw him.

'Marcus?' she asked, pulse now racing for a different reason.

'Hi,' he said, smiling when he saw her, pushing himself easily off the wall and walking towards her.

'What are you doing here?' she said, laughing in relief.

He stopped just in front of her with a teasing smile. 'You forgot something,' he said, his energy building, an electric tension filling the air between them, drawing them together.

She looked up into his chocolate brown eyes, and he brushed a strand of hair behind her ear. He dropped his fingers to her neck, caressing the soft skin below her ear, a smile dancing across his lips. He pulled her slowly towards him, bowing his head to meet her waiting mouth.

Shivers of energy passed between them as they kissed, slowly at first, the taste of cigars and ginger mingling with his vanilla scent. His hand went to her cheek, pulling her to him, deepening the kiss, his tongue probing hers. Anita was lost, the ground disappeared, her head spun, senses useless as she responded to him.

Marcus pulled back, both hands now on her cheeks, his face an inch from hers, hungry eyes full of unsated desire. She dropped her gaze, raised her hands to his waist, ran them upwards, over every ridge of his toned torso. Then, she pushed him back, forcing distance between them, her hands still on him as she looked up, eyes on fire.

Marcus' carnal smile showed he understood both her silent rejection and the gauntlet she'd laid down.

She closed the distance for a short, final, calculated kiss. 'Goodnight Marcus,' she said, in a slow, sultry whisper, before brushing seductively past.

'Goodnight,' he replied, matching her tone as she veered off the path towards the back of the cottage. There was nothing Marcus loved more than the thrill of the chase.

CHAPTER 8

Anita woke to the delicious smell of bacon cooking downstairs. She got out of bed, deciding to skip her usual yoga session, and headed straight to the kitchen. Cordelia was standing over the stove singing to herself, and turned when she heard Anita come in.

'Morning,' she said cheerily.

'Morning,' replied Anita, less enthusiastically on account of the banging in her head. 'What's got into you?'

Cordelia was not a morning person. It was usually difficult to get her to be cheerful about anything before eleven o'clock and at least three cups of tea. Today she was sparkling.

'You got home late last night,' Cordelia chirped.

'That's why you're happy? Because I got home late?'

'Tell me all about it,' she said, putting an enormous plate of sausages, bacon and eggs in front of Anita. Anita's stomach growled appreciatively; this was exactly what she needed.

'There's not much to tell,' she said. 'We ate, we danced, we drank, and then I came home.'

'Really. You expect me to believe that's all? You can't think of *anything* else you might like to tell me?'

Anita shot Cordelia a curious look. 'What else do you think happened?'

Cordelia changed tack, opting for the direct approach. 'And Marcus? Any news there?'

'Any news? You're going to have to be a little more specific.'

Cordelia huffed. 'Do you think you will see him again?'

Cordelia didn't need to wait long to get her answer. At that moment, a knock emanated from the back door, followed by a rich male voice, 'Hello?'

Anita jumped up and ran out of the kitchen, throwing Cordelia a look which said, *don't you dare.*

'Hi!' said Anita, as she approached the back door. 'What are you doing here?'

Marcus stepped into her space, crowding her, her senses overwhelmed. He leaned in and gave her a deep, enthusiastic kiss. 'It's lovely to see you too,' he said, pulling away. 'Do I smell breakfast?' He grabbed Anita's hand then pushed past her, dragging her behind him in the direction of the kitchen.

Cordelia couldn't contain her excitement when she saw them enter. 'Marcus, how lovely to meet you. I'm Cordelia, Anita's grandmother. She's told me all about you,' she lied.

Marcus flashed a charming smile. 'It's an absolute pleasure to meet you too,' he said, shaking her hand.

Anita gave Cordelia a stern look from where she was standing behind Marcus. 'Cordelia was just leaving, weren't you, Cordelia?'

Anita placed her hand on Marcus' arm to draw his attention away from her grandmother. 'She was just about to take Thorn for a walk. Do you remember Thorn?' she said, denying Cordelia the chance to dispute Anita's story.

'I certainly do,' said Marcus, shooting Anita a devilish smile.

Cordelia, who Anita had to admit, did at least know how to take a hint, rolled her eyes heavily. She placed a second plate of food on the table. 'There you go, Marcus. Come on Thorn,' she said, not trying to hide her disappointment as she set off out of the back door with her dog.

Anita and Marcus finished breakfast, then Marcus waited downstairs while Anita got dressed. She had lessons today, and he said he would walk her to the temples as he had to go there anyway.

'How did you get here so quickly last night?' Anita asked, as they left the house. 'We came straight here, but you got here first.'

Marcus smiled and looked pleased with himself. 'There's a back way that cuts across our estate, so nobody uses it. It's much more direct,' he said smugly.

But of course, thought Anita. They walked on in silence for a few minutes before she said, 'So... what did Austin say last night?'

Marcus didn't reply for several paces, seeming to contemplate what to tell her. 'He wasn't happy. He thought the dance was inappropriate and made a mockery of the occasion, and he blamed you for everything.' Marcus smiled at Anita and she raised an eyebrow, both of them acknowledging the absurdity of Austin's assumption.

'Amber, Dad's Chief of Security and Research, was there too; he's always worse when she's around. Anyway, long and short of it, Dad doesn't like you. He thinks you're a bad influence, and *not the sort of person a future Descendant should be dating.*'

Anita ignored the dating bit, even though it sent a thrill through her; they could deal with that later. 'He

132

must be annoyed that you came here last night and again this morning?' she said.

'He doesn't know,' he said, 'but even if he did, he can't stop me from seeing you, or anyone else for that matter. Eventually he's got to realize I'm not twelve years old any longer and he can't dictate what I do and who I see.'

'I'm not sure he wants to realize that.'

'He doesn't have a choice.'

His words send another burst of excitement through her veins, and she linked her arm through his.

'So how come the Descendants get to skip weekend classes when the rest of us have to suffer?' Anita asked, firmly changing the subject.

'Because they make us study three times as hard when we're children. When you lot were all running around playing after school, we were still in lessons, learning how to be Descendants.

'We're not born with all the skills we have; most can be taught. Something like Alexander's ability to read energy, you're born with or without, but pretty much everything else you can learn, if you work hard enough.

'Descendants have to be adept in all disciplines, and we have to work hard to get there. It was bad back when I was eight, but it has its advantages now, like, for example, not having to go to school at the weekend.'

'Is that why you were all at the front of the Chase?' she asked.

'Yep.'

'So even though I'm appallingly bad at Mind disciplines, there's hope for me yet?'

'Yep, maybe even for you,' he said, nudging her playfully.

'Have you ever seen anyone move anything using just their mind?'

133

'Of course I have; I've done it myself once or twice.'

'Really?' said Anita, her voice heavy with skepticism.

'Really,' he replied, absolutely serious.

'Could you teach me?'

'It's not something you can learn to do overnight. You need to be great at the basics first and build up to it. I've spent my entire life learning Mind disciplines, and I've only managed it a couple of times.'

'But we could try?' Anita wasn't sure why she wanted to. She'd never liked Mind disciplines, but somehow private lessons with Marcus made it sound appealing. Besides, it was a challenge now she knew moving objects with one's mind was actually possible, although she wouldn't one hundred percent believe it until she saw it herself.

Marcus looked indulgently down at her. 'Would you take no for an answer?'

Anita smiled at the ground before looking Marcus defiantly in the eye.

'As I suspected,' he said, rolling his eyes. 'Yes, Anita, I suppose we could try.' He draped his arm around her shoulders and kissed her hair.

They arrived at the temples, Anita relieved when Marcus removed his arm. They ran into Cleo and Bass outside the Mind Temple, which was good, because they could walk in as a group.

They entered the temple, and Marcus told Anita he would find her later, when he'd finished what he needed to do. He left them and headed for the hole in the floor, descending effortlessly.

Bass, Cleo, and Anita chose seats as close to the back as they could. Anita's hangover was abating, but the other two, along with the rest of the class, didn't look in such great shape. Their lesson was subdued.

The Spirit lesson was a total waste of time, most of them requiring concentration just to stay awake. Meditating was a distant dream.

As usual, Anita didn't attend the Body lesson, telling the others she was going for a run. However, as she left the Spirit Temple, she thought about what Marcus had said. If someone like Peter could master the art of meditating, or the Mind disciplines, through nothing more than practice, then she could do it too.

There was the added benefit that if she hung around the Spirit Temple enough, she would have to bump into Alexander eventually, so she turned and walked back into the temple. She picked an open space on a large rectangular mat near the back, and sat down to meditate.

She closed her eyes and cleared her mind, trying to push away thoughts of kissing good-looking men in the middle of the night. After minutes of sitting with blankness in her mind, the image of an eagle soaring high above the world slid through her thoughts. The eagle descended towards the ground, Wild Land all around.

There were no houses and no people, just heather and trees and rocks, but as the eagle swooped closer to the ground, she could make out a large, earth colored yurt in a clearing. The eagle flapped its wings and suddenly she was falling. She landed, like a cat, next to the yurt's entrance. It felt safe and familiar here, so she stood and walked towards the tent, pushing aside the canvas and stepping inside.

She emerged into a boring old yurt, filled with an odd, too-bright light. A low bed covered with animal hides sat on one side, several small tables and chairs dotted around, made from bits of wood lashed haphazardly together. A rack of drying herbs stood near the fire.

135

In the center of the yurt, sat on top of a waist high pillar, was a brass cylinder. It was alien in this space, and Anita was suddenly uneasy. She made her way towards the cylinder, about to pick it up to see what was inside, when she felt an overwhelming urge to leave it and turn around. She turned, and to her surprise, saw Alexander sitting on the bed, hair unkempt, shirtless, glorious torso on display. A potent pang of desire filled her, and it was all she could do to keep herself from running to the bed and jumping on top of him.

Anita's energy was at an all-time high, and Alexander smiled knowingly. 'Anita, you need to leave the cylinder alone. You need to make it disappear. Reject it from your mind and it will go.' He spoke to her, and she could hear him, but his lips didn't seem to move.

'Why do I need to leave it alone? What is it? Why's it here?'

'I can't explain now; we need to be careful, but trust me, you need to reject it.'

'How?'

Alexander got up and moved towards her. He stood in front of her so he could see the cylinder behind her back and looked into her eyes. 'Do exactly what I tell you.'

Anita nodded, no idea what was going on.

'Imagine the cylinder lifting off the pillar,' he said. 'It will be difficult and heavy, but lift it up. You're strong; use your strength to raise it.'

Anita concentrated. She did everything she could to lift the cylinder, but it wouldn't budge.

'Try harder, Anita,' said Alexander, his command gentle yet firm.

She tried, but nothing she did would lift it. Trying drained her; she was tired, and she dropped her eyes to the floor.

'Anita, look at me. I'm going to help you, but it's very important you stay focused on the cylinder, okay?'

Anita nodded.

Alexander reached forward and touched Anita's index finger lightly with his. The cylinder went light as a feather. She could easily lift it now and made it fly into the air behind them.

'Very good, Anita. Now, I need you to imagine the cylinder falling to the floor, but before it gets there, it vanishes, okay?'

Anita nodded again, Alexander's finger still touching hers. She was concentrating on the cylinder falling when the mood shifted. Another presence blasted into her consciousness and Alexander's finger left hers. The cylinder fell, but bounced when it hit the floor, and rolled through the door out of the tent.

Alexander had disappeared, and a furious voice invaded her mind. 'What the hell do you think you're playing at?'

Anita jolted back to the temple and almost fainted when she got there. She looked up to see Marcus and Alexander standing over her, Marcus livid.

'I was teaching her a thing or two about the arts of the Spirit,' Alexander replied, unruffled. 'Maybe you should think about doing the same with the Mind disciplines, so she's not so vulnerable to attack.'

'What?' said Anita and Marcus together.

'You attacked her?' spat Marcus, squaring up to Alexander.

Anita, still trying to wrap her head around what had just happened, had to suppress a smile; the idea that Marcus could beat Alexander in a fight was pretty funny.

'Don't be ridiculous; I didn't attack her. But given what I just saw, it wouldn't take much for someone else to; they would almost certainly succeed.'

'Who would want to attack me?' asked Anita, her thoughts slow and sticky.

Alexander rolled his eyes, giving her a *do we really have to recap already* look, but Marcus answered.

'It's just a good idea for you to know how to defend yourself,' he said. 'It's basic training for Descendants, and I'm not sure why it's not taught to everyone. It just means that if some crazy person tries to get into your mind, you'll know about it, and can defend yourself. Much as it pains me to admit it, he has a point; I'll have to teach you.'

Alexander laughed openly. 'You think you can teach her? You can barely defend yourself. Doesn't your girlfriend deserve expert tuition?'

Marcus was furious, energy steaming off him. Anita and Alexander stood still, watching as Marcus calmed himself, turning over the options in his mind.

'Well, I suppose, seeing as I've already agreed to teach you about the Mind disciplines, it would be a bit intense for me to teach you about the Spirit ones as well. And I'm not too proud to admit that, although I am far from a beginner, I'm not a Spirit expert. Alexander would be a more suitable mentor.' He rounded on Alexander. 'But if you lay so much as one finger on her, you'll regret it.'

'Marcus, I'm not in the least bit interested in Anita. I am interested in someone close to you being vulnerable to attack. I would say the same thing if any of the Descendants were in this position.'

'I suppose you have a point. We don't want someone getting at me via Anita,' said Marcus. His tone was cringingly pompous, containing strong echoes of Austin, but Anita let it go, so close to getting what she desperately wanted.

'Although... I'll obviously have to lay a finger on her in a plutonic way, for the meditations that require it.'

'There is no requirement for you to show her those poses.'

Alexander looked at Marcus as though he were a petulant child. 'Marcus, you know I need to show her every pose if she's to be properly protected.'

What could the offending poses be? Again, best to keep her thoughts to herself for the time being.

'Fine,' spat Marcus, 'but not until she's ready.'

Alexander gave Marcus a terse look and walked away. 'Meet me here tomorrow evening at seven, Anita. Marcus, don't even think about coming too.'

Marcus helped Anita to her feet, his face like thunder. Alexander was right; Marcus was possessive. Half of her loved it, while the other half couldn't stand it. She wanted to spend more time with both of them, but she'd had no say in the matter, and she wasn't happy about it.

Marcus took her hand, running his thumb over her skin. She softened, her anger chased away by the sparks of energy radiating out from his touch.

'When do we start my Mind lessons?' she said.

'Tomorrow morning at mine?'

She nodded, kissed him lightly on the lips, and sauntered out of the temple.

* * * * *

Anita went for a run along the river, heading for one of her favorite climbing spots. She'd felt fuzzy since the meditation and hoped the combination of fresh air and adrenaline would help clear her head. She arrived at the cliff, lost in her thoughts, startling when a voice called her name, Helena jogging into view.

139

'Helena. Hi!' said Anita. 'What are you doing here?'

'It's a nice day for a climb,' she said, descending the steep grassy slope down to the riverbank where Anita stood.

'Great minds,' said Anita, warmly. 'In fact, it's probably a good thing you bumped into me,' she smirked, 'at your age, it's a wonder you can still make it out here.'

'Alright, enough of that, thank you,' said Helena. 'I'll still beat your sorry little ass up that cliff.'

They grinned at each other, just like they used to.

They were free climbing; body types had a healthy scorn for safety. They were halfway up the cliff, just reaching a tricky overhang, when Helena said, 'You and Marcus are getting along well.'

'For the love of the Gods, not you too?'

'What do you mean, *not me too*?'

'I didn't have you down for a gossip.'

Helena laughed. 'I'm not. I was wondering how Austin feels about your relations with his son? You should be careful of him,' she said, launching herself upwards to grab a hold that had been just out of reach.

'Ah, you fall into the *save Anita from Austin* camp,' said Anita, placing her foot and all her weight on an impossibly small crease next to her waist.

'There's an entire camp of us?' said Helena.

'It's a small but growing assembly.'

'Well, Austin's dangerous, and that woman Amber comes in a close second. She's adept at getting into peoples' minds. If I were you, I'd stay away from her.'

'What do you mean *getting into peoples' minds*?'

Helena paused, looking over at Anita. 'I mean, in the same way as we have Body skills not taught at school, there are also Mind and Spirit skills that most people don't know about. Amber is extremely good at some particularly manipulative ones, and is exceptionally good at getting into peoples' heads.'

Anita's face betrayed her confusion.

'Sometimes Amber simply uses the power of suggestion,' said Helena, 'planting things into conversations, repeating words or phrases a number of times so people unwittingly remember them. She's also launched full-scale attacks. She'll find a way into a person's mind, when they're meditating, or praying, or concentrating hard, and plant something in there. Most people won't even realize she's done it. Only those who know how to meditate to the places in their mind could uncover the truth.'

Helena lifted herself over the lip of the cliff, Anita following just behind. They sat with their legs dangling over the edge, admiring the view, but Anita was quiet, dread settling over her.

'Are you alright?' asked Helena.

Anita paused, considering her answer, because she wasn't really sure. 'What's the purpose of planting something in a person's mind?' she said, eventually.

'Well, it depends. It can be an effective way to kill a person and make it look like natural causes, although there are less risky ways to kill someone. Or it can be a way of gathering information... to do that is tricky though, because you need someone with expert Mind skills to plant the idea and a skilful Spirit to extract it through meditation. Or it can be a way to store or pass information secretly between people without there being any physical evidence or conversation.'

'What?' said Anita, her mind reeling.

Helena laughed. 'If I wanted to pass a secret message to you, I would find a way into your mind and plant a brass cylinder. The next time you mediated, you would discover the brass cylinder, open it, and recover the message. The only problem, of course, is that it's hard to tell if the cylinder is friendly or an attack. Some are powerful enough to kill upon opening.'

Anita's stomach plummeted at the mention of brass cylinders. 'This is crazy,' said Anita. 'How is this kept under wraps?'

'Only a handful of people practice planting and extracting any longer; the world is a much safer place now than it used to be. Only academics, or people like Amber, bother to keep those arts alive.'

Anita contemplated Helena's words. After the first mention of death, she'd been on the verge of telling Helena about her experience in the temple, but now she wasn't so sure. 'Can you work out when something was planted? That way, you could agree a time to plant a cylinder, so you would know it was safe?'

'No. Not unless you caught the person in the act. That's difficult to do, as they'd typically choose a time to plant when you're concentrating hard on something else. The only thing you can do is learn to protect your mind from attack, so there are barriers to get through before planting.

'The Descendants are trained to protect themselves in every way possible, as they're obvious targets for attack. Austin takes it a step further, taking Amber with him everywhere he goes, just in case he wants to launch an attack himself.'

'But why do I need to be careful of Austin? Why would he be hostile towards me?'

'You're powerful, and Austin doesn't enjoy having powerful people around; it makes him feel vulnerable. He does all he can to identify and either use or get rid of those he sees as a threat.'

'And when you say *use*?'

'He employs people for their skills. In the same way he uses Amber's planting skills, he might want a powerful Spirit as an extractor, or a powerful Body to seduce somebody, or to beat someone up.'

'Seduce somebody? I would have thought that would be a Mind trick too...'

'There's a lot of crossover. Yes, Minds are proficient in seduction and manipulation, but a Body can be good at seduction too. Instead of using their mind to seduce, they use their body. Everyone has a mixture of the three Gods in them, making it impossible to split skills into only one area.

'You might be a strong Body but have very little Mind at all, meaning you may find seduction hard. You may be a strong Spirit but have a lot of Mind, meaning you master both planting and extraction. You may have a little of all three and be passable at everything but excel at nothing. There's no set formula.

'There are a handful of academics who research skills inheritance, but they haven't found much to go on. The same way we don't understand energy jolts, or know how to control the energy.'

Anita thought about telling Helena what she'd felt when she'd kissed Marcus and touched Alexander. She was dying to understand more about it, but there was only so much she was comfortable sharing.

'Anyway, the point is that you would be wise to steer clear of Austin and Amber, which also means giving Marcus a wide berth, especially after your display the other night, spectacular as it was.'

'Thanks,' Anita half laughed, 'I think. But what if I don't want to give Marcus a wide berth?'

'Then you're taking a tremendous risk. Marcus is Austin's son,' said Helena, turning serious, 'remember that. He's becoming more and more like Austin, and I wouldn't want you to get caught in the middle of that transformation.'

'It's not a foregone conclusion that he'll turn into his father,' said Anita, prickling. 'And anyway, Alexander, your fellow *protect Anita* club member, seems to think the safest place for me is with Marcus. You two should have a *'protect Anita* convention' and align your advice.'

Helena ignored Anita's tone, saying cautiously, 'Just how close are you and Marcus?'

'Not that close,' she said, growing uncomfortable, 'not that it's any of your business.' Anita had never had to explain any of her previous relationships, and she wasn't going to start now.

'Anita, if Alexander thinks you're safest with Marcus, then it's probably gone too far already. Marcus has always been possessive, just like Austin, which will work both in your favor and against you. It means Austin is unlikely to harm you and less likely to recruit you, but it also means if you ever want to walk away, you could be in serious danger. Marcus might not want to let you go.'

'This gets more and more crazy,' said Anita, exasperated. 'Marcus and I hardly know each other. If what we have develops into a relationship, it's not like I'll suddenly belong to him.'

'That's what Marcus' mother thought, and look at her now.'

'Marcus is not Austin.'

'And you are not Melia.'

Anita didn't know what she meant by that, but it couldn't be anything good, so she didn't ask. Unfortunately, Helena seemed to think it was something Anita needed to know.

'Melia was, and indeed still is, an extremely adept Mind academic. When she fell in love with and married Austin, she brought a lot of influential supporters with her. When they separated, which had a lot to do with

144

Austin turning into a carbon copy of his father, Tobias, by the way, Austin lost a lot of those supporters.

'He couldn't harm Melia, or he would have risked a faction forming within the Temple of the Mind. Obviously, given how fragile the balance is at the moment, Austin should leave you alone whilst Marcus wants you. If Marcus changes his mind, or you want to leave him, you won't have any protection.'

'The fragility of the system seems to be the topic of the moment,' said Anita, angrily.

'The possibility of a revolution is not something to be flippant about. It could happen. The Institution is growing, and given the current bloodline situation and energy crisis, now seems like a likely time, don't you think?'

Anita looked blankly at Helena. 'The Institution?'

Helena rolled her eyes. 'It amazes me how little your generation knows, lacking in political zeal; so unlike your parents.'

Anita wasn't sure whether Helena meant her parents specifically, or just her generation's parents. It took all of her determination not to ask.

'The Institution is a group of powerful individuals,' said Helena. 'Mostly academics, councilors, and a few traders, whose purpose is to ensure the energy stays steady.'

'I thought that was the job of the Descendants?'

'Theoretically, yes, but the Descendants have never been interested in ruling for the good of all. Historically, they've been more preoccupied with personal gain and adoration. They have no interest in sending the Relic back to the Gods, given that to do so runs counter to their personal interests, regardless of what they swear at their Crownings.'

'I guess that makes sense.'

'The Institution formed centuries ago to ensure the energy remained stable. They have dedicated themselves to freeing the world ever since.'

'But only the Descendants can free the world.'

'If the only freedom you consider is from the Gods. What if freedom was from the rule of the Descendants?'

'But why wait until now? Why hasn't the Institution acted already?'

'The Descendants have a bargaining chip. They possess information they'd use to discredit the Institution if we tried to act. We've been at a stalemate since they stole it. If we overthrow them, they'll discredit us. The world will descend into chaos, and the energy will most likely plummet. It would mean destruction of the world as we know it and the Institution would have failed in its mission.'

'When you say *we*... you're part of the Institution?' said Anita. 'Why are you telling me all this?'

'Because we need powerful people like you to join us,' Helena replied.

'But what's the point of growing if you can't act?'

'Because, as you know better than most, the energy is failing. If we don't act now, then it may be too late.'

'How are you going to deal with the stalemate?'

'We're going to get the information back.'

'How? Information isn't something you can just steal...'

'I can't say any more, unless you agree to join us.'

Anita almost laughed, but saw the look on Helena's face.

'Join you? A minute ago you were warning me about Marcus and Austin, and now you want me to join an underground political movement?'

'I'm not saying it wouldn't be dangerous, but having you with us may be the key to retrieving the information.'

'How did you work that out?' asked Anita, shocked.

'Think about it. If your relationship with Marcus develops, you'll be able to probe about the whereabouts of the information. You could find out how heavily it's guarded… you may even be able to recover it for us.'

'You want me to spy for you, right under Austin and Amber's noses?'

'It's dangerous, but you'd be helping to protect us all.'

Anita looked away; it all seemed so absurd. 'Helena… until a few minutes ago, I didn't know the Institution even existed. Now you're asking me to make sure my relationship with Marcus develops so I can spy for you and steal from him? It's a bit full-on, don't you think?'

'I know it is, but that's the world we live in. The energy's plummeting and the Descendants are doing nothing. You have some of the strongest energy I've ever known, and I wouldn't have told you about the Institution if I didn't trust you, or think you could do it. You don't know it, but you've been wrapped up in this for a very long time.'

Anita rounded on her. 'What's that supposed to mean?'

'I can't tell you that until you join us and prove you're committed. If you get the information, I'll tell you everything.' She paused for a moment then added, 'Including all about your parents, who I knew very well.'

'You were friends with my parents and you never told me? Through all the time we spent together, you never thought to mention it?'

Anita was partly furious, partly hurt, and partly captivated. Helena could answer all the questions she'd never been able to ask Cordelia, or anyone else for that matter. She desperately wanted to know about her parents. If they had been part of the Institution, maybe it wasn't so bad? But what if her parents had been bad people? She'd never known them… maybe she should stay as far away from the Institution as possible. Maybe this was the reason they'd ended up dead…

She was so confused. Half of her wanted to agree to anything Helena asked of her, but the other half knew she should be cautious. Helena admitting something was dangerous meant it was really dangerous, and that wasn't something to be taken lightly.

'I couldn't. If I'd told you about your parents when you were younger, it would've put both of us, and many others, in danger.'

Anita was ravenous for more, but didn't know what to say.

'By all means, take some time to think about it, but please don't tell anyone about this conversation. No one at all. It would be dangerous for you and could get me killed.'

Anita felt suddenly cold, and sick. She'd never had to consider that someone might want to harm or even kill her for something as simple as a conversation. Sure, she knew how to use a bow and arrow, and had trained to fight with knives, and her bare hands, but that had all been a game, or for practice. She'd never considered she may actually have to use the training someday, or that someone else might try to use their training on her.

'I won't tell anyone,' she promised. There was no one she could tell something like this anyway.

'Thank you. I'll find you in a few days to hear your decision. You have unparalleled Body skills, and you learn quickly; if anyone can help us, it's you.' Helena squeezed Anita's arm, got up, and jogged away. 'See you in a couple of days,' she called back over her shoulder.

Anita couldn't believe it. She'd had lessons with Helena every day for years, and she'd never hinted at any of this. Helena hadn't even tried that hard to recruit her to be an academic, and now this?

Helena hadn't really been warning her off Marcus, nor had she accidentally bumped into her at the river. Helena had been watching, had seen an opportunity, and wanted to use it to her advantage. But none of that would help Anita decide what she should do.

And then there was the brass cylinder in her head... could it be something hostile that was waiting to kill her? Alexander had wanted to destroy it... She didn't think Amber had had an opportunity to plant something, but then, Anita didn't know what to look for and she had no idea how long the cylinder had been there. It could've been anybody, for any reason, over the course of her life. It could have been Helena for all she knew.

* * * * *

The following day, Anita ran to the castle for her first Mind lesson, still processing her conversation with Helena. She arrived and almost ran headlong into Austin and Amber descending the steps. She was instantly on guard.

'What are you doing here?' Austin snapped, shooting a questioning sideways glance at Amber. Amber ignored him and stared intently at Anita.

Anita stood her ground, wondering again if the cylinder in her head was hostile and had been put there by this woman.

149

'I'm here to see Marcus,' Anita replied cheerily, pretending she hadn't noticed their hostility.

'What for?' he asked in crisp rounds, not happy about the prospect of Anita spending more time with his precious son.

Luckily, as Anita was contemplating her answer, Marcus came striding out of the entrance towards them. 'Anita, hi!' he called.

'Hi,' she said, the tension draining out of her.

As Marcus reached her, he put an arm around her shoulders in a plutonic, brotherly way and shepherded her into the castle. 'See you later, Dad,' he called calmly over his shoulder.

Marcus didn't say a thing until they were safely up the stairs and in his suite. He closed the door firmly behind them and took a deep breath. 'That was almost very interesting,' he said, frivolously.

He took a cavalier step towards her, and she casually moved away. The energy changed, charged at the realization they were now alone in Marcus' suite, no prying eyes. Marcus changed too, his movements becoming calculated, reminding Anita of a big cat stalking its prey. 'Nothing like a dangerous encounter to liven up a morning,' he purred, his predator's eyes fixed on her.

'Is that so,' she said, moving to one of the enormous light grey sofas. She sat, tucking her legs underneath her. She pulled a large, patterned cushion protectively in front of her, trying to ignore the delicious reaction she was having to Marcus' honed form stalking her every move.

'What am I learning today?' she said, meeting his gaze. She wanted to keep him focused on the matter at hand, but was finding it difficult to make herself obey, let alone him.

Marcus smiled as he sat next to her, a knowing, victorious smile, casting aside her weak attempts to divert him. His energy soared as he leaned in towards her, and despite herself, her own energy responded, her skin prickling as the heady smell of vanilla invaded her lungs, eroding her resolve.

Impulsively, she moved towards him, meeting his lips with hers. They kissed with urgency, tingles shooting all over her body as Marcus put his hands on her waist and pulled her astride him. She grabbed handfuls of his hair, kissing him more deeply while his fingers explored. He found the chink between the back of her running tights and her vest, pushing his way under, caressing her back.

But Anita stiffened as he did it, pulled her lips away, placed her hands either side of his face and rested her forehead on his, closing her eyes. Marcus removed his hands, alarmed, pushing her backwards so he could see her face. She dropped her hands from him and in one supple movement, removed herself from his lap, curling herself against the arm of the sofa.

'What's wrong?' he asked, reaching for her hand, a look of concern on his face. She didn't let him take it.

She briefly met his worried eyes. 'Marcus,' she said, then paused, trying to work out what to say next. 'Why did you invite me to the ball?'

He looked confused, his eyes wide as he considered the question. 'You intrigued me. You're different; I find you exciting.'

'And so far this has all been a game,' she said, cryptically.

'I don't understand,' he said.

Anita could see in his eyes he knew what she meant.

'Yes, you do. I didn't react to you like everyone else, so you chased me. And because I knew that, I

151

pushed you away, which made you chase me more. But now we're here, in your bedroom, and we're in too dangerous a position to play games.'

'I suppose that's one way of looking at it,' he said.

'It's the only way to look at it,' she snapped. 'You know Austin doesn't approve of me and we live in a dangerous time. I need to know you're not playing a game now.'

'Anita, I'm not. I like you. I genuinely like you. You're confident and clever, and ballsy, and you don't cower at the sight of my father, and you're reckless and sexy, and… I can talk to you. I've never spoken about my mother to anyone, but with you… it felt natural.' His voice had taken on a pleading edge.

Anita softened, her defenses falling away. She wasn't totally sure he was telling the truth, but she wanted to believe him. She took his hand and kissed it gently, then said again, 'What am I learning today?'

He smiled, leaned forward, and placed a gentle kiss on her lips, then led her by the hand to his bedroom. 'Today you're going to learn the arts of suggestion and persuasion,' he said brightly.

'You mean manipulation.'

'Call them what you will, but they're powerful skills.'

They spent the next two hours playing chess, with Marcus teaching Anita the basics of suggestion and idea planting. She was supposed to distract him with their chess game, then casually drop an idea into the conversation. He was supposed to pick up the idea and think it was his own. By the end, she hadn't got very far.

Marcus assured her the main problem was that he knew what she was trying to do. He told her she should practice on other people. He said it was best to start with people who trusted her implicitly, or who were

152

naturally gullible, and after a brief internal moral debate, she decided Bass was the best person for the job.

Anita left the castle frustrated. She didn't like it when she couldn't do things, and Marcus had told her to 'be careful with Alexander' as she left. She would do what she damn well wanted, and anyway, judging by what everyone kept telling her, it wasn't Alexander she needed to worry about.

* * * * *

Anita had just about thrown off her anger by the time she arrived at the Temple of the Spirit to meet Alexander. Her stomach flipped as she thought about his piercing blue eyes.

She fought to get her energy under control as she climbed the steps into the temple. As she entered, on the dot of seven, she saw Alexander striding towards her. His cloak billowed out behind him and his hair was wild, as though he'd repeatedly run his hands through it in despair.

Even tired and worn as he was now, he was exceptionally attractive. Her energy responded mischievously to her thoughts and Alexander looked up, no hint of a smile on his face.

'We'll start here, at the back, where you were meditating yesterday,' he snapped.

Anita's energy deflated at the curt greeting. Obviously he wasn't as pleased to see her as she was to see him. Or was he hiding it…

'How do you hide your energy?' said Anita.

He paused, glaring at her. 'I think we should master the basics first. Seeing as you seem to have particular trouble keeping your energy under control, that may never be something you manage to grasp.' The words were quiet and menacing.

Hurt, embarrassment and confusion slammed through her.

'Sit down,' he said, pointing to the place on the mat where she'd sat yesterday. Anita did as she was told, saying nothing. Her energy plummeted, excitement chased away, empty and deflated. She wasn't angry, her usual reaction, but drained.

Alexander sat down in front of her, the knees of his crossed legs so close to hers that she swore she could feel a tension in the air between their skin. Alexander looked Anita in the eye, and it was all she could do to hold his gaze, searching his lovely blue eyes. They were lovely, but they were cold, like shards of ice.

'Close your eyes, clear your mind, and breathe deeply,' he said softly.

She did as he said. She relinquished control, following his instructions to the letter, but felt curiously tired. As she closed her eyes, Anita was transported to the sky above the clearing with the yurt, was falling, landed in front of the door.

Again, Anita pushed the curtain aside and entered the unexpectedly light space. It was exactly as it had been last time, apart from the brass cylinder, which had disappeared.

She looked over to the bed to find Alexander where he'd been last time too, still topless and disheveled, and she made her way towards him. As she neared him, she felt a warm nudge at the edge of her energy, similar to the nudge at dinner, during the ball. She smiled.

'So that was you,' she said, encouraged, although her lips didn't move as she spoke.

'You can feel that?' said Alexander, surprise clear on his face.

'Of course,' she said, sitting down next to him, bringing her legs up to sit cross-legged.

154

'What happened when you got rid of the brass cylinder?' he asked, changing the subject.

'I don't know, as I didn't.'

'What?' he said, alarmed. 'Then where is it?'

'It hit the floor and rolled out of the door, but it wasn't in the clearing outside when I came in a second ago.'

'Great.'

'What does that mean?'

'It means you have a brass cylinder roaming around in your head and we have no idea where it is. Have you ever meditated to other places inside your mind?'

Anita laughed. 'No. I didn't even believe this was possible until recently. I only had conclusive proof when I saw you here yesterday.'

'Gods, they really teach you nothing.'

'It's looking that way,' she said, testily. 'Where is this place?'

Alexander looked at her as though she'd just landed from another planet. 'You're kidding?'

Anita shook her head and frowned.

'You don't know where you are?'

'Nope.'

'Anita, this is your Centre.'

'My what?'

'Your Centre. The place that comes together around the time you turn thirty?'

'Well yes, obviously I've heard of my Centre, but I always thought it was bullshit made up to keep people in lessons after school. You're telling me this is the place that will *come together* when I'm thirty? What does that mean anyway?'

Alexander took a deep breath. 'This place reflects your most prominent skills, the ones you're most comfortable with and that come most easily to you. For you, it's a mixture of Body and Spirit with very little Mind.

'There are other places inside your head that represent different combinations of skills, and any of those places can be developed. When your Centre comes together, all the different places in your mind merge into one new Centre that you will have for the rest of your life.

'Why that happens when it does, no one knows, but from that time it becomes difficult, if not impossible, to develop new skills. The reason you're so tired…'

Anita gave him a questioning look.

'… and I know because I can read your energy, remember?'

Oh, yeah.

'You're tired, because this morning you had a session with Marcus to develop your Mind skills. They don't come easily to you, so it takes a great deal of effort to build up your abilities. Like when someone practices Body skills and they're tired and stiff while their muscles recover, your mind is doing the same thing. You'll feel empty and drained until you've had time to get over it.

'Hopefully, as you have a lot of Spirit in you, these sessions won't take as much of a toll. Given that the Mind sessions will drain you, you're going to need to be vigilant; you'll be especially vulnerable to attack.'

Normally Anita would have said Alexander was being ridiculous; who would want to attack her? But she was beginning to believe that he and Helena might be right. The way Austin and Amber had looked at her this morning…

'And Marcus is probably watching us right now,' said Alexander. 'He will for the first few sessions, until he trusts that I'll behave myself.'

Anita remembered the look on Marcus' face when they'd said goodbye earlier and knew he was right. But part of her didn't want Alexander to behave himself…

'At least he can't tell what's going on in here,' she said.

'No, not exactly, but there are tells that give clues. We need to be careful not to give anything away about that cylinder of yours, but we also need to find it.'

'Or it might explode in my head and kill me?' Anita laughed.

Alexander gave her another stern look. 'Yes, and you can find that funny if you want to, but if you die when I'm in here, I could die too. I'd like to take this seriously if you don't mind.'

Anita went pale. 'You think someone may actually have put it in my head to kill me?'

'Who knows? What I do know is that we need to find it and get rid of it, before we learn the hard way.'

'But what if it contains something really important, from a friend?'

'Do you have any friends who need to pass important messages to you through cylinders in your mind?'

'Not that I know of, but you never know…'

'And what if Austin or Amber put it here to kill you?'

'I know they don't like me seeing Marcus, but do you really think they would kill me because of that? You said yourself they wouldn't risk upsetting Marcus.'

'Believe me, they've killed for less, and they could use the cylinder any time they like. They could have planted it just in case you and Marcus don't work out, so they have a convenient way to kill you then.'

'Austin gets away with things like that?'

'There aren't many people queuing up to stop him.'

'Are you trying to stop him?'

Alexander ignored the question, changing the subject. 'We need to find and get rid of the cylinder. I need to teach you how to hide your energy. I'll teach you all the meditation poses, and then we may get on to visiting the Centers of others and extraction, depending on how quickly you learn.'

Would she get to visit his Centre? Just the prospect sent shivers up and down her spine. 'Where do we start?' she said.

* * * * *

Alexander and Anita spent the next hour trying to locate other places in her mind, searching for where the cylinder may have hidden. Alexander didn't tell Anita this, but it was surprising that the cylinder had run away. It meant that someone powerful, more powerful than Austin or Amber, and with a mix of Mind and Spirit, had planted it. It would be difficult to get rid of, but they would cross that bridge if they got there.

They located two other places in Anita's mind; one by the river in Empire and another on top of a beautiful cliff looking out over the sea. Alexander knew this place well, the cliffs overlooking Kingdom, but neither showed signs of the cylinder. Both places were steeped in Spirit and Body, hence why they were the first and easiest places to find.

Anita's energy dipped even further; she was exhausted.

'We're done here for today,' he said, taking one last look out to sea from the cliff that was so familiar.

Anita nodded, following Alexander's instructions to lift herself out of the meditation and back to the temple.

* * * * *

Anita woke to find her vision filled with Alexander's concerned features. She smiled at the softness he'd hidden before.

'That was amazing,' she said, groggily, 'thank you for showing me. Who knew all that stuff was in my head?'

'If I were you, I wouldn't go into too much detail about it with Marcus when he takes you home,' said Alexander, in a low voice, helping Anita to her feet. Blood rushed to her head as she stood, her vision blurry, and she swayed on her feet, grabbing his arm to steady herself. His muscles flexed under her grip, straining to keep her upright as he wrapped his other arm around her waist, supporting her weight.

Anita's vision cleared as her body recalibrated, and she straightened, finding herself in Alexander's space, his hands still on her. Tingles crept across her skin from where they touched, his woody citrus smell all around her, warmth radiating off him. Her energy leapt, and so did his.

Marcus broke cover and hurried over to them. He pulled Anita out of Alexander's grasp, slipping his arm around her.

Anita leaned into him, exhausted; she needed sleep.

Alexander turned to leave. 'Same time tomorrow,' he said, striding away.

'Hey,' Marcus whispered, as he pulled her into a hug, kissing her hair as he wrapped his arms around her.

'Hi,' she said weakly, worried she might fall asleep right then and there.

Marcus bent, put one arm behind her knees, and scooped her up into his arms. He carried her out of the temple to his waiting car, and Anita couldn't have been happier to let him. She fell asleep in his lap before he'd even closed the door.

* * * * *

They reached Cordelia's house and Marcus lifted Anita out of the car without her so much as stirring. He carried her to the back door and straight up the stairs, pausing for a moment to work out which was Anita's bedroom. He went for the smaller of the two, as it had the dress Anita had worn to the ball hanging on the outside of the wardrobe, and gently placed her on the bed.

She woke as he put her down, smiling a drowsy half smile up at him. He crouched beside the small double bed and pushed a stray hair behind her ear. She reached out and cupped his neck, pulling his lips towards hers, kissing him sleepily.

'Thank you for bringing me home,' she mumbled.

'My pleasure,' he said, leaning in to kiss her forehead, then getting up to leave.

'Don't go yet,' she said, rolling to the other side of the bed, so he had space to lie down too.

Marcus hesitated for only a split second before lowering himself down next to her.

They lay there, face to face, Anita struggling to keep her eyes open, his warm breath landing on her lips.

Anita's eyelids fluttered closed and Marcus kissed her softly on the lips. He rested his hand over the one she had placed on his neck and gently played with each finger in turn, mesmerized by the rise and fall of her sleeping body. He turned his head carefully, lifted her palm to his mouth, and kissed it, before placing it next to her head on the pillow. Then he used every ounce of his resolve to tear himself away.

CHAPTER 9

Anita woke early the following morning, feeling drained. She hadn't felt this way in years, not since she'd first started training with Helena when she was thirteen. At least it shows I'm doing something, even if it's not the right thing, she thought, prizing herself out of bed to do some yoga.

After her workout, she showered, ate breakfast and headed to the observatory. She felt a bit better, but every action was harder than usual.

Her Mind task for the day was to practice what she'd learned yesterday. She was going to try and plant an idea in Bass' head, but still hadn't decided what it should be. She pondered as she strolled, walking at a more sedate pace than her usual march, as she considered her options.

She could plant the idea that Bass should invite Anita to sing in his band… but if he took her up on the offer, he might make her sing a love song with him… She could try to make him suggest they play a game of chess together… but that was probably a stretch, given her current level of skill; Bass hated chess with a passion, and it wasn't like Anita was keen on it either.

Eventually, she settled on trying to get Bass to want to go for a swim in the river. The weather was cooling off, so he wouldn't naturally suggest it. If he did, she could claim the plant as a triumph.

Anita climbed the observatory's spiral staircase and stepped onto the middle floor. Bass and Patrick were having a heated debate, presumably about the current energy predicament.

'Hi,' she said loudly, so they would have to look up. 'I just came from the river, it's lovely down there today.'

They looked at her, bewildered, like she must have had a nasty fall and hit her head.

'If you say so,' said Patrick, looking at her suspiciously. 'We're already seeing adverse effects on crop yields as a result of the energy drop.'

'Really?' she said. 'Are we seeing effects anywhere else? In the river, for example?'

'Um, no, not yet,' Bass said slowly, giving Anita an *are you alright,* kind of look. 'The autumn crop yields are down a bit on last year. Austin's harping on about it being a coincidence. He's apparently convinced it's all down to the weather; idiot.'

'There's a surprise,' said Anita, sitting down at a dashboard. 'How can someone so well educated, who has access to so much information, be such a prat?'

'I don't know,' said Patrick, 'but he'll have to pay attention eventually, unless he has a way to produce food out of thin air. I'd like to see how he explains away shortages…'

'Mmm, that wouldn't be pretty,' said Anita.

They got to work, sitting in silence for a few minutes, until Anita tried again. 'Thorn jumped in the water this morning; it looked so refreshing.'

Bass and Patrick looked at each other. 'Is everything alright, Anita?' asked Bass.

'Of course. Why do you ask?'

'Because for the entire time I've known you, which is quite a long time, you've never once volunteered any information you didn't have to. You've done it twice now in one morning.'

Anita went red. Damn, she thought. She really was hideous at this Mind stuff. 'Sorry for being chatty,' she retorted, furious at herself for failing to plant the idea. 'I'll keep my thoughts to myself in the future.'

'And she's back,' said Patrick, giving Anita an infuriating wink.

Anita sat in silence for the rest of the day, angry at herself, and plotting who to target next.

After work, Anita tried Cleo over drinks at The Island, then Elistair, who she bumped into on her way home, and then Cordelia. Everyone thought she was being weird. Cleo had even realized what she was trying to do.

Idiot, she chastised herself; Cleo was a terrible choice for idea planting practice. Cleo was, after all, a Mind, and manipulation was one of her strongest suits; of course she'd know what Anita was doing.

'Sorry,' she said. 'I'm getting Marcus to give me Mind lessons and he told me to practice planting ideas. But as you can see, I'm rubbish at it.'

'Well, my advice, for what it's worth, is that you've got to play to your strengths. When you try to plant an idea, don't impersonate what a Mind would do; use your Body and Spirit skills. You can't be someone you're not; use the skills you have.'

Anita nodded and quickly changed the subject. She didn't know how to do what Cleo was saying, and was cross with herself for being so easily caught out.

* * * * *

The following weeks contained classes with both Marcus at the castle and Alexander at the temple (with Marcus always finding some reason to be in the area).

Austin had extended the Descendants' stay in Empire, although nobody knew for how long. Not that Anita was complaining.

The lessons couldn't have been more different. Marcus was prescriptive and controlling, trying to force Anita to imitate the way he did things, whereas Alexander let Anita find her own way, there to guide if she needed him.

Anita left Marcus' lessons frustrated and exhausted, and usually wanting to hit him. She left Alexander's lessons drained, but somehow liberated, content. They found several more places in her mind during their lessons, including the boat she had visited with Cleo. Alexander told her it contained a good mix of Mind, Body and Spirit, so it made sense that Cleo and Anita would have ended up there.

They found a waterfall that Alexander said was full of Spirit, as well as a stable with a beautiful chestnut mare that was a mixture of Body and Spirit. There had been no sign of the cylinder, Alexander convinced it had run to a Mind dominated space. But there were only so many locations in any person's mind; it was only a matter of time before they found it.

Anita didn't tell Marcus about her successful Spirit lessons. The Mind sessions were going so badly, and Marcus was forever probing for evidence that his lessons were better than Alexander's. 'Maybe there's a reason most people aren't taught all the skills to such a high level,' he said pompously, after a particularly disastrous Mind lesson.

'Yes, maybe,' Anita agreed, inwardly sneering.

As the weeks went on, three things became evident. Firstly, Marcus and Anita would not get anywhere with their Mind lessons. Secondly, if Anita and Marcus wanted to continue their relationship, they should stop the Mind lessons. And thirdly, that the

Mind place in Anita's head did not want to be found. Alexander decided to stop searching for a while and move on to work on other skills, specifically, how to hide energy.

The conversation with Marcus to end their lessons did not go well. At first, he took it as an affront to his teaching skills. Then he switched tack, blaming her lack of progress on all the time she was spending with Alexander.

Anita eventually brought Marcus round, reassuring him it was nothing to do with his teaching skills. She blamed herself, saying how useless she was at Mind skills, telling him it was pointless to flog a dead horse. She sealed the deal by pointing out they would be able to spend more time together as a couple, and not as teacher and pupil.

Maybe she was better at Mind skills than she let on, she thought, as he softened.

Anita knew Marcus was bored of teaching her anyway, especially as she never seemed to improve, so he finally relented.

It was a much harder sell to convince Marcus not to turn up to her future Spirit lessons. It shocked her when he acted like a spoilt child. She hadn't quite believed the warnings about Marcus' possessiveness, but when she saw it with her own eyes, she wondered what she'd got herself into. She avoided a serious argument with flattery and a good measure of flirting.

'It's not that I don't want you there,' she said, sitting on his lap and wrapping her arms around his neck. 'It's that we're working on hiding energy next, and when you're around, my energy soars. It's impossible to control,' she said, playfully biting his earlobe.

It didn't placate Marcus entirely, but it distracted him. He threw her back onto the bed, climbed on top of her, and pinned her arms above her head.

'Fine,' he said sulkily, 'I won't come to your lessons.'

'You promise?' she said, matching his tone, looking up at him through her lashes.

'I suppose so,' he said, leaning down, running the tip of his nose down the length of hers, then kissing her lips.

* * * * *

Anita was happy with where she and Marcus were now. She was even more happy that she'd used the Mind skills he'd taught her to get there. That thought soothed her conscience.

She could barely contain her excitement as she headed to her Spirit lesson, away from Marcus' prying eyes. Today she would learn to control her energy. Apparently, it could be an emotional skill to learn, so Alexander had suggested meeting in a more private location by the river.

'Hey,' said Anita, reaching the large flat rock Alexander was already sitting on, cross-legged, above the angry water below.

'Hi. No chaperone today?' Alexander mocked.

'No,' she smiled triumphantly. 'Marcus has agreed to give me some space during these lessons.'

'I see,' said Alexander, surprised. Anita felt his energy rise, then quickly diminish as he motioned for her to sit down. Interesting.

'Learning to suppress your energy is different from finding places inside your mind,' he said. 'You must understand how you react to situations and to others around you. You need to anticipate your reaction and divert the energy. You can't get rid of it, but you can channel it elsewhere.'

'And how do I do that?'

166

Alexander smiled. 'You push it through your feet.'

'Right. What the hell does that mean?'

'It means exactly that. You push all the energy towards your feet, so it's utilized elsewhere, and nobody can read your reaction.'

'How does the energy get used up?'

'By propelling your body upwards.'

Anita laughed. 'What?' This was ridiculous.

Alexander looked disappointed. 'It's the same principle as energy cars and trains,' he said. 'When you push your energy down, it propels you upwards. Most people aren't powerful enough to actually walk on air, but it can make you look weightless, almost like you're floating as you walk. But, of course, you learn to hide that too, so only those who really know what to look for can tell what you're doing.'

Anita wasn't sure if he was joking; it sounded ridiculous. But then, it was how energy cars worked… 'Alright, so how do I do this... pushing downwards?'

'First, we need to make your energy rise,' he said, cocking a mischievous eyebrow.

Anita blushed. 'And how are we going to do that?' Her energy didn't react the way it used to at the mere sight of him, thank goodness.

Alexander leaned sharply towards her. 'I can either challenge you or seduce you,' he said, the mood shifting wildly as his eyes bored into hers.

Anita's energy reacted immediately, full of shock and delightful anticipation at the prospect of either.

Smug at her instant reaction, Alexander reached out and took her hands.

She thought she might burst, tingles shooting all over her body at the first contact of their skin in weeks.

'Good,' he said gently, pulling her to her feet. 'Now, think the energy downwards and imagine yourself being propelled upwards.'

Anita did as she was told, and, surprisingly, felt some weight leave her.

'Good,' said Alexander again, doing nothing to hide his energy's rapidly rising tide. 'Now, push down on my hands and imagine someone is tugging on your hair, pulling you upwards.'

Again, Anita did as she was told, and her weight completely left the ground. She panicked, and the weight returned. Her feet reconnected unsteadily with the ground, Alexander catching her as she stumbled into him, preventing her from tumbling to the floor.

'By the Gods, Anita. I've never seen anyone levitate on their first attempt,' he said. 'How did it feel?'

'Great,' she beamed, as much because he hadn't taken his hands off her as from the levitation.

This is so much more fun than Mind lessons, she thought, her energy once more rising as she looked up at Alexander, her hands enjoying the muscular contours of his chest.

'Let's try again,' she said eagerly.

'Okay,' he breathed, his energy still singing as he stepped back and held her hands.

Anita relished the tingles, different, more intense with Alexander than with Marcus.

Anita did it a second time and even took a few steps in the air, with Alexander's support, before she lost concentration and came crashing back down. She was drained, her energy dropping like a stone.

'I think that's enough for today. I don't want to wear you out completely or Marcus will be after me,' he said seriously, but Anita detected an ironic edge. 'Tomorrow we can work on sending only some of your energy downwards, so you stay connected to the ground. If you levitate in public, it defeats the point of trying to hide your energy!'

'Okay,' said Anita, attempting to hide her disappointment. 'Are you walking back to Empire?'

'I will do in a bit, but it's best that Marcus doesn't see us walking back together. He may have agreed to give you some space for the lessons themselves, but I doubt he's too far away. He won't be keen on us being seen together.'

Anita nodded, annoyed by how Alexander spoke about her boyfriend; was he her boyfriend? His words were probably true, but it was still annoying. 'See you here at the same time tomorrow?'

'Sure,' he said, sounding disinterested. 'Same time tomorrow.'

Anita walked away, confused; she'd felt his energy rise when they'd touched. He'd been the most warm she'd ever seen him today, probably because Marcus wasn't watching, but now he was all aloof again. Did he see them as friends? Did he want more than that? Could he care less? Was he doing all this just to make sure the Descendants were protected from attackers?

Most strange was that they'd spent so much time together, yet had barely had a conversation. It took so much concentration to meditate, there was no room to chat; she knew nothing about him. Before stopping to think, Anita turned and called, 'Marcus, Cleo, Bass and I are going to The Island for drinks later. You should come too.'

'Do you really think that's a good idea?' he said, after a pause.

'Of course it's a good idea. Why wouldn't it be?'

He gave her a look.

Obviously she knew why it wouldn't be, but if they all spent time together socially, she was sure Marcus would relax.

Alexander half laughed and shrugged. 'Alright. See you there.'

'Great,' she said triumphantly. More Mind skills must have rubbed off on her than she'd originally realized. 'See you there at eight.'

Alexander took a deep breath and hung his head, shaking it. 'What are you doing?' he said, when she was gone.

CHAPTER 10

'You always know how to brighten my day,' Amber teased, kissing Austin before climbing off him, buttoning her shirt and pulling down her pencil skirt.

'I aim to please,' he smirked, standing from his office chair, securing his trousers, and heading for the drinks cabinet. 'Brandy?'

'Why not?' she said, sinking into a chesterfield and curling her legs up under her. She took the glass Austin offered, savoring the first mouthful. Austin sat down next to her, and knowing this was as good an opportunity as she was going to get, she launched her assault.

'I think we should talk about Anita.'

Austin stiffened, took a slow, deep sip, then said, 'Go on.'

'She may be more of a problem than we originally anticipated. Marcus is still interested in her; he's become possessive, and he's following her around.'

Austin's face told Amber everything she needed to know; he was furious. 'What happened to infatuation and lust?' He said, hissing the words.

'It would seem the lust hasn't been sated and infatuation is turning to something more. I think it might be time for you to have a gentle word with him. Talk some sense into him.'

'I told you we should've put a stop to this at the start,' he snarled. 'Now who knows what damage has been done?'

'Austin, there's still time to solve this. We just need to focus his attention elsewhere; get him more involved in your business activities. Make him feel more important; give him something to concentrate on other than her.'

'Can't we just get rid of her?'

'Not yet,' she laughed. 'You know we can't. If he grows apart from her, we can take action, but we can't take her away from him; the consequences would be dire. As I said, he's protective of her and he won't appreciate being told what to do by you, me, or anyone else.'

Austin's mood was deteriorating; time for Amber's exit. 'Just think about it,' she said, getting up and slipping on her stilettos. She leaned back over him and ran her hands through his hair. 'If anyone can make him see sense, it's you,' she said, giving him a brief kiss on the lips.

By the Gods, I hope this all works out, she thought, walking to the door and closing it behind her, resting her head back against the wood. She didn't want to consider what might happen to her otherwise.

* * * * *

Austin heard Marcus return from wherever he'd been and followed him to the kitchen, doing a quick sweep to make sure they were alone. They were, so he moved to the enormous range cooker and put the kettle on. 'Cup of tea?' he asked, as Marcus pulled out a tin of shortbread.

'Sure,' said Marcus, suspicious. Had his dad ever made him tea?

172

'Had a good day?' asked Austin.

'Yep, fine thanks. You?' It was a lie. Marcus had been in a dreadful mood since Anita had left for her lesson with Alexander. It was killing him.

'Yes, fine thanks; all very mundane today, nothing exciting going on. What have you been up to?'

Marcus was really suspicious now. His dad being chatty was an extreme rarity, but he thought it best to play along. 'I went to Empire. I had a few things to do at the temple.'

'Good... good. Been seeing much of that Anita girl since the ball?'

Knew it, thought Marcus. Austin's ulterior motive came to light just as the kettle boiled.

'Yep, been seeing her a bit.'

There was silence as Austin made them tea. Marcus picked up a large piece of shortbread and took a bite.

'I think you should be careful, Marcus. I wouldn't want you to get hurt.'

'Oh?' said Marcus, innocently.

'I don't trust her.'

'Any particular reason why?'

'Because she's very powerful, and she's latched onto you since the ball.'

'She hasn't *latched* onto me. She's nice. We have a lot in common, so we spend time together. I don't see much harm in that.'

'Marcus, don't you think you should find someone more appropriate? Someone from a better background...'

'... what's wrong with Anita's background?' he said hotly.

Marcus wasn't sure he wanted to hear the answer; from it, he would be able to tell how strong Austin's feelings were about Anita. If Austin admitted that he'd looked into Anita's background, it was dire. If he made

173

a comment about her not being from a council family, it was still bad, but better.

'I just think you'd be better off with someone more like us. What about one of the councilors' daughters? There are lots of nice, well-connected girls who are a far more suitable match.'

Marcus released a relieved breath. 'Well, I'm afraid I disagree. I like Anita; she's interesting. Thanks for your concern, but I'm confident I'm right about her.'

With that, he picked up his tea, along with another piece of shortbread, and headed up to his suite, baffled. It was unlike Austin to pussyfoot around the edge of a topic; the direct approach was more his style. Marcus was surprised Austin hadn't tried to ban him from seeing Anita again. It wouldn't have worked, but it would have been more in character. Something was going on…

* * * * *

Marcus made his way to The Island later that evening, still confused by his father's words. He knew Austin didn't like powerful people, but Anita was hardly a threat.

He arrived, excited at the prospect of spending an evening with Anita, even more so now he knew how much his father disapproved.

He walked in and scanned the room, smiling as he spotted Anita, Bass and Cleo, before recognizing Alexander's unwelcome form. Alexander's leg was dangerously close to Anita's as he sat with the others at Cleo's favorite table.

In the name of the Gods, what is he doing here, Marcus silently cursed. Anita smiled at something Alexander said, and Marcus' mood blackened. He made a point of greeting everyone warmly, except Alexander.

Marcus sat next to Anita, leaning in to peck her on the lips. The table's whole focus was on them. Marcus carried on as though what he'd just done was normal.

Pleased with himself, he celebrated by ordering a bottle of Ginger Champagne.

* * * * *

A mix of embarrassment and excitement rose in Anita as Marcus kissed her, because, unlike Marcus, she could feel the reaction from everyone as he did it.

Anita, now sandwiched in a booth between Marcus and Alexander, with Bass directly opposite, was intensely uncomfortable. It was delightful to be in the company of either Marcus or Alexander when they were on their own, but both together like this… what had she been thinking? Not to mention Bass, who kept shooting glances her way.

Marcus' hand made its way to her leg, and Alexander's knee was so close… were they touching? There were no tingles, but maybe that was because of their clothes. She was tempted to move her leg to see… oh, Gods, she shouldn't be thinking these thoughts. Why had she invited Alexander?

Cleo, doing nothing to hide her enjoyment of Anita's predicament, and wishing to stir the situation further, broke the awkward silence. 'Marcus, we were just discussing our trip to Kingdom this weekend. Can you believe Anita has never been?'

'Really?' Marcus looked at Anita, and she shook her head in confirmation. 'I'll have to come and show you around then.'

Cleo smirked and looked at Anita.

'I thought you had to see your mother this weekend?' said Anita, tentatively, trying to suppress a worried look.

175

'Damn, yeah, you're right. Well, go without me then and I'll give you a list of things to do. I also have a brilliant driver there, who, of course, you can use, and you must stay in the house.'

Anita was devising a tactical way to break it to Marcus, when Cleo, true to form, jumped in. 'That's so kind, Marcus, but Anita, Bass, and I are going with Alexander, so we're planning to stay with him.'

Marcus' face was a picture. Everyone held their breath to see what would come next, Anita noting that Alexander's energy was steady as a rock.

'You're staying with Alexander?' said Marcus, directing the question at Anita.

'Yes,' interjected Alexander. 'It will be more comfortable for everyone than staying in a hotel, not to mention safer.' He shot a meaningful look at Marcus. 'Besides, I'm not sure Austin would welcome a house full of guests when he's in Kingdom this weekend.'

Marcus' anger kindled and Anita knew she had to defuse him. 'I'm sure your mother's really looking forward to seeing you after all the excitement of the last few weeks,' she said, drawing his attention to her, placing a hand on his thigh.

The distraction worked, Marcus' energy mellowing a little, but it wasn't enough to make him let it go.

'And it's only for the weekend,' she continued, leaning into him. 'We'll be back before you know it.' She smiled, trying to look something like an innocent puppy. It worked, his energy returning to more normal levels.

'Okay, fine,' he said, relenting, leaning in and giving her another, much longer kiss.

Under normal circumstances, Anita would have gone a deep shade of puce, and everyone would have taken the piss out of them. But everyone, including Bass, who had suddenly found the table in need of careful study, realized that Anita had adverted a crisis, so they sat in awkward silence.

'Why are you going to Kingdom?' asked Marcus, his tone edgy.

Cleo jumped in, Anita grateful this time, as the table's focus shifted away from her.

'Alexander has some business stuff to do, Bass is going to see someone to talk about energy, and I'm going to see my dad. Dad's a trader, so he's been out in the Wild Lands for ages and I can't wait to see him. He's very fond of Anita, so she's coming along for the ride.'

This wasn't entirely true. The way it had really happened was that Cleo had told them she was going to Kingdom to see her dad. Alexander had said he was going too, and asked Bass if he wanted to come along to meet some energy guy. Bass had jumped at the chance, and Cleo had announced to the table that Anita was coming along for the ride. Cleo's motives were never pure, but Marcus didn't need to know that.

Marcus lost interest as Cleo started rabbiting on about the commodities her father traded and how he was hardly ever in Empire any longer.

Marcus put his arm around Anita and pulled her towards him. The message was clear: she was his, and Alexander had better not forget it.

CHAPTER 11

By the time Friday rolled around, Anita was glad at the prospect of a break from Marcus. He'd monopolized her time since learning she'd be going to Kingdom at the weekend. He met her every morning to walk her to the observatory, had spent time in the observatory asking questions about what exactly it was she did, had walked her home every day, and had insisted she spend every evening with him, meaning she'd had to cancel her lessons with Alexander.

Anita loved spending time with Marcus, but she was getting claustrophobic, and was looking forward to the weekend away.

Friday afternoon eventually arrived, and she was full of excitement as she got in an energy car with Bass, Alexander and Cleo (with Marcus there to wave them off, of course). The back seats were arranged with some facing forwards and others backwards, so they chatted easily all the way to Kingdom.

After several hours, the tension of Alexander's proximity now almost unbearable, Alexander cut across the conversation. 'There it is,' he said, gesturing out of the window at the first glimpse of Kingdom.

Anita felt him watching her as she saw it for the first time, knew he could feel her energy soar. The city's silhouette, despite the distance, conveyed a magnificent power that made the blood race around her veins.

Kingdom sat just above the sea, a cluster of soaring spires and elegant outlines, with a wall around the city that seemed to hug it to the coast. In its center rose three imposing spires, dominating the rest. They belonged to the temples, their sheer dominance impressive even at this range.

Whereas Empire had a stately, romantic quality, Kingdom had none of that charm. It was majestic yet harsh, untold opportunity radiating from within its walls. But it also felt dangerous, like the opportunity came with a risk, like you'd never be totally safe there, never mind who you were.

This was Anita's kind of place, where a challenge waited at every corner, and those who fought the hardest won the day.

They raced towards the city, then through the gates, flying along the ancient streets, Anita straining for a glimpse of the Relic as they passed the colossal temples.

'Don't worry,' laughed Alexander, 'we can see it tomorrow.'

They carried on through Kingdom, past an array of spectacular looking shops, restaurants, and houses, until they passed out through the gate the other side.

Anita looked at Alexander, confused. 'We're not staying in Kingdom?'

'Afraid not. My family rank privacy over convenience, so our residence is just outside. We'll be spending most of our time in the city though.'

Anita was disappointed to be leaving before having a chance to explore, but couldn't wait to see Alexander's house.

A couple of miles outside Kingdom, the car pulled through a pair of understated gates onto a sweeping drive. It swung in a wide arc, revealing a grand house, large but not vast, covered in magnificent purple flowers. Anita's energy soared when she saw the house, and Alexander's responded when he sensed her reaction, his energy tinged with worry.

She turned to face him and beamed, Cleo and Bass making appreciative noises. 'It's beautiful,' she breathed, before turning her head to the other window. Lush, green lawn rolled from the front of the house all the way to the top of a shear drop into the sea.

Anita froze, eyes wide, all color draining from her face. 'Alexander...' she said, feeling sick, then stopped, lost for words.

He studied her, his energy nervous. But before he could respond, Cleo broke the spell.

'In the name of the Gods, Alexander. That is bloody glorious,' she said, looking in the same direction as Anita, out over the sea.

Although the sea itself provided a stunning, theatrical backdrop, what had caught Cleo's attention was the view of Kingdom across the bay. It was breathtaking. Kingdom looked like it belonged in a snow dome, a perfect city contained within a neat, protective wall.

But Anita couldn't focus on that. Her pulse hammered in her ears... this was... how was this possible? Why hadn't he said anything...? Apart from the city, which didn't feature, this place was identical to the cliff in her mind.

* * * * *

To Anita's surprise, she was afraid. She had never been here before. How was this place in her head, and why without Kingdom?

Alexander studied her, then sent a nudge to the edge of her energy field, but it had no impact. Anita's mind raced. Was it someone from Alexander's family who'd put the cylinder in her head? Was that how the cliff had got there? Did Alexander know something? Had he brought her to Kingdom under false pretenses?

They pulled up to the front door, Cleo talking at a hundred miles an hour about how wonderful the house was, but nobody was really listening.

They climbed out of the car to be greeted by the housekeeper, Mrs. Hudson, who ushered them inside. They entered to find themselves in an enormous, glass-topped atrium that basked an internal courtyard in light.

Alexander didn't give them time to dwell, whisking them away from the feathery space to show them to their rooms. They climbed one side of a double staircase, turned left at the top, and followed the corridor to the end. Alexander opened a door to reveal Cleo's gargantuan quarters.

'You'll be in here, Cleo. Your bags should already be waiting for you. We'll see you downstairs for supper at eight. Hopefully that should give you enough time to freshen up?'

Cleo barely heard what he said, preoccupied with the extravagant four poster bed and view over the bay. 'Uh-huh. Yep, sure thing. See you downstairs,' she said, not even sparing the others a glance.

Alexander dropped Bass off in the room next to Cleo, before leading Anita over to the other side of the house. He opened an understated door into a smaller, but truly beautiful room.

Anita, who had thought nothing but suspicious thoughts since she'd seen the view, softened as she took in the proportions. It was big, but not ostentatious, full of gorgeous draped fabric. It had a weightless, carefree, quietly opulent air.

The floor to ceiling windows let in so much light that the room basked in a golden hour glow. Through them, Anita had an uninterrupted view over the perfectly manicured lawns. They skipped to the edge of the cliff and then jump off into the sea below. But the jewel in the crown was the sight of Kingdom, seeming to levitate above the sea.

There must be so much power in the city, thought Anita, that it wouldn't be surprising if it was suppressing its energy, propelling itself off the ground.

Alexander had been watching Anita as she took in the room and the view. 'Anita,' he started, hesitantly, 'I'm sorry.'

She turned slowly to face him, quizzing him with her eyes, energy furious, but didn't say a word.

'When we arranged to come to Kingdom,' he said, 'I knew I had to tell you. I was going to tell you in our next lesson, but Marcus hasn't let you out of his sight long enough for me to get anywhere near you.'

Anita could see Alexander was telling the truth and could feel it in his energy, which he was making no attempt to hide, but she wasn't ready to let him off the hook quite yet. 'Why didn't you tell me when we first meditated to the cliff?' she asked, her tone neutral.

'I don't know,' he said. He paused… embarrassed.

The impervious Alexander, embarrassed.

'I thought you'd be suspicious if I told you, that you wouldn't trust me. I have no explanation for how the cliff got into your head, and I thought it best to keep anything personal out of our lessons. You know how Marcus feels about us spending time together; can you imagine how he'd react if he found out one of the places in your head was here?'

'How would he find out?'

'You might have told him.'

His words were matter of fact, like an arrow through her arm. Not a fatal blow, but painful; he didn't trust her.

'I need time to get ready for dinner,' said Anita.

Alexander looked for a moment like he might not leave, then whirled around, gliding back through the door, energy suppressed so Anita couldn't read it.

Alexander opened the door next to Anita's and entered his room, resisting the urge to slam it closed behind him.

* * * * *

As eight o'clock neared, Anita left her room and went to find Cleo. She tiptoed past Alexander's room in her gold sandals and a floor length goddess gown she'd had to buy especially for the occasion, and went in search of her best friend.

Anita got to Cleo's room just as Cleo was coming out. She looked spectacular, as always, in a floor length silk chiffon dress that wafted around her legs. 'Hey,' said Anita, 'you look amazing.'

'Thanks. You don't look too bad yourself,' she said, feigning surprise.

'Very funny.'

'Ready to make our grand entrance? I think the boys have already gone down.'

Anita nodded, turned around, and headed for the staircase. They made their way down the sweeping stairs and into the atrium, where the others were already sitting, sipping spectacular looking cocktails from crystal glasses. The men stood up when they entered, Anita thinking how funny it was that getting dressed up could bring out one's best behavior.

Alexander stepped forward, grabbed the two remaining cocktails from a silver tray, and handed them

183

to Anita and Cleo. Cleo walked off to admire a large piece of art.

'Anita, this is Anderson, he's a Relic specialist,' said Alexander, introducing her to a tall, skinny man with a mop of ginger hair. 'Anita's an energy specialist. She works in the observatory with Bass,' he said to Anderson.

Anita blushed. 'I'm not sure I would describe myself as a specialist,' she said, 'but I work with Bass, who definitely is one. You're a Relic specialist? How interesting,' she said, deflecting the conversation away from herself, 'I didn't know such a profession existed.'

Anderson's energy turned shifty, and he couldn't hide it from his face. 'Well, it doesn't really, not officially. The Descendants, specifically Austin, banned it a few years ago... not sure why... but they let me get on with it.' He smiled a smile that said *no more questions please* and turned to introduce his wife. 'Anita, this is Bella, she assists me with my research.'

'Hello,' said Anita, warmly. Maybe she could make friends with Bella, who could shed some light on what exactly a Relic specialist did. 'It's so nice to meet you. We're going to see the Relic tomorrow... why don't you join us?'

Anderson looked shifty again, like he was trying to find the right way to say *no*, but before he could, Bella said, 'Yes, of course; it would be our pleasure.'

Anita knew from Bella's guilty energy that she had an ulterior motive, but Anita couldn't care less.

After another lethal-yet-delicious cocktail, Mrs. Hudson ushered the group into the dining room. It was like the rest of the house; large, spacious, light and sophisticated, but not in any way grand or stuffy. The parts of the house Anita had seen so far would fit on a mountain top amid the clouds, and the dining room was no exception.

Anita found herself between Alexander and Anderson at dinner. She pointedly turned away from Alexander, shutting him out of the conversation. She was still hurt that he didn't trust her and had no intention of making life easy, not for a little while anyway.

The meal was delicious, and they were just getting onto a spectacular cheese course, when Bass said, 'Anderson, if I'm not mistaken, you used to study energy, especially energy transfer? What made you change your focus?'

Anderson smiled, his energy pleasantly surprised. 'Yes, I did. I worked with your father at one point; I spent a great deal of time at the observatory when I was younger. Energy transfer and destruction are fascinating areas. Of course, there's no way to destroy energy, you can only hinder its transfer from potential to actual, divert it, or use it.

'Energy transfer is a much more delicate topic. I studied it for years, but interest waned with its diminishing use. It's how people used to transfer secret messages...'

'... hang on, what?' interrupted Cleo, shocked at the sudden swing to her specialist subject. 'What do you mean, people transferred secret messages? Who did, and why?'

Anderson waited for a few moments, clearly hoping someone else would step in and explain. Nobody took up the reigns, so he continued. 'A few decades ago, the world was a dangerous place. Peter was born into the Body bloodline and, as he was a man, this caused widespread disruption, panic, conspiracy theories, prophecies that the world was now doomed...

'Powerful factions formed. Some rallied behind the Descendants, believing they would free the world before Peter ever came to power. Some turned to the academics for answers and funded research into the Relic and the energy. And one group formed with the aim of keeping the energy steady, so we could go on with our lives regardless of what happened with the Relic.

'This group was called the Institution; they were elusive. They took great pains to hide their work from anybody and everybody, but especially from the Descendants. They had a significant disregard for the establishment, of the opinion the Descendants weren't doing their bit to free the world.'

Anita shot a look at Alexander to see how he was taking this slight, but his face was as steady as his energy.

'But,' said Anderson, 'as I am sure you can imagine, views questioning the authority of the Descendants were seen as treason. The Institution had to operate in the shadows, passing messages carefully and without evidence between members.

'To do this, they used energy transfer to pass secret messages, planting them into the brain of another, the message taking the shape of a brass cylinder.'

Anita went cold. The Institution used brass cylinders…

'When the person next meditated,' said Anderson, 'they would come across the brass cylinder, open it in private, and respond in the same way. Nobody to this day really understands how it's possible, hence the research.'

Anita knew from Cleo's energy, not to mention how still and upright she had grown in her seat, that she had hundreds of questions she was dying to ask. Instead, she nodded along with everyone else, pretending to understand exactly what Anderson was talking about.

'Everything eventually settled down,' said Anderson. 'I think people tired of having to look over their shoulders, and people started to use brass cylinders to store energy instead. Either they would store information and memories that they wanted to share with people, or information and memories they wanted to hide.

'The fascinating thing about this was that if someone stole a cylinder containing someone else's memories, the energy would strain to get back to its rightful owner. This breaks all the rules we understand about how energy works, which is why it's a topic that lures so many academics; it's truly baffling.

'I used to study energy transfers of this sort, however, I came across the idea that sending the Relic back to the Gods could have something to do with energy transfer, so turned my attention to the Relic instead.'

'How did you come across the idea?' asked Anita, captivated, like everyone else, except Alexander, who was observing Anita.

Anderson closed down as soon as the words were out of Anita's mouth, and she immediately regretted saying them. Alexander came to her rescue. 'Poor Anderson. I invited him for a friendly dinner, and he's ended up doing a post-dinner key-note. Let's have coffee and nightcaps in the library.'

Anita shot a grateful look at Alexander, then followed the others out of the dining room. Something interesting definitely going on there, she thought, as she entered the library and helped herself to a walnut liquor on the rocks, in a beautiful crystal tumbler.

Several hours later, after Cleo and Bass had retired to bed, Bella announced it was time for her and Anderson to leave. They thanked Alexander for a

187

wonderful evening, and he got up to show them out, leaving Anita alone in the library.

Pent up after skirting around the edge of so many interesting topics, Anita left the library and headed to the cloakroom. She selected a floor length, black cloak for herself and a floor length, red cloak for Alexander. She swung her cloak around her shoulders and fastened it, using the ornate broach attached to its neck before heading for the front door.

Alexander appeared just as Anita got to the door. Before he could take in what she was doing, she threw the cloak at him and disappeared outside, without so much as a backward glance to see if he would follow.

Alexander stood dumbfounded for a second, watching Anita take off across the grass towards the cliffs. He briefly weighed his options before giving into temptation, flying down the steps, throwing his cloak over his shoulders as he went.

Anita could sense Alexander chasing her and her energy soared as he closed in, her sky-high heels slowing her down as she ran. Adrenaline pumped through her, pushing her energy higher still, her cloak and dress streaming out behind her, an ecstatic smile on her lips.

She was nearing the edge when Alexander caught her. He grabbed hold of her hand, slowing her to a stop before spinning her around to face him. An explosion of tingles cascaded through their fingers, racing around their bodies.

They locked eyes to question and at the same time affirm that the other could feel it too. Without moving his eyes from hers, Alexander pushed his hand flat against Anita's, raised them to chest height, then mirrored the position with his other hand. Anita responded, lifting her free right hand to place it flat against his open left palm. The tingles intensified into a torrent as the loop between them closed, energy coursing around the circle of their arms.

Alexander half smiled, then very slowly moved first his left, then his right hand a millimeter away from hers. She inhaled deeply, spellbound as the tingles continued even with a gap between them.

He leaned his head forward and murmured, 'Sit down,' his piercing blue eyes caressing hers.

They sank to sit cross-legged on the grass, hands and eyes maintaining their positions. His intention was clear, so she lightly closed her eyes and made her way to her Centre, where she knew she would find him waiting.

She moved towards him, noting that this felt different to normal. She was more connected to him, almost as though she were in his warm, protective embrace.

She sat on the bed in front of him and was about to speak when the world around her blurred and she jolted to a new location. She looked around and realized she was on the lawn she'd just run across in the real world. So funny, she thought, that she was in the same place inside her head as out. But it was different to usual. Normally, when they meditated here, sunlight streamed down, playing on the water below. Now it was nighttime, the moon and stars casting a soft, romantic glow.

Strange for it to be night here, when her Centre was bathed in light...

She looked around to see where Alexander was to ask him, her eyes finding his toned form pelting across the lawn towards her, echoing their game from minutes before.

Without thinking, Anita's body responded, and she whirled towards the sea, running as fast as she could towards it, her dress, heels and cloak slowing her down as before.

Alexander, also dressed as he was in the outside world, caught her. But this time, as he spun her around, he pulled her to his chest, face inches from hers. His hands went to her waist, then slid around her.

His gaze was mesmerizing, Anita's stomach somersaulting as he bowed his head and lightly pressed his forehead to hers. She closed her eyes to savor the moment, breathing deeply to drink in his wood and citrus scent.

Her breath caught in her throat as his lips brushed lightly against hers, shivers of energy shooting out from the contact. He pulled away, Anita waiting for a beat for him to return. When he didn't, she opened her lust filled eyes and looked up at him. She could see the conflict alongside his desire and lifted a hand to his stubbly cheek. He exhaled, closing his eyes.

His resolve broke, his hand sliding up her back, into her hair, as he kissed her again. She felt the kiss everywhere, her mind blank of anything but this, Alexander's arms the only reason she stayed upright. Their mouths explored, working together in deep, confident movements.

They eventually pulled apart, Alexander stealing a brief final kiss before pulling her down to sit as they were in the world outside, cross-legged on the ground. Although in here, their knees touched, hands joined.

After a few moments of silent and surprised contemplation, holding each other's gaze, guilt invaded Anita's thoughts, so she broke the silence. 'Why's it dark?' she asked. 'It's normally daytime when we come here.'

Alexander gave her a cautious smile. 'Because we're no longer inside your head.'

'This is a place in your head too?'

190

His energy relaxed at her reaction. 'Yes, but as you can see, there are some differences. In my head its nighttime and the house and Kingdom are here. For some reason, they're not in your version; it's baffling why this place is inside your head at all.'

'But you have a theory?'

'Yes, I have a theory, but I don't want to talk about that now.'

'Why not?' she asked, a hint of annoyance in her tone.

'Because there are so many other things to discuss.'

'Like what?' she said, Alexander's bait successfully averting her attention.

'There isn't anything, after all the conversations this evening, that you want to ask me?' He smiled indulgently as she realized this was her chance...

'Why did Austin get rid of all the Relic specialists but leave Anderson alone?'

'I don't know the whole answer to that, but Austin decided a while back that studying the Relic was to be outlawed. Nobody knows what caused the decision, but he sprouted some stuff about not wanting to give people false hope.

'Why he left Anderson alone, I don't know; I've often wondered myself. The best I can come up with is that either Anderson has something on Austin, or that Austin has some specific interest in Anderson's work. That's just speculation though.'

'What made Anderson connect the Relic and energy transfer?'

'Again, I don't really know. I think he must have discovered something either in a book, or been told something by a scholar, or maybe he discovered something during his time in the Wild Lands. I don't think the idea came from the accepted academic texts or any of the current academics. Nobody else is working on the assumption that energy transfer and sending the Relic back are connected.

'Although, even if they were, they wouldn't be able to talk about it in public, given Austin's decree. I doubt Anderson would've told anyone, except perhaps Bella; it's not the kind of thing he'd want in the public domain. The world is much safer than it used to be, but that doesn't mean it's safe.'

'Do you think Anderson's working with the Institution?'

'No.'

'How can you be so sure?'

'Anderson hates the Institution. He thinks they were responsible for a great deal of unnecessary suffering a couple of decades back. And Anderson finds it suspicious that they're not fully behind sending the Relic back. It wouldn't take much for the Institution to get into bed with the Descendants, and Anderson can't stand the Descendants.'

Anita laughed. 'Need I remind you that you're a Descendant and he just came over for dinner?'

'The Spirit Descendants have always been less… fundamentalist than the rest of them. More philosophical and less power hungry. We're open to ideas different to our own, which means people like Anderson find us to be easier and more trustworthy than the others.'

'Is he right to trust you?'

Alexander pulled back. 'Why wouldn't he be?'

'I don't know… maybe your withholding information from me makes me think you would do it to him too.'

'Anita, the only reason I withheld information from you was because Marcus hasn't let me anywhere near you since he found out we were coming here together. I was going to tell you.'

'You had plenty of opportunities to tell me before that night at The Island. We've been meditating together for weeks.'

'As I've said before, Marcus is a jealous person. Whether or not you choose to believe it, you'll be in danger if you two drift apart, or worse, if he thought you weren't totally loyal to him. I didn't want to get any closer to you than needed to help you protect yourself. Sharing a place in our minds...'

'What do you think of the Institution?' asked Anita, her change of tack taking him by surprise; his energy had been preparing for a fight.

'Why do you ask?'

'I just want to know.'

'To be honest, I don't know. I used to be wary of them; it's what Descendants are taught from an early age. But then, they want energy stability, which is a noble goal for the good of everyone. But if they're willing to prevent the Relic from being returned to keep the energy steady... I don't agree. Why? What do you think of them?'

'Would you help them if they asked?' said Anita, ignoring his question.

'It would depend what they asked me to do. If you're asking me if I trust them, then the answer is most definitely no. They have their own political agenda... why the sudden interest? Have they asked you for help?'

'You have a political agenda.'

'Do I?' The mood between them sharpened, turning wary, almost hostile.

Anita said nothing for a few moments, then raised Alexander's hand to her lips and kissed it. She'd pushed him as far as he would go tonight. 'Doesn't every Descendant have a political agenda out of necessity?' she asked softly.

Alexander searched her eyes as he considered his answer.

She rocked lightly forwards onto all fours, cat-like in front of him, her hands on his knees. She leaned in and kissed his lips, then broke contact to wait for his response.

He did nothing.

She waited a beat, two, before leaning in and kissing him again. She knew the impact she was having on his energy, knew he was fighting an internal battle. If she pushed him too hard, he would run away.

Again, she waited, then bowed her head to kiss him for a third time. This time, as she was pulling away, he responded to her touch. She froze, her energy a mix of excitement and terror that any movement would shatter the spell.

He kissed her, his mouth opening against her warm lips. Anita moved her hands to his neck, pulling him gently towards her, tongues caressing each other.

They became confident, then urgent, Alexander rising to his knees. His hands pulled at her lower back, pressing her to him before lifting her and pushing her backwards. He laid her on the ground, her cloak fanned out beneath her, following her down, pinning her with his weight.

She ran her fingers through his hair as he kissed and nipped her neck. She tugged at the clasp of his cloak, pulled off his dinner jacket, slid his shirt free from his trousers. Her fingers made their way under his shirt, greedily taking in the firm, athletic contours of his back.

He kissed his way down her neck, reaching her breasts as he slid her silk dress up over her hips. Anita arched, pushing her body into him, reveling in the contact. He smelt like ripe oranges and she closed her eyes, inhaling deeply, shivering as he brushed his fingers down her spine. But when she opened her eyes, the world began to blur, slipping away, no matter how hard she tried to pull it back.

Anita's eyes few open in the real world and she sat, facing Alexander, palms out in front of her, just as she had been when they entered the meditation.

'What happened?' she asked, confused and disappointed, moving her hands back to her lap. The tingling had stopped, and she felt robbed, craving his touch.

'I think the guilt we were suppressing forced us out. Our brains were caught in a dilemma, not knowing what to do... it's probably for the best...'

'You feel the tingles too?'

Alexander's breath hitched. 'Yes.'

Anita nodded. 'I get tingles with both you and Marcus,' she said, looking sheepish at bringing him up, 'but I've never felt them with anyone else.'

'With Marcus too?'

Anita nodded again.

'Interesting,' said Alexander, pausing. 'The nudges and tingles are caused when energy is exerted by one person on another, that much we think we know. They only seem to take place when the energy is pleasurable or supportive and certainly positive. There have never been reports of tingles due to negative energy, but it's rare to come across people who can feel them. There's a theory that both parties have to be able to feel them for either to be aware... does Marcus?'

'I'm not sure; he's never brought it up, but there's been no sign that he can. It sounds like the research is limited though... how many people have been studied?'

'As far as I know, only a handful.'

'Have you been?'

'Gods, no,' he laughed. 'No Descendant would ever submit themselves to academic testing. Nudges are

195

more easily studied, as we can learn to control them, but there's nobody who can control tingles, at least nobody who admits to being able to.'

'We could try. Maybe it's something to do with desire? The tingles have lessened with Marcus now, maybe because of my lessened desire for him, or maybe it has something to do with the unknown? I know what to expect when I see Marcus now, I didn't when I first started spending time with him.'

'Lessened desire?' Alexander asked, his facial expression almost making Anita laugh out loud, clearly surprised at himself for saying it.

'Only a little lessened, not entirely,' she smiled.

'But you have slept together?' he asked tentatively.

'No,' she said stiffly. 'Not that it's any of your business.'

'And Marcus is still following you around like a lost puppy? He doesn't suspect that you may... um... have interests elsewhere?'

'Who says I have interests elsewhere?' said Anita, enjoying the power of making Alexander squirm. 'And anyway, so long as he still wants me, he'll be more interested if I don't sleep with him than if I do. Marcus likes a challenge, and I'm his current one. He'll keep trying until he gets what he wants, or until something new and shiny catches his attention.'

'I thought you didn't like the Mind disciplines,' said Alexander.

'I don't. But Marcus does.'

Anita shivered.

'Come on, let's get back inside,' he said, getting up and taking Anita's hand. A shiver of energy ran through their fingers and Anita smiled as she got to her feet, her dress and cloak cascading to the floor.

She took his outstretched arm, and they wandered back across the lawn, talking about what they would do for the rest of their time in Kingdom. They entered the house and Alexander walked Anita to her room, tension growing, conversation more stunted as they approached. They stopped outside her door and Anita turned to look at him.

'You've spent all this time pushing me away,' she said. 'You keep telling me how much danger I'd be in if Marcus changes his mind about me, or even if he thought we were friends. You've barely said two words to me outside of lessons, I know nothing about you, you normally shut down any question I ask, yet tonight you let me ask you whatever I wanted. Why?'

Smoke filled Alexander's eyes as they studied hers. 'Because life's too short not to flirt with danger when it's worth the risk.'

Anita smiled, then turned to open her door. 'Goodnight Alexander,' she said, 'thank you for an illuminating evening.'

* * * * *

The following day, Alexander woke early, his mind plagued by emotions. He knew trying to sleep was futile, so got up and headed for his grandfather's library. It was a good place to think.

The study was small and pokey with piles of books and manuscripts littered about, along with old energy meters, works of art, and the odd piece of furniture.

The room had heavy drapes across a large window that overlooked the garden, but the drapes were kept closed for fear the light would damage a priceless book or piece of artwork. Alexander had always thought someone tripping over a stack of invaluable manuscripts was more of a risk…

He turned on the lamp by the door and used its dim light to guide him to the comfortable brown leather chair in front of the large, leather-topped partners' desk. He turned on the lamp at the corner of the desk, sat down in the chair, and surveyed the scene.

He immediately relaxed. Strange how such disorder could make him calm, help him find perspective. His mind raced over recent events before centering on Anita, the Body Descendant. She hadn't taken it well when he'd withheld information from her before. He was guessing she wouldn't be pleased if she found out from someone else what he suspected about her bloodline.

Then there was Helena's recent proposition for him to join the Institution. And what the hell was Austin was playing at... why was he so against doing anything about the energy?

Alexander spotted his grandfather's old music player in the corner and maneuvered his way past several stacks of books and scattered artefacts to turn it on. He'd expected dulcet classical tones to waft through the air. To his surprise, a wistful modern melody rippled out instead, complete with a smoky voice and poetic lyrics.

He made his way back to the desk, but toppled a brass model of the world onto the floor as he edged past the last pile of books.

'Damn,' he said out loud, as the model rolled under the desk. He crouched down on all fours and followed it under, reaching around to locate the missing artefact. After a few unsuccessful moments, he reached for a small lamp from a nearby table, pulled it to the floor, and switched it on. He spotted the world near the back and crawled further under to reach it.

As his fingers closed around the model, he heard a soft click under his left knee, near the edge of the drawer section of the desk. He moved back out of the way and lifted the rug covering the area, surprised to see that a panel in the floor had sprung open, revealing a small metal object inside. He reached in and fished out a tiny brass key, closing the panel and replacing the rug before examining it in detail.

After a lengthy inspection, Alexander concluded that it was a normal key, seemingly with no notable features. If anything, it was boring, with no ornate head, no engraving, no suggestion as to which lock it fitted, nothing.

He tried the key in all the locks he could find in the study; the desk, the door, the windows, the cabinets, but it fitted none of them; it was far too small. Bloody grandfather, he thought, hearing voices down the corridor and realizing everyone else must be up. He pocketed the key and turned off the lights, taking one last look around to make sure he hadn't missed anything obvious. Frustrated when nothing jumped out at him, he closed the door and stalked down the corridor to see his guests.

'Morning,' came Cleo's singsong voice as he entered the breakfast room, another room basked in light through enormous sash windows.

'Morning,' grunted Alexander.

Anita looked up from her breakfast, concern all over her face. He pulled himself out of his mood for long enough to send her a reassuring smile. She went back to her bacon and brioche.

'Everything alright?' asked Cleo, somehow sensing gossip.

'Couldn't be better thanks,' he said with a disarming smile. He helped himself to a lavish portion of smoked salmon and poached eggs on lightly toasted walnut and raisin bread, covered in hollandaise sauce. He joined the others at the table, and after a couple of generous mouthfuls, his mood lifted.

'I thought we could head straight to the Relic after breakfast, if everyone's happy with that?' said Alexander. 'We can send a message ahead to Anderson and Bella and ask them to meet us there.'

'Sounds great,' said Bass, excitedly. 'I've been wide awake since six o'clock.

* * * * *

Bass' excitement was radiating off him by the time they bundled into Alexander's car.

Alexander and Anita sat next to each other, with Bass opposite Alexander and Cleo next to Anita. They were giving Mrs. Hudson and the chef a ride as well, so the chef was in the front with the driver and Mrs. Hudson sat next to Bass. Anita and Alexander's legs were touching, shivers passing distractingly between them.

She pulled away, certain someone would notice their soaring energy, but the sensation continued. Anita wasn't sure if it was a repeat of what had happened last night, or a phantom.

Alexander sent a nudge to the edge of her energy; did this count as flirting? A pang of guilt stabbed her gut. Last night she'd been full of alcohol, caught up in the moment, but in the cold light of day, she knew what they'd done was wrong. She had feelings for Marcus too.

She promised herself that nothing more could happen with Alexander, in their minds or anywhere else, until she'd figured out what she wanted. That would mean at least until she saw Marcus again...

Her energy dropped as she shut herself off to Alexander's charms. He turned to look at her, trying to hide his concern as he felt the change.

They arrived up at the Temple of the Spirit and once Bass, Cleo, Anita and Alexander had got out, the driver pulled away to take the chef and Mrs. Hudson to the market. They made their way into the temple, which, although broadly similar to the temple in Empire, was on a much grander and more impressive scale.

The star-clad ceiling seemed to reach up into the sky, the pillars' stonework exquisitely intricate. The space was light and airy. Walking through it was like balancing on the crest of an elegant wave as it curled its way towards the beach. Just like a wave crashing into the sand, the walls of the closed off center blocked their way. Inside were Alexander's chambers, and only he, or those he invited, were allowed inside.

They circumnavigated his domain, all politely ignoring that they were dying to see inside. They took the walkway that led to the home of the Relic; a courtyard at the joined center of the three temples.

The Relic was an odd-looking piece of rock, not any particular shape and not at all pleasing to look at. It was a disappointing shade of greyish brown, with ugly ridges and edges that jutted out rudely from its core. It was a little bigger than a human head, but gave the impression that it was much heavier, like the modern metal structure supporting its weight might collapse at any moment. The Relic sat under a twisted old olive tree that added to its mystery, shielding it from the world above.

The courtyard was a series of contradictions, its boundaries forming a circle that joined the points of each temple. It was open to the elements above and around the edges, devoid of walls, yet sheltered by the bulk of the temples themselves. It was accessible from every angle, yet intimidating, the olive tree hovering threateningly, protectively over its charge.

It was awe-inspiring to see the Relic, but the space was strangely off kilter. Anita felt uneasy, on edge, and out of place.

'Hi,' said Bella when she saw them, bounding over to greet them. 'Thank you so much for such a wonderful evening last night,' she gushed, clearly not immune to Alexander's electric blue eyes and rugged charm. Anita had a pang of, what? Jealousy? Which she quickly suppressed.

'It's so great of you to show us around,' said Anita.

'It was the least we could do to say thank you,' she replied, although Anderson didn't seem to share Bella's sentiment. He'd barely looked up from the Relic to acknowledge their presence, evidently not as keen on this private lecture as Bella.

Bass, realizing this was his opportunity to corner Anderson, took care of him, and Bella talked the rest of them through the history of the Relic.

'Of course, the Relic hasn't been here forever,' said Bella, reveling in the attention her audience were paying her. 'That is to say, it's been in the world since the beginning, but we've only known of its existence for around three hundred and fifty years, since the year 1000. But I mustn't get ahead of myself; I'll start from the beginning.

'As you know, in the beginning, the three Gods created three worlds, and in our world, they created people with skills that resembled their own. At the same time, the Gods put the Relic in the world, but hid it deep within a cave system, far out in the Wild Lands.

'Along with the Relic, they hid drawings and inscriptions, and if you ask me, that is the most exciting bit. People come from all over the world to see the Relic and many leave again without realizing the significance of the inscriptions on the walls surrounding it.' Bella made a sweeping gesture with her hand around the courtyard.

'Here,' she continued, pointing to an image, 'you can see three people around the Relic. Our best guess is that each represents a Descendant. As you can see, there are two males and one female.'

Anita wasn't sure she subscribed to this; to her they looked a lot like three smudged stick people with no clear gender… maybe she lacked an expert's eye.

'Over here, we have the same three people pointing to the sky and the Relic floating towards the heavens. They're returning it to the waiting arms of the Gods, depicted here by these three symbols,' said Bella, pointing to three shapes above where a blob of color (the Relic apparently) sat.

'But what are most illuminating, I think, are the inscriptions,' said Bella. 'There are three inscriptions, and again, our best guess would suggest that they each relate to one of the God's lines. The first, we think, relates to the Spirit discipline and says, 'Look to the light', the second, we think has its origins in the Mind tradition, and says, 'Knowledge is power', and the third, from the Body, we are almost certain, because of the gender reference, says, 'She who dares will surely triumph'.

'We're not without doubts as to their exact meaning. However, academics are broadly agreed that they're likely to be words of encouragement to Descendants to fulfil their quest to return the Relic. There's complete agreement that they're motivational in some sense or another.

'Anyway, as you know, the Gods put the Descendants in the world around the year seven hundred and seventy, about six hundred years ago, but the Relic was only discovered in the year 1000. It was at this point that the true purpose of the Descendants became clear and these grand temples were built in spectacular celebration.

'Of course, a place for the Relic was designed as the centerpiece, and the Crowning ceremonies were modified to include the oath that Descendants would devote their lives to freeing the world. That was when Kingdom really took over as the premier city from Empire. Aside from the splendor of the new temples, it made sense for our principal city to be by the sea; more accessible that way.'

Bella finally stopped talking as she approached the piece de la resistance, the Relic itself. She stopped several feet away, paused, and was just about to launch into another monologue, when Cleo said, 'Who discovered the Relic, and who moved it here, along with the inscriptions?'

Bella gave Cleo a piercing look.

'A group of academics discovered the Relic out in the Wild Lands,' said Anderson, 'while on a research trip. They brought it back with them, but didn't think anyone would believe them without seeing the inscriptions as well, so they extracted sections of the cave walls.'

'Who were the academics and how did the Descendants take it?' Cleo asked, her instinct for gossip piqued.

'They were relative unknowns,' said Anderson, 'their names escape me now. The Descendants' reaction wasn't documented, so we really don't know.'

'Nothing at all?' said Cleo, surprised.

'No,' said Anderson, in a final tone.

Cleo knew when to drop a topic, so she nodded in defeat, but resolved to investigate the matter further when she got back to Empire.

Bella seized the opportunity to retake control, turning back to the Relic with a flourish. 'And this is the much-discussed Relic itself,' she said. 'But Anderson is the one who should tell you about it; he knows the subject backwards and will do it far better than I.'

Bella smiled warmly at Anderson, who looked as though he'd rather not, but knew the path of least resistance was to do as he was told.

'As you can see,' started Anderson, in a commanding voice, 'the Relic is a totally irregular shape. It has no particularly unique markings and looks very much like any other piece of rock you might find in a cave. Except, that is, that the Relic is made of an element we cannot find anywhere else, including in the Wild Lands around where it was found.

'Other than what the inscriptions tell us, we know nothing about the Relic, which is why it's been a source of fascination since its discovery. Well, that, and the promise it brought with it, of course.

'Many academics have devoted their lives to the Relic, but no one has made any headway with how to send it back. The Descendants, uncomfortable with the prospect of losing their power, haven't historically shown much support for the cause.

'We try to keep a low profile,' said Anderson. 'Attention is not good in our line of work.' With that, he turned away from the group and got back to it; it was clear they'd outstayed their welcome.

'Well, it's been a fascinating morning,' said Cleo. 'Thank you so much for the guided tour, we really appreciate it. I promised my father that I would meet him for lunch, so I'd better get going,' she said to Alexander and Anita, heading back into the Mind Temple. 'See you back at the house later.'

'And we should head off too,' said Alexander. 'I promised Anita I would show her around Kingdom. Anderson, thank you so much for taking the time to show us the Relic,' he said, shaking Anderson's hand.

'Bella, a pleasure as always,' he said, kissing Bella briskly on both cheeks.

'Bass, are you coming?' asked Anita, as Bass sat down next to Anderson, making himself comfortable.

'Uh... no... I don't think so. I'll catch up with you two later. I'm going to stay and help Anderson for a bit.'

As Anderson seemed to perk up at the prospect, Anita just nodded and threw Bass a smile. 'See you later then,' she said, thanking Anderson and Bella, then following Alexander into the Temple of the Body.

'I've never seen him take to anyone like that before,' said Alexander, when they were out of earshot.

'I guess he and Bass have a lot in common, and Bass might even be able to help him. Sounds like Anderson's spent a lot of time out in the Wild Lands recently, so he probably isn't up to date with all the energy developments. Anderson's probably as excited to have Bass around as Bass is to learn about the Relic. I know Bass doesn't always come across as an authority, but after Elistair, nobody knows more about the energy than him.'

Alexander nodded. 'I suppose that makes sense.'

Anita and Alexander walked past Peter's chambers, emerging in the main section of the temple. It was breath-taking. Not nearly as open as the Spirit Temple, but equally pleasing.

Where the Spirit Temple was one vast chamber with pillars stretching to the ceiling, the Body Temple was segmented into sections, the lines of the arches tight and pleasing. They invoked images of a ballet dancer bending elegantly backwards, supported by a strong, muscular partner.

The sections reminded Anita of secret gardens, the kind of place she would like to have a romantic picnic, secluded but open, welcoming and cozy. The place was stuffed full of wonderful, dusky pink flowers, the pillars wrapped in flowing fabric. She longed to explore, but Alexander was already striding towards the entrance, so she reluctantly followed.

They emerged into the crisp sunlight and meandered towards the center of Kingdom, their conversation wandering. The tension between them was a tangible thing, Anita entirely absorbed by his proximity, the gap between them agonizing. They'd been walking for a while when they rounded a corner into a secluded area with an enormous pair of bolted gates. Alexander stopped sharply, as though surprised to find himself here, then noticeably bristled.

'Austin's house,' he said, through gritted teeth, nodding his head toward the gates.

'Really?' said Anita, looking in wonder at the pretty-yet-imposing house that stood the other side. It was hard to work out where the neighbouring buildings ended and it began, despite being surrounded by its own protective wall. The red brick construction had a secretive look about it, as though it were guarding many highly incriminating secrets.

'It's not what I imagined,' she said, unable to tear her eyes from the building, 'not that I'm sure what I imagined, really.'

'Why?' asked Alexander, doing his best to sound conversational.

'Because it's so different to the castle in Empire. Everything about it is different; the stone, the size, the style, the proximity to the center of the town. This seems like a wonderful home right in the thick of things, whereas the castle is a statement of power sitting above Empire.'

'Yes, I suppose so,' said Alexander, offhandedly. 'Anyway, there's something else I'd like to show you,' he said, purposely moving the conversation away from Austin and, by default, from Marcus.

'Over here,' he said, taking her hand, pulling her around the side of Austin's house. A jolt pulsed through her as their skin made contact, shooting to her core.

'Where are we going?' asked Anita, confused and disorientated, as they approached what seemed to be a solid brick wall.

'Through here,' he said, leading them around what was, in fact, an overlap in the wall, concealing a small gap through to the other side. They appeared in a space that was half-room, half-tent, with stone walls and a canvas roof. The space was full of beautiful swathes of fine silk, in a vast array of deep, rich colors.

'Wow,' said Anita, stunned, as they emerged from the fabric into a bustling street jammed full of similar stalls. 'I wasn't expecting that.'

'Welcome to the market,' said Alexander excitedly, not letting go of her hand. 'This is where the traders come with goods from the farms, sea, and Wild Lands. You can buy almost anything here; silks,' he said, running his hand over a bright pink one, 'all manner of foods, clothes, cosmetics, precious metals and stones, brass cylinders, energy mechanisms, herbs and spices.'

He gently tugged her past a stall with piles of brightly colored powders on display, Anita's mouth wide open in wonder.

They passed a shop with early energy mechanisms chugging away in the window, brass cogs whirring. Anita tried to enter, but Alexander pulled her back. 'We can't linger. Most people recognize me and kindly leave me alone, but if we go into that old junk shop, we'll cause a scene.'

'It doesn't look like a junk shop to me,' said Anita, indignantly. 'There could be untold treasures hidden in there, just waiting to be found.'

'Unlikely, given the number of traders around… come on, we haven't got time to hang around.'

Alexander finally let go of Anita's hand as they approached the city's wall, his recklessness abating with every person they passed. They ducked through an opening in the wall and followed a perilous, winding stone staircase down to the sandy beach below.

'This place is a rabbit warren,' said Anita. 'I didn't realize we were so close to the beach.'

'That's why the Descendants like it so much. It's easy to disappear with all the passages and hidden passes. If things turn bad, we can easily slip away.

'And Kingdom's close to the action; if someone finds something interesting in the Wild Lands, the market is the place to find out about it.'

'It'll be a wonder if we ever get Cleo back to Empire then,' said Anita, laughing.

They walked in silence for a few beats, listening to the calming rush of the waves. 'Why are you so comfortable with Anderson's work with the Relic?' said Anita.

'Why do you ask?' he replied.

'The Descendants' interests run contrary to everything Anderson's trying to achieve. He even said as much. If he finds a way to send back the Relic, you lose your authority, and the people get to decide who they want to rule.'

'Why do you think I want to rule?'

'Well you are, aren't you? So you can't be dead set against the idea.'

'I rule because it's my duty to do so until we return the Relic. I swore an oath to do that.'

'But the other Descendants aren't helping, quite the opposite in fact. They're doing everything they can to stop the world from being freed, even if that means destroying it.'

'You think I'm like the other Descendants?'

'Not exactly, but that's why I asked the question. Why are you so comfortable with his work, given your position in this world?' Anita was getting frustrated... he was being obtuse.

'I have no interest in abusing the power and authority bestowed on me. I'm no different from anybody else, really. I'm powerful, yes, but so are others, and I have no desire to rule in a world where people aren't happy.

'I told you, Sprit Descendants are different from the rest. We're philosophical and less power hungry. Maybe that's something to do with the skills of our bloodline. Minds respect grand displays of mental and physical power, as do Bodies. Spirits acknowledge that it only takes one person to change the course of history. Maybe Anderson is that one.

'Austin can put as many barriers in Anderson's way as he wants, but if Anderson continues to fight, maybe he'll be the one to free the world from energy instability. To a Spirit Descendant, Anderson's work, motivated by a desire to do the right thing, is far more wonderful than the prospect of ruling for eternity.'

'But what if sending the Relic back causes chaos?'

'I don't buy that. People are good at accepting change when they have to, especially when it's change they've been requesting for centuries. And besides, as you pointed out, the world is heading for chaos as it stands anyway.'

CHAPTER 12

Helena bowed before the Great Spirit Leader. She perched precariously on a small, round, stone ledge above a heart-stopping drop down the mountain. It had been designed to put visitors on edge, to help the Spirit Leader get the measure of his guests.

Helena had been here several times before, and not once had she managed to keep her energy stable. She tried in vain to hide her reaction, and her failure made her angry. The Great Spirit Leader could, of course, read her energy like an open book. Coming here was always a stressful, frustrating experience, so she didn't relish her visits to the mountain.

'So nice to see you again, Helena,' said the Spirit Leader, in calm, even, almost bored tones.

He sat in the center of a mat, in the middle of a small, pillared room, open on all sides to the elements. The wind gently toyed with the fabric draped from the ceiling. He was a short-ish man of medium build, with thick, wavy, sandy colored hair. His voice had a way of penetrating to a person's core; one couldn't help but sit up and listen. He had wise features, gravitas, and an aura of severity, the kind of person you would always want on your side.

'The pleasure is all mine,' replied Helena, her words louder than she had meant them to be. 'How can I be of assistance?'

The Spirit Leader chuckled. 'Typical Body,' he said. 'No preamble, just straight to the point.'

'My sincere apologies,' said Helena, 'how's the family?'

He snickered.

Helena's blood boiled; she hated not being in control.

'Very well, have it your way,' he said. 'I summoned you here to see how you're getting on with Anita.'

He hadn't moved a muscle the whole time she'd been here, and even now, as his words hit her ears like bullets, he sat still, watching for any slight reaction.

Helena froze. Who had let slip? Did they have a mole? 'How do you know about Anita?' she said. He would've already read her surprise, so there was no point in trying to hide it.

'There isn't much I can't find out if I put my mind to it, Helena, you should know that by now.' He sent a meaningful look her way, then stood in a swift, seamless movement. He made his way to a small stone table at the edge of the open room. 'Please,' he said, waving his hand towards the chair next to his, 'come and join me.'

Helena went to the seat, making a point of doing so at a dignified speed. A shock of cold hit her as she sat on the stone chair, and it was all she could do not to gasp. She'd never worked out how he could meditate here all day in such unpleasant temperatures, dressed only in light robes. He seemed to radiate warmth, and she wondered if he cheated and snuck a hot-water bottle under his clothes. She'd asked him about it once and he'd spouted something about harnessing the power of the Mind, her least favorite discipline, so she'd left it there.

'How are you getting on with Anita?' he repeated, patiently.

'I'd be getting on a lot better if I hadn't had to come all the way here. I told her I'd be expecting an answer several days ago. I haven't been able to follow up, given that I've been travelling.'

'I wasn't too late with my invitation then. Good.'

'What's that supposed to mean?'

He fixed her with eyes that made Helena feel like an impatient schoolgirl. 'Anita needs time,' he said. 'Your natural inclination is to bully her, but she won't respond well to that approach; she's a lot like you.'

'That's why you summoned me here? To bully me into doing things your way?'

'Touché. Hopefully, by the time you get back, she'll have had enough time. Until next time, Helena.'

'I'll look forward to it, I'm sure,' she replied through gritted teeth, making no attempt at all to hide her angry energy.

The Spirit Leader's face remained neutral as he got up and made his way back to his mat. He sat down and meditated, ignoring Helena's continued presence.

As she made her way out, making sure she walked close enough to him to disturb his energy field, she marveled, as she always did, at his age. He was no older than her…

Helena had reached what most would consider dizzying heights at an early age, but he had reached the pinnacle. She'd always been jealous. 'One day I'll find out how you did it,' she said under her breath, as she made her way down the stone steps to the main chambers below.

* * * * *

213

Alexander sat at Philip's desk, pondering recent developments. Anita had been distant since they'd returned to the house and he didn't know what to do about it, or if he should do anything at all. Maybe a healthy distance between them would be a good thing, although he couldn't think of anything worse...

Then there was the key he'd found, still bugging him, mostly because he didn't know where to look next. He sprang to his feel and started pacing, but the mess everywhere thwarted his efforts, until he was so wound up, he kicked over a stack of books.

He grabbed hold of the curtains and yanked them open; it was stupid not to let any sunlight in. Bloody Philip, he thought, as light poured into the room for the first time in an age and the true extent of the mess became apparent. Philip had always harped on about the 'illuminating power of light', and how wise the one who came up with the Spirit motto, 'look to the light' had been. Hypocrite.

Alexander's irritation abated a little as a result of his reckless acts. He stooped down to reassemble the pile of books, then turned to redraw the curtains; it was disrespectful to overturn Philip's wishes so soon after his death. As he snuffed out the last chink of light, he froze, an idea finding root in his mind that grew into an epiphany. *Look to the light.*

Alexander reached for the patterned lamp on the desk and turned it over. What if the key unlocked a light? Philip had loved when the literal and metaphorical collided. What if he'd taken the motto literally, and the key unlocked an actual light?

Unfortunately, the lamp on Philip's desk had a smooth base with no keyhole to be seen. Undeterred, he inspected the rest of the lights in the study. When none of those produced a result, he went to Philip's old bedroom and inspected each of the lights there, but again, nothing.

Finally, he tried the garden sheds; Philip had loved his garden. There were only single bulbs dangling dejectedly from the ceiling and nowhere to hide a hole for a key.

Deflated, Alexander returned to the study and sat back down in his Grandfather's leather chair.

'What does the key unlock, you old sod?' he asked out loud, pulling the desk lamp towards him once more, hoping for inspiration.

He rested it on its side and re-inspected the base, trying to think of any other way that a lamp could hide a keyhole. Finding nothing, he set it upright, but as he was doing so, his fingers felt a tiny, almost invisible seam running around its base. He paused, the first flutter of hope taking hold, then turned it onto its side again and carefully inspected the seam.

The line ran all the way around and looked like nothing out of the ordinary, except, on closer inspection, the color of the base was very slightly different from the rest. He tried to slip a fingernail into the seam, but the join was too tight. He tried twisting instead. To his amazement, the base swung smoothly outwards from a point near the edge, exposing a second layer of brass below.

Alexander's heart almost stopped as his eyes made out a perfect key-shaped hole in the center of the newly exposed metal. 'By the Gods,' he said out loud.

He reached into his pocket, retrieved the key, and inserted it into the hole. He twisted lightly, and it turned easily in the lock, making a delicate clicking sound as a panel at the top sprung open.

He swung the panel cover back, noting the exquisite craftsmanship, and carefully retrieved the piece of folded parchment that sat inside.

Unable to contain his excitement, he unfolded the paper and held it up to the light, moving his face closer to make out the words. There were several lines of text, and, to his surprise, the first contained only one word: his name.

Alexander,
Remember the lessons from Philip & Fred.
Be a good scholar.
Jeffrey will help you unlock the light.
Destroy this note when you have memorized my words.
I have faith in you.
Philip

Alexander felt sick. How had Philip known he would find this? Why had he written it? What did it mean? And why had he gone to such pains to hide it so thoroughly?

As far as Alexander could see, it contained nothing contentious. Philip & Fred were nicknames that Philip had used for two famous children's authors. They'd written a book of fairy tales that Philip had read to Alexander when he was young. The stories varied, containing moral messages similar to most other books for children.

Philip's favorite story had been about a princess whose father, the King, had banished her. He'd gone mad when a group of powerful sorcerers came to court. The story was about the princess' quest to retake her rightful position and rid the land of the evil sorcerers, which, naturally, she did. She also found her prince and lived happily ever after, of course.

Alexander stiffened as Austin's last words to Christiana came flooding back to him, 'We are the only two left that know the truth now that Philip has gone'. Philip had known the truth about Christiana's bloodline. Was that what Philip was talking about here? Did he consider Anita to be the princess in the story?

The second line was clear enough. Philip had often used the words *be a good scholar*. He meant one should question everything, even the facts we think we know for certain. What Alexander was supposed to be a good scholar in relation to, however, he did not know.

The third line was confusing. Who was Jeffrey, and why, or more to the point, how, would he be able to help *unlock the light*? What did that even mean?

Alexander racked his brain, but could think of no one he knew called Jeffrey, either in the real world or in a storybook.

Philip's instruction to destroy the note seemed a little melodramatic, however, given that Philip had hidden the note so well, Alexander thought it prudent to follow his instructions. He picked it up and took it to the fireplace, making sure that he both remembered what it said and that he hadn't missed anything.

He took a match from the mantelpiece, lit it, and set the paper alight. He held onto the parchment for a few seconds before placing it in the fireplace. He waited to ensure there was nothing left but ash before turning to the shelves, picking up an old, worn book: the stories of Philip & Fred.

* * * * *

The trip back to Empire was subdued. Cleo had, for the first time all weekend, stopped talking. She was lightly dosing with her head propped against the window. Bass was silently staring out, watching the scenery go by, presumably contemplating all he'd learned and discussed with Anderson over the last two days. Anita was sure they'd see each other again; she'd

217

never seen two people get on so well after such a brief acquaintance.

Anita had been trying her best to avoid speaking to, looking at, and certainly being alone with Alexander. She was so confused about what she should do, what she felt for who, and how she should proceed. She spent the journey looking out of the window, feeling hollow as she considered her options. She could sense Alexander's scrutiny, so worked to keep her energy steady, not giving anything away.

The problem was that she had feelings for both Marcus and Alexander, her energy reacting to each of their special allures. Marcus was, for the most part, fun and carefree, flirtatious and frivolous in a way that Alexander could not be. Alexander was a ruling Descendant. Marcus was yet to assume the heavy burden of responsibility, living instead under the ominous cloud of his power-hungry father.

Alexander seemed to carry the weight around with him, understanding the world's perilous position, and that it was his duty to address it. Marcus, on the other hand, was light as a feather, as though there were nothing in the world that should be worried about with any kind of gusto.

Alexander was closed and protective of himself. Marcus had opened up to Anita, had told her about his family, and to some extent, his past. But what if Marcus did turn into Austin over time? He was already protective of her, possessive even...

Alexander was trying to do what he thought was best for her... or was he? Maybe he'd pushed her towards Marcus because his feelings weren't that strong after all...

Anita turned it around and around all the way home, but was more confused at the end of the journey than she had at the beginning.

They dropped Bass off first, then Cleo, Anita feeling Alexander turn to look at her when they were finally alone in the car. Alexander closed the glass screen separating them from the driver. 'Is everything alright?' he asked, his energy uncertain.

Anita looked at him, searched his glorious blue eyes. 'Not really,' she replied, dropping her eyes to her lap, surprised at her honest response. 'I think I need some time to work all this out. I don't know what to do.'

She paused and looked out of the window. 'I have feelings for Marcus. I feel guilty and I don't want to hurt him, but I don't want to hurt you either,' she said, looking back at him. A horrible thought erupted in Anita's head. Her eyes went wide. 'Sorry,' she said, her cheeks reddening, 'you might not...'

They pulled up outside Cordelia's house, and Anita made for the door. She swung it open, but Alexander grabbed her hand, gentle tingles spreading underneath her skin. She stopped and looked back at him.

'I do,' he said huskily, quietly, so the driver, now unloading Anita's bags, couldn't hear.

A car turned into the end of the road, ostentatious enough that it could only be one of Austin's. Alexander begrudgingly let go of Anita's hand. 'Looks like you have company,' he said, as the car stopped.

Marcus threw open the door, his long, lean body moving rapidly in their direction.

'See you soon,' said Alexander, sending a nudge to the edge of her energy field.

Marcus took hold of Anita's hand and drew her away from the car, into his space.

'Alexander,' said Marcus, nodding curtly; he would take things from here.

'Marcus,' said Alexander, nodding back. He pulled the car door closed, stealing one last look at Anita before his driver pulled away.

* * * * *

The following morning, Anita headed to the garden for her usual yoga session, but her mind wasn't in it, vivid flashbacks from the previous night rudely interrupting. She ditched yoga in favor of something more vigorous, donning her running trainers, and headed for the river.

As she ran, she contemplated, revisiting the conundrum that had been preoccupying pretty much all of her conscious thought for the last two days: Marcus or Alexander?

Last night had been fun. They'd gone to some councilor's daughter's twenty-fifth birthday party and had danced for hours. Marcus had ignored everyone but Anita for the whole evening, much to the annoyance of all the female guests, as well as the councilor hosting the event. He'd kept trying to find reasons for Marcus to dance with his daughter, but Marcus had refused every time.

Gwyn had been at the party too and had made a snipe at Anita as she and Marcus passed. Marcus was oblivious to it, and when Anita had brought it up, he'd unhelpfully suggested that Anita might be paranoid. How were men so blind when it came to the relationships between women? How could they so successfully ignore what was right in front of them?

After the party, they'd walked along the river back to Cordelia's house, dancing as they went, pausing every so often to kiss in the starlight. Marcus had brought up the weekend, clearly unhappy about the trip. He warned Anita off Alexander, saying it was bad enough she had

220

to have lessons with him; weekends away took it too far.

Marcus had resembled a pompous, puffed up bird, feathers all ruffled. He'd told her that next time he would show her Kingdom, as, unlike Alexander, he knew the city's best sights.

Anita had distracted him by saying she'd seen Marcus' home, telling him how enchanting she thought it was. The conversation had been lighthearted and fun for the rest of the walk, until they'd reached Cordelia's gate, where Marcus suddenly turned serious.

Marcus kissed her, hinting in every unspoken way that she should invite him to stay. She didn't take the hint. Instead, she'd thanked him for a fun evening, gave him a lingering yet firm goodbye kiss, then turned away.

Anita snapped out of her daydream to find herself a good five miles further along the river than she'd expected. She turned around and headed back in the direction she'd come, trying to work out her next move.

Guilt was her constant companion, and she knew she was going to have to do something soon. Marcus would eventually find an excuse to put an end to her lessons with Alexander, and she couldn't expect Alexander to continue as they were indefinitely.

And she owed Helena an answer. The decision weighed on her, but deep down she'd known what she would do all along.

Anita arrived home, showered, changed, and then headed to the Body Temple to find Helena. As luck would have it, Anita didn't have to look for Helena at all; she bumped into her just outside the temple.

'Anita, hi,' said a surprised Helena. 'I was just coming to find you.'

'Great minds think alike,' said Anita, 'I was coming to find you too. I've considered what you said,' she continued quickly, before Helena could intervene, 'and

I've decided that I can't do what you asked. It's not fair on Marcus, regardless of who his father is.'

Helena paused, giving Anita a penetrating look, then softened, Anita breathing a sigh of relief.

'I'd like to show you something,' said Helena. 'Do you have time now?'

Helena's response took Anita off guard. It was unlike her to ask so nicely; she usually assumed that nobody had anything better to do than comply with her will.

'Of course,' said Anita. 'What do you want to show me?'

She gave Anita a frank look. 'It's better for you to see for yourself.'

Anita knew there was no point in arguing, so she nodded. 'Lead the way.'

* * * * *

Helena led Anita to an energy car and climbed into the driver's seat, Anita taking the seat next to her. Helena fired up the car in her usual brisk fashion.

Helena drove out of Empire and into the countryside beyond. They travelled in silence, neither knowing what to say.

After only a few miles, Helena turned onto a small, almost hidden track, which wound its way to a large, rundown farmhouse. Helena stopped the car and got out, swinging the squeaky door closed behind her. Anita followed, Helena already halfway across the yard, heading for a storage barn. She pulled the enormous door open on its runners, signaling for Anita to look within.

Anita peered into the relative dark, waiting for her eyes to adjust, but unless she was missing something, it looked like there was nothing to be seen. 'I'm not sure I understand,' she said, turning to look at Helena. 'There's nothing in there.'

'And that is precisely the point. Usually at this time of year, this barn is full of grain. Since the news of Christiana's death, crops have started to fail, fishermen have found dead fish floating in the rivers, and as you know from your work at the observatory, we've seen no evidence of the bounce back predicted by Austin. Come with me,' she said, turning away from the barn, heading for an old wooden gate into a field.

'Look at that,' said Helena, gesturing to a flattened wheat crop. It was black and grey, a far cry from its characteristic golden brown.

Anita looked gravely at the sight. 'How widespread is it?'

'Very. Farmers all over the world are reporting issues, some worse than others. This is an extreme example; the farmer has lost nearly everything this year. His farm won't survive another harvest like it.'

'Will it push up food prices? Is it bad enough to cause shortages?'

'Prices will increase, but this year we'll probably survive without severe shortages. If it continues into next year, it'll be a different story. Although, prices going up could lead to protests in itself.'

'Protests?' said Anita. She'd heard of protests a couple of decades back, but never in her lifetime. 'Who would risk Austin's wrath? And honestly, what can he do about it anyway?'

'Your generation has no political sense! We used to protest about a whole host of things that mattered. About the Descendants not taking their vows seriously, the education system, draining natural resources in the Wild Lands... until Austin stole that information, and now we can't do a thing.'

'What would you do if you got it back?'

'Protest, rebel, help people see that there could be freedom under the Relic if we overthrew the Descendants. We'd give people hope, a better way to live, even if the bloodline is broken. We'd put pressure on the Descendants, make them do what they promise in their vows, make them reinstate the Relic experts.'

Helena was waving her arms around, caught up in her words. 'We've got to do *something*, we can't just sit back and take it lying down. Can you imagine a world where you can't get food without having to fight for it? Or where you're not sure when you'll next be able to eat? You'll be alright if you keep in with the Descendants, they're probably stockpiling already, but if this goes on unchecked... just think of the consequences.'

'When the Descendants find out the full extent of this, they'll have to take action.'

Helena laughed a cruel laugh. 'You think Austin's going to come to the rescue of the people?'

'There are two other Descendants,' said Anita, a warning in her tone. 'Alexander will fight for action, and how could Peter refuse to join him?'

Anita's words lit a fire under Helena. 'Open your bloody eyes, Anita. Peter is spineless; he'll never stand up to Austin. So it's Alexander against Austin, who has Peter's silent support. That's two Descendants against one; Alexander will never win that way.'

'But Marcus has influence over Austin. He could make Austin see sense.'

'By the Gods, Anita, have you really let your feelings for Marcus cloud your judgement to such an extent? Marcus had no power over Austin. He's a puppy following his master, nothing more. The only way Marcus will ever get more power is if he becomes who Austin wants him to be. The only way to get them to listen is to take direct action, and that's why we need you.'

It was like Anita was thirteen again, receiving a lecture from Helena. But she was no longer Helena's pupil, and if Helena wanted her help, she could damn well ask nicely.

'Tell me, Helena, why is it I should trust you? You were my teacher and mentor for years, but never once told me anything about my parents, despite knowing how desperate I was for any shred of knowledge.

'You come to me representing a shady organization that I've never heard of, talking about starting a revolution to overthrow the rule of two of my friends. You want me to steal information from them, but you refuse to tell me what it's about. And worst of all, you dangle the carrot of my parents to force me into helping you. I've made up my mind; you'll have to find another way.'

Anita vaulted the gate into the field; she would walk back to Empire. She couldn't stand being around Helena another second.

* * * * *

Anita crossed two fields that looked exactly like the first, covered in blackened, flattened crops, so she knew Helena wasn't lying, at least about that. Obviously something had to be done, but she was sure the Descendants, even Austin, would have to act once they really knew what was happening. There was a council meeting in a week; they'd take action then.

As Anita crossed the next field, movement in her peripheral vision caught her attention. In the top corner of the field stood a small stone structure that she recognized as a shrine to the Body God Tatiana. In front of the shrine were two men, one holding a struggling goat, the other holding a knife up to the sky.

She couldn't hear what they were saying, but after a few moments, the man with the knife lowered his hands and slit the goat's throat. The animal's body collapsed to the floor.

The two men placed the carcass in the shrine and Anita stopped, stock still, shocked at the sight. She'd heard of sacrifices to the Gods, who hadn't? But she'd never actually seen one. She could only imagine the desperation that had driven these men to such an act. The men knelt in front of the shrine and prayed.

* * * * *

Helena was furious; it couldn't have gone any worse if she'd tried, and worst of all, it was all her fault. The Spirit Leader had warned her about trying to bully Anita, and she'd failed none the less.

There was nothing that wound up Helena more than her own mistakes, and she hated herself for it. She beat herself up and replayed their discussion in her head, supposing what might have happened if she'd gone about it differently. Maybe she should've told Anita something about her parents, or made something up about the information they were trying to get back? Either way, Anita's faith in the Descendants, especially in Austin's desire to do the right thing, was worrying.

Was Anita really so blind to the truth? If she was, then there was no hope... but Anita was the only way... 'Damn it,' she said furiously, mostly because of her own incompetence, 'how could you be such a stupid, blundering idiot.'

She slammed her balled up fist into the roof of her car before yanking open the squeaky door, clambering in without her usual grace, and slamming the door as hard as she could behind her.

* * * * *

Austin knew Amber was right. If he was to prevent the loss of his son to Anita, he'd have to bring him into the fold. But there was a lot that Austin didn't want Marcus to be involved with, or even know about, and he'd been racking his brain for something suitable for weeks.

He needed something far enough removed to keep Marcus out of the contentious stuff, yet significant enough that Marcus would find it interesting. He needed something that would make Marcus feel like he was in the inner circle.

In the end, it was the troublesome Anita herself who had sparked an idea. Anita and Marcus had been discussing her friend Cleo's newfound interest in the archives. Cleo was on some mission to uncover something about something, not that that was important, but the archives would be a great place for Marcus to start; at the family vault.

Each of the three bloodlines had a vault in the archives. Hardly anyone knew they existed, and they came equipped with impressive security systems. Austin had stored some explosive stuff there over the years, along with a load of old family paraphernalia.

The vault was a place where Marcus could learn things that seemed important, where he could be let in on certain secrets. He would learn about the family's history, but wouldn't have involvement in Austin's day-to-day business... it would be a while before Marcus was ready for that, if he was every ready.

Austin thought back to what he'd been like at Marcus' age; exactly like Marcus was now. Young, idealistic, hedonistic, carefree and with no idea how his father really operated. If his father, Tobias, had introduced it to Austin too early, he would have shied away, and Marcus would react the same way. This though was genius. It would seem the troublesome Anita had some perks after all.

Austin opened the concealed door in the paneling under the main staircase at the castle. He stooped through the gap and ran lightly down the small, cramped flight of stairs within, down to the dungeons, the headquarters of Amber's security team. He greeted the guard sitting behind the desk in his usual curt way. 'Keys to the vault.'

The guard got up and turned to a cabinet behind him, retrieving a set of large brass keys. He handed them to Austin, saying, 'There you are, Sir. Anything else I can help you with?'

'No, not today. I'll return these this evening.'

The guard didn't respond. He half nodded, waited for Austin to leave, and then sat back down. 'You're welcome, arsehole,' he muttered under his breath when he heard the door click shut at the top.

* * * * *

Marcus came down the stairs as Austin emerged from the dungeon. Austin had told Marcus to meet him in the entrance hall at ten, ready for a day of education, whatever the bloody hell that meant. Marcus couldn't think of anything worse than an 'educational day'. In his experience, education and enjoyment did not go hand in hand. However, he was intrigued by what it was Austin wanted to show him, so he'd agreed without argument.

'Morning,' said Austin, cheerily.

'Morning. Ready to tell me where we're going yet?'

'No. It's a surprise.'

'I see,' said Marcus, deeply suspicious and a little nervous. This was out of character for his father, and that was worrying.

'Come on; the car is waiting.'

Austin and Marcus travelled without conversing, Austin not noticing that this was strange and Marcus not knowing what to say to break the silence.

'Why've you brought me *here*?' asked Marcus, as they pulled up outside the archives. 'I've never considered myself a great historian, Dad.'

'And I wouldn't consider myself a historian either, Marcus, however, I find what's inside extremely exciting and I'm sure you will too.'

Marcus looked dubious. 'If you say so.'

Austin barely heard Marcus' reply, already striding off up the steps, through the front door and into the beautiful old building that housed the archives. The building had been a lovely country manor house, large and square with high ceilings and enormous full-length windows. It had been one of the earliest buildings constructed in Empire and the stonework had a lovely worn finish that fit perfectly with the ancient artifacts inside.

Austin breezed past the plush reception area without saying hello to the startled receptionist. He made for a door leading to a staircase to the floor below, Marcus trailing in his wake. The archives had originally been upstairs, but they'd soon needed more space and the light from the windows wasn't good for the artefacts, so they had moved everything to subterranean levels.

Austin and Marcus descended a further two flights of stairs and came out onto a dimly lit floor filled with racks of books, manuscripts, letters, energy meters, brass cylinders, and many other relics of the past.

Austin walked to the back of the floor, to a door separating two racks of books. He checked there was nobody around, pulled out the brass keys he'd picked up earlier, and crouched. He inserted the larger key into a hole in the wall near the floor. To Marcus' surprise, this made a panel in the rack's side, to the left of the door, swing open, revealing a small keypad and fingerprint scanner.

Austin quickly entered a code, then placed his finger on the reader, before swinging the panel shut, leaving no trace, or at least not in the dim light, anyway. Austin stood, then used the second brass key to unlock the door as you would any other. He pressed down on the handle and swung open the door.

Marcus could not have been more disappointed. After all that, the room held nothing but artefacts similar to those outside. Austin had brought him here to make a song and dance about some stuff from the past? Great.

Austin entered the room and gestured for Marcus to follow him before closing the door behind them. 'Welcome to the family vault,' he said with a flourish. 'This is where we keep the family secrets Marcus, along with documents about our history, and the sacrifices we've made in service of the world.

'Each Descendant family has a vault here, protected by similar security. We use them to keep things locked away that we would rather not be in the public domain. The best thing is that nobody suspects a thing, as this is the last place anyone would imagine a Descendant would keep secrets. We've had countless raids on our properties over the years, but not a single raid here.'

'Why have you brought me here?' asked Marcus. Why was his father showing him this now, or indeed at all? Austin had exerted a great deal of effort to keep Marcus away from anything interesting.

Austin looked surprised. 'To let you in on the family secrets. To get you more involved in the work I do, the work you will one day do as a ruling Descendant. To bring you up to speed on our history. These things are essential in preparation for power.

'When you rule, you'll find it beneficial to see how previous Mind Descendants acted when faced with challenges. You can draw on their experiences to shape the decisions you make. But, most importantly,' said Austin, looking uncertain, 'I'm showing you this because I hope you'll find it interesting.'

Marcus felt a pang of guilt that he wasn't being more enthusiastic. After all, this was the first time Austin had ever shared anything with him. It was a pretty big deal, if for no reason other than that.

'It's great, Dad,' said Marcus, with all the enthusiasm he could muster. 'Where should I start?'

Austin perked up. 'Over here, with the brief history of the family. We keep a biographer on hand to document all significant occasions and events. At the end of each reign, they compile a book about each Descendant, with a summary added to the brief history. I'm afraid these days it's not overly brief. It is, however, a good place to start. Once you've cracked that, we can move on to other areas.'

'What are those over there?' asked Marcus, pointing to a row of brass cylinders, the one on the end a little apart from the rest.

Austin's face pinched. 'We'll deal with those at a later date. They're memories of important things that happened in the past. I store them here for safekeeping, but you'll need a good grounding in our history before we go into those.

'Remove nothing from this room, and think carefully before letting anyone else know it exists. As I mentioned, part of the success of the vaults is that very few people know about them, and I'm sure I speak for all the Descendants when I say we would like it to stay that way.

'I've had your fingerprint programmed in and the code is here,' he said, handing Marcus a piece of paper. 'You can collect the keys from the dungeon any time you want, the guards know to give them to you.

'I hope you find this room inspirational and informative, and if you have questions about anything you find, my door is always open. For now, I'll leave you to explore the brief history in peace. Just lock the door when you leave and the security will reset.' Austin handed over the keys, leaving Marcus bemused.

Marcus stood for a moment, wondering whether he was in some bizarre dream, then looked around, contemplating where to start. He was tempted to walk straight over to the brass cylinders, or to rummage around in the other piles of stuff that looked much more interesting than a not-so-brief history of the family. But given this was the first time Austin had shown Marcus anything interesting, he thought it best to comply with his father's wishes, at least to start with.

So he picked up the history, turned on the light suspended over one of two worn old armchairs, sat down heavily, and read.

CHAPTER 13

'Again, Bass, you seem to have misunderstood your brief,' said Austin. 'You are here to monitor the energy and report your findings to the council. We do not keep you on hand to interpret those findings in an exaggerated manner, and present them here as fact.'

Every fiber in Bass's being was still as the words hit him, his face carefully neutral.

'Frankly, Bass,' said Austin, with disgust, 'this is tantamount to scaremongering, and that is something that this council must take extremely seriously. We all know the effect comments like yours can have on the energy...' Austin was visibly enjoying himself, until a calm, even voice cut him off mid-sentence.

'... we can't ignore what's right in front of us, Austin,' said Alexander, standing up and walking towards the lectern, throwing visible weight behind Bass.

'Bass' report is consistent with information I've been getting from farmers and fishermen all over the world,' said Alexander. 'The crops are failing, fish are dying, it's only a matter of time before we see food shortages.

'I'm sure everyone in this room will be fine; we have the means to secure food and protect it. Others, those we have a responsibility to protect, will not be so fortunate. We must take action now,' he said, turning pointedly to Austin, 'or we'll have a rebellion on our hands.'

Austin screwed up his face. 'This is the problem with young Descendants,' he laughed, self-assurance seeping out of every part of him. 'They have no experience of life, have never seen situations like this before, have never witnessed situations like this blowing over, running themselves out of steam.

'When life carries on as it always has, regardless of the Body bloodline, everything will go back to normal. The energy will stabilize and food will be in abundance once more.

'Now, I think we've had enough of these hysterics for one day. Bass, I would advise you to carefully contemplate what you say in this chamber during your next update, or we may have to reconsider your position here… we did appoint you at a very *young* age...'

Bass was about to explode with indignation.

Alexander intervened, both before Bass did anything stupid, and because his own frustration was at boiling point. 'No, Austin, this conversation is not over. I am a ruling Descendant with as much of a say here as you, regardless of my age, and we must take action.

'You cannot use the past to predict the future, especially as our world has never faced this challenge before. People think the bloodline has been cut, that there's no hope of freeing the world. That isn't something people can easily bounce back from.'

'Luckily,' said Austin, 'we have three ruling Descendants, which comes in handy at moments like these.'

Austin rounded Peter, who had shrunk so far back into his seat that he looked like he was trying to escape through it. 'Peter, we come to you for the deciding vote,' said Austin. 'More time for this discussion, as the young bucks suggest, or should we move on to more pressing matters?'

Peter sat still, like a rabbit in headlights, the cogs of his mind turning. 'It seems to me,' he said, slowly, 'that we are weighing the merits of youthful energy versus experience.' Peter paused. 'In this delicate matter, experience should guide us. If we see no improvement, we can revisit the topic at a later date.'

Peter looked deflated, and Alexander knew from his energy that his words did not match his emotions. Austin's intimidation tactics had worked their magic once more. But right now, he had to get Bass out of the chamber before he said or did something stupid.

'We'll repeatedly revisit this topic, as the energy continues to drop,' said Alexander, walking over to stand right next to Bass, 'and when it does, we can all gain first hand, front row experience of the chaos that drop will cause. Maybe in the future, if this happens again, we'll have some *experience* to tell us how not to deal with it. For now though, I think we've all had quite enough.'

Alexander turned and looked Bass straight in the eye, his head giving a tiny twitch in the direction of the door. Bass nodded and he and Alexander wheeled towards the exit, striding in perfect, confident unison, the doors opening for them as they departed.

They quickly exited through the Temple of the Spirit and almost ran straight into Anita and Marcus, who were walking towards the Temple of the Body.

* * * * *

Anita detected their energy before she saw them, a mix of rage and comradery. 'Hi,' she said tentatively, as they marched down the steps, oblivious to everything around them, consumed by their thoughts.

They looked up together, both reacting when they saw Anita and Marcus. Anita was glad Marcus wasn't a reader and almost laughed aloud as their energy changed; their rage redirected towards Marcus. Anita knew they didn't really like him, but this was a bit much...

Their comradery extended to Anita, who was grateful they weren't mad with her, but this served to further confuse her; what the bloody hell was going on?

Then, to her surprise, sheepishness crept into Alexander's energy, which he quickly suppressed. Maybe a reaction to Anita's energy spike at seeing him, which she was now desperately trying to hide. Sometimes, Anita wished she was as oblivious as Marcus to all this, although even he could tell something was wrong.

'Is everything alright?' asked Anita, tentatively.

'No, everything is not alright,' said Bass. 'His father,' he said, throwing an accusing look in Marcus' direction, 'is an arrogant, blind, fool who is about to sink the world into chaos via starvation, while happily ignoring his duty to do something about it.'

Marcus and Anita looked blankly back, so Alexander stepped in. 'We've just had a council meeting and Bass gave an update on the energy. He reported the facts, which are, as you know only too well, Anita, that the energy is showing no signs of bouncing back. In fact, it keeps falling, and the consequences of that are becoming clear.

'It's only a matter of time before the weather reacts, and then who knows what might happen. What if the water supply dries up? What if we're ravaged by endless storms? Only the Gods know what else could be in store...

'The council, particularly Austin, has no appetite to accept the facts, nor do anything about them. It's

Austin's opinion that because the energy has always bounced back in the past, it will continue to do so in the future: pompous fool.'

Anita reached out and squeezed Marcus' hand. She didn't like Austin, but it couldn't be easy to hear others talking about him like this. Surprisingly, Marcus' energy was stable as he took stock of what he'd heard.

'So, what happens next?' asked Anita. 'How bad does it have to get before they finally decide to do something?'

'Who knows,' said Bass, 'but the Descendants have the means to look after themselves for a great deal longer than the rest of the world. Maybe it will take starving people revolting in the streets before they do anything. Even if that happens, I doubt Austin would show much compassion.'

This finally incited a reaction from Marcus. 'He's only doing what he thinks is right, based on what he and my ancestors have seen in the past,' he said, pressing on, even though they'd all rounded on him. 'Dad may be many things, but to imply that he'd intentionally hurt others for his own gain is pushing it too far. He would never do that.'

'Really?' said Alexander. 'What makes you so sure?'

'Because I know him; he is my father, after all. I know he can be severe and difficult to deal with, but he does genuinely want what's best for the world.'

'But you can't agree that what's best for the world is to do nothing?' said Anita. 'To take no action? To ignore the facts in front of us?'

'What facts?' said Marcus, tentatively. 'All we have are a few observations. We've had bad crop yields before; maybe this is just another poor year. Maybe it'll pick up again next year. Who really knows?'

This was too much for Bass. 'I thought Descendants were given a decent education, especially

237

about the role the energy plays. It's fundamental to everything. It feeds into everything, and everything feeds into it.

'The change in the levels *is* manifesting as poor crop yields. Who knows what will be next? Otherwise, you're hypothesizing that a significant dip in the energy could have no effect on the world, something we know categorically to be false.'

'Yes, but we don't know that the energy dip is manifesting through the crop yields and fish stocks, it could be having an impact elsewhere, on something we have yet to find. The low yields could be simply because it's been a bad year... we have had a lot of rain.'

Anita couldn't believe what she was hearing. 'Are you serious? It's as clear as day that the two are linked. You're ignoring the evidence because you don't want to admit your father's wrong.

'Marcus, the world is on the brink of a crisis, the likes of which we have never seen. There's nothing in the past that can help with what we're facing. We need to interpret what we have in front of us and act on that information. Don't you think we should take action?'

Anita immediately regretted her words; she'd backed Marcus into a corner. To agree with her would be to go against his father. Marcus seemed to genuinely believe that his father would do the right thing eventually, that Austin took his duty seriously.

'All I know is that Dad wouldn't act in a way he thought would harm the world,' said Marcus, 'which means he must know something more about what's going on than we all do. Maybe we should trust that he's been around for longer... he has more experience, can bring a unique perspective.'

Bass and Alexander had had enough. 'I've already heard this bullshit from one member of the Mind line today, and luckily, I don't have to stand here and listen to any more of it,' said Bass. 'Just wait and see what happens when we take no action; you'll look like a fool then, along with your father.'

Bass and Alexander left Anita and Marcus, storming off in the direction of the observatory.

Anita stood still for a second, trying to process what Marcus had just said. She turned slowly to face him. His energy deflated, shoulders hunching forward, usual confident swagger momentarily deserting him. 'Did you mean that?' asked Anita. 'Or were you just saying it so as not to insult your dad?'

Marcus' energy was uncertain. Anita felt the moment his resolve snapped into place.

'Anita, nobody's one hundred percent sure what's going on. We've never encountered this situation before, so we can't be sure what will happen next. I don't think the right thing to do is scaremonger about disaster and destruction; that won't help anyone.'

'So we should do nothing?'

'It's a delicate situation. I don't think we should do anything rash.'

'What your father's doing is something rash. To not act at all is criminal, and you're burying your head in the sand.'

Anita turned away and started walking towards the Body Temple.

Marcus followed her.

'I'll see you later, Marcus. I need some time alone,' she said, taking the steps two at a time.

'You're going to let a council debate come between us?'

She wheeled back to face him, a look of disbelief plastered across her face. 'You're going to let some ridiculous view held by your father come between us? Open your eyes, Marcus, it's a big scary world out there and Daddy is villain number one.'

* * * * *

Marcus watched her go, trying to sort through his own thoughts. Which side was he on? His mind raced, locked in an endless loop of uncertainty. He was angry, confused, hurt, embarrassed, worried, and most of all had a deep sense of foreboding that this situation would not blow over as he would like.

He didn't want to lose Anita. It had surprised him how much he'd missed her when she'd gone to Kingdom, and he'd seen her pretty much every day since. But he couldn't take a stand against his father, who had only just started to involve him. Nothing he'd seen so far showed that Austin, or indeed any of the previous Mind Descendants, had ever done anything out of line with their duty.

But, come to think of it, it was a little strange that nobody had ever put a single foot wrong... maybe he was being lied to...

Austin terrified everyone, but until now, Marcus had assumed that was because he had a powerful position and an unpredictable temperament. He would never purposely hurt someone without good reason. Would he?

* * * * *

Anita reached the top of the stairs, agitated, angry, emotions coiling tighter and tighter inside her. How could Marcus be so stupid? She'd felt his conflicting emotions, but he'd sided with Austin when deep down he knew action needed to be taken. He'd sided with Austin when he could've easily sided with her, once the others had gone.

She understood Marcus couldn't publicly trash his father, especially in front of another Descendant, but surely he trusted her enough to tell her what he really felt? Not only had he not trusted her, but he'd let her down in front of the others. She looked like a fool for being so close to him... she needed to punch something.

'Anita?' came a voice from behind, startling her. How had someone got so close without her knowing they were there? She whirled around to see Helena standing next to a pillar, a strange look on her face, almost nervous.

'I'll do it,' said Anita, surprising them both equally. Action needed to be taken by somebody; it may as well be her.

Helena walked forward. 'Er... what we discussed the other day?' she said, cautiously. 'You'll do it?'

'Yes,' she said, holding her breath, wondering if she was really doing this.

'Let's go for a run,' said Helena, in a low voice. 'We don't want to be overheard.'

Helena led Anita to a small cottage around the corner from the temples, pulled out a key, and let them in. 'Here, I'll be back in a minute,' she said, throwing some running tights, a t-shirt, and trainers to Anita before making her way up the small spiral staircase to get changed.

A few minutes later, they were running in the direction of the river, Anita relishing the vent for her frustration. She pushed the pace faster and faster, her energy lifting with every stride.

By the time they reached the river, Anita felt good; she felt great; she felt invigorated. They paused by the water's edge, stretching and watching the lively water ripple its way downstream.

'What made you change your mind?' asked Helena.

'The Descendants won't do anything. Austin's determined not to, but somebody has to do something. You've offered me a way to help. I would be as bad as they are if I didn't act either.'

'What about your relationship with Marcus?'

'If all goes well, he'll never know, and we can carry on as we are.' Her features puckered. 'What exactly do you need me to do? Where will I find the information that needs to be retrieved?'

Helena took a breath. 'We don't know. That's part of what you're going to have to do. All we know is that a memory was stolen from me. I obviously can't remember what it was, but it was something about the origins of the Institution, something that would undermine us if we ever challenged Austin.

'It was stolen a couple of decades ago and is the reason the Institution went quiet. All I know is that it's stored in a brass cylinder with red rings around each end. We only know that much because Melia, Marcus' mother, got inside Austin's head, just before they separated. Unfortunately, Austin realized something was wrong before she could find out where the cylinder was.'

'How am I supposed to find it? Marcus won't know anything.'

'Ask him.'

'Are you mad?' said Anita.

'You might have to tap Amber or Austin for information, or maybe one of the security guards.'

'Wonderful. Just out of interest, what do you think will happen to me if they catch me?' She said it flippantly, but the thought gnawed at her.

'I wouldn't get caught if I were you. One thing I can guarantee is that it won't be pleasant if you do. They probably won't kill you; you mean too much to Marcus, but Amber can be most unpleasant.'

'I'll bear that in mind. Anything else to mention before I jump into the fire?'

'No, I think that covers it. We should cut all contact between us; I don't want anyone to get suspicious. When you succeed, send me a message, and then, as promised, I'll tell you everything about your parents.'

'That's not why I'm doing this.'

'I know. But surely you want to know?'

'Not if you tell me something I don't want to hear...' she said, angrily. 'I've wondered my entire life about my parents... but I can't think about that until I've got the cylinder. I'm doing this to stop Austin and help stabilize the energy. I want to hear about my parents, but not as payment. I'm doing this because I want to, not because it's part of a business transaction.'

'Understood,' said Helena. 'I just want that cylinder back in our hands so we can focus on re-stabilizing the energy. I'd love for you to help us do that too...'

'Let's not get ahead of ourselves. I could end up in Austin's dungeon for the rest of my life. One step at a time.'

'Right you are. In which case, I'll look forward to your message. Good luck,' said Helena, heading off towards Empire with nothing to soften her goodbye.

'Thanks, I'll probably need it,' said Anita, heading in the opposite direction. She found a place to cross the river and set off for the castle; there was no time like the present.

* * * * *

Anita and Marcus had made up, neither one really apologizing and neither one changing their point of view; Anita thought he'd be suspicious if she had. They accepted that their opinions differed on the energy and acknowledged that this would happen from time to time. They agreed to draw a line under it and move on.

For a few days after that, their relationship was tense, but the tension eventually wore off, their dynamic back to how it had been before. Regrettably, a silent agreement materialized between them that Anita would no longer see Alexander. She hadn't seen him, apart from bumping into him outside the temples, since they'd got back from Kingdom. She put off Spirit lessons, spending the time with Marcus instead.

Marcus relaxed when he realized Anita wasn't seeing Alexander, and their relationship strengthened, but he was also becoming more controlling as the days went by. He wanted to know where Anita was going and who she was seeing, and he tried to go with her practically everywhere she went.

The only saving grace was her work at the observatory, which gave her some much needed space. Even this was unpleasant for a while, Bass appalled that she was still with Marcus.

Bass couldn't stay mad with Anita for long, his disdain wearing off after a couple of weeks, but Anita found herself on the roof, lying on the same old energy receiver, even more often than usual. She craved time by herself.

The quest to find Austin's brass cylinder was going the same way as the quest to find the one in her head had: nowhere. There were no clues anywhere, and Marcus didn't let her near Austin and Amber, or any of the security guards, so she had no chance to probe them for information.

The closest Anita had got to anything interesting was when she'd seen a guard emerging from an invisible door under the stairs one day. This had taken her by surprise, but that the castle stretched down into the ground wasn't remarkable. Although it could be where

Austin kept his secrets… With nothing more than that to go on, Anita was not doing well so far.

To compound her problems, Marcus had decided he wanted to meditate with her. He kept harping on about how she'd meditated with Alexander, so it was only fair that they should meditate together too.

She kept putting it off, but knew that would only fly for so long before he became suspicious. She worried they might accidentally find the cylinder in her head… what would happen then? She needed advice from Alexander before they meditated, but Marcus barely ever left her side. Luckily, Cleo saved the day.

Anita had been skirting around Marcus' possessiveness on one of her rare evenings out without him. Cleo had mentioned that Marcus was spending a lot of time in the archives when Anita was at the observatory. She didn't know what he was doing there, as she only ever saw him coming and going, and was wondering if Anita knew.

Anita had replied honestly, saying that she had no idea, although it did seem a bit strange.

Cleo was looking into the Relic discovery and the reaction of the Descendants, but hadn't yet found anything. This wasn't surprising, given that the Descendants controlled the archives, but Cleo was sure it was only a matter of time until something cropped up.

* * * * *

The following day, Anita went to the observatory as usual, allowing Marcus to drop her off. Twenty minutes later, having received a message from Cleo that Marcus was safely in the archives for the day, Anita left the observatory and headed for the river.

Cleo had delivered a message to Alexander, and unusually for Cleo, she hadn't made a suggestive comment or questioned why. Maybe something in Anita's worried face had put her off, or maybe Cleo just wanted some excitement. Either way, Anita had been grateful.

Anita reached the river, the arranged meeting spot, with a hive of bees in her stomach. She felt Alexander's powerful energy waiting for her in the trees. Her energy soared, as did his when he sensed her presence.

She stepped into the trees, her heart pounding as her eyes took in his beautiful, rugged form. It took all the self-control she possessed to prevent her from running to him and throwing her arms around him; she hadn't realized until now how much she'd missed him.

She stopped a few feet away, feeling a nudge at the edge of her energy, and without hesitation, sent one back. He closed his eyes until the sensation had passed, a pained look on his face when he reopened them.

They stood in silence, Anita taking in the contours of his face, Alexander doing the same to her. She finally broke the spell. 'I missed you,' she said, his energy reacting to her words.

He took a step towards her, reaching out to place his hands either side of her face, pulling her to him, tingles shooting through her body even before their skin made contact.

The shock of his fingers on her cheeks was so strong, she worried they might fuse together, his eyes boring deep into hers, confirming he felt it too. He closed his eyes and placed his forehead against hers, his brow furrowed as he fought desperately to get his boiling energy under control.

Anita finally steeled herself, using every ounce of control she had to pull away from him, the aroma of oranges swirling around her, fogging her mind, screaming at her to kiss him. 'I need your help, Alexander,' she said, forcing herself a safe distance away, to focus on why she had come.

She sat down on the trunk of a fallen tree and waited as he took deep breaths, recovering from the effect of her touch.

'Anything,' he said, moving towards her.

Anita put her hand up to stop him. 'Please don't come too close,' she said. 'This is difficult enough as it is.'

'What's wrong?' he asked, his eyes sweeping over her as though searching for the cause of her distress.

She looked dejectedly at the floor; meeting his gaze wasn't a good idea. 'Marcus wants to meditate with me. I've put him off so many times already, it's only a matter of time before I'm going to have to do it. I'm worried we'll stumble across the cylinder in my head. I don't know why it's there or what it contains, but I know I don't want him to know about it.'

Alexander's energy lost its panicked edge.

'It's always risky to let someone into your head, but there are ways to control it. In the same way that I made sure we only ever meditated to places in your mind until that night in Kingdom, you can keep the meditation in Marcus' mind, which will protect you.'

Anita pushed away the flood of memories of his lips, the feel of his skin under her fingers.

'Marcus will probably buy some story about you wanting to explore his head because you're fascinated by him. You need to think of your energy pushing into Marcus' head when you meditate. That should take you into his mind. You'll need to be forceful, as he might try to do the same thing to you. The Gods only know when Marcus last meditated; Mind Descendants don't think it's a necessary skill to maintain, so you shouldn't have too much trouble.

247

'Just make sure you keep the pressure up the whole time, so you stay in Marcus' head. It's a lot like when you suppress your energy downwards, but instead of pushing it down, push it into Marcus. If he insists on visiting somewhere in your head, go for the boat on the sea. It's the place you're least attached to, and it contains a lot of Mind. Marcus will feel comfortable there, and you should be able to push him back into his head from somewhere like that.

'Avoid your Centre if you're worried about divulging information, and it goes without saying to stay away from the cliff in Kingdom. Even though the house isn't there, Marcus will recognize it…'

Anita felt calmer than when she'd arrived, but was still worried.

'You'll be fine,' he said, 'you're a natural at this stuff.'

'And he can't get into my head unless I'm there too, when we're meditating? There's no way for him to keep me occupied in his head and then sneak off into mine?'

Alexander tried to hide his smile. 'It is possible, but Marcus can't do it. I've managed it occasionally and there are a handful of skilled Spirits who can too, but you're safe with Marcus.'

Alexander hesitated before adding, 'You should be more worried about him getting into your head when you're asleep though; anyone can do that.'

'That's not a problem,' she said, looking directly into his eyes, her face neutral, 'as I haven't recently been asleep in his presence.'

Alexander couldn't hide the uplift in his energy, and Anita smiled inwardly. 'I really do miss you,' she whispered, a pang of guilt ripping through her. She averted her gaze.

'I miss you too,' he said, looking as though he might close the distance she'd placed between them. 'Why can't we start up lessons again?' he said, a note of desperation in his tone. 'Nothing will happen between us, I promise.'

'But I don't promise. We don't even have to touch for there to be tingles between us; what's it going to be like if we meditate together?'

'What about drinks with Cleo and Bass some time? Drinks in a crowded bar with other people can't be anything to worry about?'

Anita laughed. 'There's no way Marcus would let me have drinks with you without him there.'

Alexander went still. 'Then leave Marcus and be with me,' he said, catching her off balance as he swiftly closed the gap between them. 'I'll look after you,' he said, kneeling, grabbing her hands, looking into her eyes, surges of energy shooting through her. 'Austin won't try to hurt you if you're under my protection.'

Anita bowed her head, her insides contracting. 'I can't,' she choked, 'at least, not yet.'

'Why?' he asked, reaching his hand to her face, lifting her chin so her smoky grey eyes met his, urging her with every fiber of his being to change her mind. 'What do you mean *not yet?*'

'I can't go into it now,' she said, her eyes begging for forgiveness as she placed her hands on his shoulders and pushed herself to her feet. She tore herself away, putting a safe distance between them. 'I'll tell you as soon as I can, I promise.'

'When?' he asked, standing.

'I don't know,' she said, shaking her head, tears in her eyes. 'I have to go; it's too dangerous to stay any longer. I need to get back to the observatory.'

'If there's anything I can do, come and find me, or send Cleo. I'm here if you need me.'

As Anita made to leave, Alexander's energy turned cold.

'What is it?' she said.

He hesitated for a split second. 'Nothing. Just let me know if there's anything you need.'

She sent him a grateful look. 'Thank you.'

She reached out and touched his arm as she passed him, causing an eruption of tingles so strong they almost stopped her in her tracks. She said nothing and nor did he, using all her energy to keep away from him.

Anita left, Alexander tracking her as she ebbed away.

CHAPTER 14

Anita returned to the observatory just in time to see Marcus' car pulling up outside. She hadn't been that long, had she?

'Hi,' she said, walking over, kissing him as soon as he climbed out of his car.

'Hello,' he said, grabbing her waist. 'Where have you been? Slacking?'

Anita laughed, if you only knew the half of it, she thought. 'Just went for a quick walk. You know what us Body types are like; if we stay still for too long, we get antsy.'

'That is true,' he said with a smirk, then pushed her back against the car, kissing her. 'I got bored, so thought I'd come and persuade you to skip work.' He flashed her his most charming smile.

'Alright,' she said, leaning in and whispering in his ear, so Marcus' driver couldn't hear, 'I feel like meditating.'

Marcus' energy soared. He looked at her like a child in a sweet shop, a mix of excitement and awe, but with some concern that the candy would be snatched from his grasp. She laughed, nodding her head.

'Are we just going to stand here all day?' Anita asked, in mock frustration. 'Or are we going to go?'

Marcus pulled her into the car, his delight contagious. He clasped her hand all the way back to the castle. When they got there, Marcus burst through the door, pulling her along in his wake, Anita giggling uncontrollably at his unrestrained elation. They raced each other up the stairs, taking them two at a time and, unusually, Marcus won, Anita still trying to control her laughter.

They entered Marcus' room, and he pinned her against the door as he closed it, kissing her enthusiastically. His unbridled joy lifted her energy, and Anita fought to get herself under control as he led her to a rug in front of one of the full-length windows. She focused herself, concentrating on what she needed to do to push the meditation into Marcus' head.

Anita sank down and sat cross-legged on the rug, expecting Marcus to sit opposite her, but he shook his head. 'I think we should practice the love pose.'

'The love pose?' asked Anita, confused and a little apprehensive.

'You don't know about the love pose?'

'No,' she said honestly.

Marcus' energy rose even further at her words.

'The love pose is the only pose practiced lying down and the only pose where you touch the person you're meditating with. It gives you a sense that the meditation is all-encompassing; it's a deeper, richer experience, and has a more profound effect on those doing it.'

'So, what do we have to do?' said Anita, fighting to keep the worry from her voice.

'Lie down on your back, or on your side, and turn your head to face me.'

She obliged, lying on her side, which felt less vulnerable than lying on her back. Marcus lay down next to her, also on his side.

'Now we intertwine our hands,' he said, taking her hand so the back was close to his lips and vice versa. 'And now we meditate as you would normally. See you on the other side,' he said, smiling broadly, brushing his lips across the back of her hand, shutting his eyes.

Anita tried to adjust to these surprising circumstances, while focusing on pushing her energy into Marcus' head. Immediately the meditation was different to normal, although this was probably to be expected, as the only person she'd ever properly meditated with was Alexander. It wasn't more intense than usual either, if anything it was less so, but she pushed the thought aside as she focused on pushing her energy towards Marcus.

She found herself in thick woodland when the meditation settled. She looked around but couldn't see Marcus anywhere, so started walking in the direction that felt best. She soon hit a small stream, sunlight spilling down through the trees, illuminating the water and moss-covered floor. She leaned against a tree, watching the trickling water as she waited for Marcus to find her.

After a few moments, Marcus' voice pierced the silence. 'Over here,' he beckoned, drawing her towards a small wooden cabin with a veranda overlooking the stream.

'It's beautiful here,' she said as she reached him, taking hold of his outstretched hand. 'Where are we?'

'I don't know exactly. I've been meditating here since I first had Spirit lessons, but to this day I don't know where it is. Funny that, don't you think?'

'Yes, I suppose. I wonder how these places get inside our minds... places we've never knowingly been.'

'Some think they're inherited through our bloodlines,' said Marcus, as Anita sat down on one of the large rocking chairs on the veranda. 'I don't know if

I believe that, though. Dad would never share something as intimate as the places in his mind with me, and I can't even remember my grandfather, so I don't know what his were.'

'What about your mother?' asked Anita, hoping Marcus wouldn't mind her probing further. 'Would she tell you about the places in her mind?'

'She might, but I'd never ask her. It's very private, and many minds would see it as a weakness for others to know something so unique about them. What about the places in your mind? Do you know where they all are?'

Anita hesitated. 'Not all of them. There's one where I'm in a boat on the sea, but I don't recognize anything about it. I've been sailing many times, but neither the boat nor the coastline are familiar.'

'Can we go there?' he asked hopefully.

She paused, but her instincts told her she should let him in; he'd be suspicious otherwise. 'Sure,' she said, before concentrating all of her energy on the boat, and moments later, she and Marcus were sitting on the deck as it sailed itself in the gentle breeze.

Marcus' face darkened. 'Is this some kind of joke?' he spat, looking nervously around.

'What do you mean?'

'You expect me to believe you don't know where we are? I'm not that naïve Anita.'

'Marcus, I honestly have no idea. Where are we?'

The next thing Anita knew, she was back in Marcus' room lying on the floor. Marcus yanked his hand away, jumped up, and put distance between them. 'Anita, that was my Grandfather's boat, *Aphrodite*.'

'What?'

'Tobias, my dad's dad.'

'How's that possible?' she asked, drawing her knees to her chest and hugging them to her. How could she have something like that in her head? 'But Tobias must have died when I was only three or four, and I'm pretty sure I never even met him. How can his boat be in my head?'

'How am I supposed to know?' he said, voice raised. 'But that was Tobias' boat; I saw a picture in the archives only yesterday.'

'Why are you shouting at me?' she said, flying to her feet and storming towards him. If he was going to yell at her, she could yell too. 'You said only minutes ago, you don't know where that place in your head is. What if that's somewhere my grandmother has a connection to?'

'Well, how do you explain it?'

'*I can't.*' She stressed the words, standing inches from him and looking up as though he were truly stupid. 'In exactly the same way that you can't explain how that place got into your head.'

At that moment, something in Anita's brain fell into place. She replayed Marcus' words: *I saw a picture in the archives only yesterday...* Why was he spending so much time in the archives? He hated history, and he wasn't researching anything that he'd told her about, yet he was looking at things that had belonged to his grandfather.

Marcus shared every waking thought with her, much to her irritation, yet he hadn't even mentioned the archives, where he was spending time every day. Why? She had to see whatever it was. She had to get him to take her there, which meant she needed to smooth things over. There was nothing for it...

Anita and Marcus stood, faces inches apart, tension building, eyes clouded with fury, when Anita's intention changed from rage to furious passion. She tilted her head upwards, lifted her hands to Marcus' shirt, and pulled him to her, her angry lips meeting his with fervor.

Marcus responded instantly, kissing back with equal force, lifting his hands to her face, drinking in her urgent kisses. He pushed her back against the wall, pinning her like prey, holding her there with his hips. He released her long enough to pull her dress over her head before lifting her off the ground, pushing her back against the wall. She wrapped her legs around him, a hum of pleasure escaping her as he kissed her neck.

She clawed at his shirt, pulling it out of his trousers, unable to get it any further because his hands were busy unclipping her bra. Marcus turned, easily holding Anita's lithe body, carried her to his bed, and threw her roughly down. He removed her lace underwear, discarding the fabric on the floor.

Anita lay naked, looking up at him as he studied every inch of her. She sat up, grabbed the hem of his shirt, and pushed it upwards, hands skirting over the ripples of muscle on his torso. She stood, sliding the shirt over his head, relishing the sensation as Marcus' hands returned, ghosting down her spine, sending shivers everywhere. His hands kept moving, coming to rest over the contour of her behind.

She reached for his trousers, ridding him of his remaining clothes, then spun him round. She pushed him back onto the bed, climbing on top of him like a cat, kissing her way seductively from his navel, to his torso, to his neck, to his lips.

Marcus retook control. He grabbed her waist and rolled her onto her back, following her over, pinning her to the bed. She wrapped her legs around him and he pushed into her, intense shivers of pleasure shooting out from everywhere they touched.

Anita lifted her hips to meet him, grabbing his hair with her hands and pulling his mouth to hers. They moved faster, tension building, loud gasps of pleasure escaping unnoticed from their mouths. Anita found the edge, bucked her hips, and tipped over, convulsions racking her body. Marcus came with her, then collapsed onto her, a sea of sensation erupting across Anita's skin as their bodies came flush together.

Marcus rolled off her, turning his head to look into her eyes. He pulled Anita's back to his chest, wrapping a protective arm across her, holding her tightly against him. He used his free hand to pull her hair back off her neck, planting light kisses on the exposed flesh. She played her fingers across his arm, then lifted his hand to her lips, kissing the palm gently.

He ran his teeth over her ear. 'Sorry,' he whispered, so quietly she could barely make out the word. 'I overreacted. I was just so shocked that my grandfather's boat was in your head.'

This was her chance. 'Why were you looking at a picture of it?' she asked.

'Because I've been learning about my family. Dad recently introduced me to some family history that I never knew existed, so I've been spending time at the archives looking into it. It's been fascinating; there's so much I never knew about the Mind line, and there's still so much to learn.'

'Can I see the picture?' she asked. Damn, way too forward. Surely that would scare him off...

'Why do you want to see it?'

'Because I'm as intrigued as you are about how Tobias' boat found its way into my head. There may be a clue in that picture. How would you feel if I had a picture of the wood in your head? Wouldn't you want to see it?'

Her words seemed to hit home, and his energy softened.

'The thing is, I can't take the picture out of the archives,' he said.

'But we can go there,' she said tenderly, not conceding an inch. 'I'd love to see your family's history; what's important to you is important to me too.'

He took a deep breath. 'Okay,' he said, kissing her shoulder, 'let's go now. We can go for a walk afterwards. The sun will be setting by then and the archive gardens are beautiful at that time of day.'

'Thank you,' she said, rolling into him and gently kissing his lips.

* * * * *

They stopped at a herbalist on the way to the archives, Anita buying a contraceptive tea. She downed the sweet liquid in a few swift gulps.

They arrived at the archives, and Marcus led Anita down three flights of stairs. Halfway to the back of the floor, they bumped into Cleo, who looked shocked to see them.

'Hey!' said Cleo, giving Anita a quizzical look. 'I don't think you've come here more than twice in your entire life, have you?' She laughed. 'What are you doing here?'

Marcus looked uncomfortable.

'Nothing much,' said Anita. 'Marcus spends so much time here I thought I'd come and see what all the fuss is about.'

Anita threw Cleo a look, pleading with her not to ask any more questions. Thankfully, she took the hint.

Marcus, whose energy had been coiling tight, visibly relaxed. 'Anita, I'll come and get you in a minute, there's something I have to do,' he said.

'Okay,' she agreed without hesitation, not wanting to put him off now she was so close.

* * * * *

Austin descended the stairs to the basement and asked the guard for the keys to the vault. He'd seen Marcus leave earlier with Anita, so now would be a good time to remove a couple of choice artefacts before Marcus explored too widely. 'Keys,' he barked at the security guard, who looked back blankly.

'I'm afraid Marcus came and collected them earlier, Sir.'

'What? You gave them to him when he was with Anita?'

'He was with Anita? It was only Marcus who came down here.'

Austin's fuse was lit. If this were not resolved quickly, then he would explode, and no one in the castle would be spared his wrath.

'Amber,' he bellowed.

She appeared at her office door, face full of concern. 'What is it?' she asked.

'This blundering employee of yours gave Marcus the keys to the family vault when he was with Anita.'

'Are you sure?'

'I just saw them leave together.'

Amber reacted instantly, barking orders back into her office and at the guard behind the desk. 'I need a team of four people, now. Bring round the cars. Alert the archives that they're not to allow Anita to leave until we get there. Are you joining us, Austin?'

'Of course I'm sodding joining you. Let's go.'

* * * * *

Marcus walked off and Anita realized that Cleo being here could work to her advantage. 'I need your help, Cleo,' she whispered.

Cleo looked eager; she loved nothing more than a conspiracy. 'What do you need me to do?'

'Distract Marcus. He's about to take me into a separate room and I need you to come snooping around just after we enter. He's showing me a picture, but I need you to buy me some alone time in there so I can have a look around.'

'Anita,' called Marcus, striding back towards her. 'Are you coming?'

Cleo nodded at Anita. 'I'm in,' she said happily, her voice low.

Anita walked towards Marcus, who led her through a very normal-looking door into a very average-looking room. It housed artefacts that resembled those on the shelves outside. Deathly boring. Until she spotted a row of brass cylinders on the far side of the room. A single cylinder sat slightly apart from all the others. It had red rings around the top and bottom, and she could swear that it called her name.

Her stomach lurched and adrenaline flooded her blood as she turned back to look at what Marcus was showing her. 'As you can see, *Aphrodite* is definitely the boat in your mind,' he said, voice full of wonder.

'By the Gods, you're right,' she said, genuinely shocked. Although her focus was on something altogether different, the picture still fascinated her. Anita took it from him and scanned every inch. Of course, there was nothing that gave the slightest clue as to why it was in her head.

At that moment there was a light knock on the door and the color drained from Marcus' face.

'Marcus?' said Cleo's voice through the door.

'Keep her occupied,' said Anita. 'I'll be out in a minute; I just want a bit more time with the picture.'

He turned, clearly conflicted. Anita made a big show of sitting down and studying the photo as though engrossed. Marcus huffed out a breath and went to deal with Cleo.

As soon as the door clicked shut behind him, Anita abandoned the photo and made for the brass cylinders. She picked up the cylinder with red rings, the metal smooth and cold in her hands. It was heavier than she'd expected, and as she placed it in her coat pocket, something curious happened: it started to shake.

Anita turned to make for the door, not wanting to stay for a moment longer than she needed to in Austin's treasure trove of secrets. But, as she was about to push down the door handle, the conversation she'd had with Anderson in Kingdom came back to her. He'd said, 'if someone stole a cylinder containing someone else's memories, the energy would strain to get back to its rightful owner'.

If that were the case, she had the wrong memory. It had only started to strain when she'd stolen it; it had been still before that. She looked back at the shelf to see which cylinders were straining, so she could select one of those to take with her, but they were all standing entirely still. None of them seemed uncomfortable where they were. She looked frantically around, hoping to find more, but there were none to be seen.

Anita had a horrible moment of clarity: Helena had lied to her. She wasn't here to take back one of Helena's stolen memories; she was here to steal for the Institution. To steal from Austin.

Anita hurried back across the room and replaced the cylinder in the exact location she'd found it, set slightly apart from the others. But, as her hand left the cylinder and it reverted to a still, lifeless object, the door flew open. Amber, Austin and four security guards came hammering in.

Amber took in the scene and reacted instantly, running forward and grabbing Anita by her arms. Anita countered instinctively; she was, after all, an adept Body, and used Amber's forward momentum to flip her onto her back, making her release Anita's arms.

Anita valiantly fought her way through three of the four bodyguards, however, as she reached the fourth, the others recovered, and collectively wrestled her to the ground. Two of them pinned her down with all their weight.

Marcus appeared at the door, aghast as he took in the sight of Anita under a mass of bodies. 'Leave her alone,' he ordered, moving towards them, but Amber intervened, placing herself in his way.

'She was stealing from your father,' she said smugly, her words like poison.

'No, she was not. She was here looking at a photo of Tobias' boat.'

'Then why, when we came through the door, was she reaching for that brass cylinder?' Amber asked triumphantly, gesturing towards the cylinder, that moments before, Anita had held in her hand.

'I was just having a look,' Anita spluttered, gasping for breath, finding it difficult to breathe with such an immense weight holding her to the ground. 'I've never seen cylinders so delicate. I just wanted to see them up close.' She felt faint, desperately trying to refill her lungs.

'Do you really believe that?' laughed Amber, looking at Marcus as though he were a bug to be squashed.

'Yes, I do,' he spat, turning to the so-far-silent Austin standing in the entrance. 'She was looking at this photo of *Aphrodite*,' he said, picking up the picture and waving it in front of Austin's face. 'What's wrong with that?'

'Aside from the fact you brought her here at all, Marcus, and that you left her alone to explore to her heart's content, and that we found her reaching for one of my brass cylinders, nothing, I suppose.' His sarcasm was chilling. 'And why exactly did you show Anita this picture?'

Anita prayed he wouldn't tell Austin about their meditation, or that the boat was a place in her head. She had a feeling it wouldn't be a redeeming factor.

'Because we got talking about boats and sailing and I told her I'd just come across a photo of the most exquisite boat I'd ever seen. Anita asked me to show it to her, so I did.'

'You expect me to believe that someone as manipulative as her came here just to see a photo?' Austin laughed cruelly, exchanging a look with Amber, clearly a commentary on his son's incompetence.

Marcus' temper flared. 'What makes you think Anita's manipulative? I tried to teach her Mind skills, and she's useless at manipulation.'

'Don't be so stupid, Marcus. How else would someone from Anita's background get so close to someone like you if not by manipulation? She was probably feigning ignorance to reinforce the ruse. It's time to see her for who she really is.'

'Don't treat me like a child. Anita is not who you paint her to be. Now let her go, and stop being so melodramatic. There was no harm done. I'm sure if Amber calls off her guards, Anita will apologize for the confusion and we can all move on from this embarrassing misunderstanding.'

'You have a lot to learn,' said Amber. 'Boys, take her back to the castle and put her in a cell.'

'No,' Marcus ordered, 'let her go.'

Everybody ignored him, Austin turning to leave the room, followed by Amber, then the guards, dragging Anita between them.

Anita threw Marcus a last pleading look, mouthing the words, 'I love you,' to him as they took her away.

Austin, it would seem, was right about one thing: she did have a manipulative side.

* * * * *

Cleo hid, crouched behind a rack of artefacts, watching them take Anita away. She'd dragged Marcus to the other side of the room, saying she wanted to show him something. When they'd got there, she'd acted as though she'd misplaced whatever it was and rummaged through a pile of papers. Marcus had lost patience and said he needed to get back to Anita. He'd asked Cleo to give them some space.

Cleo had let him go, hoping Anita had had long enough to explore. But when Marcus was halfway back to the door, Austin, Amber, and four large guards had burst onto the floor, running towards the door, reaching it before the startled Marcus.

Cleo hadn't been able to hear what happened inside, but had watched, appalled, as they dragged her best friend roughly up the stairs towards the entrance, a furious, flapping Marcus in tow.

He kept appealing to Austin, saying, 'Dad, please, don't do this,' but Austin ignored his son's words entirely, carrying on as though nobody had uttered a sound.

The only time Marcus' words had any effect was when he had said, 'Dad, I love her, please don't do this.'

At this revelation, Austin and Amber had rounded on Marcus, each fixing him with a terrifying stare. They'd said nothing, presumably given the location.

They'd turned back and followed the guards up the stairs, Marcus following in their wake.

Cleo had stayed put for a full fifteen minutes after they'd gone, terror and shock fixing her in place. When she was convinced they weren't coming back, she cautiously climbed to her feet and made her way out of the building, making sure nobody saw her leave. The last thing Anita needed was for the only person who knew she'd been taken to be spotted by one of Austin's informants.

Once she was free of the archives, Cleo ran back to town, heading directly for the Temple of the Spirit. The only person she could think to tell was Alexander. She hoped desperately that he was there… she didn't know where else to look if he wasn't.

She reached the temple and raced to the circular slab in the center of the floor. She got down on all fours and pounded the stone, hoping he could hear her. To her amazement, within seconds, the slab in the floor slid aside. Cleo scrambled out of the way in time to see Alexander ascending the stairs.

'Cleo, what is it?' he asked, grabbing her arm.

'It's Anita,' she garbled. 'Austin has her.'

'What? What do you mean?' Alexander looked around, noticing the few people in the temple taking an interest. 'Come on, we should talk downstairs.'

Normally this would be a source of great excitement for Cleo; nobody else she knew had been inside the chambers below the temples. Right now though, she was just grateful that Alexander was here and might be able to help.

They quickly descended the spiral staircase and came out into Alexander's study. He sat Cleo down in one of the large, brown, leather chairs and made her a cup of hot, sweet tea, saying, 'Tell me what happened,' as he did it.

Cleo recounted what had happened. Alexander looked drawn and worried when she finished, sitting opposite her, considering what she'd said.

'There's one more thing,' said Cleo, looking down into her tea, struggling to find the best way to say it. 'As they were leaving and Marcus was trying everything to get Austin to free Anita, Marcus said he loved her. Austin and Amber rounded on him. They looked like they might lock him away too, but they didn't say a thing. They just left, and Marcus followed them.'

'Those words might be all that keeps her alive,' said Alexander, with a pained expression. 'But then again, they're another reason for Austin not to want to let her go…'

* * * * *

Once Cleo had left, Alexander carefully weighed his options. He considered contacting Marcus to try and work with him. He thought about storming over to the castle and demanding Austin release her. He even considered killing Austin, but quickly put that thought aside.

In the end, Alexander reasoned it was most important to maximize the chances that they would keep Anita alive. The best way to do that was to let Austin know that Alexander, along with others, knew she was being held. It would be too risky for Austin to kill her outright, and it would buy Alexander time to work out a way to free her.

Alexander drove to the castle, the light from the windows blazing out into the pitch-black sky. He walked up to the imposing front door and pulled the handle that rang the bell.

Amber answered, looking at him suspiciously. 'Why are you here?' she asked, full of hostile surprise.

'I have something important I need to discuss with Austin.'

She gave him a look that told him to elaborate.

Alexander met her gaze, remaining silent.

'And the important topic of conversation is…?' she said.

'… none of your business,' he replied severely, pushing Amber aside as he swept into the castle. 'Since when have Descendants had to explain themselves to the likes of you?' This was the kind of thing Austin would say, so Alexander hoped it would resonate.

She looked petulantly back at him, but her eyes said she knew she was beaten. 'I'll see if Austin is available.'

A few minutes later, Alexander was standing in front of Austin's desk. Austin pretended not to know why he was there, and made a point of not offering Alexander a seat.

'I have something of a sensitive nature to discuss with you,' said Alexander.

Austin raised his eyebrows in mock surprise. 'Oh?' he said. 'How can I help?'

'It would appear as though you have detained one of my students. I would like you to release her into my custody.'

'Which student is that?' he asked casually, lifting a tumbler of honey colored whiskey to his lips.

Alexander looked at him for a few beats before replying. 'I think we both know I'm referring to Anita. She's close to your son, is she not?'

Austin's nostrils flared. 'Tell me, why is it you think I should release someone who tried to steal from my family's vault into your custody?'

'As I said, she's one of my students, which makes me partially responsible for her. I should like to resolve

267

this quietly and as a matter of urgency, so there is no embarrassment for any party.'

'I see. Well, I'm afraid I can't do that. I'm yet to finish questioning her, and It's important we conduct a thorough investigation into what happened. I'm intrigued why she tried to steal one of my memories, for example.'

'What could Anita possibly want with one of your memories?' Alexander laughed. The laughter didn't reach his eyes.

'I don't know, Alexander. That's what I intend to find out.'

'And when you've found that out? Will you release her into my custody then?'

'That all depends on what I find,' he said. 'I might decide it's best to lock her up for a couple of years instead.'

'I hope that's not the case,' Alexander said, turning to leave. 'Marcus wouldn't be happy.'

Alexander left the castle with mixed emotions. He'd never expected Austin to hand Anita over, and now at least he was unlikely to kill her. But the spiteful look on Austin's face was not something to be taken lightly.

* * * * *

Amber stood over Anita. They had cuffed her hands and feet together, pushed her onto an uncomfortable wooded chair, and attached her hands tightly to the wood. They'd given her no food or anything to drink since they'd tied her up, and after twelve hours of sitting in the same position, her muscles were cramping and her mouth was dry.

'You're quite the troublemaker,' Amber said slowly, threateningly, circling the chair like a shark would its prey. Amber's energy was giddy with anticipation; she would draw this out.

Amber took her time as she walked, high heels clipping menacingly on the slabs of stone. 'And let's not forget that you're quite the manipulator, from what we've seen so far. It would seem you've caught the attention of not only Marcus, but Alexander as well, if our reports are anything to go by. What will Marcus do when he sees pictures of you and Alexander holding hands while walking the streets of Kingdom?'

Anita said nothing. What could she say? Deny she was manipulative? Justify the photos? Anita knew Amber would say or do anything to elicit a reaction. Amber's powers of manipulation surpassed anything Anita could do... she just had to stay calm. One problem at a time.

Even if Marcus saw the photos and freaked out, holding hands with Alexander was a minor offence compared to what Amber and Austin were doing to her now. She was sure such innocent pictures wouldn't change his mind about her. He'd said he loved her. It would take more to turn him against her, at least, she hoped it would.

'Not answering, are we?' Amber said, pausing directly behind Anita and bending over to whisper ominously in her ear. 'Don't worry, I wouldn't want you to, not yet anyway. That would be too easy. Tell me, Anita, why were you trying to steal one of Austin's memories?'

Anita kept silent, looking obstinately forwards as Amber circled round into her peripheral vision. Out of nowhere, Amber raised her hand and swiped it as hard as she could across Anita's face, making a slapping noise that reverberated around the hollow room. Anita's head whipped to the side, face throbbing from the impact.

'I can't tell you how long I've wanted to do that,' Amber purred, continuing to circle, 'and I'm sure you'll be pleased to hear it was everything I'd hoped it would be.'

'Let's try a different question,' Amber continued. 'What do you hope to achieve through your relationship with Marcus? Was it just about getting access to the vault, or do you have something else planned? Maybe you're working with someone? A group of academics? The Institution?'

Anita kept looking forwards, so didn't see that Amber had picked up a whip from the back of the room and was advancing darkly towards her. 'I'll give you one more chance to say something,' said Amber, 'and if you do, I promise to go easy on you. It will ruin my fun, but I like to reward good behavior.'

Anita said nothing. She knew there was nothing she could say that would really help her.

Amber paused for a couple more seconds before raising the whip high into the air, cracking it down onto Anita's unsuspecting legs. It too made a sickening noise on impact that bounced around the empty, grey, windowless room.

Anita let out an involuntary gasp of pain as Amber struck again, this time on her stomach, then a third time across her upper arms. Apart from her cries of pain, Anita uttered not a single sound. She gritted her teeth against the agony, focusing on a small stone on the floor.

She was empty, removed from the skin that sung from the impact of the whip. It was like she was floating above her tied-up form, neither connected to what was happening, nor fully detached. Her energy was the lowest it had ever been… powerless.

* * * * *

The questioning and torture went on for hours. Austin joined Amber for the later stages, waiting for the moment that Anita would break; he was sure she would.

She didn't.

By the end, Amber was furious, having extracted not a single word. Indeed, the only sign that Anita was still alive were the whimpers of pain she uttered at every fresh injury.

Anita's body was covered with wounds; the whip had cut her flesh, she had several broken ribs, a black eye was forming, and still, she wouldn't talk.

'You're losing your touch, Amber,' Austin taunted. 'I wouldn't have thought this one would be a hard nut to crack.'

Austin's ridicule drove Amber over the edge, and she rained blows down on Anita with such ferocity, that by the time she'd finished, Anita was unconscious.

'Stupid bitch,' spat Amber, before regaining her composure, turning towards Austin and smoothing down her pencil skirt. 'Can't we just kill her?'

'Alas, no,' replied Austin sternly, holding Amber's chin, then kissing her, full of dominance. 'Marcus complicates matters, and Alexander knows we have her. He requested we release Anita into his custody. Killing her, I am afraid, is off the table.'

'By the Gods, she gets around. We should've tried to recruit her when we had the chance. Manipulation skills like hers are really quite rare, especially for someone with such profound Body abilities.'

'Indeed, but that doesn't solve the problem of what we should do with her, given that killing her isn't an option.'

'Say she confessed to stealing on behalf of some group or other and lock her up for a few years. Marcus and Alexander will move on.'

'A nice idea, but it won't fly. Marcus has never been interested in a girl for longer than a week or two, and I can't recall Alexander ever sticking his neck out for anyone. I don't think this is going to blow over. Locking her up will lead to more problems.'

'Then what? Let her go?'

'Maybe. But I'm going to make Marcus question her first.'

Amber and Austin turned and left the room, closing the heavy grey door behind them. Anita heard the key turn in the lock and the bolt clunk home. No escape through there, she thought, and no escape anywhere else either. There were no windows and only tiny ventilation holes in the wall. Even if she could get out of her cuffs, there was no way to get out of the cell.

* * * * *

Austin climbed the stairs, photos in hand, and knocked lightly on Marcus' door. The door swung open and Marcus looked at Austin with disgust. 'What do you want?' he sneered.

'I want to talk to you about Anita and then I'd like you to question her for us.'

Marcus laughed coldly. 'Why would I do anything to help you after the way you've treated her? You hauled Anita off like some common criminal, ignoring both my wishes and my judgment. I'm trained, just like you, to identify deception and deceit. I can assure you Anita's shown no signs of either.'

Austin handed Marcus the pictures of Alexander and Anita holding hands in Kingdom. 'No deception or deceit at all?' he asked triumphantly.

Marcus took a long look at the photos before casting them aside. 'All I see is Alexander dragging Anita through the streets of Kingdom, during a visit that happened several months ago, before we were properly seeing each other. Alexander and Anita are friends; she had lessons with him in the Spirit disciplines.

'What did you expect me to do,' he smirked, 'fly into a jealous rage because Anita's holding another man's hand? Show me pictures of them kissing, and maybe then you'll get your reaction, but this means nothing at all.'

Marcus was jealous, very jealous, but there would be time for that later. First, he needed to get Anita out of here. 'I'll question her for you, so we can clear this whole thing up and let her go.'

Marcus pushed past his perturbed father and made his way to the dungeons. Austin followed him, trying to keep up while maintaining a dignified pace.

Marcus burst into the dungeon, snapping, 'Where is she,' at Amber. Amber looked to Austin, who was coming down the stairs. Austin nodded.

'Right this way,' said Amber, leading the way down the corridor, unlocking the cell with Anita inside. 'Knock when you want to come out,' she said, standing aside and motioning Marcus through the door.

Marcus saw Anita's slumped form and rushed past Amber, hearing the door shut and lock behind him as he sank to his knees in front of her, lifting her head with his hands.

'By the Gods, what have they done to you?'

She looked at him through her swollen eyes and smiled weakly.

Marcus breathed a sigh of relief; they hadn't broken her spirit. 'I'm so sorry, Anita. This is all my fault; I should never have left you alone in the vault.'

'Don't say that...' Her voice was a whisper.

'What were you doing?' he asked softly.

'The cylinders... they're well crafted. The energy equipment at the observatory is made of brass. It needs to be precise. I was going to ask who made them.'

She tried to take a deep breath, but winced at the pain in her chest. 'I was about to pick one up when Amber, Austin and the cronies burst in, saw me reaching for the shelf, and assumed I was trying to steal something. The rest you know.'

'I'm so sorry, Anita,' he repeated. 'I'll get you out of here, I promise. You haven't done anything wrong; they can't keep you here.'

'I'm sure they'll find a way if they want to,' she said in a low, cynical voice.

'I'll find a way,' he whispered, placing a gentle kiss on her forehead. 'I have to go, but I promise I'll get you out. I love you.'

'I love you too,' she said, in a voice so small it was barely even a whisper.

CHAPTER 15

Marcus left the castle without stopping to talk to his father. Much as he hated him, it was time to work with Alexander; he had power as a ruling Descendant that Marcus did not.

Marcus made his way to the Spirit Temple and rapped on the stone covering Alexander's chambers, not having to wait long for a response. 'Marcus? What are you doing here?' said Alexander, as the stone slid aside.

Marcus stood silently for a moment, not quite believing he was about to say what he was. 'I'm here because I need your help to free Anita. I saw you at the castle earlier and listened to some of your conversation with Dad. I know you want to free Anita, and I can't do it on my own. You have power that I don't and the only way we'll get her back is if we force Dad's hand.'

'I went to the castle to make sure your dad keeps her alive. He and Amber would kill her if they thought they could get away with it.'

'I, uh...' Marcus wasn't sure what to say. It had opened his eyes, seeing the state of Anita, so he supposed there was no reason to assume Alexander was wrong. But he couldn't believe his father would murder someone without good reason... 'All I know is that Anita's in a bad way. Amber didn't show her any kindness during the interrogation. She seems to have a couple of broken ribs and wounds everywhere.'

Alexander's hands clenched into fists. 'What are they accusing her of?'

'They think she was trying to steal a brass cylinder of Dad's. It contains some memory. Anita says she wanted to look at the brass work; she said she noticed it because of her work at the observatory. I'm not sure Dad will buy that though.'

'How do you suggest we go about freeing her if they won't believe her?'

'I think we need to use your power as a Descendant to threaten Dad. The one thing he cares about more than anything is his reputation. If you threaten to embarrass him publicly, then he may opt to let her go.'

Alexander perked up. 'What do you suggest I use to embarrass him?'

'Luckily, I've been researching my family's history. There's a lot I've cross-referenced with other sources to get the real story, including what caused Mum and Dad to separate, for example.'

Alexander leaned forward. 'Go on.'

'It turns out Dad was having an affair.'

'With who?'

'I'll only tell you that on a need to know basis. It should be enough just to threaten him.'

Alexander nodded. 'What do you want me to do?'

'I'll go back to the castle, tell Dad I think Anita's innocent, and explain the misunderstanding. When he says he thinks I'm naïve and don't know what I'm talking about, I'll tell him you're willing to blackmail him over the affair if he doesn't let her go. Hopefully that should be enough. If not, then we have to go through with it, and we keep digging up embarrassments until he's willing to set her free.'

'You would do that to your own father?'

'If he keeps Anita locked up, yes. I love her, and she's done nothing wrong. It's my fault she was in the vault; I've got to get her out.'

* * * * *

Marcus went back to the castle, stood outside Austin's office, took a deep breath, and knocked sharply, walking in without waiting for an answer. He entered to see Amber and Austin sitting on a sofa drinking whiskey, laughing in a way that made Marcus cold.

'Marcus,' said Austin, surprised that his son, who usually waited obediently at the door, had waltzed straight in. 'Join us for a drink,' he said, recovering.

'No, thank you. I have something I need to talk to you about... privately,' he said, looking Austin straight in the eye.

Amber got up to leave, shooting Austin a knowing look that Marcus chose to ignore.

'Dad, you need to let Anita go. She's done nothing wrong. She was looking at the brass work on those cylinders, nothing more. You must know how rare they are, and she has an interest because of her job at the observatory. If you want to punish anyone, then punish me. I was the one that took her to the vault and then left her alone. If I hadn't, this would never have happened.'

'And why did you leave her alone?' Austin asked.

'Because we bumped into Cleo, and true to form, she was snooping around. I went out to ask for some privacy and walked her to the stairs. She went back upstairs, presumably to where she'd been working. As I was walking back to the vault, I stopped to look at an artefact that caught my eye, and that's when you burst onto the floor.'

His story wasn't entirely accurate, but he didn't want to get Cleo into trouble too. It was best to downplay her presence. Marcus was sure it was all innocent, but Austin would be unlikely to see it that way.

'And you think it's a coincidence that Cleo happened to be at the archives when you took Anita there?'

'Yes. Cleo's at the archives almost every day and has been since before you showed me the vault. It would have been surprising had she not been there. Anyway, it was an impromptu visit by Anita and I, and Anita couldn't have got a message to Cleo to meet her there without me knowing.'

Austin seemed to accept this. 'So you want me to just let her go? You know I can't do that, not when she has such a hold over you. She's using you, Marcus. We have to find out what she's using you for.'

'Why do you see a conspiracy everywhere you look? Can't Anita like me for the same reasons I like her? We have fun together and have a lot in common. Most people either suck up to me or are terrified of me, but Anita's normal; it's refreshing. Unlike you, I don't want people to treat me differently.'

'You're acting like a naïve child. Why can't you trust that I know best?'

'Because you don't always know best, and one day I'll be a ruling Descendant. I can't stay in your shadow forever.'

'You're not even close to being ready to rule,' said Austin. 'You're a lost boy, led astray by a girl. You can't even admit you might be wrong when we caught her red-handed.'

This was the point of no return, but Marcus knew that to get anywhere with his father he had to fight fire with fire, it was the only way to win his respect. 'If you don't let her go, then Alexander will expose details of the affair you were having just before you and Mum separated.'

He said it then stopped dead, the air around them seeming to crackle as Austin took in the words.

'What affair?' he asked.

'Don't play with me, Dad. You know exactly what I'm talking about.'

Austin looked at him, impressed. 'You would do that to your own family? Bring embarrassment down on yourself as well as me?'

'You're trying to play the family card when you locked up Anita, who I love? You ignored my wishes to set her free, beat her up, and then refused to listen to her perfectly reasonable explanation. I thought you'd do better than that.'

* * * * *

Marcus' resolve was impressive. The look in his eye reminded Austin of his father, Tobias, and it filled him with pride. He knew now that Marcus had it in him to enter the family business. If he was happy to blackmail his own father, then only the Gods knew what else he was capable of.

However, it was important, now that Marcus had found his teeth, to keep him on side. Austin had to bring Marcus firmly under his wing. Amber would have to take orders from him; she wouldn't like that, but Marcus had to see incremental benefits, or there was a danger he would defect. And, much as it pained him, Anita would have to be set free. He could deal with her later, after he'd driven a wedge between her and

Marcus. He was confident that wouldn't be too difficult, not now that Marcus had shown his true colors.

'Alright, consider her freed. You can take her home if you'd like.'

* * * * *

Marcus froze, holding his breath. Was he dreaming, or had that really been so easy?

Austin laughed. 'Son, I'm proud of the way you've dealt with this. You've leveraged a piece of delicate information to your advantage; I couldn't have done it better myself. Only... does Alexander really know about the affair?'

'He knows there was one, but he doesn't know who it was with. I said I would only tell him if he needed to know.'

'But you know who it was with?'

'I guess we'll never know now, will we,' said Marcus, smugly, turning for the door. 'Come on, I need you to call off your dogs.'

Austin chuckled, getting up from his desk.

They made their way to the dungeon, Marcus still not totally convinced he wasn't dreaming. A part of him worried Austin was playing some cruel joke and was about to change his mind. They reached the desk where Amber was talking to one of her guards and Marcus said, 'Amber, please come with me. We're setting Anita free.'

Amber sniggered, clearly about to rebuke him. But she looked up and saw Austin, a smile playing about his lips, waiting with interest to see what she would do next. Amber narrowed her eyes, face setting in fury.

'Of course,' she replied through gritted teeth. Marcus was trying to keep his expression even, but couldn't totally hide his amazement. Who would've thought that blackmailing his father would have such positive effects?

He followed Amber to the cell and watched while she uncuffed Anita's hands and feet. Anita looked worried, unsure what was going on, whether torture was to follow.

'Dad's letting you go,' said Marcus, in a gentle voice, helping her to her feet. But as she tried to put weight on her legs, they gave way. She would've fallen if Marcus hadn't scooped her into his arms and carried her out of the room.

He didn't stop for a second on the way to his car, still concerned Austin would change his mind. Anita said nothing, resting her head limply on his chest.

Marcus placed her on the back seat, being as careful of her broken ribs and bruised flesh as he could. He sat opposite her, taking her hand as his driver set off towards Anita's home.

* * * * *

Anita said nothing on the short journey, her energy not responding as she would have expected to freedom. She was still empty and drained, and although she knew she should be thankful to Marcus for getting her out, she felt nothing.

They arrived at Cordelia's and Marcus picked Anita up again, pushed the gate open, and walked to the back door. It was ajar as usual, and he didn't stop before making his way inside, calling for Cordelia.

'Hello?' he said urgently. 'Cordelia? Are you here? I need your help.'

Cordelia came rushing out of the sitting room, where she and Cleo had been talking by the fire. 'By the Gods,' she said, seeing the state of Anita. 'What have they done to you?'

Cleo burst into tears at the sight of her best friend.

'Bring her in here,' said Cordelia. 'Cleo, clear the sofa so Marcus can put her down.'

Cleo did as she was told and Marcus placed Anita on the sofa, then knelt on the floor and took her hand protectively.

Cordelia rushed to the kitchen to get a glass of water and a sponge. They needed to hydrate her, and Anita wouldn't be able to sit up and drink normally in her current state.

Anita was aware of the activity around her, but still felt detached. Her energy had deserted her; it was even an effort to breathe. She lay motionless and let them fret.

She knew she'd be alright; the wounds would heal with time and the emotional scars would fade. Right now, though, that didn't seem to matter, and she wallowed in her stupidity. She should have realized what Helena was up to. She deserved to be locked up, given her foolish, reckless actions. She deserved the pain. Why wouldn't they stop fussing and leave her alone?

* * * * *

After Cordelia had fed her some sugary water, Anita drifted off to sleep. Marcus, Cordelia, and Cleo discussed what to do next. They'd been debating it for some time when Cordelia put her foot down.

'It's simple,' she said, shutting down any further conversation on the matter. 'She will stay here and I will look after her until she is better. I will allow few visitors in that time, and even you two can't be here all hours. She needs to rest, recuperate physically and spiritually, and come to terms with what has happened. She cannot do that with people around her twenty-four seven. Do I make myself clear?'

Cleo and Marcus wanted to argue, but Cordelia's body language told them not to. They nodded their silent agreement.

'Good, I'm glad. Now, thank you for your concern, but I will take it from here. Come back tomorrow, and if Anita wants to see you, I will let you in. If not, you'll have to wait until she's ready.'

They were gearing up to argue again, but Cordelia fixed them with a look that made them think twice.

'Okay,' said Cleo, turning to Marcus. 'Come on. I'm sure you've got some recuperating to do too, and there's nothing more we can do for Anita at the moment. Cordelia has it under control.'

'Alright,' he said in a strained voice, 'but I'll be back early tomorrow to see her.'

'That's fine, but I'll only let you in if she wants to see you.'

Cleo took Marcus' arm and gently but firmly steered him out of the house. 'See you tomorrow, Cordelia. Let us know if there's anything at all we can do.'

* * * * *

Marcus and Cleo said goodbye when they reached the gate, Marcus climbing into his car, Cleo resisting the temptation to ask for a blow by blow account of what had happened. Marcus slumped in the back seat, looking tired and drawn, and Cleo watched as the car pulled away. This couldn't have been easy for him either, she supposed… Cleo headed for the temples, to tell Alexander all she knew.

283

* * * * *

Alexander rushed to Cordelia's as soon as he heard. He couldn't quite believe that Marcus' plan had worked, but was relieved that it had. Cordelia, surprised to see a second Descendant on her doorstep, had reluctantly let him in, but only after he'd agreed that, under no circumstances, would he do anything to wake her. Cordelia left them alone, satisfied that Alexander would keep his word.

He entered the sitting room and took in Anita's battered body, lying lifeless on the sofa. Her energy was so low that it was barely recognizable. He walked slowly, silently to her side, crouching by her head, delicately moving a strand of hair off her swollen face. There were no tingles now, no excitement at his touch, but her energy lifted a little at the contact, or at least, he told himself that's what it was.

He sat by her side for an hour, not moving a muscle, willing her energy to recover, but it stayed where it was, with no movement at all. Eventually, he got up, brushed his lips lightly against her forehead, and left, thanking Cordelia and saying he would be back in the morning to see how she was.

As he was leaving, he paused, turning back to Cordelia. 'Her energy is dangerously low. We have to do this at her pace. Don't let Marcus force her into doing anything more quickly than she wants to; she's going to need time.'

Cordelia nodded. 'Goodnight, Alexander. I will no doubt see you tomorrow.'

* * * * *

The following morning, Anita woke and sat bolt upright, the pain hitting her like an express train. She hadn't been able to feel it the night before, but now it was... her mind went fuzzy, she worried she would faint. She froze, waiting for the pain to abate a little before gingerly swinging her legs to the floor.

She stood, carefully testing that her legs would take her weight before fully committing. Another shot of pain stabbed through her chest, but this time she was expecting it, which somehow made it more bearable. She hobbled to the door and made for the stairs, but Cordelia heard her footsteps and headed her off before she could reach them.

'Good morning,' said Cordelia, appearing from the kitchen. 'I'm glad you feel well enough to walk, but what exactly do you think you're doing?'

'I'm going to my bedroom,' Anita said weakly. It was taking all her energy and concentration to make it to the stairs.

'May I ask why, when you have everything you need down here?'

'I want to be alone,' she said, now tackling the stairs, one painful upward step at a time.

'Alright. I'll bring you breakfast; you need to eat.'

Anita didn't answer. She knew it would be futile to argue and was more concerned with reaching the top of the stairs by herself than with Cordelia bringing her food. She reached the top and paused, waiting for the worst of the pain to ease before pressing on towards her room. Luckily, given the size of the cottage, this didn't present too much more of a challenge.

She reached her bed and lay carefully on top of the covers; it was too much effort to crawl under them. She curled up, bringing her knees to her chest, and cried.

Anita stayed in her room, refusing to see anyone but Cordelia for a full week. She fluctuated between sobbing uncontrollably and staring blankly into space for the first two days, the sobbing doing nothing to help the pain in her ribs.

When she slept, she had flashbacks of Amber torturing her, Austin's cruel face looming in the back of her consciousness. When she was awake, her stupidity consumed her. How hadn't she seen through Helena? And the guilt of lying to Marcus… She didn't love him, not yet anyway, and Amber had been right, she had been manipulating him.

She heard Marcus and Cleo downstairs demanding to see her, but Cordelia sent them away day after day, saying they had to do this at Anita's pace; they couldn't force her to do things she didn't want to do.

Alexander's visits were different. Instead of demanding to see her, he asked if she wanted visitors. He asked questions about what she was eating and if her energy was bouncing back. Anita's energy was coming back, slowly, but it was nowhere near its normal level.

She heard Alexander explain to Cordelia that it would take a while for her to recover. She was a Body and currently unable to exercise, the thing that would normally lift her spirits. He suggested to Cordelia that she encourage Anita to meditate instead, to help with her psychological healing.

Cordelia was careful to talk to visitors at the bottom of the stairs, so Anita could hear their words. Anita could decide for herself what she wanted to do and not do. Taking Alexander's advice, she began to mediate. It helped clear her mind, her anger at herself fading, becoming less consuming.

After a week in her room, Anita ventured out, heading downstairs to the kitchen. The pain in her ribs had mellowed, the cuts and bruises healing, the swelling in her face gone. She made herself a sandwich and took it to the sitting room, where she sat down by the fire.

As she finished her first complete meal since coming home, there was a knock on the door. She heard Cleo's voice searching for Cordelia.

'Cleo,' Anita called, her voice cracking as she spoke.

Cleo heard her and came rushing in, embracing her. 'Ouch,' said Anita, Cleo a little overzealous with the pressure of her hug.

'Sorry, but I'm so happy to see you up and about. I've been so worried about you, we all have: Marcus, Alexander, Bass, Cordelia, Elistair, everyone. How are you feeling?'

'I've been better, but I'm getting there. My energy is picking up. That's been the worst thing… I haven't had the will to get out of bed. Until this morning, I was either totally empty, or full of anger and loathing. Today I woke up and felt a bit better.

'It's so good to see you. Thank you for all your help. It must have been terrifying, trying to get out of the archives.'

Cleo laughed. 'Probably not as terrifying as being tied up and tortured,' she said, then, realizing what she'd said, followed it with, 'Sorry, didn't mean to bring that up like that.'

Anita smiled. 'It's alright. That's what happened, after all. Anyway, what have I missed?' she asked, changing the subject. 'Fill me in on all the gossip.'

'Well, to be honest, everything pales into insignificance next to what happened to you, but Marcus and Alexander seem to have made up. Or, at least they can tolerate spending time together, so that's good, I suppose.

'A couple of council kids had a party and trashed their dad's three hundred-year-old energy meter; it was a particularly fine piece, apparently. Austin and Amber have gone to Kingdom, and everyone's speculating as to why… sorry… didn't mean to bring them up again.' She paused. 'To be honest, I'm more concerned with how you're doing and if there's anything I can do to help?'

Anita averted her gaze, blinking away the first prick of tears. 'Not right now. I need to work out what to do about Marcus and Alexander, but I can't face them yet. You could come for a walk with me though? I'm dying to get out of the house.'

Cleo jumped at the offer. 'Maybe I'll be able to keep up with you now,' she said, helping Anita to her feet.

CHAPTER 16

Anita spent the next couple of weeks building her strength, both physically and mentally. She went for long walks with Cleo and spent hours meditating in the garden. However, she refused to see either Marcus or Alexander until she was feeling more like herself and had had time to decide what to do.

She'd told Cleo everything; how Helena had approached her, asking for help, and that Helena had known about Anita's parents all along. Cleo deserved to know.

Anita had expected Cleo to react badly, to tell her she was stupid to have gone along with someone as dubious as Helena, but she didn't. Cleo had said she understood. She'd said Anita was the kind of person who needed to act, especially if everyone else was shying away from action. Helena had offered her a way to do that, so it wasn't surprising that Anita had taken the bait.

Cleo said if it had been her, she wouldn't have turned Helena down the first time. She would've bitten off Helena's right arm to have found out information about her parents. Cleo assuaged Anita's worries, saying everyone made mistakes, that nobody's perfect, and that as far as ruses went, Helena's was pretty believable. Cleo told her not to be so hard on herself.

After a couple of weeks, Anita felt more like herself again, ready to let people back into her life. The time was fading her scars, and Anita was starting to forgive herself. She turned her attention to what she should do about Marcus and Alexander.

They both still came to visit every morning, having settled into a routine of who arrived when, to avoid being there together. Cordelia turned them away every time without fail, saying that Anita would let them know when she was ready to see them. She'd had a couple of near misses, where they'd altered their visiting time for whatever reason.

Anita had had to duck behind a tree on one occasion, to make sure that Alexander didn't see her. Of course he would have known she was there, but he'd respected her wishes, continuing into the house to see Cordelia as normal. He'd returned, again, not stopping, a couple of minutes later.

After a great deal of consideration, Anita decided to see Marcus first; she was his girlfriend, after all. He'd also been the one to rescue her, and although he didn't know it, she'd deceived him. She owed him a lot.

The following morning, Anita sat in the garden at Marcus' normal visiting time, on a bench near her usual yoga spot. She sensed him before she saw him and steeled herself as the sound of his footsteps disappeared onto the grass.

As he rounded the corner of the cottage, he saw Anita and stopped dead, blinking, mouth falling open. When he was sure it was really her, he flew across the lawn to where she sat and dropped to his knees in front of her. He hugged her, pulling her head to his shoulder.

'Anita, thank the Gods you're alright. I'm so, so sorry. How are you?' he garbled into her hair, his energy disbelieving and full of guilt.

She pulled back and smiled at him, running her hand down the side of his face. 'Marcus, this wasn't your fault. It was mine. I should've respected that you took me to a place of great importance to your family and should've known not to pry.

'I'm so grateful that you showed me the picture; if anyone should be sorry, it should be me.' Tears of shame and regret welled up in Anita's eyes, bursting free, trickling down her pale cheeks.

Marcus looked aghast. 'Dad locked you up and tortured you when you'd done nothing wrong. You have nothing to be sorry for.' He moved to sit next to her, pulling her into his arms, softly stroking her hair, willing her to come to her senses. 'Anita, please don't blame yourself. Dad's reaction was crazy. It was unforgiveable. I'm just happy you're still able to stand the sight of me.'

His kindness caused the tears to flow vigorously, and she pulled herself closer to his chest, Marcus wrapping his arms more tightly around her. He bowed his head forward, kissing the top of her head, his warmth radiating through her.

The tears finally stopped, and Marcus helped Anita up, taking her inside. He made them a pot of tea and they sat on the old, worn sofa next to the fire. Anita cuddled into him and Marcus gently stroked her hair.

They talked intermittently, sitting for periods in silence, just enjoying the contact with the other, until Marcus told her quietly that he had to leave. She kissed him, his lips soft and comforting. She didn't want him to go.

'Can't you stay?' she asked, willing his answer to be yes, her forehead furrowed with distress. 'Just for a little longer.'

Marcus faltered, his energy anguished. 'I've got to go. I'm going to be late as it is, but I'll be back as soon as I can, I promise.'

'Where are you going?' she asked, hoping to find an argument to make him stay.

He hesitated, obviously battling with what to tell her. Resolve settled over him, a worried look spreading across his face. 'I'm going to meet Dad,' he said sheepishly.

'What?' Anita breathed, her mind muddled at his words, her body sending a shot of adrenaline through her veins.

He looked guilty and embarrassed, but he continued. 'Since I blackmailed Dad to make him release you, he's developed a newfound respect for me. He's involving me with his business activities, and Amber even has to take orders from me now. The relationship is far from good with either of them, but I'm learning so much that'll be invaluable when I'm a ruling Descendant.'

The little color she'd had drained from Anita's face. She was living a nightmare. After everything Austin had done, how could Marcus be working with him? How could Marcus be closer to him now than he had been before? She went cold, started to shake. Marcus tried to pull her back towards him, but she pushed him away. She just wanted him to go.

Whereas moments before she'd felt safe in his embrace, now she was scared. 'I'll see you later,' she said, pulling her knees up to her chest, closing herself off to him.

Marcus deflated. 'I… I have to go, but I'll explain everything later,' he said. 'I'll be back as soon as I can.'

She nodded, and he placed a soft kiss on her cheek, but she barely responded. She was a different person from the girl who'd kissed him just moments before.

He got up and made for the door. Anita's energy plummeted as he went.

As soon as Marcus left, Anita got up and headed for the door. She needed to get out, to do something, to think. She ran as soon as she left the house, not knowing where she was going, ignoring the dull pain in her chest.

She couldn't believe it; was he choosing Austin over her? After everything they'd been through? After they had beaten her to within an inch of her life? The thoughts spun round and round.

Anita halted abruptly, realizing she'd run to the temples, the ancient buildings climbing majestically into the sky. She ran straight past the Temple of the Body and headed to the Spirit Temple instead; meditation would help. She settled down at the back of the temple, in the place she and Alexander used to meditate, and closed her eyes.

The news from Marcus had taken her by surprise, but when she thought about it, it would be both difficult and dangerous for Marcus to cut all ties with Austin straight away.

She'd never, not for a second, entertained the thought that Marcus would go back to work with Austin. She'd wondered if father and son would ever even speak again. She'd thought they might have a similar relationship to that of Austin and Melia, avoiding each other. But maybe she should give Marcus a chance to explain.

Maybe he hated his father too. Maybe he was stepping closer to him only because it would work to his advantage in the long run. Or maybe he was doing it to make sure Austin didn't come after her again… She'd overreacted to the news. She should hear him out.

Anita was about to get up and go back to Cordelia's, when she felt Alexander's powerful energy enter the temple. She closed her eyes and pretended to meditate, not ready to see him yet, especially as she was so confused about Marcus.

Alexander saw Anita and paused, leaning against a pillar, watching her rise and fall as she breathed long, slow breaths. He toyed with the idea of sitting down opposite her, joining her meditation. But aside from that being an invasion of her privacy, he knew he had to respect her wishes; she'd talk to him when she was ready. He dragged himself away, heading to the temple's center, and descended into his chambers.

Anita watched his graceful, flowing movements as he went. She couldn't deny her feelings for him, the ache in her chest. She craved the feel of him, the smell of him, longed to meditate with him, his presence in her mind like a heady, potent drug. She wanted to wrap herself around him, to taste him... she... had to stop.

After everything that had happened with Marcus, after she'd manipulated him and lied to him, she didn't want to abandon him, not now, when he was so vulnerable to his father.

CHAPTER 17

The next few weeks were hard for Anita. She wanted to make things work with Marcus: how could she want anything else given what he'd done to get her out? But he was falling ever more under Austin's influence, his views becoming more radical and more entrenched.

She sought the calm safety of the Spirit Temple and started meditating there every day. She told herself it was nothing to do with Alexander, but every day she sensed him, watching her from afar. He never came over, giving her the space she needed, but she had to hide the spike in her energy whenever she felt him there.

It was a beautiful late Autumn day, the sun sparkling low in the sky, the air crisp and sharp, the ground covered in leaves that crackled under every footstep. Anita was lost in her thoughts as she walked to the Spirit Temple for her usual meditation, wrapped up warmly, only her face exposed to the wind.

As she approached the temples, she looked up, sensing powerful energy ahead. She caught sight of Helena descending the steps from the Body Temple, conversing animatedly with someone Anita didn't recognize. She froze, her energy turning to hatred, anger at Helena, and disgust at herself flooding back.

Anita pushed the emotions aside, looking around for somewhere to hide; she wasn't ready to face Helena yet. Given the limited options, she selected a large oak tree, scrambling behind it before Helena spotted her. Helena passed, not seeing Anita, or at least not letting on if she had, and disappeared, still deep in conversation.

Anita had been wrestling with what to do about Helena. She'd considered confronting her, demanding to know what she'd been playing at. She imagined telling Helena she knew it was one of Austin's memories that Helena had been trying to steal. Anita tried to picture her reaction.

In the end, she'd decided the best course of action was not to do anything. The thing that would annoy Helena the most would be not knowing what had happened. No doubt she'd heard the rough story on the grapevine, but not to hear it straight from the horse's mouth would be killing her.

Helena had no problem with confrontation, in fact, she enjoyed it. She hated being kept in the dark, so that was exactly what Anita would do. Anita still wanted to know what the memory was about, but there was no chance Helena would tell her, and nobody else but Austin knew.

Anita waited to make sure Helena was definitely gone before proceeding to the Temple of the Spirit, sitting cross legged in her normal spot. She didn't have to wait long before Alexander appeared and she smiled, not making any attempt to hide the effect he had on her. His energy rose in response and without stopping to think, she sent a nudge to the edge of his energy field.

He responded immediately, striding over to where she sat, sinking down in front of her and taking her hands. A delicious jolt of electric energy hit her.

'I've been so worried about you,' he said softly. 'How are you feeling?'

'I'm getting there,' she said, enjoying the closeup view of his face, especially those glorious eyes. 'How are you doing?'

He looked at her indulgently. 'How am I doing? I'm fine.'

Alexander dropped her hands, sensing others about to walk into the temple. 'We shouldn't talk here,' he said. 'I don't want Marcus to hear rumors, especially now he's working more closely with Austin.'

Anita nodded and Alexander led her to the center of the temple, the stone above his chambers sliding aside. They descended the steps, Anita excited to see what lay beneath for the first time.

They entered a room that housed Alexander's desk and several worn leather chairs. It was crammed full of books and pictures, but had a warm, cozy character, the fire in the corner reminding Anita of home.

'It's amazing,' she said, wandering around, looking at the contents of the shelves.

'I'm glad you like it,' he said, tracking her every move. 'I can't take credit though, I've hardly touched it since I took over from Philip. All this stuff belonged either to him or previous Descendants. I've barely started working through everything. It's terrible, I'm probably sitting on a treasure trove.'

'A happy task,' she said, spotting a rare energy book and taking it off the shelf to flick through the pages. 'Quite a significant treasure trove if this book is anything to go by,' she said, putting it carefully back on the shelf. She turned to look at him. 'What do you know about what's going on between Marcus and Austin?' she asked abruptly, his energy telling her she'd caught him off guard.

He took a deep breath. 'From what I can tell, Marcus is being brought further and further under Austin's wing. Since he convinced Austin to free you, their relationship has changed; Austin seems to respect Marcus now, in a way that he didn't before. He's even making Amber take orders from Marcus, not a move he would've played lightly. It's probably to make Marcus feel like he has some control.

'In reality, he has no control at all. Marcus is being groomed to follow in Austin's footsteps, as Austin was by his father. No doubt Marcus thinks he's learning invaluable lessons that'll help him in the future. He may even have some naïve notion that he'll be able to bring Austin round, so he'll do something about the energy when everything gets really bad.

'The truth is, Austin has Marcus exactly where he wants him. He'll get Marcus so involved in his *business* activities that he can't get out. He'll encourage Marcus to do things for him, each more dubious that the last, only a small step further than what he's done before.

'Eventually, Austin will force Marcus to make a choice, to do something so bad that he passes the point of no return. At that point, Austin will have won. Marcus will no doubt hate himself for a time and wonder how he's become entangled in such a web of deceit. He'll tell himself that the only hope of a way out is to go further into the clutches of the trap.'

Alexander paused, running a hand through his hair. 'You may still have influence over him, but you'll have to be careful how you use it. For the first time in his life, Marcus' father is treating him like he's worth something, like the Mind line is lucky to have him. Marcus has wanted his father's acceptance forever; it would take something significant to make him give that up.'

Anita sat in one of the leather armchairs, digesting Alexander's words. 'Do you think an ultimatum would work?' she asked carefully, avoiding his eyes.

'No,' he said. 'The worst way to deal with Marcus is to force his hand. He needs to learn for himself what Austin's doing and decide if he wants to be part of it. It'll take time. He's unlikely to give up Austin right now, not when he finally feels like he's getting somewhere.'

'Then what should I do? His views are more extreme by the day. He can't see the things he and Austin are doing are wrong. They're forcing farmers, who fear losing their farms, whose crops are failing, who feel responsible for the impending food shortages, to pay full rent. They're taking livestock as payment.

'They have a responsibility to the people of the world and all they care about is collecting what they think they're owed.' She stood and started pacing.

'All you can do is to suggest an alternative,' said Alexander. 'Every time you take him head on, he'll go defensive. He'll try to justify his actions rather than consider the wisdom of your words.'

Anita nodded; what Alexander said made perfect sense. She struggled with such a round-the-houses approach, but she knew she'd have to try.

'Anita, regardless of what happens, it won't be your fault.'

She turned away, tears filling her eyes. He closed the space between them.

'Austin's been setting this up since Marcus was born. You can't expect to bring him round on your own.'

Anita turned to face him, standing so close that his breath skipped across her face. She met his electric eyes, heady at their proximity, her energy leaping, as did his. Anita bowed her head, stepped forward, and wrapped her arms around him. He pulled her tightly to his chest.

Anita felt full within the circle of his muscular arms, his lips on her hair.

They stood, cocooned together, neither wanting to pull away. Eventually, Anita pulled back, looking up at him. 'Meditate with me?'

'Of course,' he said. 'I want to show you something though. There's somewhere special I want us to meditate.'

Anita smiled, intrigued. 'Where?'

'Just come with me,' he said, taking her hand and pulling her further into his chambers, into a room with an enormous, luxurious looking bed.

She faltered as he pulled her towards the bed, grateful and surprised to see the shelves next to it swinging towards them, revealing a secret passage behind. Alexander stuck his head through and looked both ways to check there was no one there.

The passage was dimly lit with lanterns along the ground and Anita wondered who maintained them... surely not the Descendants.

They made their way through a maze of tunnels, pausing only once, when Anita thought she heard something. Alexander waved it away, explaining that it was probably someone up in the temple above.

They finally arrived at a large, ornate door. Alexander turned to Anita, smiling conspiratorially, then pushed its heavy baulk open, standing back to let her enter first.

She walked through and looked around. Here too, the only light came from candle-filled lanterns, so it took her a few moments to understand her surroundings in the dim glow. She'd stepped into a columned space that circled around something in an open area in the middle. She could hear the soothing sound of running water, and, as she stepped forward, through a beautifully constructed archway, she finally realized where they were. She spun violently to face Alexander.

Alexander laughed. 'It took you a while.'

'We're directly below the points of the temples?'

He nodded. 'It's a shame more people don't get to see it; it's really quite beautiful.'

She looked around. He was right; it was. A raised pool sat in the center, which was somehow surrounded by lush green grass. Climbing plants trailed sweet-smelling flowers as they wound round the columns and reached for the ceiling. There were rose bushes, blooming with enormous white flowers, not the tight, uniformed variety, but the looser, freer kind. And there was a tiny pinhole in the ceiling, that, by some trick, let in enough light to illuminate every inch of the pool's shimmering surface.

The pinhole connected the sacred pool below to the temple points above.

'What do you think?'

'It's incredible,' she replied. 'It's so calm, like the energy is totally even, without even the smallest ripple.'

'It is even,' he said, 'in the same way that the pool under the observatory absorbs the energy noise in the area there, this pool does the same thing here. It has a more potent effect here, given how secluded it is. There's less background energy to start with and the place has a special balance, being under the points of the temples.'

'We're meditating here?' she asked excitedly.

He nodded. 'I want to share something with you and here seems like the best place to do it.'

'This isn't what you wanted to show me?'

'No. I want to show you something inside my head.'

She smiled, moving, so she was standing right next to the pool, and lay down on her back; she didn't feel vulnerable with him.

He hesitated. 'Anita…'

She turned her head and sent him a calm, level look. 'Sush,' she said, stopping any further words, placing her hand beside her, ready for him to hold.

He moved to her and lay on his back, arm down by his side, taking her waiting hand. He turned his face to look at her, curved his head forward so their foreheads touched, and they both closed their eyes.

Alexander determined their destination, Anita relishing the trust she had for him, letting him take her wherever he wanted to go. The intensity in this pose was astounding, the energy coursing between them almost painful, like it might rip them to shreds. She felt… powerful, light, like she was floating off the ground, Alexander floating with her, supporting her, lifting her up.

The meditation settled, and Anita looked around, confused, wondering if something had gone wrong.

'Hey,' said Alexander, 'everything okay?'

'I have literally never felt better,' said Anita. 'The energy, it's… you can feel it too?'

'It's extraordinary,' he breathed.

Anita sat up a little to make sure she wasn't missing anything. 'The pool is a place in your head?' she asked.

Alexander pushed up on his elbows, making sure he kept hold of her hand. 'It's more than just a place in my head,' he said softly. 'This is my Centre.'

'This is your Centre?' she repeated, stunned, trying to work out what this news meant. 'Why?' she asked; the best she could come up with.

'Why is anyone's Centre what it is? People say we inherit them from our ancestors… but it's so personal… Philip would never tell me what any of his were. And so few people know how to meditate properly... You're the only one that knows any of mine,' he said.

She turned her head to look at him, rolling towards him, placing her free hand on the side of his face. She looked into his blue eyes, a reflection of her longing, and dipped her head to kiss his lips.

As their lips touched, a rush of tingles raced through her, so strong they knocked the breath from her lungs. Alexander wrapped an arm around her, pulling her to him, fisting a hand in her hair.

He rolled her backwards, lowering her to the ground, pining her with his weight. The meditation seemed to swirl. She didn't know if she was sitting, lying, standing, floating. She was lost in his mouth, his smell, the hard contours of his body. She was grounded, supported by the grass pushing up against her back, but also suspended, drifting in mid-air.

Alexander pulled back, breath ragged, looking hungrily down at her. He planted slow, soft kisses over her face. Anita's fingers skirted the exposed skin at his neck. He bit her lip, exquisitely, seductively, and Anita's stomach clenched. She kissed him, then pushed him gently away, sitting up to face him.

'I think I love you, Anita,' he said, his voice husky.

She ran a hand through his hair. 'I think I love you too.'

He pulled her into his lap, folding his arms around her, caressing her back, her hair, her arms, heat sparking between them. Anita tipped her head back as his lips caressed her neck, and she moaned at the sensation.

'We should wake up now,' she said, trying to clear the lust from her mind. 'This is so perfect, what I'm about to say isn't allowed in here.'

Alexander pulled them abruptly out of the meditation. They woke up to the sensation of falling, their stomachs lurching upwards as they landed on the ground with a heavy thump.

'What was that?' asked Anita, alarmed.

Alexander looked astonished. 'I don't believe it,' he said with delight.

'What?'

'We were floating, when we were meditating. I've heard about this happening, but only ever at the Spirit Temple in the clouds. I can't believe it,' he said, grabbing her and pulling her into a rough, excited embrace.

Anita had never seen him like this... so unguardedly happy...

Alexander released her. 'What did you want to talk about?' he said.

She paused. 'I love you, but nothing more can happen between us until I've ended it with Marcus. I owe him that much.'

'Is that all?'

'Yes! What did you think I was going to say?'

'I don't know... that we couldn't be together, or something equally horrible.'

She took his hand. 'When I meditated with Marcus, it was also in the love pose. I'd never even heard of the pose, let alone practiced it. You stayed away from it for obvious reasons, but when I meditated with Marcus, it was less intense than when you and I meditate normally.

'I thought maybe that was just because Marcus is a Mind and you're a Spirit, but after what I just felt, I know that can't be all it is. I don't feel for Marcus what I feel for you,' she said, then hesitated, 'but I can't cheat on him. He made Austin release me...'

'You've been through a lot together.'

'I just hope it won't push him further towards Austin.'

'It might,' Alexander said, 'but Marcus and his choices are not your responsibility. He has to account for his own actions and you have to account for yours. To stay with him when you don't love him wouldn't be good for either of you.'

'I know,' she said. 'I just need to talk to him. We should go. The longer we're alone together, the more likely my resolve is to break.'

He smiled as he got up, taking her hand and helping her to her feet. They left, Alexander closing the door behind them, still holding her hand as he led her back the way they had come.

Neither of them noticed Gwyn hiding in the shadows, watching them leave, her energy suppressed as low as she could make it go. She'd been in the tunnels earlier and had heard their voices. She'd ducked into a side tunnel and suppressed her energy, hoping they wouldn't see her. She'd kicked a lantern, a muffled scraping noise floating to their ears. They'd paused at the sound, however, when nothing had followed, they'd carried on.

Gwyn had silently followed them to the pool, had watched as they'd entered and closed the door. She couldn't follow them inside, but she'd waited, determined to find out what they were up to.

To her great disappointment, they moved silently back towards Alexander's chambers, giving her nothing, but they were still holding hands... that was suspicious enough for Marcus to want to know about it. If her boyfriend had been down here with another girl, she would want to know, and anyway, she didn't like Anita, so it would give Gwyn great pleasure to cause her some pain.

CHAPTER 18

Gwyn went straight to the castle. Amber let her in, sending her up to Marcus' suite. Gwyn climbed the stairs and knocked on his door, Marcus surprised to see her when he answered.

'Gwyn?' he said. 'What's up?'

She hadn't stayed long, just long enough to tell him what she'd seen, twisting the knife by adding an embellishment here and there. Marcus had remained composed, which had surprised her; she'd expected a jealous rage. He thanked her and showed her out.

Marcus tried to stay calm, tried to determine the best way of handling the situation. But he couldn't think of a single legitimate reason for them to be at the pool together, especially not holding hands. He would talk to Anita about it. He barked for Amber to get him his driver and headed to Cordelia's.

* * * * *

Anita sat on one of Cordelia's worn sofas, still on a high from what had happened with Alexander. They hadn't kissed when they'd said goodbye, respecting Anita's wishes to tell Marcus first, but this had only added to the tension.

Anita was replaying their most recent meditation kiss in her mind when Marcus' voice pierced her daydream, his footsteps following his call.

'Anita? Are you here?'

'Hi,' she said, a little off balance. Why was he here? 'Good day?' she asked, getting up, trying to buy herself time to get back on kilter.

'There's something I need to discuss with you,' he said tersely, irritation painted across his face.

'What is it?' she asked, concerned. The only saving grace was that this couldn't be about what had just happened with Alexander...

'Tell me,' he said, 'how is Alexander?'

Shit. 'He's very well. I've just seen him, in fact,' she said, trying hard to keep her temper under control.

'Really?' he said. 'Why did you see him?'

'We're friends. It was good to catch up, and we meditated together. As you know, I've found meditation helpful, after what happened.'

'I think it would be best if you don't see Alexander any longer,' said Marcus, as though this were a perfectly normal statement.

'I'm sorry, what?' Anita spluttered, half laughing. They'd had an unspoken understanding that Anita would stay away from Alexander before, but he'd never actually said the words. And she'd only gone along with it because she'd been working for Helena, and had needed to keep him on side.

'I think it would be best if you don't see Alexander any longer,' he repeated.

'Yes, I heard what you said, I'm just in shock that you think you can dictate who I'm allowed to see.'

Marcus faltered; obviously not the reaction he'd expected. 'But I think it's for the best, don't you?'

'What does that even mean? Why would it be for the best for me to stay away from a friend?'

'Because I'm uncomfortable with you holding hands with your male friends.'

Anita went cold. How could he possibly know?

'It's not like this is the first time you've been caught holding Alexander's hand in public.'

By the Gods, how had he found out? Surely not from Alexander?

'Do you know who you sound like?' she said. 'Your father. You can't order me around, or force me to do things I don't want to do, whether you think it's for the best or not. I'm an adult, quite capable of making my own choices, and I choose to spend time with Alexander.'

She paused, steeling herself for what she was going to say next. 'And… I… I choose not to spend time with you anymore.'

The color drained from his face. 'What?' he whispered, looking lost. 'You can't break up with me. I love you.'

Tears pricked at Anita's eyes. She didn't want to hurt him, but there was no other way.

'Marcus, since,' she paused, taking a deep breath. 'Since you convinced your father to set me free, you've changed. Austin has let you into his inner circle and you're obviously happy about that, but I don't like the person he's turning you into. He's closing your eyes to what's really going on in the world, he's making you kick people when they're down, he's turning you into someone like him.'

'You're wrong,' he stuttered. 'I'm not turning into him, I'm making sure I can protect us.'

'You think Austin isn't clever enough to see through that? He's immersing you in his shady world so that one day you'll be so far in you can't get out. I don't want to be a part of that,' she said, the tears overflowing, 'and I don't want you to be either.

'You're a fun, genuine person. You take life at face value, and that suits you. It makes you daring and carefree; it's what drew me to you when I first met you. But I can't be part of this any longer; you need to work out who you want to be on your own. If you want to be like Austin, then carry on as you are, if not, then you need to get out before you're trapped forever.'

'I thought you loved me?' he choked, looking at her expectantly, as though this would make a difference.

'I do, but I don't want to be under your control. Trying to stop me from seeing my friends isn't love. A relationship like that isn't equal, it isn't healthy, not for either of us. It's Alexander now, but what if you decide you don't like Cleo, or Bass, or you think that someone looks at me the wrong way? I can't live like that. I don't want to live like that. I'm sorry, Marcus, but it's over.' She said it as gently as she could while conveying the finality of her decision, wiping away the tears still trickling down her face.

Marcus turned to leave.

'I'm sorry,' Anita said as he left, sinking to the sofa and pulling a cushion towards her, unable to stop the tears. She'd known it wouldn't be easy, but it hurt more than she'd expected.

She felt horrible and hated to think what Marcus might do now. She hoped he wouldn't run back to Austin, that some of what she'd said had gone in.

'Hello?' called a voice from the corridor, Cleo appearing, rushing over to her best friend when she saw the tears. 'What's wrong?' she asked, her concern palpable as she put her arms around Anita. 'What happened?'

'I just broke up with Marcus,' she sobbed, 'and he didn't take it very well.'

Cleo pushed Anita away so she could look at her face. 'You did what? Doesn't that put you in danger?'

'I don't care about that. If Austin wants to come after me, then he'll come after me, but Marcus was so hurt, I feel horrible.'

'Why did you do it?'

Anita had never acted like this before; she'd always been so tough. Cleo wasn't sure how to handle a teary Anita.

'Because I realized I love Alexander.'

'I see,' said Cleo, her tone turning firm. 'So, you're sitting here, sobbing into a cushion like some silly girl, when you broke up with Marcus because another Descendant wants to be with you? Please get it together.'

Anita looked blankly at Cleo, shocked at her lack of compassion. 'I feel like a bitch for hurting him,' she said defensively.

'Well, I'm sure you'll get over that as soon as you're gazing longingly into Alexander's beautiful eyes. Bloody hell, some people,' she said, getting up and pacing across the room.

Cleo's reaction had a sobering effect on Anita. Maybe she was being a little melodramatic; it wasn't like her to let things get to her like this. 'Is everything okay, Cleo?' Anita asked, wiping away the last of her tears and putting aside the offending cushion.

'No, everything is not bloody well okay. It's alright for you, Miss *I've got two men chasing after me, but boo hoo I've just had to tell one Descendants I'm not interested because I'd rather have the other one*, but for those of us living in the real world, men are total shits who don't turn up for dates when they say they're going to.'

Anita realized that, because of all the drama going on in her own life, she'd totally neglected her best friend. 'I'm sorry. What's going on?'

Cleo looked relieved to get her story off her chest and sat back down on the sofa. 'Well, you know I've been seeing that councilor's son off and on, the one I went to the ball with?'

Anita nodded. 'Of course: Henry.'

'Yes, Henry. Well, we've been seeing quite a lot of each other recently and it's been going really well. He was going to take me to the open mic night tonight; I was thinking about taking to the stage… you're coming too, right?'

Shit, she had forgotten all about it. The chances of Cleo actually making it to the stage were minimal, but still, she needed to pull it together on the friend front. She nodded. 'Of course.'

'Anyway, Henry was supposed to pick me up earlier. We were going to go for dinner and then on to the open mic from there, but he stood me up. I walked into town, thinking he must have lost track of time or something, but as I walked past Temple Mews, I saw him all over some other girl outside the flower shop.

'I went over to him and tapped him on the shoulder. When he saw it was me, he turned away dismissively and said he would see me later. I slapped him; a little melodramatic perhaps, but it made me feel better, and then I stormed off; I didn't want to make a proper scene. Stupid arrogant arsehole,' she said, looking happier already.

'What an idiot,' said Anita. 'The councilors' children always think they're something special, and they're not.'

'Well anyway, I won't be seeing him again. Pity, the sex was good.'

Anita smiled indulgently. 'Come on, or we'll miss the open mic, and you never know, you might find fresh meat.'

'Let's hope so,' she said frivolously.

'Cleo,' said Anita, stopping before they left the house.

'Uh huh?'

'I'm really sorry I've been so self-absorbed for the last few weeks. I promise not to be from now on.'

'Don't be silly, you've had a lot going on. I forgive you. Just don't do it again. That includes the getting kidnapped bit as well.'

Anita laughed. 'I'll do my best. Nice touch with the slap, by the way.'

'Thanks, I thought so.'

CHAPTER 19

Anita and Cleo arrived at the clearing by the river just as Bass was taking to the stage, to enthusiastic applause. They sat down in a spot at the back, near the tree line, and listened as Bass' raw, melodic voice filled the air around them. They sat in silence for a few minutes before Cleo occupied herself with the group of guys next to them.

Anita was happy to be alone. She focused on the words of Bass' song, blocking out any thoughts of Marcus, blocking out the guilt. She made herself notice the cool Autumn wind against her skin, the chill of the ground beneath her, the sun on her face. She lay back on the grass and her mind turned to Alexander. She closed her eyes, replaying their meditation again and again, lips tingling at the memory.

A song finished, the crowd clapped wildly, and Anita felt familiar, powerful energy wash over her senses. She opened her eyes and looked up to see two electric blue eyes looking down at her, her energy lifting as she lost herself in his gaze.

'You shouldn't sneak up on people,' she said, as he crouched next to her.

'You shouldn't be grumpy when someone comes to find you especially,' he replied, stroking her cheek. 'Come we with?' he said, offering her his hand. She took it and they got to their feet, Anita realizing that this meant he knew…

'How have you heard already?' she asked, astounded and a little annoyed.

'News travels fast around here; you should know that by now.'

'Hmmm.'

Alexander led her into the woods, heading further up the river. When they were safely out of sight, he stopped and tugged her towards him, sparks surging between them as their flesh met. They laughed excitedly, elated by their newfound freedom.

'How did it go with Marcus?' asked Alexander, running his thumb across her cheekbone.

'It could have been worse,' she said, taking his hand, continuing along the path. 'He came to see me because he knew we'd been to the pool together. Someone saw us there, holding hands, and he told me I wasn't allowed to see you anymore.'

'Oh.'

'So, as I said, it could have been worse. It was the right decision, and I warned him about Austin. I doubt he'll listen, but at least I tried. I feel guilty though, after what we went through, and I think he really does love me.'

Alexander squeezed her hand as they rounded a sharp bend. It revealed a graceful waterfall, the path coming to an abrupt halt by its side. The water cascaded into a deep plunge pool, throwing up a fine white mist.

'It's beautiful,' she said, unable to take her eyes off the water, the sun creating rainbows in the spray.

She turned towards him when he didn't answer, met his gaze, stepped into his space. The mood between them altered as she reached for his lips.

'Wait,' he said, moving a hand to her neck, looking down into her eyes, his thumb caressing the delicate skin behind her ear. 'There are some things I need to tell you before this goes any further... there can't be secrets between us.'

Anita felt robbed. She'd been fantasizing about their first kiss in the real world for a long time, but what he said made sense, even to her preoccupied mind.

'There are some things I need to tell you too, but I have one condition,' she said, looking up at him.

'Name it,' he said, his pupils dilating, their bodies close, breath mingling.

'Kiss me. If you hate me after what I have to tell you, or I hate you, at least we'll have that.'

Alexander said nothing. He closed the gap between them, lowering his face so their skin almost touched. Anita tipped her head back, lost in his eyes.

He placed his hand on her stomach and pressed her backwards, her body complying without hesitation to his touch. Her back came flush against rock, the cold stone halting her movement, holding her in place.

He moved a hand to her face, ran his thumb across her lips, then closed his beautiful eyes, lowering his mouth, so it hovered just above hers. He touched his nose to hers, breathing deeply, Anita relishing the tension that stretched to breaking point between them. She breathed him in, his citrus scent, savoring the contact of their skin, the hum of energy.

Their mouths finally met to a shower of tingles, Anita forgetting everything but him as his lips caressed hers. They started with slow, sensual touches, each of them learning the territory, fireworks of pleasure going off in Anita's mind. It was all-consuming, nothing else existing, only the kiss, only Alexander.

The kiss deepened, tongues testing, tasting, savoring. He pushed his body into her, the kiss more demanding, desire pooling in Anita's core, her hands fisting his hair.

315

Alexander broke away, pulled back, turned his head from hers, his brow furrowed. He took deep, shuddering breaths, wresting himself back under control, strengthening his resolve, before returning for one last gentle kiss.

'I hope you forgive my secrets,' he said, moving his face dangerously close to Anita's before pushing himself away, leaving them both shaken, wanting more.

'Me too,' she said, a deep sense of loss welling up inside her. She tried desperately to regain some composure, her energy going crazy, her instincts urging her to demand more. Who cared about secrets anyway?

Alexander sat on the grass next to the plunge pool, just out of range of the spray. Anita sat next to him, leaning back against a rock, toes still tingling from the kiss.

'Shall I go first?' she asked. She wasn't sure she wanted to hear what Alexander had to say.

'Sure,' he said, taking her hand, 'fire away.'

Anita told Alexander everything. She told him how Helena had approached her, and how she'd agreed to help. She told him about the cylinder with Austin's memory, about being beaten up, and about how she'd felt for the past few weeks.

Alexander's energy remained calm the whole time. He stroked her hand when she told him about the beating, the emptiness, the self-loathing, and how stupid she'd felt.

When she finished, he said, 'You thought you were helping. You didn't know Helena was lying to you. We can only make decisions based on the information we have in front of us. You chose to do something rather than sit back and let the world suffer. I would probably have done the same thing, especially if the proposal had been from someone I trusted.'

'But I should have known not to trust her. She's been lying to me for years about my parents.'

'Things look different with hindsight; you were just trying to help.'

Anita took a deep breath. She didn't want to talk about it anymore, although she was glad Alexander knew the truth. 'Alright, your turn,' she said, smiling. 'Make it quick; we have better things to do.'

Alexander stalled, kissing her temple. Her chest contained an entire aviary of birds, all flapping their wings furiously inside her. She held her breath.

'When we first arrived in Empire, we came because Christiana was ill; she wanted to find someone, a girl, before she died. Austin agreed to it because he thought Christiana only intended to see the girl from a distance. Christiana had other ideas; she wanted to tell her the truth about something that happened a long time ago, that Christiana had regretted ever since.

'I've had to piece together the story, and I don't know for sure, but it seems they altered the bloodline so we could never send back the Relic. I don't know why, or why Christiana had a change of heart, but Christiana thought it was wrong for them to play God. She wanted to set the record straight and tell the girl what had happened.'

Alexander paused, steeling himself. 'The most plausible candidate for that girl is you, Anita.'

His words hit her like a hammer. 'What?' she laughed. 'Have you hit your head? You think I might be a Descendant?'

'You've got to admit you're powerful. You're probably the most adept Body I've ever met.'

'But I also have a significant Spirit influence; I wouldn't be a reader if I were the Body Descendant.'

'Christiana was a reader.'

'I'm not a Descendant.'

'Really? Why not? Who were your parents?'

'Gods, Alexander, that's a bit much.'

'I'm sorry, but just entertain the idea for a second before you dismiss it... and there's more.'

Alexander told Anita about the conversation he'd heard between Elistair and Peter, confirming she was the Descendant, about the note from Philip, and that Austin had killed Christiana to keep her quiet. The bit Anita was most surprised about was that Elistair was involved. He had always looked after her... surely this couldn't be the reason?

'It all fits perfectly,' said Alexander. 'I'm just sorry I didn't tell you sooner.'

She sat numbly, staring at the water, processing his words. 'It's going to take some time for me to get my head around this,' she said slowly.

'I know,' he said, stroking her hand. She entwined their fingers, savoring the low hum of energy that pulsed between them. He pulled her into him, wrapped his arms around her, and she rested her head against his chest. They sat there, only the sound of the water piercing the quiet, their breathing aligned.

'I still want to kiss you,' she said eventually, twisting and pulling his head down towards her. Alexander looked relived, placing a quick, promising kiss on her lips.

'Good, because I want to kiss you too,' he said, wrapping her back in his arms, kissing her hair.

Anita tried to get up, but he tightened his grip. She had to resort to tickling to make him let her go. He threw his hands up in defeat and let her wriggle around to face him. She pulled herself up onto his torso and kissed him before pulling away and getting to her feet. 'Come on,' she said, 'I think we should go somewhere more private.'

318

'I won't argue with that,' said Alexander, getting up and putting his arm around her, pulling her close to his side as they made their way back towards Empire.

They walked in silence, full of blissful content, Anita not quite believing this was happening. They stole glances at each other every now and again just to check it was real.

They emerged from the woods onto the track that led back to Empire. They waited for the energy van that was coming down the road to pass by. However, to their surprise, as the van pulled level with them, it screeched to a halt, and the side door opened.

Four hooded men dressed all in black jumped out and bundled them inside, where another four men were waiting to restrain them.

They struggled wildly and Anita tried to scream, but a gloved hand covered her mouth, stifling her cries. They quickly realized that to struggle was futile, so they stilled. There were eight men against the two of them, and they already had cuffs clamped around their wrists. They could do nothing now but wait.

The van travelled for what seemed like forever, the path it followed winding this way and that, nobody saying a word. They sat with their backs to one another, not even able to share a reassuring look.

The van stopped abruptly, and the door opened, two men dragging Anita out and two dragging Alexander. The others flanked them, presumably in case they tried to make a bid for freedom. Although it was pitch black, the place felt familiar to Anita, like she had been here before, but she couldn't quite place it.

The men dragged them roughly into a barn, then towards an open hole in the middle of the floor. They were forced to jump into it one at a time. It wasn't deep, and they each landed lithely on their feet. Several more guards were ready to collect them when they landed, the hole's cover replaced as soon as they were in.

The guards shoved them along a rudimentary corridor and into a small, box-like room, then forced them down onto wooden chairs, their hands and feet tied to the struts. It reminded Anita of her time spent in Austin's dungeon, wondering if he was behind this too.

The men filed out of the room as three new figures entered. Two of them Anita didn't recognize, but the third she knew only too well. Helena? Why would she do this? They'd been gagged, but Anita's eyes flew wide with surprise.

'So good to see you both,' said Helena. 'Sorry about the unfortunate circumstances, but it was the only way.'

Helena sat down, taking her time, making herself comfortable before speaking again. 'Now, Anita, let's have a little chat about that cylinder in your head.'

I hope you enjoyed Queen of Empire. Book two, Temple of Sand, is out now!

I'd really appreciate it if you left a review on Amazon, Goodreads, Instagram (#TheRelicTrilogy #QueenOfEmpire #FantasyRomance), or any other place you can think of... authors aren't fussy! Just a few words, or a line or two would be perfection. Thank you for your support.

CONNECT WITH HR MOORE

Are you a Mind, Body, or Spirit? Sign up to HR Moore's newsletter to find out! You'll also get all the latest news about releases, book recommendations, and freebies too!

Sign up here: https://www.subscribepage.com/r2a0n6

Find HR Moore on Instagram and Twitter:
@HR_Moore
#TheRelicTrilogy
#QueenOfEmpire
#FantasyRomance

See what the world of The Relic Trilogy looks like on Pinterest:
https://www.pinterest.com/authorhrmoore/

Like the HR Moore page on Facebook:
https://www.facebook.com/authorhrmoore

Follow HR Moore on Goodreads:
https://www.goodreads.com/author/show/7228761.H_R_Moore

Or check out HR Moore's website:
http://www.hrmoore.com/

ABOUT THE AUTHOR

Harriet's British, but lives in New Hampshire with her husband and two young daughters. When she isn't writing, editing, eating, running around after her kids, or imagining how much better life would be with the addition of a springer spaniel, she occasionally finds the time to make hats.

TITLES BY HR MOORE

The Relic Trilogy:

Queen of Empire
Temple of Sand
Court of Crystal (coming mid 2021)

In the Gleaming Light